Praise for
the #1 *New York Times* bestselling
Stalking Jack the Ripper series

*"A marvelous yet somewhat gruesome mystery...an unexpected twist makes the ending worth the wait. A must-have."

—*School Library Journal* (*starred review*)

"There are plenty of suspects and red herrings as well as tense escalations....A scenic, twisty mystery."　　—*Kirkus Reviews*

"Maniscalco has created a serious, sharp-minded, and forward-thinking protagonist in Audrey Rose, whose fearlessness will endear her to readers looking for an engaging historical thriller. Abundant red herrings and a dash of romance round out this gruesome but engrossing story."　　—*Publisher's Weekly*

"Audrey is a young woman eager to use her brains and willing to flaunt society's rules....This mystery pays homage to classics like Doyle's Sherlock Holmes and Mary Shelley's Frankenstein [and] will satisfy those readers looking for historical mystery, a witty heroine, and a little romance."

—*School Library Connection*

"Audrey Rose is a witty, resourceful feminist who refuses to bow to Victorian-era gender norms. This dark, gothic landscape is peopled with nuanced, diverse characters who keep readers enthralled. A gripping mystery with a compelling heroine and just the right touch of romance."　　—*Kirkus Reviews*

"Every sentence of this novel drips with decadence. The settings and Moonlight Carnival performances are lush yet dangerous, beautiful yet terrifying. It was easy to understand just how Audrey Rose comes to be so enthralled with the Moonlight Carnival and the performers because, as readers, we're put under the same exact spell. . . . Masterfully crafted."

—*Hypable*

"Audrey Rose Wadsworth prefers breeches to ball gowns, autopsies to afternoon tea, and scalpels to knitting needles. . . . Maniscalco's portrayal of scientific invention in a newly industrial era will serve as a fine first foray into Victorian classics."

—*Booklist*

Escaping FROM HOUDINI

Escaping
FROM
HOUDINI

KERRI MANISCALCO

JIMMY PATTERSON BOOKS
LITTLE, BROWN AND COMPANY
NEW YORK · BOSTON · LONDON

Copyright © 2018 by Kerri Maniscalco
Bonus content (tarot-card art) © 2019 by PhantomRin (Irina Plachkova) and (text) © 2019 by Kerri Maniscalco
Excerpt from *Capturing the Devil* © 2019 by Kerri Maniscalco

JIMMY Patterson Books / Little, Brown and Company
Hachette Book Group
1290 Avenue of the Americas, New York, NY 10104
JimmyPatterson.org

First Paperback Edition: September 2019
First Edition: September 2018

JIMMY Patterson Books is an imprint of Little, Brown and Company, a division of Hachette Book Group, Inc. The Little, Brown name and logo are trademarks of Hachette Book Group, Inc. The JIMMY Patterson Books® name and logo are trademarks of JBP Business, LLC.

The publisher is not responsible for websites (or their content) that are not owned by the publisher.

The Hachette Speakers Bureau provides a wide range of authors for speaking events. To find out more, go to hachettespeakersbureau.com or call (866) 376-6591.

Photographs courtesy of Alamy: RMS *Etruria*, p. 2.

Photographs courtesy of Etsy: Justice Tarot, p. 62; Houdini promotional poster, p. 94; Victorian contortionist, p. 86; Late nineteenth century circus performers, p. 122; acrobat, p. 136; vintage absinthe posters and labels, p. 168; The Fool, p. 186; plague doctor, p. 258; ten phunny phools, p. 332.

Photographs courtesy of the Billy Rose Theatre Division, The New York Public Library Digital Collections: "Circus tents," p. 52; "Harry Houdini with wife Bess," p. 290; "Harry Houdini," p. 388.

Library of Congress Cataloging-in-Publication Data
Names: Maniscalco, Kerri, author.
Title: Escaping from Houdini / Kerri Maniscalco.
Description: First edition. | New York; Boston: Little, Brown and Company, 2018. |
    Jimmy Patterson Books, 2018 | Summary: In 1889, the ship *Etruria* departs Liverpool,
    England, for New York carrying Audrey Rose Wadsworth and her crime-solving partner,
    Thomas, a famous escape artist, and a cold-blooded killer.
Identifiers: LCCN 2018023093 | ISBN 9780316551700 (hc) | 9780316487177 (Barnes &
    Noble Special Edition) | 9780316487160 (Barnes & Noble Signed Edition) |
    9780316527392 (international edition) | ISBN 9780316551724 (tpb)
Subjects: | CYAC: Mystery and detective stories. | Cruise ships—Fiction. | Ocean travel—
    Fiction. | Serial murderers—Fiction. | Magic tricks—Fiction. | Houdini, Harry,
    1874–1926—Fiction. | Great Britain—History—Victoria, 1837-1901—Fiction.
Classification: LCC PZ7.1.M3648 Esc 2018 | DDC [Fic]—dc23
LC record available at https://lccn.loc.gov/2018023093

10 9 8 7 6 5 4 3 2 1

LSC-C

Printed in the United States of America

To those who believe in the magic of dreams.
Everything is possible.

"Hell is empty
And all the devils are here."
—*THE TEMPEST,* ACT 1, SCENE 2

WILLIAM SHAKESPEARE

Escaping FROM HOUDINI

RMS *Etruria*

ONE

MOONLIGHT CARNIVAL

RMS ETRURIA
LIVERPOOL, ENGLAND
1 JANUARY 1889

New Year's afternoon aboard the *Etruria* began like a fairy tale, which was the first indication a nightmare lurked on the horizon, waiting, as most villains do, for an opportunity to strike.

As our cruise liner prepared to leave port, I ignored twinges of unease in favor of the lush fantasy world before us. It was the start of a fresh year, a new chapter, a wonderful opportunity to put dark events of the past behind us and stare ahead into the bright future.

A future that might soon bring a wedding...and a wedding night.

I took a steadying breath and glanced at the stage in the center of the grand dining saloon. Heavy velvet curtains—an ink blue so dark they appeared black—shimmered with tiny sparkling gems whenever light caught them. Aerial performers in diamond-encrusted bodices twirled on silver threads, beautiful spiders spinning webs I was hopelessly caught up in.

Round tables dotted the floor like well-placed constellations, their moon-white linens strewn with flowers in purples, creams, and blues. Among many modern conveniences, the *Etruria* boasted a hothouse, and the scents of jasmine, lavender, and other midnight notes wafted around, inviting yet dangerous—not unlike the masked performers soaring above us. They swung effortlessly from one trapeze to the next, letting go without fear of falling as they flew through the air and snatched the next bar with ease.

"The long trains on their costumes make them look like shooting stars, don't they? I should love to have a dress made with as many gemstones one day." Miss Prescott, daughter of the chief magistrate across the table, sighed deeply. With her caramel hair and cunning brown eyes, she reminded me of my cousin Liza. She set her champagne flute down and leaned close, dropping her voice to a conspiratorial whisper. "Have you heard the legend of Mephistopheles, Miss Wadsworth?"

I tore my gaze from the hypnotic scene above once more and shook my head. "I can't say that I have. Is that what tonight's performance is based on?"

"I suppose it's time for a story." Captain Norwood, the proud captain of the *Etruria,* cleared his throat, gaining the attention of our table, including the Prescotts; Uncle Jonathan; my chaperone, Mrs. Harvey; and the wickedly enchanting Mr. Thomas Cresswell, the young man who'd won my heart as deftly as any cardsharp winning hand after hand at his game of choice.

Accompanied by my uncle, Thomas and I had spent two grueling days traveling from Bucharest to Liverpool to board the *Etruria* before it set out for New York. We'd found creative ways of stealing kisses on our journey, and each secret encounter flashed through my mind unbidden—my hands in his dark brown hair, his lips igniting flames along my skin, our—

Miss Prescott gently nudged me under the table, returning my attention to the conversation.

"...if, of course, legends are to be believed. Named after a character from German folklore, Mephistopheles is a demon in the Devil's employ," Captain Norwood said. "Known for stealing the souls of those already corrupt, he's full of magic and trickery, and he happens to be one spectacular showman. Here, look at these tarot cards he's made for the tables. Each card features one of his performers." He held up a gorgeous set of handpainted cards. "I guarantee you're in for a week of unparalleled magic and mystery," he continued. "Each night will bring a new carnival performance, never before seen. This ship will be the talk of legends, mark my words. Soon every cruise liner will host similar entertainments. It will be the start of a new era of travel."

I raised a brow at his near-reverent tone. "Are you suggesting you've hired a demon to entertain us and it's sure to become all the rage, Captain?"

Thomas choked on his water, and Miss Prescott shot me a mischievous grin. "Is there a church or chapel on the ship?" she asked, all round eyes and innocence. "What shall we do if we're tricked out of our souls, sir?"

The captain lifted a shoulder, enjoying the mystery. "You'll both have to wait and see. It shan't be much longer now." He returned his attention to the adults, when Miss Prescott leapt up from her seat, startling me and earning a disapproving glare from her father.

"One more little clue, please?"

Maybe it was the devil in me, but I couldn't help adding, "I would hate to be so overcome with hysteria that I abandoned the ship. We're not too far from port, are we? Perhaps I might swim..."

Miss Prescott slowly blinked in appraisal. "Indeed, Captain. In fact, I feel a bit of a fainting spell coming on this very moment! Do you think it's Mephistopheles?" she asked, voice rising in pitch. "Does his trickery work from a distance? I wonder how many he can affect at once."

I peered at her, leaning in as if to medically inspect her. "You do appear a bit pale, Miss Prescott. Does your soul feel attached to your person?"

Thomas snorted, but didn't dare interrupt this new show taking place. With my deep blue silk evening gown, midnight gloves that extended past my elbows, and sparkling jewels draped over my collarbone, I felt nearly as bedazzling as the acrobats flying above us.

Miss Prescott wrapped her gloved hands around her throat, eyes going wide. "You know, I *do* feel strange. Lighter, even." She swayed on her feet and clutched her center. "Should we call for smelling salts, Captain?"

"I don't believe it's necessary," he said, inhaling deeply, no doubt regretting pairing the two of us together. "I assure you, *this* Mephistopheles is harmless. He is just a man pretending to be a legendary villain, nothing more."

"I swear my soul is getting weaker. Can you tell? Do I look more...transparent?" Her eyes grew nearly to the size of saucers as she dropped into her seat and glanced around. "I wonder if there's a spirit photographer aboard. I've heard they can capture such things on film. My clothing isn't becoming indecent, is it?"

"Not yet." I bit my lip, trying to keep the smile out of my voice and off my face, especially since Mrs. Prescott seemed ready to burst from fury at her daughter's act. "We might be able to weigh you to see if there's any difference."

Uncle paused his conversation with Thomas, shaking his head ever so slightly, but before he could comment, an attendant hurried over and handed him a telegram. He read it, twisting the ends of his pale mustache, and folded the paper up, shooting me an inscrutable look.

"If you'll excuse me." Uncle stood. "I must tend to this at once."

Miss Prescott's eyes sparkled. "Your uncle must be off on secret forensic business. I've read stories in the papers regarding your involvement with the Ripper murders. Did you and Mr. Cresswell truly stop a vampire in Romania from slaying the King and Queen?"

"I—what?" I shook my head. "People have been writing about me and Thomas in the papers?"

"Indeed." Miss Prescott sipped her champagne, eyes following Uncle as he exited the room. "Most everyone in London has been whispering about you and your dashing Mr. Cresswell."

I could not focus on the spectacle my own life was taking on. "Pardon me. I must get some…air."

I half rose, unsure if I should follow Uncle, when Mrs. Harvey patted my hand. "I'm sure everything is fine, dear." She nodded toward the stage. "It's about to begin."

Tendrils of smoke unfurled around the inky curtains, the scent strong enough to evoke a few coughing fits throughout the room. My nose burned, but it was a minor nuisance compared to how quickly my pulse now raced. I wasn't sure if it was Uncle's swift departure, the information regarding Thomas and myself being known for our forensic skills, or the anticipation of tonight's performance that was to blame. Perhaps it was all three.

"Ladies. Gentlemen." A deep male voice intoned from everywhere at once, forcing passengers to twist in their seats. I craned my own head around, searching for the man behind the disembodied voice. He must have engineered some mechanism to project himself around the room. "Welcome to the show."

A buzz shot through the saloon as those few words echoed. In the silence that followed, cymbals trilled lightly, building into a crescendo that clashed as servers lifted silver cloches from our plates, revealing a meal fit for royalty. No one seemed to notice the mushroom-gravy-topped filets or fried potatoes that were arranged in a grand pile, our hunger no longer for food, but to hear that mysterious voice once more.

I peeked at Thomas and smiled. He moved about in his seat as if hot coals had been placed randomly and he had to shift or remain still and get burned.

"Nervous?" I whispered as the aerial performers gracefully descended, one by one.

"Of a performance that boasts of causing arrhythmia, according to this program?" He flicked the black-and-white-striped show bill he held. "Not at all. I cannot wait for my heart to burst. Really livens up an otherwise monotonous Sunday evening, Wadsworth."

Before I could respond, a drum thundered and a masked man emerged from a cloud of smoke in the center of the stage. He wore a frock coat the color of an opened vein and a starched shirt and trousers that were an endless black. Scarlet ribbons and silver bullion trimmed his top hat, and a burnished filigree mask covered everything from his nose up. His mouth curved in wicked delight as every eye in the saloon went to him and each jaw dropped.

Men jumped in their seats; women's fans snapped open, the sound akin to a hundred birds taking flight. It was unsettling, witnessing a man materialize, unscathed by the tempest raging about him. Whispers of him being the Devil's heir reached my ears. Or Satan himself, as Miss Prescott's father would have it. I nearly rolled my eyes. I should hope he'd have better judgment as a chief magistrate. This was clearly the ringmaster.

"Allow me to introduce myself." The masked man bowed, mischief sparking in his eyes as he slowly drew himself back up. "I am Mephistopheles—your guide through the strange and magnificent. Each night the Wheel of Fortune will choose your entertainer. However, you may barter with performers after the main show and indulge in any of our acts. From flame swallowers to lion tamers, fortune-tellers, and knife throwers, your wish is our command. I warn you, though, beware of midnight bargains, taking your fate in your own hands is poorly advised."

Passengers fidgeted, probably wondering at the sort of bargains they might make—how low they might fall in the pursuit of pleasure so far from society's watchful shores.

"Our tricks might appear sweet, but I promise they are not treats," he whispered. "Are you brave enough to survive? Perhaps you'll be another who loses their heart and their head to my midnight minstrel show. Only you can decide. Until then?"

Mephistopheles prowled onstage, a caged animal waiting for an opportunity to strike. My heart thudded wildly. I had the distinct impression we were all prey dressed in our finest, and if we weren't careful, we'd be devoured by his mysterious show.

"Tonight is the first of seven in which you will be dazzled." The ringmaster lifted his arms, and a dozen white doves flew from his sleeves into the rafters. A few excited cries erupted, Mrs. Harvey and Miss Prescott among the first.

"And horrified," he continued, a slight croak now in his voice. From one blink to the next, his tie was no longer made of cloth—it was a writhing snake, wrapping itself about his neck. Mephistopheles clutched his throat, his bronze face turning a deep purple under the filigree mask. My own breath caught when he bent over and sputtered, gasping for air.

I almost stood, convinced we were bearing witness to this man's death, but forced myself to breathe. To *think*. To compile facts like the scientist-in-training I was. This was only a show. Nothing more. Surely no one was going to die. My breath came in short gasps that had nothing to do with the corset of my fine dress. This was utterly thrilling and horrible. I hated it almost as much as I loved it. And I adored it more than I cared to admit.

"Good heavens," Miss Prescott muttered when he dropped to his knees, wheezing. His eyes rolled backward until all I saw were their whites. I held my own breath, unable to release the tension in my spine. This had to be an illusion. "Someone help him!" Miss Prescott cried. "He's dying!"

"*Sit down,* Olivia," Mrs. Prescott whispered harshly. "You're not only embarrassing yourself, but me and your father as well."

Before anyone could aid the ringmaster, he pried the serpent away and drew in air as if he'd been submerged in the seawater we traveled through. I slumped back, and Thomas chuckled, but I couldn't quite pull my gaze from the masked man onstage.

Mephistopheles shoved himself into a standing position, staggered a bit, then slowly lifted the snake above his head—light from the chandeliers caught his mask, turning half his face a furious orange-red. Perhaps he was angry—he'd tested us and found us lacking. What well-dressed monsters we must seem, carrying on with our elegant supper while he fought for his life, all for nothing more than our mere entertainment.

He spun in a circle, once, twice, and the slithering beast disappeared. I leaned forward, blinking as the ringmaster proudly bowed to the audience again, hands no longer occupied by the serpent. A roar of applause went up.

"How in God's name?" I mumbled. There were no boxes or places for him to have hidden the snake. I sincerely hoped it didn't find its way to our table; Thomas would surely faint.

"You might even fall..." he called as he somersaulted across the stage, top hat remaining in place without his touching it, "...in love."

Mephistopheles tipped the hat and it tumbled down his arm as if it were an acrobat vaulting over a trapeze. Like any great showman, he held it out so we could see it was a regular top hat, if not a bit gaudy. Once he'd made an entire circuit around the stage, he tossed it in the air, then snatched it back with a snap of his wrist. I watched, unblinking, as he stuck his arm in up to his elbow and yanked out a dozen ink-blue roses.

His hat had been utterly ordinary. I was almost certain of it.

"I warn you once more—do not get too attached." Mephistopheles's voice boomed so loudly I felt an echo of it in my own chest. "While we boast death-defying acts, no one escapes its grip forever. Will tonight be the end for some? Will you lose your hearts? Or perhaps," he grinned over his shoulder at the crowd, "you will lose your heads."

A spotlight illuminated a crudely painted harlequin doll—which hadn't been there a moment before. Pivoting in a single, graceful movement, the ringmaster threw a dagger across the stage. It flew blade over handle, sinking into the doll's neck with a *thwack* that hushed the audience. For a taut moment nothing happened. All was wretchedly still. We sat there, scarcely breathing, waiting. The doll's body stubbornly remained pinned to the board it had been propped against. Another moment passed and Mephistopheles *tsked*.

"Well. That won't do." He stomped his feet. "Everyone...do as I do!"

Stomp. Stomp. Stomp.

Passengers obliged, slowly at first, then sent the dining saloon into a vibrating frenzy. China rattled, silverware scuttled across tables, goblets sloshed merlot onto the expensive linens, our tables now appearing more like crime scenes than elegant spreads. Deciding to let go of my well-bred reserve a bit, I stomped along. Thomas, a bemused expression on his face, followed my lead.

Stomp. Stomp. Stomp.

The pounding drummed into each of my cells, prompting my blood to pump to the beat. It was animalistic and feral, and yet so...*thrilling*. I could not believe so many lords and ladies and

11

highborn passengers of first class were swept up in the hedonism and debauchery.

Mrs. Harvey brought her gloved fists down on the table, adding a new fervor to the sound thrumming in my ears. Miss Prescott did the same. A breath later the doll's head thumped to the floor, rolling toward the ringmaster's gleaming boots.

Stomp. Stomp. Stomp. It seemed no one was quite ready to give up the devil's rhythm once it had started. Mephistopheles was the conductor of this wicked symphony, his hand punching the air as the *stomp stomp stomping* reached a fever pitch.

"Silence!" he shouted, voice booming above everything else. As if he were a puppet master snipping strings, the clomping of feet ceased. Some in the crowd stood, cheering, while a few men in silk top hats whistled loudly.

Miss Prescott rose from her seat, face flushed and eyes bright, completely unaffected by the glare her parents leveled at her. "Bravo!" she called out, clapping. "I said bravo!"

Mephistopheles gazed at the severed head with a thoughtful expression, as if he was reliving a memory that haunted him, something wretched enough he'd never escape it, no matter how far he'd run. I imagined, like his elaborate illusions, nothing was quite as it seemed where he was concerned. To my astonishment, he picked up the doll's head and kicked it into the air, where it exploded in fireworks that sprinkled down like fallen stars, burning out before they reached the black-and-white-tiled floor. Silence fell upon us all.

"So, I inquire once more, which will you lose before the week is through? Your heart? Your head? Perhaps," he drawled, face cast in shadows as the chandeliers dimmed slowly before winking out, "you will lose your life, your very soul, to this magical traveling show."

I gasped and held my gloved hands up, but could only make out the barest hint of them. My heart pumped faster as I glanced around the pitch blackness, enraptured yet terrified of what monster might be lurking. Seemed I wasn't the only one intrigued. Excited murmurs rippled through the darkness. The promise of death was as alluring, if not more so, than the prospect of falling in love. What morbid creatures we were, craving danger and mystery in place of happily-ever-afters.

"For now," he continued, his voice a smooth caress in the dark, "enjoy an evening of magic, mischief, and mayhem." My palms dampened and I couldn't help sitting forward, needing another word, another clue, another bit of the surreal. As if he'd heard my inner longings, Mephistopheles spoke again. "Esteemed passengers of the *Etruria*...please indulge your senses in the greatest show from sea to sea," he crooned. "Welcome to Mephistopheles's Magnificent Minstrel Show, or as it's better known...the Moonlight Carnival!"

Lights flashed on, the brightness stinging as I blinked dark spots away. A moment later, Mrs. Harvey shoved away from our table, face as pale as a specter. Thomas reached out to steady her, but she raised a shaking hand.

I followed her gaze and bit my tongue hard enough to taste copper. Miss Prescott—the young woman clapping with delight moments before—lay facedown, unmoving, in a pool of blood with nearly a dozen knives stuck deep in her velvet-covered back.

I stared, waiting for her to gasp out or twitch. To toss her head back and laugh, having fooled us with her performance. But that was an illusion of my own making.

Miss Prescott was truly dead.

TWO

FROM DREAMS TO NIGHTMARES

DINING SALOON
RMS ETRURIA
1 JANUARY 1889

For a moment, nothing happened except for the growing ringing in my ears. Thomas might have been calling my name, but I couldn't focus on anything other than forcing myself to breathe. I needed to be rational and analytical, but my emotions weren't quite ready to comply. I studied the dead, but sitting beside a person who'd been murdered was incomprehensible.

The room twisted as I stood and everything became scorchingly hot. I tried convincing myself it was a terrible dream, but Mrs. Prescott's guttural scream erupted, drawing a hundred pairs of eyes our way, and I knew it was real.

Passengers at other tables gasped, their expressions filled not with repulsion but... delight as they spied the young woman lying in her own blood with ten dinner knives following the length of her spine. I slowly blinked at the people who were starting to clap, stomach churning, until the truth hit me: they thought this was another act.

To most in the saloon, Miss Prescott's "murder" was simply part of the dinner show—and what a magnificent one it was, according to a man at the next table. Thomas was already out of his seat, his attention torn between his sobbing chaperone and me, all the while scanning the perimeter for threats. I wanted to assist him, to be productive and useful, but I could not stop the shrill ringing in my ears or the fog that had descended over my thoughts. Everything seemed to move slowly. Everything except for my heart. That thundered against my ribs in frantic bursts. It was a warning beat, urging me to action, begging me to flee.

"Olivia!" Mrs. Prescott clutched her daughter's body, tears dripping onto her velvet dress. "Get up. Get *up*!"

Blood smeared across the tablecloth and Mrs. Prescott's bodice, the color as dark as my churning emotions. Miss Prescott was dead. I could neither process it nor will my heart to harden and be of use. How could this be?

Captain Norwood was suddenly out of his seat and yelling commands I could not decipher through the relentless ringing in my head. Movement around the table finally forced my gaze away from the knives and blood; diners were being escorted out, though the merriment in the room hadn't quelled. Except for a few at nearby tables, no one looked especially alarmed. I stared down at the horror, uncertain how anyone might mistake it for an illusion. There was so much blood.

"Wadsworth?" Thomas touched my elbow, his brow crinkled. I stared at him without truly seeing anything. A lively young woman lay dead next to me; the world no longer made sense. "Ghastly though it sounds, pretend it is an equation now."

Thomas bent until I met his gaze, his expression as strained as I imagined my own. This wasn't easy for him, either. And if he could turn that cool exterior on, then I could, too. Shaking myself from my own horror, I rushed to Mrs. Prescott's side, and gently took her hands in mine. It was both to comfort her and preserve the crime scene. Through my storm of emotions I clutched at one fact:

a murderer was on board this ship and we needed to isolate clues quickly. As gruesome as it was, we couldn't disturb the body. At least not yet.

"Come," I said as tenderly as I could.

"Olivia!" Mrs. Prescott wailed. "Sit up!"

"Look at me, Ruth. *Only* at me," Mr. Prescott interrupted his wife's screams. There was an edge in his voice that carved through her growing hysteria. She straightened, though her lips trembled. "Go to our chambers and instruct Farley to give you a warm brandy. I'll send Dr. Arden at once."

I made to go with her when a warm hand came down on my shoulder. Thomas squeezed it in comfort, his golden-brown eyes serious as he inspected me. "I'll escort Mrs. Prescott and Mrs. Harvey to their chambers, then fetch your uncle."

He didn't ask if I'd be all right staying with the body; he trusted I would be. I stared at him a moment more, his confidence proving a balm to my raw nerves, soothing my fears. I nodded once, took another deep breath, then faced the table. Captain Norwood stared at a playing card stuck to Miss Prescott's back I hadn't noticed. It was directly in the center of her spine. My blood chilled. Whoever had thrown the knife had impaled the card through the blade first. A potential warning and a clue.

"I'll need this area to be left precisely as it is, Captain," I said, falling back on months of forensic training while Thomas guided the two women out. Uncle would be proud; I'd collected my emotions like anatomical specimens and stored them away to dissect later. "You'll also need to question everyone in this room."

"The lights were out, Miss Wadsworth." Norwood swallowed hard, his focus sliding back to the knives in Miss Prescott's spine and the torn card. "I doubt they witnessed anything useful."

I longed to smack him upside the head with that obvious remark.

The lights had only been out briefly—someone might have noticed suspicious behavior prior to that.

"Humor me then, sir," I said, using my best authoritative tone. The captain clamped his jaw. It was one thing to hear commands from a man, but from a seventeen-year-old girl it was quite another. For the sake of the murdered woman before us, I let my annoyance go. "My uncle is an expert with reading a crime scene," I added, sensing the captain's wavering decision. "It's what he'd advise."

He ran a hand down his face. A death on the first night of the Moonlight Carnival didn't bode well for his future plans. "Very well. I'll send crew to everyone's rooms tonight."

At a signal from the captain, attendants swept into the saloon like a well-dressed army, ushering members of first class out as calmly as they could. A few guests threw nervous glances our way, but most were excitedly chattering on about how lifelike the performance was. How real the blood appeared. And how on earth had the ringmaster managed to make the knives in the back look so authentic? Captain Norwood said nothing to confirm or deny these theories. He stood, face grim, and bid the passengers good evening.

As the room emptied, an uncomfortable feeling tingled down my own spine. I turned, surprised to find Mephistopheles staring from the stage, expression impossible to read behind his mask. Unlike the others, however, his attention wasn't on the murdered girl. He was watching me. His gaze was heavy, almost tangible, and I wondered what he'd seen or might know. I took a step in his direction, intent on asking him these questions and more, but he faded into the shadows and disappeared for good.

The chamber we'd been offered for Miss Prescott's postmortem reminded me of a dank cave.

We were deep within the bowels of the *Etruria,* and being so near the boiler system, the temperature was unpleasantly warm and the lights flickered a bit too often, as if the ship itself was nervous about what dark deeds were to come. I was grateful for the refrigeration on board—we wouldn't keep the body in this chamber for long, lest it swell with rot overnight and attract vermin.

Gooseflesh tickled my skin despite the heat. No matter how hard I fought to think otherwise, I could not escape from memories of another sinister laboratory. One where the *whirl-churn* sounds still managed to tiptoe through my nightmares some evenings. The bad dreams were less frequent than in weeks past, but they haunted me from time to time, painful reminders of all that I'd lost during the Autumn of Terror.

Ignoring the hiss of steam emanating from an exposed pipe, I focused on Uncle Jonathan as he rolled up his shirtsleeves and proceeded to scrub with carbolic soap. When he finished, I walked around the examination table, sprinkling sawdust to soak up any blood or fluids that might leak onto the floor. Rituals were necessary parts of our work. They helped keep our hearts and minds clear, according to Uncle.

"Before I remove the knives, I want physical details written down." Uncle's tone was as cool as the metal scalpels I'd laid out on the makeshift tray. "Height, weight, and so on. Audrey Rose, I'll need my—"

I handed his apron over, then tied my own about my waist. I hadn't changed out of my evening attire, and the juxtaposition of my fine silk gown against the plain apron reminded me of how unpredictable life could be. I doubted when Miss Prescott woke this morning she feared she'd be lying facedown on our examination table, stabbed with knives starting from the base of her skull and ending just near her tailbone.

Thomas picked up a notebook and nodded toward me, expression determined. He and I were well versed in our macabre roles, having practiced many times in more than one country. It seemed no matter where we went, death followed, and like greedy misers, we stored data away, profiting, in a sense, from loss. I'd provide the scientific findings and he'd record them—a team in all ways.

I dug around inside Uncle's leather medical satchel until I found the measuring tape. I held it from crown to toe as I'd been taught, my mind clearing with the familiar task. Now wasn't the time to reflect on all the things Miss Prescott longed to do in life. Now it was time to read her corpse for clues. I didn't believe in revenge, but it was hard not to seek justice for her.

"Deceased is a female named Miss Olivia Prescott, approximately one hundred and sixty-five centimeters, and eighteen years of age," I said, pausing for Thomas to scratch the information down. He looked up, my signal to continue. "I'd put her weight around seven and a half stone."

"Good." Uncle lined up the scalpels, bone saws, and scissors I'd need for the internal examination next. "Cause of death."

I tore my gaze from the cadaver. "I beg your pardon, sir, but there's nearly a dozen knives protruding from her back. Isn't her cause of death rather obvious? I'm sure one or more of them either pierced her heart or lungs, or severed her spinal column."

He turned his sharp, green-eyed focus on mine and I fought the urge to shrink away. Clearly, I'd forgotten an important lesson. "As forensic examiners, we cannot shut off other avenues to search. What have I taught you about trusting only that which you see?"

As far as admonishments went, it wasn't the worst, but my face still flamed under his scrutiny. "You're correct...it's...I suppose it's possible the knives have been poisoned. Or that Miss Prescott was killed through other means and the knives were a distraction. She did expire rather quickly and quietly."

"Very good." Uncle nodded. "It's imperative we keep our emotions and theories in check while performing a postmortem. Otherwise we run the risk of influencing our findings. Or becoming so distraught we work ourselves into a fit, like your aunt Amelia."

Uncle closed his eyes and I had the distinct impression he hadn't wished to speak of her.

"Aunt Amelia?" I drew my brows together. "What's happened to upset her? Is Father all right?"

An uncomfortably long pause followed my question and Uncle seemed at a loss for words. I gripped the measuring tape in my hands, knowing anything that took this long for him to compose a response to couldn't be good. He finally shot Thomas a pinched-lipped look—as if he wasn't certain he wanted his other protégé to hear what he had to say, then sighed.

"It seems Liza has gone missing."

"Missing? That can't be right." The shrill ringing in my head from earlier was back. I took an unsteady step away from the corpse, lest I faint onto it. "I received a letter from her only last week." I shut my mouth, trying to recount when my cousin's letter had been dated. I couldn't recall. But there hadn't been anything out of the ordinary. She'd been happy, secretly meeting with a young man. There was no harm in innocent flirtations. "Surely Aunt Amelia is overreacting. Liza is probably off with..."

I hadn't seen Thomas stand up, but he caught my eye across the small room. If Liza had run off with the young man she'd last written about, it would be a devastating blow to our family and reputation. No wonder Uncle had hesitated in front of Thomas.

Uncle rubbed his temples. "I'm afraid the news comes from your father. Amelia is beside herself with grief and hasn't left her chambers in more than a week. Liza went out one afternoon and never returned home. Your father worries she may be dead."

"Dead? She can't—" My stomach seemed to fall through my knees. Either it was the ocean travel or the news, but I was about to be sick. Without offering another word, I rushed from the room, not wanting to witness the disappointment in my uncle's eyes as my emotions erupted from the box I'd set them in and consumed me.

I huddled into my cloak, watching from the chilly promenade deck as the sun dipped toward the horizon, turning the dark, churning waves the color of clotted blood. The steady sound of water striking the hull was like a siren's call, luring victims in, promising all would be well if one simply took a leap of faith and entered her underwater dominion.

"What have you gotten yourself into this time, Cousin?" I sighed, the puff of warm air mingling with the cold ocean mist. In response, waves bashed against the side of our ship, distressed and restless, and perhaps a little desperate to shove us back to England. Back to where I had a chance—even a bleak one—of finding Liza.

How quickly dreams dissolved into nightmares.

Despite the impossibility before me, I refused to submit to the fact that I was stranded at sea, powerless to assist those I loved. I could not believe Father allowed me to leave England without telling me my cousin was missing. I'd thought we'd gotten past his sheltering ways after he'd permitted me to study forensic medicine in Romania, but I was clearly wrong. Even though it wasn't my fault, I felt as though I'd already failed Miss Prescott. And now Liza...

"I will not fail again," I swore aloud. There was only one line I would never cross—murder. Taking a life from a person—that would make me no better than the murderers I hoped to thwart. A cruel voice in my head whispered that I'd never actually *stopped* them.

I simply gathered clues made of blood and bone, and tried piecing them together before more bodies were added to the unending tally.

To truly end a murderer, I'd need to become one.

I eyed the lifeboats hanging against the wall of the promenade, wondering if I possessed enough physical strength to wrangle one down and row myself back to England. I clenched my teeth and faced the water. Salt and sea mist stung my nose, the spray rising in the icy air and coating my face. It woke me up from nonsensical visions.

Behind me a door swung open, revealing a tall figure gilded by light—the background din of staff cleaning up after the terrible opening show accentuated his own silence. He stood there, too shrouded in shadows for me to make out his features, but judging from the involuntary flutter in my chest, it was Thomas.

As he approached the railing where I stood, I noticed a telegram peeking out from his overcoat pocket. I wondered if it was from my father and if he'd sent word to everyone aboard this ship except for me. If anyone had hurt Liza, I would kill them. Slowly.

I almost smiled, finding the thought didn't disturb me one bit.

"If I didn't know any better, Wadsworth, my dear," Thomas said, voice laced with teasing, his typical method of distracting me from my darkness, "I'd believe you were about to perform your own escape act. Am I to be your assistant, then?" He stared down at himself, frowning slightly. "I left my sequined dragon frock coat in London and this one's a bit plain. It doesn't particularly scream 'carnival chic.'"

"Actually, I was contemplating murder."

"Not mine, I hope." He leaned over the railing and glanced sideways at me. "Though I am rather handsome in this suit. I suppose if it's my time to go, I might as well go in style. Be sure to keep my face intact. I want you to swoon and mourn at my funeral."

I nearly groaned. "That's in poor taste, considering recent events." I nudged him with my elbow as he sighed. "I still choose you even with your shortcomings, Cresswell."

"It's my wit, isn't it?" Thomas faced me, a tentative smile starting. "You can't bear to be apart from it. Honestly, I'm surprised you haven't informed your uncle about the claim you've staked upon me. Seems like news you'd enjoy sharing."

There was a question in his eyes, but I quickly gazed back at the ocean, pretending to have missed it. The stars were out in full force tonight, twinkling and shimmering across the undulating sea. It reminded me of the painting Thomas made for me the week before: an orchid that held the entire universe within its petals. It amazed me that the world could resume its orbit no matter what destruction had been wrought. I wondered how Mrs. Prescott was feeling, if she'd been given her brandy and was floating somewhere between dreams and nightmares.

Perhaps I ought to join her.

I felt Thomas studying me but no longer had the urge to mask my expression as I used to. He opened his mouth, then shut it, causing me to puzzle over what he might have said. Perhaps he'd grown as weary of having the same debate. I didn't wish to tell anyone of our eventual betrothal until we'd spoken to my father. Thomas saw it as hesitancy on my part, a notion so ridiculous I refused to acknowledge it at all. We simply did not have the luxury of time to visit with Father and inform him of our intentions while we raced to the ship, as much as I wanted to. There wasn't any part of me that didn't long to be with him forever. After everything we'd been through over the last month, I thought he'd know that.

A moment later, he wrapped an arm around my shoulders and tugged me near, safe in his indiscretion, since we were alone on the freezing deck. I relaxed into his embrace, letting the warmth of his body and the scent of his cologne comfort me.

"I cannot promise all will be well, Audrey Rose."

I exhaled loudly. "This is one of those times it's all right to lie, Thomas. I'm quite aware of how dire things are, but I'd like to pretend otherwise. At least for a few moments."

"Right," he said, turning his thoughts inward. "What I mean is, I promise to stand by your side through whatever comes our way. You'll end up being the hero, no doubt, but I'll look good beside you. And that's what truly counts."

"Honestly?"

He drew back, feigning being affronted. "You can't possibly have *all* the glory. Good looking *and* the hero? This is one of those times it's all right to lie, Wadsworth."

"Have you no—" He brushed his lips against mine and I forgot about my worries, just as he'd intended. The kiss started off tentative and sweet, a distraction and promise itself, but soon turned deeper and more urgent. I wound my arms around his neck, bringing him closer, getting lost in the rhythm of both the sea and our kiss. Even on the coldest night, he could ignite a fire within me. I worried that one day the blaze might consume me entirely.

Much too soon, he broke away. In times like this I thought he was right—we ought to announce our intentions and marry immediately. Then I might kiss him whenever I pleased.

"Shall I say the thing I'm not supposed to?" he asked, his tone serious.

I drew in a deep breath. For him to acknowledge hesitance meant I most certainly did *not* want to hear it. "We've promised not to lie to each other."

"All right. Here are the facts." He studied me again, his expression controlled but kind. "There's nothing to be done about Liza from here. We can make arrangements to return to London once we reach America, but for now we have the very real issue of a murderer aboard our ship. It may be an isolated incident, but I don't believe it will be."

Gooseflesh marched along my arms. Thomas's deductions were hardly ever wrong. If he believed there might be more murders, it was only a matter of time before we found the bodies.

"What do you suggest we do?" I asked, rubbing my hands over my sleeves.

"I'm glad you asked. I've been thinking on this quite a bit."

"And?"

"I'm in favor of hiding in your chamber for the remainder of the week." A smile twitched across his lips as I raised a brow. "Drinking, kissing, debauching ourselves until we arrive in New York." He sighed dreamily. "You must admit, we'd be safe from the murderer. Deliriously happy. And both of those options are much better than standing over cadavers."

I rolled my eyes. "Or we could finish the postmortem and see what we find."

"A less fun but more valiant choice as always, Wadsworth. Though your uncle wishes to resume the postmortem tomorrow per the captain's request." He exhaled, though there was a troublesome gleam in his eyes. "I've been tasked with escorting you to bed, a difficult job, but one I shall take very seriously, I assure you."

I shook my head. Thomas had dragged me from the deepest parts of my worries and restored my focus . . . all while managing to steal another kiss. I couldn't say that his method wasn't appealing as we made our way down the promenade, arm in arm.

THREE

ACE OF CLUBS

An attendant braided my hair and helped me into a cotton night-gown with lace-trimmed sleeves without uttering a word—while the majority of passengers still believed Miss Prescott's murder was an elaborate show, most of the crew aboard the ship seemed to hold their breath along with their tongues, unsure if another nightmare would soon be unleashed.

Once she'd gone, I released an exhausted sigh and glanced around. My chambers were handsomely appointed with a marble nightstand, a carved vanity, a small table and chairs, and a wardrobe that would have pleased King Louis with all its gold embellishments. However, the industrial-sized bolts and steel surrounding the small window couldn't hide the truth of where I was. Despite the lavish dressings, a chill seeped in through the cracks.

Our luxurious ship was nothing more than a floating prison.

I pulled a pair of thick stockings on and lay on my bed, know-ing sleep was the last thing I'd accomplish with so many thoughts spinning through my mind. I picked up the Ace of Clubs I'd found staked to Miss Prescott's body and inspected it. What connection did it have to this murder? I mulled over a few potential clues, the most prominent having to do with magic tricks.

Sleight of hand was something I'd not given much thought to before, though I'd seen street magicians roll cards across their knuckles in London. They must practice for long hours to make it appear so fluid a motion, their deception flawless to an untrained eye. Not too different from a cunning murderer.

Crime scenes were filled with their own sort of sleight of hand. Murderers tried fabricating scenes, manipulating them to cover their true intentions and identity. Mephistopheles was gifted in the art of misdirection, something based in fact, not fantasy. He made a person look one way when they ought to do the exact opposite. If he hadn't been onstage when Miss Prescott was killed, he'd be the most likely culprit.

I sat up, heart racing, as I finally understood my earlier preoccupation with the young ringmaster. I wanted to learn his very particular skills—utilizing that part of my brain while placing myself in the minds of deviants and murderers would be most beneficial. Something niggled around the edges of my mind, some hazy, far-flung idea that would be nearly impossible to pull off. If I could mislead Thomas Cresswell, make him believe the impossible—that my feelings had shifted—then I'd know for certain I was an expert at that art form...

Abandoning that plan, I settled back into my pillows and flipped the Ace of Clubs over, searching for significance. It was sliced through its center and stained with dried blood, but the back had the most interesting design. A raven—dark as ink—opened its wings against a silver moon. Vines and thorns were intricately woven around the card's edges in thick black strokes. On both the top and bottom center, a strange double eight lay on its side, overlapping itself.

I avoided touching the place where the knife had torn it, still in denial that Miss Prescott had been slain right beside me and I hadn't been any the wiser. If only Uncle hadn't—

A soft knock came at the door connecting my room and my chaperone's, startling me from my ruminations. I pushed myself up, deposited the card on my nightstand, and wrapped an embroidered orchid dressing robe about me. Gooseflesh rose, though it wasn't from surprise. The watered silk was cool and smooth as liquid against the parts of my skin not covered by my nightgown.

"Come in."

"It's only me, dear." Mrs. Harvey opened the door, a small tea service balanced on her ample hip. "Thought you could do with something warm. I also brought my traveling tonic just in case you'd like something a bit *warmer*."

I smiled, recalling the clever name she'd given her spirits when we'd traveled to Romania last month. Her engraved flask teetered on the tray. The sharp scent of alcohol was detectable from where I sat and I decided it would indeed warm me quickly. And perhaps burn a hole through my stomach in the process.

"Tea will do for now, thank you." I went to join her at the small table, but she stopped me with a firm shake of her head. She poured tea, then tucked me back into bed, pushing the steaming cup into my hands. Bergamot and rose immediately scented the air, relaxing me at once. "Thank you."

"There, there, child." She plopped down beside me and took a generous swig of her tonic. "No need to thank me. I was simply in need of a bit of company myself. Makes the traveling tonic go down easier." Her gaze drifted over to the card on my nightstand. "Wealth."

"Pardon?" I asked, wondering if she'd already been sipping her tonic.

"My husband used to dabble in cartomancy—reading fortunes in playing cards—in his youth. It was how we met." A wistfulness entered her expression. "He was dreadful at it. God rest his soul. Though he was quite talented in other areas."

"How are you faring?" I asked, quickly changing the subject. I didn't wish to find out which talents she was dreamily recalling. "It's been quite a day."

"I don't know how you and my Thomas do what you do and keep your wits about you," she said, snapping back to the present, "but I'm proud of you both. You make a fine pair, you know. In your apprenticeship and in other ways. Has Thomas made his intentions clear?"

I stuck my face in my cup, hoping the steam could be blamed for the flush creeping onto my skin. "Yes...well...that is, I believe he wishes to speak with my father."

"He's not conventional. Lord help him, he's got much to learn about using those manners of his, but his heart is good." Mrs. Harvey took another sip, eyeing me over her spectacles. "You will make him very happy, Audrey Rose. But, most important, I believe he will also make *you* very happy." She wiped at wetness in the corner of her eye. "It's not proper...but...here."

Without saying more, she handed over a folded note. There was no name on it and no envelope. I looked up quickly. "What's this?"

Mrs. Harvey gathered her flask and moved toward the door, lifting a shoulder. "I haven't the slightest notion what you mean, dear. I'm simply an old woman who came to say good evening. I sleep like the dead, so you'll have to shout if you need me. I most certainly wouldn't hear if your door opened and closed."

With a wink, she closed the door to our chambers, leaving me gaping after her. Clearly she hadn't been as unaware of Thomas's flirtations last month as she had appeared. Without thinking too hard on how he'd convinced her to take part in this new scheme, I unfolded the paper. A short message in neat script greeted me. I wondered who'd written it until I read it.

If you'd please, I beg for you to meet me near the starboard side of the bow at midnight.

Alone.

My pulse thrummed at the proposition contained in one small line. It wasn't the first time Thomas had requested we meet somewhere at such an indecent hour. Unchaperoned. This time, however, we weren't in a mostly empty boarding school in Romania, far from inquisitive eyes. If we were to be caught alone here amongst the upper class—I'd be deemed a trollop, my reputation destroyed. Then again, perhaps Thomas had deduced a new theory or discovered another clue that might unveil Miss Prescott's murderer. My wretched curiosity whirled with possibilities.

I stared at the note a moment more, biting my lip, surprised Thomas would have an attendant take down such a personal message. I could pretend as if I'd never received it. Do the polite and decent thing expected of me. But that path was so utterly dull. I thought of Thomas's lips on mine, imagined his hands tangled in my dark hair, our breath coming in short gasps as his hands slowly traveled over me, exploring and teasing.

Acceptable or not, I craved his touch.

My eyes snapped to the small clock ticking away on my night-stand. It was nearly midnight now. I glanced down at my silk robe and lace-trimmed nightgown, the ruffles on my sleeves falling across my fingers. There wasn't enough time to get dressed and rush all the way to the starboard side of the boat without being seen. Yet show-ing up in my current state would cause embolisms should I run into anyone else who'd decided on a midnight stroll. Which sounded pre-cisely like the sort of deviant plan Thomas would make.

"Scoundrel." I smiled, then tossed my winter cloak on, grabbed a scalpel from my medical bag just to be safe, and hoped for the best as I crept out my door.

During daylight hours, the *Etruria* inspired feelings of grand travel and frivolity, what with its massive masts and large steam funnels. Hardwood floors had been buffed and polished until sunshine gleamed like diamonds from them, and the roof above the promenade deck was a beautiful addition to the pearly corridor of first class.

At night those same features felt haunted, dangerous. The overhang was more akin to an open mouth, waiting to chomp down on guests; the same shining floors were now reminiscent of a salivating tongue. Lifeboats secured to the wall were actually perfect hiding places instead of quaint miniatures. The immense sails snapped around as if they were wings of some enormous sea creature hunting fresh meat. Smokestacks exhaled, the fog lingering around the railing, watching. Anything might be lurking in the mist. Or, more appropriately, any*one*.

"Foolish," I whispered, pulling my fur-trimmed cloak tighter as icy fingers meandered down my skin. If Miss Prescott hadn't been murdered, I'd blame my overactive imagination for morphing the boat into a gargantuan creature. But there truly *could* be something hiding in the shadows, hoping to sink its claws into my back next. I decided I didn't care for sea travel one bit.

Thomas would do better to choose a more reasonable place for any future clandestine meetings. Preferably indoors, near a fire, far from empty corridors and thrashing waters. Teeth chattering, I hurried down the promenade, attention snagging on anything that seemed out of place, though it was hard to know exactly what didn't belong. I'd never traveled on such a vessel before.

Wind whipped down the open corridor with a low warning howl. Ropes creaked. Each new sound was like a needle pricking my veins. I held my scalpel tightly at my side, not wanting to strike out at anyone by mistake. I needed to rein in my emotions, or someone could get hurt. I longed to kiss Thomas, not accidentally eviscerate him.

As I neared the front of the ship, I slowed my pace. I didn't see my future betrothed, but surely he had to have arrived by now. I strained to see around benches and slatted chairs that had been bolted to the ground. It was hard to make out anything more than silhouettes in the cloud-covered night; the dim lanterns lining the promenade were either turned off or didn't extend this far. I swallowed my fear down. No one was out hunting me.

"Thomas?" I whispered, inching toward the prow. On this part of the ship, the wind was merciless. I tucked my chin to my chest, though that hardly helped. If Thomas didn't appear soon, I'd—

He strode toward me, a silhouette in human form. My heart raced.

"Was the dramatic meeting place truly necessary, Cresswell?"

He stopped a few feet from where I stood shuddering. I all but rolled my eyes as he scanned me and then our surroundings. He did not move any closer and my annoyance reared up. This was not the warm greeting I'd pictured as I sneaked about the frigid ship.

"Well? I'm about to catch my death. What was so urgent that we needed to meet out here at this hour? Do you have any news on Miss Prescott?"

He tilted his head to one side, considering. And that's when I noticed the slight reflection as light caught on his face. As if part of his features were covered in . . . I gasped.

"Apologies for any disappointment, miss, but my name is not Cresswell." Mephistopheles took a hesitant step closer. "Though I am intrigued a young lady of your standing would agree to such an unchaperoned meeting."

I held the scalpel up, cursing my hands for shaking. I did not want him to think my trembling was entirely due to how frightened I was.

"W-what do you want?" I managed to get out. I swore the wind bent to his will; it growled and hissed, finding every crevice in my clothing to claw its way through. Mephistopheles came forward, his cloak whipping about behind him. I did not believe in such things, but in this moment he appeared to be the devil's heir Chief Magistrate Prescott claimed he was. "S-stop. Or I swear I'll s-sever your artery. I know pr-precisely where to inflict the m-most damage, sir."

I don't know what I expected, but a surprised bark of laughter wasn't it. He removed his own cloak, his movements unhurried as to not startle me into slashing out.

"Contrary to what you may think, I'm not in the business of watching young women die. Please." He held the cloak toward me. "Take this. It's an angora blend. You won't find another garment as warm or soft, I guarantee it." I gritted my teeth against their chattering and eyed the cloak. I did not want to accept any form of help from this wicked-looking young man. He slowly grinned. "Here. I'll lay it over this chair and you can fetch it yourself." He set it down with care, then stepped back, bowing in mockery. "Your cloak awaits, fair lady."

"What d-do you want?" I repeated, holding my weapon at the ready. He simply crossed his arms, and stared pointedly at the garment. I exhaled loudly, then snatched up the cloak. I resisted the urge to rub my cheek along the downy softness. In a matter of moments warmth bloomed over my body, and my trembling decreased. He smirked, and I brandished my weapon once more, wiping the smug look from his face. "Answer my question or I shall leave."

He unfolded the nearest chair and sat, crossing one leg over the other. If he was cold, sitting there in his scarlet evening jacket as the wind howled its displeasure, it didn't show. Perhaps he wasn't entirely human. That at least would explain his seemingly inexplicable talent for magic tricks. For the first time I noticed his gloves—each one had a crescent moon stitched onto the back of it with stars across the knuckles. They were exquisite.

"I've a proposition for you." I started shaking my head, but he held up a hand. "It's a bargain that will prove most beneficial, I suspect. I saw the way you observed the unfortunate incident this evening. You were calculating and calm when others panicked. You searched for clues and details. Both are skills I am in need of."

"Yes, it's quite unfortunate to find nearly a dozen knives in someone's back," I said coldly. "What a tremendous talent you have, making the murder of a young woman sound no more horrendous than a simple act of misfortune. And then attempting to use it all to your benefit. You're disgusting."

He eyed me from his seat. "Admonish me all you wish, but one fact remains: it *is* unfortunate. Would it make you feel better if I'd shed a tear?"

I had the impression his inquiry was sincere, as if he'd relish nothing more than turning this into an opportunity to practice his performance skills. "I've had quite enough mischief for one evening. If you'll excuse me, I've—"

"I came to offer my tutelage in exchange for your assistance. I believe, based on the curiosity you displayed during the show, that you wish to learn sleight of hand. I desire to preserve something very dear to me. You can help with that."

"I have no desire to learn tricks, sir."

He offered a look that suggested I was a horrible liar. "You won't find a better teacher."

"But I may find a less arrogant one." I forced myself to breathe. It wasn't magic I desired to learn, but he was close to guessing the truth I'd rather hide. "Anyway, I'm sorry to inform you, sir, but I do not believe in such nonsense as magic. I am a scientist. Do not insult me with your cheap theatrics. If your charlatan's fortune-telling practices worked, then you'd have known not to bother."

"'Cheap theatrics'?" He jumped from his chair and took a few steps in my direction. I held my ground, watching as he slowly reached out, then pulled a card seemingly from the air around us.

36

"Magic is science. It's simply a fancier term for showing people the impossible is attainable."

I stared at the card, heart thumping as he rolled it across his knuckles. It was hard to tell in the dim light, but it appeared similar to the unique playing card stuck to Miss Prescott's body. I longed to raise my scalpel again, but didn't want to alert him to my shift in mood. Either Mephistopheles was the person responsible for Miss Prescott's death, or someone with access to his cards was. Since he'd been onstage, I knew the latter to be the most probable.

He watched me closely. Without the distance of the stage between us, I could easily see the intelligent gleam. "Do you deny the allure of sleight of hand, too? Are you only interested in one form of science, or would you care to expand your knowledge?"

"Weren't you the one who warned against accepting midnight bargains with your lot? Contrary to what you may think," I said, spitting his earlier words back at him, "I'm not in the business of being a fool. Now if you'll excuse me, it's late and this was a waste of our time. Good night, sir."

I brushed past him, not bothering to look back as he called out, "Our bargain remains yours to take. I have a feeling you'll think of it differently soon enough. After all, murder is just another form of sleight of hand, is it not?"

I hoped he hadn't noticed my steps falter as I hurried along the dark promenade, ignoring the chills that raced along my spine. Murder *was* another form of sleight of hand. And if the person responsible was talented enough, they just might get away with it.

FOUR

A TANGLED WEB

I fiddled with the pearl buttons on my gloves as Uncle rapped his fist against the chief magistrate's door. Mumbled voices rose on the other side, though they didn't stop arguing. Uncle waited a few moments before repeating the motion. He'd been up earlier than I was and had completed Miss Prescott's postmortem on his own, leaving me too much time to think over the last twenty-four hours without any distractions.

I stared blankly at the bolts surrounding the door. I'd barely slept the night before, tossing and turning until I thought I'd go mad. Aside from Mephistopheles's strange midnight bargain and Miss Prescott's murder, there was the constant weight of worry over Liza. I wanted to beg Captain Norwood to turn this ship around and sail straight back to England. Instead I had to settle for taking one wretched day at a time. Patience was a loathsome virtue.

"Have you heard anything I've said?" Thomas waved a hand in front of my face, one corner of his mouth quirked up. "It's truly fascinating when you do that."

"Do what? Think?" I batted his hand away. "Pardon me."

"No need." He grinned. "You know I don't mind when you day-dream about me."

Uncle glanced over his shoulder. "Might the two of you act prop-erly for five minutes?"

"I've done nothing!" I tossed my hands up. "The only thing I'm guilty of is thinking about last night's murder. Mrs. Harvey said something about cartomancy. It might be worth investigating."

Uncle muttered something that sounded quite rude and knocked once more. Thomas stepped into my line of view and mouthed, "And guilty of picturing me without clothing?"

Before I could offer him an unladylike hand gesture, the door swung open. In an instant, the teasing smile was gone from my friend's face, replaced by the cold calculation that always entered his features when observing people. I'd expected to see Chief Mag-istrate Prescott, but a shorter, rounder man with a receding hairline greeted us.

"Good day, gentleman," he said, not sounding at all as if he meant it. "And young lady. What may I assist you with?"

"I'm Dr. Jonathan Wadsworth of London, and these are my apprentices, Mr. Thomas Cresswell and Miss Audrey Rose Wads-worth. We've come to call on Mr. Prescott," Uncle said. "There are a few questions we need answered regarding the days leading up to his daughter's murder. It won't take but a few minutes of his time."

The stout man pulled his shoulders back, and tried looking down his stub nose, though Uncle was a good bit taller. "I'm afraid that's not possible at present. I've administered a tonic to quell his nerves." He stuck his meaty hand out. "I'm Dr. Philip Arden."

Thomas and I exchanged raised brows. Gentlemen weren't nor-mally given elixirs for nerves, a foolish societal notion claiming men didn't experience such emotions, but I was more concerned with the blatant lie. We'd just heard the two men arguing through the closed door.

Uncle nodded. "Any information Mr. Prescott may offer will do, even in his current condition."

"I'm afraid I must insist you come back another time," Dr. Arden said, slowly closing the door in our faces. "The Prescotts desire time to process the sudden death of their only daughter. Surely you understand the need for such delicacy?"

I bit down on my tongue. Part of me wanted to say I didn't understand at all, to talk sternly about the importance of ferreting out any clues before they were lost to memory. However, I knew that was a harsh viewpoint given the circumstances. Their only daughter died brutally in front of them. If they needed time to mourn, it was the least we could offer.

A door creaked open down the corridor, yet no one stepped out. I caught Thomas's eye and jerked my head in the direction. He took a small step toward the room and paused, nodding in assent. Someone was eavesdropping. I tuned back into the conversation between Dr. Arden and my uncle, hoping they'd hurry it along.

"Very well," Uncle relented. "Please let him know I stopped by. I'll return again later this evening."

I dropped a polite curtsy, but before Dr. Arden could tip his hat, I was moving swiftly down the corridor. I was about to raise my fist and knock, when I noticed Mrs. Prescott staring blankly ahead, eyes rimmed in the red of the grief-stricken.

"Mrs. Prescott…" I moved slowly into her line of vision. "Do you need me to fetch—"

"I told him we shouldn't accept the offer," she said, eyes fixed on the ocean. "It was his pride that doomed her."

I felt Uncle and Thomas hovering behind me and held a hand to stall them. "What offer made you uncomfortable? Was it something you received prior to boarding the ship?"

She blinked at me, as if realizing she wasn't speaking into the void after all. "A letter. We'd received an invitation. As did the Ardens." She laughed, the sound anything but amused. "'Esteemed guest,' indeed. Robert enjoys believing his own press—that his opinion is one to aspire to attain. There wasn't any way he'd miss an opportunity to show off. Vanity is a sin."

"Does Mr. Prescott know who sent the letter?" I pressed. "May I see it?"

A tear slipped down her cheek. Then another. She turned her attention on me and her emotions punched me in my very core. "What good will it do? My Olivia is gone."

Thomas shifted, fingers tapping his sides. He reminded me of a hound who'd scented a promising lead and wanted to hunt it down no matter the cost. I made to grab him, but he carefully sidestepped my reach.

"Mrs. Prescott, if I may offer my opinion?" he asked. I closed my eyes. Thomas was many incredible things, but subtle he was not. "You have suffered a tragedy most could neither imagine, nor endure. Yet here you stand, breathing, living. Which is the most difficult thing to do. People often admire physical strength, but I believe it's the simple things one does after a tragedy that defines them. There is no greater show of power than continuing to live when you'd like nothing more than to lie down and let the world fade. Your strength and conviction are needed now—to assist us in capturing whoever did this to your daughter. Miss Olivia might be gone, but what you do next will help her seek the justice she deserves."

I blinked back the stinging in my eyes, completely and utterly speechless. Mrs. Prescott seemed equally dazed, but recovered swiftly and disappeared into her room. I stood there, mouth agape, not knowing who this Thomas Cresswell was. He flashed a quick grin. "A lifetime full of surprises, remember, Wadsworth?"

"Indeed." I could not imagine a future that didn't include unwinding each secret he possessed. Mrs. Prescott finally made her way back to where we lingered in the doorway.

"Here," she said, sniffling. "For Olivia."

Thomas took the letter with great care, holding it to his chest. "We will find who did this, Mrs. Prescott. And they will be made to pay."

I glanced sharply in Thomas's direction. His tone sent a creeping chill across my skin. I did not doubt that he would fight with everything he had to solve this case.

Mrs. Prescott swallowed hard. "If you'll excuse me, I need to lie down again."

We bid her goodbye and continued down the promenade. Uncle glanced over at us while we walked, expression shuttered. I wondered if he was thinking about Aunt Amelia, worried that she might be in an equally horrid condition, going mad with panic over Liza's disappearance. So often we were only tasked with cutting open the dead, searching the aftermath for clues. Speaking with the living during their time of grief was much harder. It was nearly impossible to turn emotions off and disconnect from the gruesome work that needed to be done.

Once we were far enough down the promenade deck, Thomas stopped and handed the invitation to me. It was quite decadent as far as envelopes went. The paper was a shiny ink blue and the letters were a swirling silver and gold. Little stars littered the border as if someone had blown glitter across the page. It reminded me immediately of the Moonlight Carnival.

I traced my finger over the glossy finish and opened the letter up.

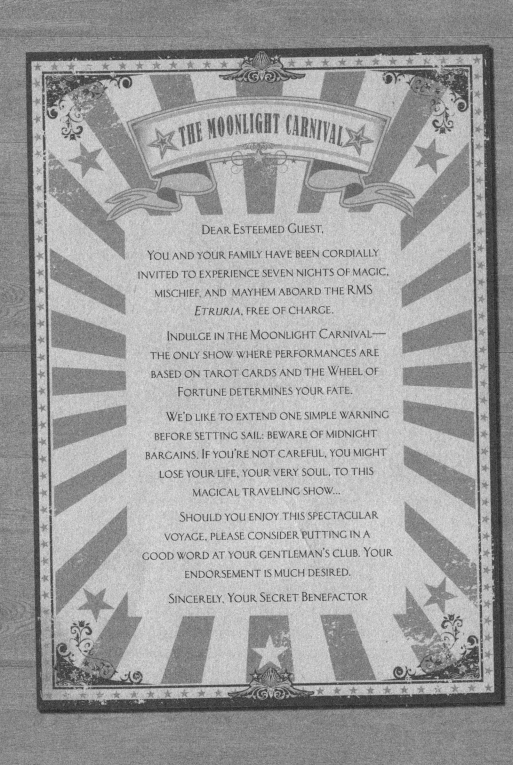

☆ THE MOONLIGHT CARNIVAL ☆

DEAR ESTEEMED GUEST,

YOU AND YOUR FAMILY HAVE BEEN CORDIALLY
INVITED TO EXPERIENCE SEVEN NIGHTS OF MAGIC,
MISCHIEF, AND MAYHEM ABOARD THE RMS
ETRURIA, FREE OF CHARGE.

INDULGE IN THE MOONLIGHT CARNIVAL—
THE ONLY SHOW WHERE PERFORMANCES ARE
BASED ON TAROT CARDS AND THE WHEEL OF
FORTUNE DETERMINES YOUR FATE.

WE'D LIKE TO EXTEND ONE SIMPLE WARNING
BEFORE SETTING SAIL: BEWARE OF MIDNIGHT
BARGAINS. IF YOU'RE NOT CAREFUL, YOU MIGHT
LOSE YOUR LIFE, YOUR VERY SOUL, TO THIS
MAGICAL TRAVELING SHOW...

SHOULD YOU ENJOY THIS SPECTACULAR
VOYAGE, PLEASE CONSIDER PUTTING IN A
GOOD WORD AT YOUR GENTLEMAN'S CLUB. YOUR
ENDORSEMENT IS MUCH DESIRED.

SINCERELY, YOUR SECRET BENEFACTOR

"What do either of you make of this?" Uncle asked. "First impressions."

"It's hard to say." I drew in a deep breath, my mind turning over the words. "On one hand I understand Mrs. Prescott's distrust—why seek endorsement from a judge? Surely there are more influential members of the aristocracy to target for that sort of thing." I scanned the letter again, then handed it to Thomas. "I'd claim it was highly unlikely to have been sent by anyone associated with the carnival. Which of them could afford to purchase passage for four first-class passengers?"

"But?" Thomas urged, brow raised. I had the impression he'd come to the same conclusion and was giving me an opportunity to shine.

"It's very close to the opening statement Mephistopheles made." I pointed to the one line that was practically identical. " 'You might lose your life, your very soul, to this magical traveling show.' Who else would be privy to that speech, if not a carnival worker?"

Uncle twisted his mustache, focus turned inward. "Perhaps someone who's attended the carnival before. This isn't the first time the Moonlight Carnival is performing."

"True," I said, unconvinced. "It still doesn't explain why they'd wish to frame the circus. Thus far there are no witnesses that we know of, no motive as to why Miss Prescott was targeted, and no decent reason to orchestrate such a tangled web to commit one murder. Why not simply wait until the lights are out, strike, then slip back to wherever they emerged from?"

Thomas paced the deck, his movements quick and precise, much like I imagined his thoughts to be. He stopped abruptly and moved to the railing, staring out at the endless sea. Uncle and I glanced at each other, but didn't dare interrupt him while he traveled into that dark, twisted part of himself. A few moments later, he half turned, shoulders stiff.

"The murderer is likely someone who enjoys the spectacle. He isn't interested in quietly committing his dark deeds—he wants drama, the thrill of seeing people recoil. I…" The wind blew a section of hair across his brow. He turned to us, expression hard. "Next time the victim will be revealed in a grander fashion, one that cannot simply be thought of as a performance. Wherever he is right now, he's seething. Enraged that more people weren't afraid of his opening act. When he strikes again, every passenger aboard this ship will be imprisoned by their fear. I guarantee he means to turn this cruise into a fantastical nightmare."

After a prolonged pause, Uncle motioned for us to be on our way. "Be on guard at all times, both of you. The last thing we need is any more trouble for this family."

While dressing for the evening show, I replayed Thomas's dire proclamation in my mind. By the time the attendant finished pinning the last rosebud in my hair, my stomach was completely knotted. If Thomas was correct, and I had no doubt he was, then another person was about to die.

Uncle had warned us to be on guard, so I'd taken his advice rather literally. In my silk off-the-shoulder gown, dyed a dark purplish black, I felt as if I were a figure that could easily blend into the shadows and observe the dining saloon if needed.

I removed my mother's heart-shaped locket from the jewelry box and handed it to the attendant, immediately comforted as its weight settled on my breastbone.

Once the attendant left, I carefully perched on the edge of a chair, mulling over facts. According to Mrs. Prescott, both Chief Magistrate Prescott and Dr. Arden received invitations to experience the Moonlight Carnival, all expenses anonymously paid. They knew each other outside of the *Etruria,* but I needed to investigate their relationship further. Which might prove difficult, as Dr. Arden had the welcoming personality of a slug. He'd taken to staying in Mr. Prescott's chamber and refused to speak with anyone for at least another day or two.

Letting that lead go for the time being, I focused on what I already knew. Miss Prescott was slain as soon as the lights went out, a coincidence, perhaps, but I didn't believe so. Someone who knew precisely when it would be dark in the dining saloon had waited to strike. Another indication that whoever committed the heinous act was somehow involved with the carnival. Or someone who might have observed any rehearsals. I made a mental notation to speak with the captain again. He'd have names of crew members on duty.

Then there was the matter of the Ace of Clubs; its connection was still unclear. Although that might be the point. Maybe the card was nothing more than a distraction. Though cartomancy was another avenue that might prove beneficial...

Someone knocked on the connecting-room door, tugging me from my thoughts. I stood, smoothing down the front of my gown. "Yes?"

I expected Mrs. Harvey, fetching me for supper. Instead Thomas waltzed in as if being alone with me in my bedchamber was not utterly scandalous. I scanned him from head to toe in his dress suit; surely looking so handsome had to be a criminal offense.

"Where's Mrs. Harvey?" I both hoped and dreaded that she would join us.

Thomas slowed his pace, inspecting me as if to gauge my emotions. Whatever he saw in my expression made his lips twitch. "In the dining saloon with your uncle, waiting for us."

"How did you manage—"

Words failed as he strode over and gathered me into his arms. His eyes, while slightly filled with mirth, were dark and deep enough for me to drown in. Our last stolen kiss felt like it had happened ages ago, and every nerve in my body tingled with anticipation.

God save me, I wanted him.

One of his hands slowly trailed down my back, and my breath hitched, igniting something in his gaze that practically undid me. Never one to disappoint, he bent his face to mine, a smile curving those wonderful lips as he tilted my chin up.

"Have I swept you off your feet yet, Wadsworth?"

Without replying, my mouth was on his. I hadn't yet pulled my gloves on, so my bare fingertips roamed over his skin, and he replied in kind. Each stroke consumed my senses until all I could think of was where his hands might explore next, and the expanding hope that his lips might follow their careful path. His love was pure yet intoxicating, sweet and powerful. I'd never tire of this—of touching him and being touched by him.

As if he knew exactly how he made me feel, he slid his hands over my shoulders and up into my hair, moving until our bodies pressed together. I could have sworn there was an electric current running over every place we made contact. He whispered my name while dropping kisses down my throat and along my bare collarbone, stopping right where my locket lay. A need greater than propriety overcame me. Heart pounding, I tugged his suit jacket off and maneuvered us toward my bed.

Thomas gently laid me down, his body hovering above mine. It might not be medically possible, but I swore if he didn't touch me again soon, I'd combust. He ran a thumb over my bottom lip, gaze thoughtful. "I love when you look at me that way."

I searched his eyes. "How?"

"Like you might possibly love me in the same extraordinary way that I love you."

Any tether of self-control I'd clutched at slipped from my grasp. I drew him down until his weight settled on me, marveling at how incredible it felt to share a bed with him. I traced the strong lines of his jaw, getting lost in the golden flecks of his eyes before slowly bringing my mouth to his again. When his tongue touched mine, I nearly lost my senses.

Kissing him was my favorite indulgence, and he certainly enjoyed spoiling me.

"Perhaps you're right. We ought to get married on the boat," I said, breathing heavily. I might be ready to do more than kiss him, especially if he kept tracing those idle circles on my bodice. With a knowing grin, he kissed me once more, then resumed his attention to my neck. His teeth grazed the sensitive skin of my throat as his hand slipped down to my hip. Saints help me. "Do you think there's a priest? Father couldn't possibly be *that* mad if we eloped. Uncle might agree to be our witness... or Mrs. Harvey."

Thomas pulled back enough to look into my eyes, his wicked grin returning. "Miss Audrey Rose Wadsworth, conqueror of my soul—you are an absolute *fiend*. You'd like to flout tradition simply because of your need for my body." He held a hand over his heart. "I swear I have never loved you more."

Warmth spread to my face. "You're impossible."

"Impossible not to adore." With a seemingly great amount of effort, he pushed himself up and assisted me to my feet. There was still a hunger in his eyes that matched my own, and I wondered which of us would go mad with want first. I dragged my gaze away from him and settled it back on the bed, devising a way to reverse a few moments in time. "Have I ever told you about our country estate?"

I blinked at the sudden change in topic. "I don't believe so."

Thomas moved his hands up my wrists to my arms, then glided them down to my waist. He brought my body to his, lips ghosting over mine, and I fought to remain in control. I had the impression that if I were to kiss him again, neither one of us would regain our composure. In that moment, I wasn't sure I wanted to do the proper thing.

"Once we're married, I'd like to take you there," he whispered. "I'll send most of the staff away. We'll have all the privacy in the world—no more sneaking about. When you look at me the way you are now, my virtue is perilously close to corruption. And I've never been a very pious man, Wadsworth."

Heat pooled in my core at such a shocking declaration. I found I couldn't wait for the day we stopped holding ourselves back. "You truly are a scoundrel, Thomas Cresswell."

He chuckled. "Ah yes, but that sparkle in your eye indicates you adore it. And I love nothing more than pleasing you, so I'll do my best at being the worst."

"How romantic of you."

"I thought so, too." He glanced at the clock on my nightstand. "I'm afraid your uncle might murder Mrs. Harvey if we don't hurry back. He was eyeing up the knives when I left, and I don't believe he was contemplating which was the correct one to use on his filet."

I forced my gaze away from his mouth. Thoughts of actual murder shattered any remaining heat I'd felt between us. I sighed. "Let's go save our chaperones, then."

Thomas shrugged his jacket on, then exited through Mrs. Harvey's room. I studied my reflection in the looking glass, adjusting dark curls that had slipped free. I touched my lips, hoping they didn't appear swollen with kisses to anyone else's eye. I couldn't wait to write to Liza, she lived for this sort of romantic detail. She'd be shocked and delighted and—I gasped as if I'd been struck a hard blow. I'd momentarily forgotten she was missing.

I bent over, pressing my hands to my center and dragged in a deep breath, trying to quell my nerves. I was a terrible wanton thing, getting so distracted by Thomas's lips. I swore to do better the rest of the voyage.

A moment later, he knocked on my outer door like a proper

gentleman escort. I pushed my worries aside, opened the door, and accepted his arm. He was right—there wasn't anything we could do for Liza while trapped on this ship. Once we made land in America, I could orchestrate a better plan.

"Ready?" Thomas asked. I nodded. We moved as swiftly as my silken shoes permitted into the inner corridor that led to the saloon.

We checked our overcoats—and Thomas's white silk muffler—with an attendant and hurried down the hall, Thomas striding confidently in his full-dress suit. I paused, gaping at a rose he wore, fastened through his dress coat's buttonhole. I hadn't noticed it before I'd taken his jacket off. Truthfully, I hadn't been thinking of much outside of our embrace.

He caught my stare and winked. "They've got hothouse flowers on board for a shamefully indecent price. Clearly, I thought of you while dressing. Do feel free to return the favor anytime. Only, perhaps you ought to do it in reverse."

My clever retort died on my lips when the doors were swept open for us by two liveried attendants. The color scheme was the same black-and-white floors and sparkling ink-blue curtains from yesterday, but tonight there were silver and gold accents. Flowers, candelabras, and strands of beads made up centerpieces, a waterfall of excess riches.

What caught my attention—and most everyone else's, judging from their wide-eyed looks—were the masked performers filing into the room, twirling silver swords as if they were batons. Light bounced around off their blades, sending a flutter into my heart.

They were an army of performers, dressed for battle. Any one of them might turn their weapon on a dinner guest. Worse yet, all of them held the power to make this feast a bloodbath.

My steps faltered. I couldn't imagine a spectacle that would please a hungry killer more and hoped I was wrong.

Circus tents

FIVE

KNIGHT OF SWORDS

DINING SALOON
RMS ETRURIA
2 JANUARY 1889

"It's all right, breathe." Thomas guided me to our table and pulled my chair out, though there were waiters at the ready. A few of them blanched, but they did not dare step forward and remove him from the task he'd assigned himself.

At Thomas's show of chivalry, Uncle Jonathan lifted his attention from his fork and knife. He stared, expression inscrutable, and Lord only knew what he thought of Thomas's careful attention to me. I doubted he could hear my heart thudding, but irrationally worried the words I KISSED THOMAS CRESSWELL MOST WANTONLY were suddenly painted above my brow.

A smile started at the edges of his lips as if he'd dissected the very thought from my head. "Audrey Rose." He nodded as my escort took the seat beside him, across from me. "Thomas. You're just in time."

Mrs. Harvey sat on my right—across from my uncle—and gave me a nod of approval. "You look beautiful, dear. That color suits you well. Eggplant is such a marvelous shade for dreary January evenings! Hides a multitude of sins, as well."

At my furrowed brow, she motioned to a slight stain on her pale dress. It appeared to be liquid in nature, though I couldn't be sure.

"Thank you, Mrs. Harvey." Before I could remark on the fashionable gown and dazzling jewels she wore, the lights dimmed. Being aboard a ship fitted with electricity was enchanting, especially when it was used it to create a thrum of excitement.

I glanced around the room, taking note of anyone who appeared nervous, but no one stood out. Captain Norwood hadn't announced the truth regarding Miss Prescott's death, mostly for his own good, but also because the Prescotts had asked for discretion. Diners chatted excitedly at their tables, silent, and swordsmen and women continued swinging their blades, and all was strangely well. Maybe Thomas was wrong. Maybe tonight's show would not end in death. I picked up my goblet and sipped, releasing the last bit of tension from my spine.

Smoke flitted along the bottom of the curtains, teasing yet promising a blaze just out of sight. My palms dampened my sheer gloves. It was almost time. I peeked over at Uncle, but he was preoccupied with his supper. He tore into his filet with a singular focus he usually reserved for the dead we studied. Apparently he didn't believe that murder was on the menu again this evening. At least not in this room.

"Esteemed passengers of the *Etruria*," the ringmaster crooned, appearing once again from the cover of thick smoke. I shuddered at the memory of him appearing just as suddenly last night. "Welcome to night two of the Moonlight Carnival! The Wheel of Fortune has chosen an extraordinary performance. For your viewing pleasure, may I present an evening of thrills. Chills. And, quite possibly, spills...of *blood*!"

Without warning, the curtains peeled back like splayed flesh, revealing a masked young woman in a corset made of crushed red velvet, and midnight stockings. And little else.

Coffee-and-caramel hair was done up in ringlets that added inches to her height. Her bustle had layers of black crinoline edged in red ribbon that was quite beautiful.

A heart was cut out between her neck and bosom, showing off her décolletage. Ties in black ribbon mimicked the back of her corset, holding the neckline together. Matching black appliqués adorned each hip. She wore a filigree mask that was a metal so dark it appeared to be frozen oil. Dressed in red and black, she donned the feminine equivalent of the ringmaster's suit.

There was a collective gasp as the crowd took in the masked woman and then the oversize sword gleaming in her hands. Much like her costume, the sword's hilt was a thing of beauty—carved in nearly black metal, it resembled a bouquet of wildflowers and bird wings. It was like a faerie blade forged in some wild, heavenly fire.

Behind the mask, the young woman's eyes met mine and widened. Why on earth—

I covered my mouth, trying to contain my gasp as recognition shot through me like an arrow. No matter how or why, I knew one thing for certain.

The girl onstage was my missing cousin, Liza.

I swallowed hard, my focus never leaving hers. Even with the mask covering half her face, I knew it was her. The ringmaster moved into view, breaking the spell between us, and I set my goblet back down with a thud. Liquid splattered the tablecloth, and an attendant, ever vigilant, swiftly sopped up the mess. *Liza.* I barely blinked, worried she was a specter I'd conjured up and would disappear just as quickly.

"Try not to lose your hearts or your heads"—Mephistopheles's eyes gleamed—"and lovely Liza will try to keep hers as Jian Yu the Invincible. The incredible. The superior Knight of Swords, saws her in half!"

While the crowd roared in delight, I gulped down my growing horror.

"Well, this is an interesting development," Thomas whispered. I stared at him, unsurprised that he was practically bouncing in his chair. He adored riddles and unexpected pieces to sort out—tonight had just become one of the grandest puzzles of all.

"If by 'interesting' you mean absolutely horrid, then yes, I agree."

Uncle inhaled sharply and I knew he'd recognized our wayward family member as well. I refused to look at him, knowing he must be furious. What she'd done was far worse than simply run off. Maybe not in my eyes or Uncle's, but in society's she might as well brand herself a harlot.

Mephistopheles cleared his throat, spurring my cousin into action. Liza grinned seductively at the crowd and lifted the sword above her head, strutting along the stage as if she were born to do so. My pulse thundered. I was both speechless and proud.

"Your aunt would have a stroke if she were to witness Liza in such a state," Thomas said, earning a swift glare from my uncle. He drew his brows together. "Is it not true?"

"Thomas," Uncle warned. "Enough."

In spite of the terrible circumstances, I smiled. My cousin was living out her romantic dreams, uncaring what the world thought of her. I admired her, though a sliver of worry slipped in as I recalled Mephistopheles's fateful words. It appeared Liza had lost both her heart *and* her head to his carnival. Suddenly, her last letter came back to me. She'd mentioned being secretly courted by an escape artist.

Gasps went up around us and I shifted to see what had caused such a stir. A sound of ominous hoofbeats filled the room as Jian Yu the Invincible, the Incredible, the Knight of Swords, rode a black horse dressed in chain mail through the saloon. The animal's liquid eyes flashed their whites, and it reared up into the air, hooves crashing onto the tile with enough force to rattle glasses. Mrs. Harvey clutched my arm, and a few women seated close enough shrieked.

Jian seemed as hardened as the armor he wore. His silver mask completely covered one eye and ended in a series of points sharp enough to pierce skin on the other side. It appeared as if a crown of swords had melted and formed itself around his head. He was the living embodiment of the Knight of Swords tarot card, and his costume reflected it perfectly.

In his wake, the other sword-wielding performers sheathed their weapons, with a sound that sent spikes into my veins, and dropped to their knees as if in supplication. Gooseflesh rose along my arms. The whole scene was terrifying, made even more so by the silence that buffered Jian.

He rode the horse up the stairs, his gait unhurried—he wanted us to admire him as he went by. Long dark hair was tied back at the nape of his neck, offering the crowd a good look at his equally dark angular features—sharp enough to slice through a few hearts, judging from the fans snapping open and the excited chatter coming from the women. Mrs. Harvey took a long pull of her ice water, and Thomas rolled his eyes.

"Is a muscular physique truly that inspiring, or is it the dangerous scar over one eye?" he asked, though Mrs. Harvey didn't trouble herself with answering. Or tearing her gaze from the young man now onstage. Jian hopped down from his steed and thrust the reins at Liza, jerking his chin toward the curtains.

"Have you been studying those journals I gave you, Audrey Rose?" Uncle interrupted, pulling my attention to him. "I'll need both you and Thomas to be well versed in marks made with an—"

Uncle fixed his gaze on something across the room, piquing my curiosity. A second assistant rolled a coffin-type contraption onto the stage. Holes were cut out near the top, bottom, and sides of the strange box. Lengths of rope were lassoed about each end and also looped over the shoulders of the female assistants.

"Oh, good," Thomas said blandly, "I was hoping they'd wheel the dead out before dessert. Entrails go better with the main course, don't you agree, Wadsworth?" He crinkled his nose. "Totally wrong for sweets."

"Be serious." My heart raced despite my admonishment. "No one is going to spill entrails."

He cocked his head. "I am being serious. That box is used to saw people in half. One wrong move and those in the front row will have blood splatter and severed organs sloshing onto their tables. Messy business for the mousse and berries. Though if we do have a murderer aboard, this might be the spectacle killing we feared."

Jian sheathed the swords he'd been swinging about and made a show of inspecting every inch of the wooden box. Liza and the second assistant stood to either side, smiling broadly as if one of them might not be cut open before our very eyes. I subtly wiped my hands down the front of my skirts. Part of me was morbidly fascinated. And the other part disgusted by that same fascination. Some days I despised the contradictions of my mind and the darkness in my heart.

"You don't think Liza will be the one…" I stopped speaking, eyes fastened to Jian as he stepped up to the edge of the stage and lifted a hand to his face as if he were shielding his eyes from the sun. The dining saloon quieted a bit, but noise persisted.

"A volunteer," he grumbled, a slight accent apparent. "Now."

No one seemed inclined to offer themselves up as a potential sacrifice. And I couldn't blame them. Who in possession of their logical senses would do such a thing? Jian's mask glinted as he stalked to the opposite end of the stage. He glared at a table full of young gentlemen. "You are all cowards—not worthy of meeting my blades." He turned to the assistants onstage. "Liza!"

My cousin's smile was frozen, though her throat bobbed and her knees locked, betraying her fear. She took a deep breath and stepped forward. Before I knew what I was doing, I was out of my seat, tossing my napkin onto my half-eaten food.

"Wait!"

"Ah." Jian grinned, wide and toothy. "We have an assistant after all."

Even though I was standing, half ready to run across the stage and throw myself into that box of death, the knight's gaze was not directed at me. He was looking across from where I stood, knees wobbling, to where Thomas was already making his way up the stairs and onto the stage, steps sure and unhurried. The precise opposite of my heartbeat. Everything inside my body went numb and prickly at once.

"Thomas, please don't." I stared, hands clenched at my sides, as he paused before the coffin and, after winking at me over his shoulder, climbed inside.

"Sit, dear," Mrs. Harvey whispered, reaching for my arm. "You appear a little peaked, have some wine. It soothes the nerves." She signaled to a waiter who poured a deep red blend from the carafe he held. I tried not to think of Miss Prescott's blood as it sloshed into my cup. "There you are, be a good girl and take a few sips."

Without argument, I plopped back into my chair and took the proffered glass, bringing it to my lips, barely registering the sour-grape taste as it slid down my throat in quick drabs. I didn't care much for wine, but it did distract me. Briefly. I dabbed at the corners of my mouth with a linen napkin, attention straying to where Thomas poked his head, arms, and feet out from the coffin-shaped box, then stayed perfectly still.

Flashes of him lying dead on a morgue table assaulted my senses, and it took every last bit of my self-control to not rush the stage and drag him into my arms. The rational part of my brain knew with certainty that no harm would come to him. Carnivals were in the business of selling tickets and creating spectacles. Not murdering patrons.

Even if that was precisely what had happened last night.

I could not shake the tension from my limbs as Liza and the second assistant covered the wooden box with a lid, and nodded to Jian. I sat straighter, easing the boning from my center. The room suddenly felt hotter, and I wished to be outside on the deck, the icy winter air waltzing along beside me as it drifted through the covered promenade.

Uncle huffed at the sight of Thomas shoved into the box, but I noticed the crease of worry that appeared between his brows. It did nothing to assuage my own fears. "Foolish boy."

I clutched my mother's heart pendant hanging around my neck, ignoring the bite of metal in my palm. Thomas removed his arm from view, then brandished a card when he stuck his hand back out. I could have sworn the massive ship encountered turbulence as I swayed in my seat.

People in the crowd laughed at the ridiculousness of Thomas's disembodied arm fluttering the card about, but I couldn't tear my gaze from the enormous saw both assistants walked over to the knight. Metal teeth on the blade glinted, ready to sink into the wooden box—and Thomas's flesh—should anything not go according to plan. Or perhaps his murder *was* the plan.

A bead of sweat rolled down my spine. All it would take was one false move and his lifeblood would spill—

"There, there, dear." Mrs. Harvey patted my hand. I let my breath out and she smiled. "It's only an illusion. What happened yesterday was terrible, but the odds of murder happening a second time, well, it's simply not probable. Our Thomas knows what he's doing. Hmm?"

I swallowed hard and nodded. I knew she was correct, but my heart didn't want to listen to reason. It quickened at the thought of all the horrible things that *could* happen. Thomas knew what he was doing, even if what he was doing was an *awful* idea.

Liza shot me an unreadable look over her shoulder. I tensed all over again as Jian lifted his saw above his head. I nearly ran for one of the kneeling performers, ready to seize one of their swords should Thomas be hurt.

"You can see the blade is very real. Isabella, if you would. Demonstrate." He nodded toward the second assistant. Isabella stepped forward and hacked at the saw with a sword she'd picked up from the table, the metal clanging for all to hear. I gritted my teeth at the noise. A young man at the next table covered his ears. "It is also very sharp. Liza?"

My cousin flourished a filigree mask hidden on her person and set it on top of the box. Jian carefully sawed back and forth until it snapped in two. I tried not to dwell on the fact it had only taken three passes for the blade to break the metal in half—it was much too sharp to be anywhere near my beloved Cresswell.

I took a deep, steadying breath as Jian prowled around the box, saw lifted proudly above his head. He stopped near where Thomas's center would be, then motioned to Isabella. She picked her way across stage, grinning widely, hands planted firmly on her hips like a ballet dancer. She stood opposite the knight—apparently the sawing bit required two people. I twisted the napkin in my lap as Jian fit the blade into one side of the box and pushed it over to Isabella.

"On the count of three," he ordered. "One. Two. Three!"

Metal on wood screeched in a *scritch scratch, scritch scratch* pattern, the blade sinking deeper and deeper into the box.

Justice tarot

SIX

SAWN IN HALF

DINING SALOON
RMS ETRURIA
2 JANUARY 1889

I wanted to cover my eyes, run from the room, and toss myself over-board, but forced my body to sit and be still. Meanwhile, on the stage, Thomas's hands and feet waved frantically as the saw got ever closer to his person.

A few people turned away from the show, snapping their fans out and calling for smelling salts. Should this act fail, it would likely be the most gruesome sight anyone here would ever witness, myself included. The aftermath of death and murder was difficult business, but actually watching it happen? I shut my eyes for a moment. I did not want to imagine the darkness that would be unleashed from myself if Thomas died on that stage.

"Oh, dear." Mrs. Harvey took a generous swig of her own wine. "It's terribly lifelike, isn't it? I would swear that blade was really cutting into him."

I clamped my jaw so tightly it ached. There were only a few more inches left and the saw would go through the center portion of the box. And through Thomas.

Scritch scratch, scritch scratch.

I mentally tallied where my medical bag was, how long it would take for me to sprint to my cabin in my evening gown and retrieve it, and if I'd have the skills necessary to sew him together. I hoped there was a surgeon on board. Someone more skilled than Dr. Arden, who was still sanctioned away with Chief Magistrate Prescott.

Scritch scratch, scritch scratch.

I held my breath as the saw struck the bottom of the wood, waiting for blood and viscera to gush out beneath the crack. Thomas stopped moving. My heart might have ceased as well. Murmurs went up around me, but the voices were indistinguishable noise as I stared, waiting to see Thomas bleed out.

Nothing happened.

Thomas's hands and feet suddenly moved about as if a blade hadn't sliced through his middle. I partially stood, ready to clap and have this be done, but apparently this nightmare wasn't yet over. Jian and Isabella repeated the performance with another blade. Once it sawed down to the table, each of them took one side of the box and pulled it apart.

I don't remember having decided to do so, but I screamed. It was loud and terrible enough to make Uncle drop his fork and Mrs. Harvey fumble for her wineglass. The Knight of Swords laughed, the sound dark and ominous like a storm rolling over the sea.

"A man sawn in two!"

Another few people in the crowd screamed. I clapped a hand over my mouth, trying to keep any more of my own shrieks from escaping. The two wide blades covered each end of the box, obscuring any spilled viscera from the audience's view, though I logically knew there wasn't anything to hide. My emotions won against logic, and panic settled under my ribs. Thomas's hands. I focused on them and the card he still waved about. They were moving. He was moving. This was an illusion. A terrible trick.

I blinked tears back, hating Thomas for doing this. Jian wheeled the two halves of my whole heart around the stage, proudly showing off his skill with a blade. After they did a complete turn, they pushed the box back together, then removed both saws. I gripped the edge of my seat, tethering myself to it to keep from flying up there to rip the coffin open and run my hands over Thomas.

Liza brandished a black canvas sheet large enough to conceal the box. They covered it, walked around it once more, then ripped the sheet off with a snap. They lifted the lid and...nothing. Thomas didn't emerge and his arms and legs were no longer visible. My heart thudded dully, the sounds in the room slowly becoming loud and silent at once. Part of me wished I'd thought of calling for smelling salts. Liza and Isabella exchanged worried glances that I didn't think were part of the act. I stood, heart hammering.

Jian sheathed the swords he'd been swirling about and stalked over to the box, hands fisted. Something was wrong. As he approached Thomas popped up like a jack-in-the-box, holding a second card, and Jian startled back.

The audience cackled at the expression on the knight's face—it was as sour as if he'd been sinking his teeth into tart lemons. Without warning, he yanked a thin sword from the sheath on his back, and plunged it directly through the center of the card, cutting off any more laughter.

Thomas hopped out of the box, offering a quick bow before bounding down the stairs, his cheeks pleasantly flushed.

"He looked rather annoyed by my performance," he said, breathing a bit hard. "I thought it was a brilliant touch. A little laughter to balance out the fear."

Jian and his assistants exited the stage, but I couldn't concentrate on anything other than a bit of frayed fabric on Thomas's waistcoat. My blood felt as cold as ocean water as it surged through me. "You were cut."

Thomas brushed a piece of dampened hair back, but didn't comment.

Mephistopheles reemerged from the smoke like the devil he was. He smirked out at the passengers, then motioned behind the velvet curtains. On command, they pulled back, and Jian, Liza, and Isabella swept into deep bows and curtsies. The crowd whistled and cheered, some even took up stomping their feet again, while others removed the hothouse flowers from vases and tossed them onto the stage floor. I couldn't find the will to join them.

Instead, I watched the fire flash in the knight's eyes. My friend had annoyed him and he did not seem like the sort who enjoyed being made to look foolish. A muscle in his jaw twitched when his attention settled on Thomas. I swore there was some silent promise that passed between the two of them when Thomas noticed his scrutiny.

"Ladies and gentlemen," Mephistopheles said. "Seems no one has lost their heads tonight. But will you be as fortunate tomorrow? We shall consult the Wheel of Fortune and see. Good night!"

Each performer stepped back just as the curtains drew to a close, disappearing from sight.

I turned on Thomas, hands wrapped around my goblet to avoid strangling him. "Are you quite mad? You could have been hurt!"

His gaze swept from my grip on my goblet to the tension in my jaw. He held his hands up, surrendering to my anger. "Easy now, Wadsworth. Perhaps we ought to move away from the cutlery and glass. I assure you I was perfectly safe."

I snorted. "Of course you were. Who wouldn't be *perfectly safe* while being sawn in two? Especially after someone was murdered yesterday! How very foolish of me to worry."

"Audrey Rose," Uncle warned. "Please control yourself until after dinner. I have enough to contend with after Liza's performance." He stood, tossing his napkin down. "In fact, I'm going to fetch her now. She'll be joining you in your chambers."

With that, he strode out of the room. Mrs. Harvey promptly picked up her empty glass, staring into it as if it might transport her from the table. "Would you look at that," she said, calling an attendant over to pull out her chair. "I find myself suddenly overcome with exhaustion. If you'll excuse me."

I watched her go, too annoyed to contemplate being without a chaperone once more.

"Well?" I asked. "What sort of deductions did you come to before climbing into that box to deem it safe?"

He reached for my hand, then caught himself. While we were alone at our table, we were not secreted away in my chambers. His touching me in public would be most inappropriate.

"That box had a false bottom. I noticed the slight seam in the wood, an extra few inches that weren't necessary. Once I'd gotten a better look at it, I saw that I'd actually be lying directly below the box in a sub-box in the table." He smiled tentatively. "It's really quite ingenious. The design allows the box to be cut in half while my hands and feet protrude from the holes. Whoever engineered it is brilliant. I've never seen anything like it before."

"You'd deduced all of that before lying in it?"

"Mostly." Thomas glanced at the tables that were slowly clearing of guests. Soon we'd be the only ones left. "It's adorable when your nostrils flare so dramatically. There"—he grinned, dodging my swift kick under the table—"that's the look. One day I'm going to have it captured by a grand portrait artist and hang it above the mantel in my study."

"I truly dislike you sometimes, Thomas James Dorin Cresswell."

"Even when I'm being valiantly heroic by sacrificing myself?" He removed the two cards from inside his suit jacket and waved them in front of me. "I'd wager you hate me less now."

"Marginally." I plucked the cards from his grasp. One was an Ace of Clubs, the second was a hand-drawn tarot—Justice. I sighed and set them down. "What do you make of these?"

"Well, the scales of justice appear wildly off-kilter. It seems too great a coincidence that Chief Magistrate Prescott's daughter was slain. It's worth looking into his background as a judge. Clearly, someone doesn't find his rulings fair. It might be a good motive." He tapped the playing card. "And the Ace of Spades is likely a distraction."

"What about the Ace of Clubs left on Miss Prescott's body?" I countered. "Maybe the tarot card is the distraction."

Thomas shrugged. "Perhaps they're both meant as decoys. Or maybe these simply were misplaced. I believe we ought to search—"

A terrible ruckus interrupted us. It sounded as if a stampede of elephants had gotten loose and was charging through the corridors. Which, given the presence of the carnival, wasn't entirely out of the question. Confused, I twisted in my seat, watching a few people run past the open door as waiters stuck their heads out.

Dread slithered through my limbs. People running with tears streaming down their faces were never a good sign. Whatever they were terrified of had to be quite bad indeed. They'd just seen a young man cut in half and had barely stopped eating their entrées.

"Hurry," Thomas said, gently taking my arm and rushing us toward the door. "If it's what I fear...there might be time to save the person."

"Wait!" I wrenched free and ran to the nearest table, grabbing a knife. "Better to be prudent."

Thomas wrapped his hand around mine and we moved as quickly as we could against the tide of passengers heading the opposite way. I kept the knife pointed down and close to my side. I'd never seen the promenade so crowded, and what had felt like a comfortable walking deck now felt like a funnel.

Men in top hats bobbed back and forth, some escorting their

families away from the chaos and others diving into it. A few times my hand almost slipped from Thomas's, but he was right there again, placing his body before mine as a barrier. People jostled him, but he steered us to where the crowd was the thickest.

"Please!" someone shouted, from where I couldn't quite see. "Return to your cabins. Do not run, and do not panic. I assure you all I will keep you safe."

"Like you kept her safe?" a passenger shouted back, earning cries of approval from those closest to him. "None of us are safe out here on the water. We're trapped!"

"Now, now," the first man called, "everything will be fine. Remain calm and return to your cabins!"

Thomas, using his added height, maneuvered us closer. Captain Norwood stood on a crate, motioning for crew members to disperse the passengers. My gaze traveled around him, searching out the cause for alarm.

Then I saw it.

A woman, strung up by her ankles, hung from the rafters of the promenade deck. Her skirts fell over her head, covering her identity and leaving her underthings exposed for the world to see. That would have been horrific enough, had she not also been run through with multiple swords stuck in a myriad of crazy angles all over her body. Blood slowly dripped onto the deck from each exit wound, the sound akin to water dripping from a faucet. Even with the noise of frightened passengers, all I could hear was that sinister drip. It was the single most horrendous sight I'd ever witnessed, and I'd been present for the discoveries of many of the gruesome Ripper slayings.

I held a hand to my center, forcing my breaths to come in even intervals. Rope creaked as the body twisted like a fish caught on a line. I'd thought Miss Prescott's death was terrible, but this was an entirely new level of monstrous. Wind barreled down the open-air corridor, sending the corpse swaying serenely above us. I tried to focus on anything other than the blades as blood arced around the floor.

"Oh. Dear God above, look," I said, pointing to a frayed bit of rope. "If we don't get her down soon, the ropes will snap." And the swords would be impaled even deeper, possibly decapitating her before our very eyes. My stomach flipped at the image. This poor victim did not deserve one more ounce of indignity or trauma to befall her.

Thomas scanned the crowd. "Your uncle is over there, we ought to go to him."

We stood near the railing, the wind thrashing about in fury. I rubbed my hands over my arms, only just realizing I'd not only forgotten to grab my cloak, but had also lost the knife. Thomas dropped his suit jacket over my shoulders, though he never took his gaze from the murder scene. Once the crew had managed to remove most of the passengers, Uncle motioned for us to head over.

"Please go back to your rooms." A deckhand blocked our path. "Captain's orders."

Thomas ran his gaze over the young man. "We're to assist with the body."

The deckhand's focus flicked to me. "Both of you?"

"Let them through, Henry!" Norwood barked. "And someone fetch that bloody ringmaster for me. If one of his damned performers did this, I'll string *him* up!" The captain turned on my uncle, hands fisted at his sides. "We can't leave her here indecent all night; I'll give you twenty minutes, then you can do the rest inside." He started moving down the line of crew. "Go to the cabins and see if anyone is missing a relative. This young woman didn't travel alone. Someone has to be worried by now. Oh, and make sure to send brandy to those who seem the most distraught. We don't need a full-fledged panic on our hands. Go!"

Uncle caught my eye before walking around the body. For a horrifying moment I imagined it was Liza hanging there, run through by the very blades she'd helped wield earlier. Then my logical senses took control, and I actually looked at the facts before me. The woman wasn't wearing a carnival costume. I couldn't see her face, but she appeared to be larger in height and weight than my cousin.

I took a deep breath, but it did nothing to steady my pulse as I moved toward the victim. Up close, the rope creaked as the body twisted in the breeze. The sharp scent of copper mixed with the brine of the sea, a smell I'd not soon forget.

Thomas walked around the body, face cold as the winter air around us. It was hard to imagine how he was the same person who'd been filled with such heat a few hours before. He pointed to a lifeboat that was half lying on the ground. "Someone cut the rope off one end and used it to haul her up. See?"

I moved forward and crouched down. "That might indicate this wasn't planned. If it had been, I imagine the murderer would have brought rope with him."

"I respectfully disagree, Wadsworth. That's what he hoped to portray. But look there…he used another length of rope and looped it through the piece he'd cut and then threw it twice around the rafters. There would have been plenty for him to cut the length from." He nodded to where the rope pooled on the ground. "Why go through the extra hassle of cutting the lifeboat down, and risk drawing attention?"

That was a question I had no answer to. I turned my attention back on the horrific detail of the swords. One thing was certain, whoever had run her through had to have a decent amount of strength. An oddity struck me about the whole scene.

"Why didn't anyone hear any screams? Surely she had to have cried for help. I cannot imagine standing quietly by while being impaled with a sword, much less…" I counted them, stomach souring. "Much less seven of them. There has to be a witness."

Uncle took his spectacles off and buffed them on his sleeve. I imagined he was anxious to bring the body into our makeshift laboratory. "I'm sure our examination will answer some questions. I'd like each of you to change and meet me in the laboratory." He turned, then hesitated. "Thomas, please see to it that Audrey Rose is accompanied. And be sure to leave Liza under Mrs. Harvey's watch. I'd have everyone accounted for this evening."

"Yes, Uncle." I took one last look at the scene.

"Seven of Swords," a cool, deep voice said, startling me. Thomas and I both lifted our attention to the new arrival. Mephistopheles stuck his hands in his pockets and whistled. "Reversed. Never a good sign. Then again, that's quite apparent, isn't it?"

"What are you on about?" I asked, already annoyed by his presence. He hadn't even bothered to take his mask off, heaven forbid the world see his true face. "What does that mean?"

"Honestly, have none of you noticed she's been made to look exactly like the Seven of Swords tarot card?" At our blank stares, Mephistopheles dug around inside his coat and removed a deck of cards. He flipped through them, then snatched one out with a flourish that didn't belong at a crime scene. "Does this appear familiar to anyone? Wait. Something's not quite right...oh...here you are." He turned the card upside down. "The Seven of Swords when reversed, or turned upside down, is a tricksy thing. Deceit. Shame. It can also mean someone thought they'd gotten away with something." He jabbed a finger toward the body. "Someone fashioned this scene very carefully."

Thomas narrowed his eyes. "You're awfully flippant when your carnival boasts of using the tarot for its acts."

Mephistopheles tucked the cards back into his jacket, then patted the pocket. His gaze drifted over to where I'd been staring, trying to find the bulge in the material. He tugged his coat tighter and grinned. "Care to look for the cards? I guarantee you won't find them, but the search would be fun."

I gripped my hands at my sides. "Perhaps the captain ought to toss you in the brig."

"That would be most unfortunate," the ringmaster said. "You see, I reported some objects stolen before the show began tonight. Rope. Tarot cards. And…what were those other things…" He scratched his chin in mock contemplation, then snapped, "That's it. Swords. A whole bunch of them. In fact, they no longer appear to be missing. Though I doubt Jian will want them back now. Death is bad for business."

"You're despicable," I said, unable to contain myself a moment longer. "A woman is dead, slain in a most brutal manner before you, and you've managed to make her a complete mockery."

Mephistopheles stared at me, as if truly noticing me for the first time beyond surface appearances. "My sincerest apologies, miss. I have no further information to offer other than what I've given. It is most unfortunate that another woman has been slain, but my carnival has nothing to do with it. I cannot afford to have people start believing—or fearing—to attend my shows. Many people I employ depend on it to live. I suggest you turn your sights elsewhere."

He took one last look at the staged body, then strode down the deck. I tugged Thomas's coat tighter. When someone professed innocence so loudly, it made me contemplate their guilt.

"Come," Thomas offered his arm. "I'll walk you to your chambers."

As we made our way to my room, I glanced out at the water and regretted doing so. At night it was a dark, undulating beast. Light glinted from the sliver of moon—a thousand tiny eyes watching our procession, winking and blinking as we moved along. I wondered what else the silent water might have witnessed tonight and what other secrets it might be keeping. How many other crimes might it have aided by swallowing the bodies whole?

SEVEN
A MURDER MOST BRUTAL

Thomas deposited me at my chambers with a promise to return shortly for our postmortem. When I walked into my room, I found Liza sprawled on the bed, her nose crinkled at one of my forensic journals.

"Don't take this the wrong way, dearest cousin, but how do you sleep at night?" she asked, pointing to a rather graphic dissection. "This is quite gruesome for bedtime."

"Liza...what on—"

"Honestly," she said, lifting her brows at the title. "'A Case Study of Blunt Weapons and Lacerations'?" She thumbed through the book, stopping on the pages with illustrations. "It's macabre, Cousin. Even for you. Is that someone's intestines?" She stuck a finger down her throat, doing her best impersonation of gagging.

"Your mother is an absolute wreck," I said, not commenting on my normal nighttime reading, though I was impressed by her knowledge of anatomy. She deposited the book on my nightstand, then stood. "She and Father have circulated rumors of you being unwell.

I believe everyone's under the impression you're recovering at Thornbriar. Though my father believes you might be *dead*."

"Couldn't they have at least come up with something a bit more romantic?" Liza made a face. "Your father's country estate is grand, but makes a dull story. I should write to Mother and offer up a few suggestions of my own." She picked up the Ace of Clubs from my nightstand. "Did you know that the four suits are also associated with elements?"

"I did not."

She grinned—a rare, goofy sort of smile that made me think something especially sugary was about to be served. "Harry is a wonder with creating grand tales. I swear, he makes the most ordinary things seem extraordinary. He claims there's power in how you sell something. Why call something perfume when it can be a love mist?"

"Harry?" I sat on the bed beside my cousin, fiddling with the folds of my skirts. "About that...what in the name of the queen possessed you to run off with a man you scarcely know? I hope he didn't spin you a story too good to be believable."

"Most stories are too good to be true. That's what makes them enchanting."

"And dangerous," I muttered.

Liza laid the card down and leaned into me, her head resting against my shoulder as she used to do when we were children playing in the gardens at Thornbriar.

"I have so much to be grateful for—so many opportunities that others will never even know, and yet each time I tried on a new gown for my coming-out ball, it felt as if I were being strangled. Living life, but not enjoying it. I was dressed in silks but might as well have been covered in thorns."

I sighed. It was a feeling I knew all too well.

She nestled closer to me, voice catching. "Haven't you ever

wanted to be someone else? If only for a short while. Or maybe not someone else, maybe you longed to be your *true* self. To live exactly as you pleased without consequence or judgment. I know this might all be a terrible mistake—an illusion more elaborate than those in this carnival, but for the first time, I am the master of my fate. I feel as though I've been freed from a cage and I can finally breathe again. How can I give up this freedom?"

Guilt sank its crooked teeth into me. I knew exactly what it was like, feeling chained by expectations set upon me by someone else. Everyone deserved to live freely and in honor of themselves. A basic right should not be a luxury. I wrapped an arm around my cousin and leaned my head against hers. "So...tell me about the King of Cards. I want to hear all the details while I get ready for the postmortem."

"Well, then I suppose I ought to start from the beginning."

I could hear the smile in my cousin's voice as she recited all the ways Mr. Harry Houdini had made her senses disappear. I was thrilled for her, though worry gnawed unpleasantly the more she spoke. I did not share her sentiments about a man who'd potentially ruin her on a whim, especially since no promises of marriage had been made. It seemed Houdini had nothing to lose, and my cousin had much to forfeit. I tried pushing my unease away, wanting to be as supportive as she was of me. She talked and talked until Thomas arrived and promised to finish her tale once I'd returned.

I made to leave, then turned around. "It's good to have you back."

"Of course it is, silly. I'd wager life was utterly dull without me. Now go on." She smiled, lifting my anatomy journal as if she intended to study it. "I'm not going anywhere."

I moved to the door, then froze. "Liza? Have you noticed anyone in the carnival troupe acting oddly?"

"You're not implying one of my new friends is to blame for these atrocities, are you?" She sat up straighter, eyes narrowed. "No. I haven't heard or witnessed anything except their own terror."

"I didn't mean to—"

"Go solve this horrid mystery for all of our sakes. I swear I'll be here when you return."

She crossed her heart and I hoped she'd actually keep her word.

I couldn't help but think the light above our makeshift post-mortem table sounded like a dying bee. The slight buzz and flicker did nothing to improve my mood as Uncle folded the shroud down, revealing the victim.

I studied her wheat-blond hair, the peaceful look upon her face. It was hard to imagine she'd died in such a violent manner—that was, until my attention dropped lower. There were a total of fourteen holes in her body, two in each arm, two in each leg, and ten through-out her torso. Entry and exit wounds from the swords. I wanted to close my eyes, but hiding wouldn't change anything. She'd still be deceased and I'd still need to find any clue that might lead to why. I shuddered a bit, recalling how her death had been staged after a tarot card.

"Begin your examination now, Audrey Rose." Uncle had already finished washing his hands and handed Thomas the journal and a pen. "Start with wounds this time, please."

"Yes, sir." I cleared my throat, then walked around the body, observing. "Skin around both ankles has a slight rash, though there's no indication of rope burn. If it had been present, that would indicate she'd been alive and struggling against her bonds. Since it is not, it is likely she was not struggling and therefore already deceased."

"Good. What else?"

I stared at her face again, biting my lip. There was something too serene about her. She had kohl around her eyes, but there weren't any smudges. Odd for someone who'd been murdered in a heinous way to not have shed any tears. I pointed to the clue.

"Victim's kohl is perfectly intact," I said. "Either the perpetrator applied it postmortem, which I do not believe, or we might find an elixir in her system. I doubt this woman was conscious when she was attacked."

"Brilliant." Thomas lifted his attention from his note-taking, and looked at me. "Her nails are also unbroken. There are no signs of any defensive wounds."

"Which also explains why she hadn't screamed," I said, building off our examination. "She was already either deceased or incapacitated when she'd been hung upside down."

Uncle hovered above one of the wounds. "I believe the facts are lining up with that theory. Look at the cuts. What story do they tell?"

I joined my uncle, leaning in to get a better look. At first I was unsure... they were horrendous cuts, then it hit me. There was blood, but no bruising. "The swords were likely inserted *after* death."

"Very good. Cause of death?"

I stopped seeing a deceased young woman. Before me lay a puzzle waiting to be put together. I pulled her eyelids back. "There's no petechial hemorrhaging. No bruises on the neck." I moved around the table. "She certainly wasn't strangled. Until we open her up, I'm afraid we can't be sure of cause of death. Though, given the lack of other signs, we might be looking at a poisoning."

Thomas stood abruptly, dropping his notebook as he lifted the victim's arm. He leaned close, then set it back down, face grim. "It appears as though she's been administered a shot. Or has had some bloodletting done. Look there. A small syringe might have made that mark."

My heart rate jumped. "We know of at least one doctor aboard this ship."

"One who had a connection to our first victim," Thomas added. "And he was none too keen on having us anywhere near his next patient."

"Dr. Arden admitted to giving Chief Magistrate Prescott an elixir." I had a growing feeling of dread. "And both Prescotts were absent from the dining saloon." I'd imagined they'd chosen to remain in their rooms, mourning their daughter. But what if they were unable to leave? "I know he'd said he wouldn't be attending, but did either of you notice Dr. Arden during the show tonight?"

Uncle shook his head. "I didn't see him. And Chief Magistrate Prescott didn't answer the door when I called on him again before supper. In fact, the room sounded empty. No one so much as shifted. Odd if they were both in the room as they'd claimed they'd be."

"Well, then"—Thomas grabbed our cloaks—"let's check on them at once. We'll fetch the captain on the way."

"No need." Captain Norwood leaned against the doorframe, his face more tired looking than it had been the last time I'd seen him. "I've come to give you the news myself."

I covered the body with the shroud, hoping to give her as much respect as I could. The captain wrenched his attention away from the corpse, appearing a bit green around the collar. "My crew went to each first-class cabin, hoping to find a witness. But—"

"We believe we've discovered who's responsible, sir," I said, not wanting to waste time. We needed to check on the Prescotts; hopefully we weren't already too late. "You need to locate and apprehend Dr. Arden at once. He was last—"

"Pardon me, Miss Wadsworth," he interrupted, "but I'm afraid you all may be wrong." He glanced at the covered body again, swallowing hard. "You see...we spoke with everyone...and Miss Arden, the doctor's daughter, is missing." He removed a photograph from his coat pocket and held it out for us to see. I drew back, stomach sinking. "This is the young woman on your examination table, is it not?"

I stared mutely at the photograph, mind slowly catching up with the new information and what it meant to our case. If Dr. Arden's daughter was our victim, and if there was no conflict between them, then that eliminated him from suspicion. We needed to begin again—and the task seemed daunting.

"But this isn't all you found out, is it?" Uncle nodded to another sheet of paper the captain had poking out from his coat pocket.

"I wish it was." Norwood sighed and withdrew the note. "Another family is demanding we investigate the disappearance of their daughter. I ask that you all come with me straightaway."

My knees felt weak. Already... the potential for another body. Thomas caught my eye. He needn't utter a word—two bodies and a possible third in only two days. What we had now was another career murderer. One who had only just begun his dark acts.

Crimson fabric spilled like fresh blood over the floor of Miss Crenshaw's first-class cabin, an unsightly gash in an otherwise well-appointed chamber. I stood over the mess, hands on my hips, studying the silks the way I imagined Thomas was doing beside me, trying to discern order from chaos. It was a monumental task, especially since I was all too aware of the need for discretion as her parents' gazes seared into my back. I didn't need to possess Thomas's uncanny skills with deductions to know they wouldn't be pleased by my conclusion.

Honestly, though, hers was a much-better fate than the one I'd originally feared. I stared at the crumpled gown until nearly going cross-eyed, hoping to find some clue as to where its owner disappeared to. One that would not cause a fainting spell or scandal. Lord Crenshaw was a popular figure, and I knew the reputation of his family and their good name was of the utmost importance.

I refocused on the dress. The fabric was beautiful—some of the finest threads in all of Europe from what I could see. The only con-clusion I had was that it was an awful shame to discard it on the floor in such a careless manner.

Miss Crenshaw might be reckless in personality, but that didn't mean she'd been murdered. If foul play wasn't the issue, then that meant she'd run off…and young, unmarried women typically didn't do so alone. A glance at her parents had me questioning which they'd prefer to be true. A scandal of this nature was a death in itself.

Two champagne flutes sat on a nightstand along with a half-eaten chocolate cake, furthering my suspicion that she hadn't been alone.

I flicked my attention to my uncle, but he was preoccupied with watching crew members scour the bedroom chamber, ensuring they didn't disturb any potential forensic clues. After the unveiling of Dr. Arden's daughter earlier, everyone was balanced on a scalpel's edge.

I squinted toward the porthole, recalling the constant ebb and flow of people who worked the docks prior to us leaving port yester-day. It would be an ideal place to get lost in a crowd.

"You claim that your daughter has been missing since yesterday? Before the ship left?" They nodded. "Have you questioned her lady's maid?" I toed the dress with my own embroidered silk shoes. "Some-one had to have helped her out of this garment. The bodice is quite intricate. Look at the stays on the back—there's no possible way she'd have undone that alone."

Thomas lifted his dark brows in appraisal, but didn't comment. I studied him out of the corner of my eye, noticing the smile he was fighting and wondered what I'd missed that had amused him.

"Surely this is not an indication of foul play," said Lord Cren-shaw. I noted that he didn't answer my question. I pried my attention away from his distractingly white mustache. "Our daughter might be visiting another guest. Or perhaps she changed her mind and returned to London prior to sailing."

Ready to jump at any lifeline and save his ship's reputation, Captain Norwood readily agreed. "I can say with authority it wouldn't be the first time a passenger has decided to disembark from the ship. Ocean travel can be quite daunting to some."

"Yes," Lord Crenshaw said, looking hopeful. "That's probably it. Elizabeth is deathly afraid of the water. Perhaps she didn't want to make a fuss and went home. She'd mentioned how nervous she was just yesterday morning. Which was the last time we saw her."

"Would she have taken anyone with her? A chaperone?" I asked, seeing the hesitation on Lady Crenshaw's face. It was a nice story, but most fairy tales had a dark side to them, especially when it came to a princess's fate. "A footman or maid?"

"I—I don't believe anyone else is missing," Lady Crenshaw said. "But Elizabeth wouldn't... she's such a good girl. She probably didn't wish to ruin our trip. It's not as if she's a lower-class trollop."

I chomped down on my immediate response, face burning. If *she* were a *he,* I doubted they'd call her such names. And her station had nothing to do with the matter whatsoever. Plenty of less fortunate families had more class than Lady Crenshaw had just showed.

"Have you noticed anything of value missing?" I asked. "Jewelry, trinkets..."

Lady Crenshaw shook her head. "Only an emerald ring. But Elizabeth never took it off."

"You're quite sure that's it?" I pressed.

"I haven't had anyone go through her things." Lady Crenshaw flipped open the jewelry box, rifled through it a bit, then drew her brows together. "A strand of pearls is also missing. I-I'm really not sure that that has anything to do with her disappearance, though."

Thomas bit his lower lip, an indication he was battling some inner war with himself. "Was she alone? I see two champagne flutes, one of which has lipstick and the other does not," he said. "Another obvious deduction may be that she was undressed by her lover after they indulged in some spirits."

Everyone in the room sucked in a sharp breath. I rolled my eyes skyward, wondering what I'd done to irk any higher power that might exist. It was the one thing we were all supposed to *think* but not *speak* aloud. Even Uncle stiffened.

"That would explain the hasty pile of clothes," Thomas added, undeterred by the sudden silence, "the crinkled bedding, and the subsequent absence of Miss Crenshaw. Perhaps she's run off with someone and didn't wish to tell her parents. If I had to guess, I'd say it was someone below her station. Which is all the more plausible after noticing that ink stain on her pillowcase. Appears as if someone who worked with their hands rested them there. It's also on the crystal."

"How dare you!" Lord Crenshaw said, face reddening by the second. I wondered what had aggravated him more—the thought of Miss Crenshaw running away, or potentially going off with someone of a lower class. "Our daughter would do no such thing...to even *suggest* that sort of reprehensible behavior is—"

"Don't lose your temper, dear." Lady Crenshaw laid a hand on his arm. "Let's leave them to this and retire for bed. Elizabeth is home in London. We'll write to her when we're in New York in a week's time. This was all a silly misunderstanding."

Lord Crenshaw nodded stiffly to the captain and gave Thomas a severe glare before leaving the room. Once they were gone, I set my attention back on the cabin. There weren't any signs of a struggle, and no blood splatter. Judging from the dress left on the floor, I doubted a murderer would have spent time washing the walls of blood only to leave the bed and gown crumpled. Especially given the theatrical nature of the last body we'd found. Though the second champagne flute was a troubling detail. One that didn't sit right.

It was likely as Thomas suggested—a young woman who'd

chosen a different path for herself. After spending the last half hour with her parents, I'd say it was high time she'd run off. One more hour with them and I'd do the same.

Uncle poked his head into the water closet, looked around, then pushed his spectacles up his nose. "All seems in order, Captain. From the preliminary inspection, I don't believe there were foul intentions at play here. Seems like a young girl who's maybe a bit"—his eyes moved to mine—"spirited for her family's tastes."

Captain Norwood visibly sank with relief. If one more body turned up this evening, I imagined he'd row himself back to England. "Very good, then. The remainder of this voyage *must* go smoothly. Much is at stake for it and myself." He exhaled. "Come. Let's get you three to your cabins. Have you had time to tour the auxiliary sails yet?" He placed a hand on Uncle's shoulder, guiding him toward the promenade. "Truly remarkable. When powered with the steam stacks, this ship can carve through the ocean like it's a Christmas ham."

"How festive," Thomas uttered as we fell into step behind them. "An ocean liner that's akin to a knife carving salted meat. If that doesn't suggest luxury, I'm not sure what does."

I took one more look around the cabin, but saw nothing out of the ordinary. Still, my stomach clenched a bit. I ignored it. A third young woman hadn't been murdered the second night aboard this ship. That was thankfully too terrible even for the murderer who'd run through a corpse with seven blades and posed her like a tarot card. Thomas offered his arm and I accepted it, leaving the empty cabin behind, though worry wedged itself in like a splinter and lingered just below the surface.

Victorian contortionist

EIGHT

WHAT'S IN A NAME?

UNCLE JONATHAN'S CABIN
RMS ETRURIA
3 JANUARY 1889

Liza crossed her arms over her chest, expression carefully controlled. If this were a game of chess, she seemed determined to win. Though one glance at Uncle showed he felt the same. The Wadsworths were a stubborn lot. This posturing might drag on for hours.

"I cannot possibly back out of the performance tonight," she said. "We've been practicing all week. It would be in poor taste to simply retract my word after I've given it."

"Your *word*?" Uncle drew in a deep breath as if to keep from exploding like a firecracker. "If, by your 'word,' you mean agreeing to assist a young man after you ran off, potentially destroyed our good name, and nearly broke your mother's heart, then pardon me if I fail to see the honor in that. You will either send a note to this Houdini, or I shall keep you locked up in your cabin until we arrive in New York. As it stands we'll have to turn right back around so I can escort you to London. Do not make this worse on yourself by aggravating me further."

Liza shot me a pleading look, but there was little I could do.

When she batted her lashes, I relented. I turned to Uncle, hoping to find some thread of reason to tug on. "Sir, if I may?"

He raised his brows. "Audrey Rose, I'd caution you to not try my patience, else you'll end up with your cousin's fate of being locked in your chambers."

I blew out a breath, feeling a bit like a tightrope walker as I navigated Uncle's foul mood. One small misstep and my hard-fought freedom would come crashing down. "I understand, sir. I was... what I mean to say is...the performers wear masks."

"A very astute observation."

I gritted my teeth. Snapping at Uncle wouldn't be beneficial to either Liza or myself. Though it would be immensely satisfying. "The point being, if you were to graciously permit Liza to complete her performance this evening, no one would be any the wiser. Her identity would remain safe, along with our family name." He opened his mouth to argue, but I cut him off with what I'd hoped was the winning hand. "Then she'll promise to never step foot onstage thereafter. Won't you, Liza?"

She shot me an incredulous look, as if I'd betrayed her after saving her. I held her gaze until she finally sighed. "I promise, Uncle. After this evening, I shan't agree to any more performances. I will only finish what I've committed to."

Uncle paced around the small cabin, pausing to stare out the porthole. "Need I remind you both that thus far two young women have been murdered on this voyage?" Liza and I exchanged glances. "And now you'd like for me to condone reckless behavior. Does that seem wise to either of you?" He faced us again, hands clasped behind his back. "After tonight's performance, you are to obey each and every rule I lay out until we're back in London. Do you understand?"

Liza slowly nodded, eyes fixed on her gem-encrusted shoes. "Yes, sir."

"Let me make this perfectly clear," Uncle continued, "should you even think of doing anything you're not supposed to, I will recommend you live out your days in the asylum for girls. I have an inkling your mother will listen to any diagnosis made."

I felt the color drain from my face. It was one of the worst punishments I'd ever heard, especially coming from Uncle. I stole a glance at my cousin, but she seemed more relieved than disturbed. Apparently the lecture wasn't yet over. Uncle addressed me.

"I will hold you responsible for anything that might happen," he said. I held his gaze, though I longed to sink to the floor. "I suggest you both leave my sight at once before I change my mind."

I grabbed Liza's hand and quickly obliged. Once we were out on the promenade, she clutched my other hand and spun me around. "That was brilliant! I cannot believe he listened to you. I must learn your secrets! I was near certain he'd lock us both up right then and there."

I gently pulled my hands from Liza's grasp and stared out at the ocean. It was the first sunny morning we'd had and the light was nearly blinding when it bounced off the waves.

"Liza..." I ran a gloved hand over my face. "Perhaps you ought to cancel. Uncle's brash, but he's right. Two girls have been murdered. And I—well, to be perfectly frank, I'm worried someone from the carnival might be responsible. Who else would stage a crime like a tarot card?"

Liza studied me for a moment, then reached out and drew me into a hug. "You worry too much, Cousin. And I think—well, I *know* if you met the other performers you'd not be suspicious of them. They're really quite sweet." She stepped back, still holding on to my shoulders. Her face lit up like the sun was gilding her. "I have the perfect solution. You must meet them! Come. We'll go say hello and then you will see for yourself. They're harmless."

"I don't think..." I took in the hopeful expression on my cousin's face and relented. "Very well. Introduce me to your new friends."

⌒⌒⌒

My attention steadily moved around the chaotic room. Captain Norwood had given the carnival an empty cargo hold, and they'd put nearly every inch of it to use. Women balanced on tightropes, clowns practiced jumping over barrels and drums, a girl near our age was covered in tattoos of animals, mostly of the lions and tigers she urged to jump through hoops, and a woman took a ball of fire and swallowed it as if it were a dinner roll. I gasped. "What in the name of the queen..."

"Anishaa the Ace of Wands. Each performer's act is based on the tarot card they represent." Liza watched the girl gulp down another flaming stick. "The girl on the trapeze is Cassiopeia. We call her the Empress. She's favored by Mephistopheles and is quite stuck up about it."

At the mention of his name, I inadvertently searched him out, curious as to what his practices might look like. I imagined a lot of strutting and chest puffing.

"He's not here," Liza added, brow raised. "He spends his time locked away in a cabin working on his mechanical inventions."

"Oh." I turned my attention on Cassiopeia. She somersaulted from one trapeze to another, rolling gracefully through the air as if she were a comet. Her hair fell in long platinum layers, adding to her etherealness. She was stunning. I watched the other aerial performers tumble down ropes, then swing back up them. It appeared as if gravity was under their spell as much as I was. "How do they manipulate the ropes and silks?"

"Body weight and lots of practice. Don't let their small statures fool you," Liza added. "They're stronger than most men."

A man in a black-and-white-striped leotard brought his arm round his head, laying it flat over his shoulder. I froze, heart pounding, as I took in the mechanics of it.

"He's dislocated his shoulder joint!" I whispered to Liza. The contortionist did the same move on the opposite side, then sank down, turning himself into a pretzel. My lip curled involuntarily. "That cannot be good for his health. The wear and tear on his ligaments…"

I glanced at a bemused Liza, shaking her head. "That's Sebastián Cruz. His performances are quite popular." She leaned close. "I've heard he's put his talent to good use, hiding in trunks when unsuspecting husbands come home."

I lightly slapped her arm. "That's horrible."

"Horribly scandalous." Liza grinned. "Rumors claim he's gotten into some trouble on the ship. That's why he's called the Hierophant— he must be favored by God to get out of such unholy predicaments all the time."

I stared at him a few moments longer, mesmerized by the way he folded his body up. A thought struck me. "Where is your Houdini?"

"Likely off with Mephistopheles." Liza sighed. "The two of them are always putting their heads together, coming up with some new way to dazzle an audience. I'll fetch you to meet him tonight after the show."

Unless there was another murder. Then I'd be meeting a corpse. The thought broke the wonderment of the carnival's practice session. Now as I glanced around, the performers all made my skin crawl like grave worms. Even without an audience they all wore masks, hiding from both the world and one another. A large board with concentric circles was set up at one end, firecrackers shooting out as it spun in place. Jian Yu threw blades one after the other into the center of the target, the last dagger sinking into the hilt of the blade before it. Chills slid under my silk.

"Who's the man with Jian?" I asked, watching him remove the daggers and stagger back. "Is he an assistant?"

"Goodness no. That's Andreas the Fool."

I snorted. "I would have imagined that to be Mephistopheles's stage name."

"Honestly, Cousin. Mephistopheles is not half as bad as you make him out to be. He's the Magician, naturally. And he's one of the best I've ever seen. Harry admires him and is constantly yammering on over his brilliance. The way he uses science and math is incredibly innovative. If you give him a chance, you might actually like him."

I kept my eye roll to myself. It seemed as if everyone was convinced the ringmaster could do no wrong. While I was intrigued by his form of science, I did not wish to let on about it. I nodded back at Andreas. "So why is that one called the Fool?"

"He claims to have a magic looking glass that divines one's romantic future." She shook her head. "The sad thing is, he actually believes it works. I've sat down to a reading, and thus far it hasn't informed me who my husband will be. All I see is my distorted image and an indecent amount of cobwebs. If anything, it's downright haunted!"

"Why does Mephistopheles keep him if he's no good?"

Liza looked at me as if I'd said something particularly dense. "He's incredible at the spectacle of fortune-telling. His tent is one of the most popular—he lights incense, speaks in a darkly mysterious Bavarian accent. Plus"—she nudged me in the ribs—"he's quite interesting to look at. Not exactly handsome, but arresting in a way."

"What about—"

"She shouldn't be here." Liza and I both spun around, faced with massive chest-plate armor. I dragged my gaze upward and swallowed hard. Jian turned his glare from me to Liza. "And you still don't belong here."

"Don't be so cross, Jian. It's unbecoming." My cousin simply rolled her eyes. "This is not just anyone, this is my cousin, Miss Wadsworth. She's a lord's daughter so you ought to show a smidgen of respect."

He pointed one of his blades at me, hands scarred from practices that must have gone poorly. "You shouldn't be here, *miss*."

Liza's face turned near scarlet, but before she could explode, I smiled politely. "It was lovely meeting you, Mr. Yu. Impressive knife work, you must practice often."

His lips curved up in what I imagined was an attempt at a smile but came out more like a sneer. "Sometimes I use moving targets. Keeps things interesting."

I narrowed my eyes at him. "Have you ever made any mistakes while using live targets?"

"Once."

Without elaborating, he marched back to the stationary target board and threw blade after blade into the wood. Andreas jumped back as splinters flew. It took an incredible amount of force to cause that sort of damage—the same sort of strength that was needed to shove seven swords into a corpse and string it up.

"I'm dreadfully sorry about that," Liza said as we made our way out of the practice ring. "The performers get a little sensitive about outsiders."

"You're not an outsider," I pointed out. "And he wasn't very pleasant to you."

"Once I accept them as my blood, our bond will become unbroken," Liza said, sounding as if she were quoting from some strange carnival manual. "But not a moment before."

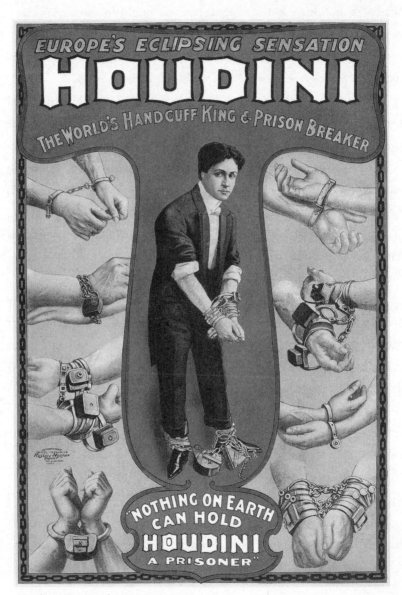

Houdini promotional poster

NINE

KING OF CUFFS

Tonight's stage was dressed in silvers and grays—like moonlight shining through cracks in the ship's hull, lighting on bits of broken glass, or, in this case, crystal decanters and bejeweled patrons. Diners paused, eyeing the preshow performers as they glided through the room on stilts, their movements surprisingly graceful despite the long poles they perched on.

Every part of their costumes was silver, from their masks to their sequined shoes. Tulle hung in tattered shreds that moved ethereally each time they stepped forward on their tall pretend limbs. In fact, the stilts they balanced upon resembled swords. They were bits of glittering beauty with an edge, blades ready to drop at any moment and slash those who least suspected it.

While my uncle and Mrs. Harvey spoke cordially over their meal, I stared at the twirling batons, mesmerized by the silver and white ribbons slicing through the air. An extraordinary amount of work and skill had gone into the creation of the garments, and I wondered at the person who'd made such fine stitches. They could be under the queen's employ, though I supposed they worked for royalty of a different sort.

"You've got the look of someone who's thinking of sewing corpses back together." Thomas grinned over his roasted-duck entrée as I snapped my attention to him. It was scary how well he knew me sometimes. He lifted his glass. "We ought to toast to that. This champagne is terribly good—the bubbles go straight to your head. Don't worry," he added with a wink, "I'll be sure to join you dancing on the table after you've had a few glasses."

"My partner in crime and debauchery," I said, clinking our glasses together. "I am a lucky woman, indeed."

Thomas seemed quite pleased by the statement.

The lights dimmed, our nightly signal that the show was about to begin. I shifted, watching the ringmaster, who promptly took the stage in a clap of cymbals and blast of smoke. His suit was tailored to his body and was a charcoal so deep it could have been mined. Both mask and waistcoat were scarlet tonight, the red bullion around his top hat mimicked splashes of blood. A bold yet decent choice, considering everything that had occurred. I tried to ignore how his knee-high boots drew the eye downward, even if the eye stubbornly wished to remain on his blasted face.

Thomas inspected the young man in the same manner he studied corpses. I couldn't tell if he desired to murder him or dissect his secrets more.

"Ladies." Mephistopheles walked the perimeter of the stage, mask casting beams of light that cut through the chittering crowd and ended most conversations. "Tonight's act is so fearsome you may faint from the strain. However"—he pulled out a small crystal vial— "we have smelling salts for any fits or vapors. Don't be shy in requesting them. Our stilt walkers have plenty on hand; alert them if you're in need."

He beckoned to someone behind the curtain. No one appeared, which likely meant something had been set in motion behind the scenes. I swallowed a bit of roasted duck that suddenly seemed stuck in my throat. I hoped Liza was all right.

"Ladies and gentlemen." Mephistopheles paced along the edge of the stage. "You may wish to look away if you have any sort of medical condition. Particularly any affliction of the heart." The ringmaster paused and glanced around, his gaze settling on my table. "For the brave and fearless among you," he continued, "tonight will forever be marked as the greatest event of your lives."

A murmur went through the crowd at that bold statement. The Moonlight Carnival was spectacular as a traveling troupe, but even their exquisite illusions couldn't live up to that show-bill claim. A sound of thunder rolling through storm clouds began a moment before a masked Liza and another assistant wheeled out a large trunk, then stepped back.

I moved my focus from the trunk to the assistants. They were dressed in sequined silver costumes that were basically just corsets, and thick white stockings. It took a moment for me to piece together that most of the colors chosen were a palette taken from the night—moon, stars, and clouds against inky skies. The ringmaster extended his moonlight revel to the smallest detail.

"Tonight you will experience a metamorphosis like no other. Tonight the impossible is possible. All the way from Appleton, Wisconsin." Mephistopheles swept his arm in a gesture of welcome. "The great. The wonderful. The man who cannot be tamed or caged—please turn your attention over to the amazing Harry Houdini, King of Cuffs!"

The audience politely clapped, but it wasn't anywhere near as wild as it had been for the ringmaster on opening night. Mrs. Harvey winked at me, then hefted her wine into the air in a toast as a young man in a tuxedo took the stage. I sat straighter, not wishing to miss even the slightest detail. This was the young man who'd been clever enough to win my cousin's affections. His dark hair was parted down the middle, and when he flashed a smile, dimples greeted the crowd.

Unlike the other performers, Houdini was unmasked. There was a presence about him, though, something that felt like a charge in the air before lightning struck. Liza smiled wide, her whole body seeming to radiate joy as Houdini lifted his arms above his head. In a booming voice that was surprising for his smaller stature, he called, "Ropes!"

Liza removed a length of rope from the trunk, holding it up for the audience before snapping it through the air like a whip. Houdini pivoted, his back now turned on the crowd.

"That's quite rude, isn't it?" Mrs. Harvey whispered. "Bad manners to turn his back on...oh...oh, I see. That *is* something."

Houdini held his arms out behind himself, nodding to Liza as she silently tied them together in a web of crisscrossing rope. I was impressed by her expert knots—Aunt Amelia would not be as pleased by her embroidery lessons being used in such a way.

"Look at those knots," Mrs. Harvey whispered, "he'll have a dickens of a time getting out of those. I wonder if he's got a knife stashed in his trousers...certainly appears that way."

Thomas choked on his water, shooting our chaperone an incredulous look.

Liza tugged and pulled, nearly knocking the escape artist off his feet. A young man at the table next to ours said quite loudly, "How boring. I bet the rope isn't even real."

Houdini spun until he faced the tables again, eyes flashing. "Two volunteers from the audience! Who wants to inspect my bindings?"

The young man who'd spoken sank into his seat, the weasel. Apparently he was one of those dogs who was all bark and no bite.

The audience kept its attention on the stage, likely hungry for the same sort of drama that unfolded the night before. Two men took Houdini up on his offer and added another length of rope around his bound hands for good measure. This seemed to satisfy the crowd, though it was a bit duller compared to the tension the Knight of Swords drew out.

I glanced around the room, unsurprised that no other performers were in the crowd, except for the stilt walkers, who still picked their way among our tables, silent and eerie as ten-foot ghosts.

"And now..." Houdini wriggled in place. "My cuffs!"

The second assistant, Isabella, brandished the handcuffs that he'd crowned himself king over. Houdini showed us his back once more, standing perfectly still as the cuffs clicked into place with finality. Houdini strode over to the trunk and climbed inside, folding himself in tight as any bolt of fabric. Seemed he'd taken some contortion lessons from Sebastián.

Thomas set his glass down when the lid was dropped and locked into place. Liza tied another length of rope around the trunk, then snapped a padlock and chains around it. We'd likely sit here all evening waiting for him to pick his way out of all those locks.

Diners slowed their chatter. Without prompting, both assistants skipped behind the stage, reemerging with a rolling cabinet that was taller than a person, the portable curtain fabrics a deep charcoal. They secured it around the locked trunk, keeping it from view. To my utter shock, Liza stepped forward, mask shimmering as lights flickered overhead, before retreating behind the portable curtains with a grand flourish of her hands.

"When I clap my hands three times—behold a miracle!"

She clapped once, and diners shifted in their seats. Twice, and talking dropped to mere whispers. She clapped a third time, and the room was a held breath, ready to gasp.

Out burst Houdini from behind the curtains Liza had disap-peared through, free as anything. He swept his arm out: "Behold! Metamorphosis!" He yanked the curtain back, revealing Liza cuffed in the trunk.

Thomas and I exchanged glances as the crowd sprang to life. The trick had literally taken three seconds—how they'd accomplished such a thing was indeed magical. I wondered if there was anything Harry Houdini couldn't escape from.

Or any trap he couldn't set for someone else. Our last victim had been hung up from her ankles; perhaps we'd just found the young man who'd accomplished that difficult feat.

TEN

HEART OR HEAD

WOMEN'S PARLOR
RMS ETRURIA
3 JANUARY 1889

"Look, Cousin," Liza whispered, an expression of awe upon her face. Up this close, the wax of her heavy makeup showed its cracks like a porcelain doll whose paint had flaked from age. "There he is. My truest love." She admired Houdini across the crowded room, and the power of her emotions crashed into me like a wave. I wished I could muster up the same level of excitement, but something I couldn't quite identify kept me skeptical about his intentions. "Isn't he the most amazing young man you've ever seen?"

"He is intriguing," I admitted, eyes straying to Mephistopheles before flicking back to Houdini. My own cheeks warmed when the ringmaster's gaze fell on me and remained there. I pretended not to notice—it seemed a dangerous sort of thing, having a young man like that interested.

Oblivious to who had captured my attention first, my cousin nodded. "Just watch the way he moves about the room. Every eye is upon him. I swear he truly does possess escape magic." I followed her gaze but was once again caught in Mephistopheles's snare. "I am most certainly bewitched in all ways and see no way out. It's the most horrid splendor of all!"

I looked sharply away from the ringmaster and studied my cousin. Two petal-sized spots of pink bloomed across her cheeks. It was obvious that she was quite taken with the escape artist. Though one glance around the room—filled with women fanning themselves—had me raising a brow and staying my tongue.

Houdini seemed to have an entire garden of blushing roses to tend to. He buzzed from one flower to another, laughing and kissing gloved hands as he went. Liza appeared utterly enchanted, while I felt my face scrunching into a most unpleasant scowl. He paused a bit too long near some women, his touch lingering well past the point of decency.

"Ladies."

I turned abruptly at the sound of that deep voice, heart knocking about my ribs. Mephistopheles stood in all his costumed glory, filigree mask curling about mischievous eyes. The very ones fixed upon mine. This close I could see the hair that fell across his brow was black. It was silky with subtle waves, the sort of soft curls that made your fingers wish to run through it on their own.

"Seems I haven't yet had the pleasure of *properly* introducing myself," he said. "Liza? Who is this beautiful creature and why have you kept her from me?"

"This is my cousin." Liza smiled proudly. "Miss Audrey Rose Wadsworth."

So much for this being our "proper" introduction. I all but rolled my eyes. "Creature? You do flatter me too much with such compliments, sir. It's no wonder that so many lose their hearts to your traveling minstrel show."

He stared at me, brows raised above his mask. Apparently sass wasn't what he expected, though he honestly should have with an opening such as that. Creature, indeed. As if women were mere animals to be fancied when it suited a gentleman.

"Such sharp words," he said. "Your tongue ought to come with a warning."

"Truth is often compared to a blade," I said. "I question those who marvel when it pricks."

Liza stood behind him, subtly shaking her head, but the smile on her face told me she approved of my comment. She was my partner in all things equality. We women could be called creatures, if only the men who said such careless words accepted our claws were fearsome things when we decided to scratch.

Much to my utter amazement, he laughed. "Miss Wadsworth, I—"

A young woman squeezed between us, a glass of champagne in each hand as her two friends pushed in beside her. She nervously stuck a glass out, offering it to the young ringmaster. He politely took it but did not sip from it—he still appeared a bit amused by my response.

"You were incredible opening night, Mr. Mephistopheles. Absolutely marvelous, even," the young woman said, taking a long pull of her champagne. She winced, likely from drinking the bubbles too quickly, her cheeks flushing bright. "A few of us were wondering if you might try a new trick just for us. Surely you can't best *all* of us."

Giggles erupted from the small crowd around us. Liza grinned. It was quite a scandalous offer, one I couldn't help smiling over myself. I liked these girls. There was something bold about them that reminded me of my friends Ileana and Daciana. A twinge of sadness pinched my core—I wished they were on the ship with us, but they were settling things in Romania after the Dracula case. They promised they might board another ship and meet us in America next month if they could, something I hoped for dearly.

The ringmaster's lips curled up at the edges, though his eyes were stubbornly stuck to mine while he considered their offer. I quirked a brow, waiting. He turned toward the young women and bowed deeply. "Of course. But only if I get to choose my next victim."

One of the giggling friends broke off her laughter. "Victim?"

"Indeed," Mephistopheles said. "I can think of no better term for the crime of seduction about to be committed, can you?"

"No, I suppose I cannot."

She shook her head and stepped closer to her friends. The handsomely dressed girls all exchanged glances; it wasn't quite what they had hoped, but it was an interesting bargain nonetheless. Two of them nodded, and the one who'd conducted the exchange bit her lip, seeming to consider accepting this or trying a counteroffer but finally assented.

"Very well, sir. Which of us do you choose?"

He indicated his prey. "Her."

I nearly choked on my own sip of champagne when I realized he was pointing at me. No good could come of this interest, indeed. I didn't know what game Mephistopheles was playing, but, I supposed, whether I wanted to or not, I was about to join him.

There was no denying the thrill that sparked through me at being chosen for this next act, though it wasn't because of the enigmatic masked man leading me to the center of the women's parlor. This was a remarkable opportunity to observe his sleight of hand up close—to dissect his performance and witness the tactics he used to distract both *victim,* as he called me, and audience.

"Ladies, I have been requested to perform for you." Mephistopheles held my gloved hand in his, raising it shoulder level for all to see. "Miss Wadsworth will be playing the role of willing victim. If you please, I'll need everyone to gather in a circle around us. Pretend as if we're about to hold a séance. I'm sure you've all attended one or two of those."

He snapped his fingers, and a liveried waiter produced a small chair from one of the side tables and set it in the center of the newly made ring. Women whispered excitedly, gazes hungry for more scandalous magic. Or perhaps they were simply happy to feast on the young ringmaster a bit more. I felt the power of their stares drift from Mephistopheles and settle on me as I stood there, unsure of where to go. Of all evenings for me to wear a sleeveless gown, I felt exposed and vulnerable.

I twisted my mother's ring about my finger, then stopped. I focused on the room, hoping to calm my growing nerves as Mephistopheles adjusted his top hat and suit. I didn't care for such scrutiny, as if I were nothing more than a slide under a microscope. Houdini slowly made his way toward Liza, his focus drifting over to the ringmaster only occasionally as he took leave of several young women.

"Next, I request the lights be dimmed." A moment later, the chandeliers pulsed with brighter light before trickling down to a dull, golden glow. "I ask that you all take one large step back on the count of three. One. Two. Three."

My breath caught. It was unnerving, hearing the entire room move as one. Mephistopheles truly did command them like a puppet master. Everyone was silhouetted in the dim light, shadow people dancing around a devil's bonfire. I could have sworn I smelled the scent of burning wood, though I knew it to be an impossibility.

I flicked my gaze to the ringmaster as he walked around the crowd and came to a halt before me. The red of his vest reflected in his mask when he tilted his face down, motioning for me to take the seat. I hesitated, recalling the two victims, then forced my feet to carry me over to whatever sinful delight Mephistopheles had planned. I would not lose my life in front of so many witnesses.

"Watch closely," he said, hardly above a whisper, "or you'll miss it."

He circled me now, hands trailing from my bare shoulders all the way around my neck, his touch almost as electric as the lights in the ship. I no longer felt the stares of the women surrounding us—I could only concentrate on his gloved fingertips, never straying from the path he'd chosen while he moved around me, picking up speed with each pass. It was almost scandalous, but not quite, the line too indistinguishable this close to decency. His movements were sure and steady, unlike my pulse.

Except for one slip of his hand caressing the nape of my neck—perhaps a kind gesture of apology—I noticed no change from when he began circling me to when he abruptly stepped back. My skin felt both scorched and ice cold where his fingers had been, as unsure as I was about the entire situation. Women snapped their fans open, the sound drawing me back to the room.

"Did you watch closely?" The ringmaster asked, voice cool and smooth as silk. As if still in a trance of their own, everyone nodded, murmuring, "Yes." I doubted they could've looked away from the charismatic man if they tried. He bent down, placing his mouth dangerously close to my ear. My skin prickled; this time I knew exactly why. "Is something valuable missing, Miss Wadsworth? Something you'd do anything to get back?"

I shook my head, hoping to set my mind straight with the action. "No, I don't believe so."

And I meant it. Though his fingers were *quite* a distraction, I kept my focus on them entirely; not once did they leave my skin. He dropped to one knee, eyes dancing when they met mine. "Strange. I could have sworn I'd just stolen your heart."

"I beg—"

"As do most young women I encounter, I'm afraid."

My face flamed. But before I could scold him, he produced the heart pendant that had been one of my mother's favorite pieces, watching as I blinked disbelief away. I fumbled around my throat, tugging at a chain. "That's impossible. I'm still wearing—"

In my hand was a pocket watch, one that did not belong to me. Thorns and a Latin phrase were etched onto the back of it, VINCERE VEL MORI. I stared unblinking, trying to understand how it was possible. Somehow, in front of all of these witnesses, Mephistopheles had switched my necklace with his watch. I swallowed my questions down. I had no idea how he'd managed such a thing without being caught, but it had to be luck mixed with sleight of hand. I wanted to know how he had accomplished it and if it could be applied in other ways, such as acting; however, that would need to wait until we were alone. Which I would make sure happened soon. Tonight.

"Very impressive, I suppose," I said, knowing I was being dishonest. It was one of the most impressive feats I'd seen, aside from Houdini's Metamorphosis trick. "Now, give it back, please."

I held my hand out and immediately had the sensation of walking into a trap. It was a well-laid snare, so hidden I'd had no idea it had been the actual trick the whole time. I wanted to curl my fingers back into a fist, but resisted the urge. Mephistopheles swiftly took my hand in his, turning it over so my palm faced down. Still on one knee, he made a ring appear and disappear across his fingers. My heart slowed.

"If you had to choose," he asked, "would you want your heart or your hand?"

Any whispers that had broken out died. All eyes turned to me once more, making my palms sweat. I could barely think, barely focus on anything other than my mother's ring and pendant in some stranger's grasp. Stealing my necklace was one thing—how he'd managed to also remove my ring was too much to process. I felt entirely undone, a dinghy bobbing unanchored in a storm.

"They are both mine." I drew my brows together. "I don't have to choose."

He watched me behind his mask, eyes searching. "Not yet. But I imagine you soon will." He leaned close, until no one could overhear his next words. "Have I earned your interest in our bargain yet?" My pulse sped up. This choice. I had a feeling it would bring chaos into my life. But the reward would be worth it. I slightly inclined my head. "I'll meet you where I did last time."

Without another word, he handed both pieces of jewelry over and stood, clapping his hands generously. "Please offer a round of applause to my latest victim, Miss Audrey Rose Wadsworth. She survived this time, but perhaps she'll lose her heart to me yet."

Liza beamed beside Houdini, bringing her hands together the loudest of everyone while he leaned in and chatted with one of the girls who'd prompted this show. I wanted to return Liza's elation, but couldn't shake the essence of trouble that hung like a mist in the air.

If Mephistopheles was that talented with pilfering objects, perhaps he was gifted enough to steal a person's sensibilities. He swooped down, kissing hands, and earning the admiration of the women in the parlor, and I wondered if I'd made a fatal mistake by agreeing to meet with him tonight.

ELEVEN
PRINCE OR PAUPER

WOMEN'S PARLOR
RMS ETRURIA
3 JANUARY 1889

I retrieved my fur stole and left the women's parlor as soon as I could extricate myself from conversations on how it had felt having the ringmaster's searing touch on my skin. For members of upper-class society, they certainly were not shying away from such devious talks. No one even cast an accusatory or judgmental eye on me, either. It was as if they'd been spellbound.

I held the fur close around me, trying to ignore the bite in the air as I exited the corridor and hurried down the empty promenade. Tiny snowflakes began falling, neither promising nor denying a storm was on the way. A figure leaning against the wall of rowboats came into view.

Mephistopheles tipped his hat back. "I'm pleased you've decided to meet me."

"Why did you choose me for that performance?"

"Truth or a lovely version of it?" he asked.

"I do not require soft versions of reality, Mr.—"

"Ah. Let's deal with one truth at a time, all right?"

He moved to the railing on the deck, canting his head toward me. Snow danced and twirled between us, though he gave no indication of being affected by the cold. I, however, nestled deeper into my furs, wishing I also had an overcoat.

"I chose you because I believe you search for the truth hidden in the lie. Others enjoy the magic and spectacle. You are fascinated with the *how*. I don't think you're taken with me or the illusion I offer...the distraction." He looked directly into my eyes, searching for what, I couldn't tell. A moment passed and his expression didn't change. "What is it you do for that old man you travel with?"

I didn't know what harm could come of admitting my chosen path. "I study forensic medicine with my uncle. Mr. Cresswell and I apprentice under him." I opened my mouth, then shut it, hesitant to speak about either the Ripper or Dracula case. Both were too raw and personal to share with a stranger. "We're going to America for a new case, actually."

"You study the dead?" He raised a brow above his mask as I nodded. "Which means you're aware of the darkness and seek to bring about the light. I cannot help being equally intrigued by that. I create chaos, and you fabricate order from it. We're not so different, you and me. We both have a core that's built of science, only different outward expressions of it."

It was eerily similar to my own thoughts. I did not wish to find commonality with such a scoundrel, but couldn't deny his assessment. Despite inner warnings to stay far from this young man, my curiosity about his mechanical inventions was piqued.

"Why did you choose the path of an illusionist?" I asked. "You might have become an impressive chemist. Don't you wish to help people?"

"Some might argue that entertaining people is helping them."

I rolled my eyes. "Producing smoke in looking glasses does not equate with creating scientific or engineering advancements that could eradicate disease and save lives."

"I politely disagree, Miss Wadsworth. There are many ways to assist people. Laughter and distraction are sometimes things people need in conjunction with medical diagnoses and treatments." Mephistopheles studied me. "You might want to explore other avenues of possibility, since you're such a gifted student of science. I may *only* offer a few hours of distraction, but for some that is enough to press on through dark times. Hope is an invisible yet mighty force. Don't dismiss its power."

I blinked, stunned by both how correct he was and how ignorantly I had viewed things. A long-ago memory emerged from the grave I'd buried it in. I'd often read stories to my mother as she lay dying, hoping to transport her from her pain, if only for a few moments. Part of me bristled at being schooled by such a devious young man, but mostly my cheeks burned with shame for not understanding his point sooner. People did need to be entertained, to have their minds occupied with thoughts other than a constant bombardment of negativity. Mother's spirits certainly seemed lifted whenever I'd open a book and take her on a new adventure.

"I am—"

Mephistopheles suddenly grasped my hand in his and pressed a chaste kiss to it. Words of apology died on my tongue as I took in the fire in his eyes and the way they shifted just over my shoulder. He was putting on yet another show, and it was not for my benefit. I yanked my hand away, but it was too late. He grinned.

"An absolute pleasure, Miss Wadsworth," he said. "Perhaps we'll meet again at our favorite spot..." He leaned in so only I might hear the next part. "Let's say around midnight? Seems our meeting has come to an abrupt end and I still have much to discuss, if you're game?" The ringmaster nodded behind me, that antagonistic smile still in place. "Good evening. Mr. Cresswell, I presume? We were just discussing you. And who is the lovely lady with you?"

I let my breath out in a deep exhale, not wanting to turn around and face Thomas just yet.

"Oh? You were discussing me?" Thomas sounded skeptical and appeared even more so when I shifted to find his gaze on me. "An honor considering I don't possess a trick hat with ink-dyed roses. Or the ability to tumble across the stage. Though I *am* darkly enchanting. I understand the draw." He paused as if considering his next words. "You're still wearing that mask, I see. Does it chafe?"

"Not at all. There's velvet on the inside." Mephistopheles turned a smile on Mrs. Harvey, so radiant I feared she'd faint from overheating. "Will you introduce me to this pretty young thing, or shall I die of want?"

"Mrs. Edna Harvey, Mr...." Mrs. Harvey drew her brows together. "Er...Mr.?"

"'Mephistopheles' is perfectly adequate, if you please." He inclined his head. "If you'll excuse me, I must tend to consortium business. Good evening to you all."

We stood together on the deck a moment, watching the ringmaster make his way to the troupe and whatever business carnival folk had postshow. Once he was out of earshot Mrs. Harvey dropped Thomas's arm and fanned herself.

"He is quite something, isn't he?" she asked. "So mysterious with that mask and name. I wonder if he ever slips—can't be an easy thing, taking on a new identity like that. I imagine he's got to take that mask off when he sleeps..."

"Maybe one of us should sneak into his rooms and find out," I said, teasing.

Mrs. Harvey's attention shot to me. "I wouldn't mind volunteering for that task."

Thomas grinned, then took Mrs. Harvey's arm once more, leading us to our rooms in a show of courtly manners I was impressed by. "I doubt any of his performers even know his true identity. There's a definite reason for the masks, and I'm sure it's not simply to create an aura of mystique. I'd wager he's either hiding from someone, or hiding a sordid past."

I snorted in the most unladylike fashion. "Is this one of your infamous deductions based on observation?"

"Mock me all you will." Thomas lifted a shoulder. "But his mannerisms speak of aristocracy. As do his boots."

Honestly, I was unsurprised that Thomas had once again divined some seemingly impossible detail from the salty ocean air. "All right. Tell me more about his boots and how they signal aristocracy in the Thomas Cresswell deduction journal."

"I bet something terrible happened to him. Poor thing." Mrs. Harvey stopped walking in front of her cabin. She glanced down the deck behind us. "Miss Wadsworth, since you're only next door, I think it will be fine if Thomas escorts you home this once. Unless you find it to be too indecent. I'm suddenly feeling quite…"

"In need of your traveling tonic?" Thomas supplied, doing a terrible job of keeping the laughter out of his voice when she poked him in the chest. "Ow."

"Hush, you," she said, not unkindly. "It's not polite to make fun of your elders. One day you'll need a nip of traveling tonic to help you sleep, too."

I ignored the silliness passing between them and smiled at our lackadaisical chaperone. It was entirely improper for Thomas to walk *anywhere* with me without a chaperone, but we'd been in more-compromising positions than a short walk, much to my father's horror, should he ever find out. "It's fine, Mrs. Harvey. Since our rooms connect—I'm sure no one will be too scandalized. Most everyone has turned in for the night anyway. We won't linger long."

"What a magical evening it's been. And not one corpse ruined the fun!" She kissed my cheeks and Thomas's, then opened her door. "I'm completely spent."

Once she closed the door, Thomas and I walked the few steps to a bench situated between my room and the next. Sensing that he had something to say, I sat down and patted the spot next to me. The snowflakes had mostly ceased, but the bite was still nipping at the air. Ever attuned to me, he shrugged his overcoat off and wrapped it about my shoulders.

"Thank you," I said. "You were saying something intriguing about shoes, I believe?"

"The soles had no scuffs," he said, glancing around once before sitting and rubbing his hands together. "Before you mention it, no, I don't believe that a good buff and shine would explain it. They are new. Or at least they haven't been worn much."

"Maybe he only wears them during his performances."

Thomas sat back, his smile heartbreakingly wicked in the dark. "A good theory, Wadsworth, but the way he runs around and tumbles across the stage...even if he only wore those particular boots during his shows, they'd show a little wear. Since none can be found, what might that indicate?"

"He purchased new ones."

"Precisely. Even a successful showman wouldn't spend so much on the fine leather he chooses," Thomas said. "He certainly wouldn't purchase expensive pairs every time. Which leads me to believe he's most definitely someone who already hails from a wealthy household and doesn't offer much thought to spending frivolously. If you knew you'd need to replace your shoes nightly, would *you* purchase the most costly ones?"

He had a point. "Well. That would also explain his insistence on wearing a mask and using a stage name, wouldn't it?" I studied my friend, taking in the familiar sharp angles of his profile. "Yet you believe he's dangerous."

"He's secretive, manipulative, capable of making harmless things feel sinister, and sinister things feel harmless. Two young women are dead. Based on those reasons alone, I do not trust him." Thomas ignored the polite rules of our world and took my hand in his, twining our fingers together, expression thoughtful. "He wants something from you. I'm not sure what, but my best guess is it's not for anything good. Whatever his motivations, they are strictly for *his* benefit or the carnival's. And if he hurts you . . ."

"I am capable of taking care of myself, as you know. I've already survived meeting him alone, there's nothing to worry over. I believe getting close to him would be beneficial in multiple ways."

Thomas stood and paced near the funnel closest to the bow of the ship, shoulders bunched either against the wind or the partial plan I'd blurted out. I slowly got up and followed, wishing I could stuff the words back into my mouth. Steam billowed out behind him reminding me of lounging cigar smokers in a men's smoke room, puffs of grayish white drifting lazily into the clouds. If only my friend was as relaxed as that imagery. He was wound so tightly I feared he'd spring into the ocean at any moment.

"Honestly," I said, watching him walk back and forth a few more times, "you know it's the best method of distraction, Thomas. It gives you a wonderful opportunity to work your Cresswell magic and it offers me time to get closer to the performers. Don't be jealous you didn't think of it first. Your sulking is unbecoming."

He stopped pacing and stared at me as if I'd grown a second head. "Stepping inside a lion's cage might be the best form of distraction, but it's not the safest means, Wadsworth."

"The very nature of our job is dangerous," I argued. "This is simply another tool to use in hunting murderers. If everyone's attention is on the drama unfolding between Mephistopheles and me, they aren't paying close attention to you or Uncle."

"Oh, really? So no one will be paying attention to your poor, heartbreakingly handsome, jilted lover while you're getting close to the ringmaster?" He arched a brow. "Perhaps I'll use myself as bait. I'm sure I could charm my way into the hearts of a few of the performers myself."

"Is that what this is about? You feel left out of the excitement?" I asked. "Your job is much more thrilling and important than flirting with the ringmaster. You get to study scuff marks on boots and calculate how they got there and who is responsible. See? Very important work."

"Then you ought to have the honor of playing my role," he said. "I'm all for equality in our partnership." I pursed my lips and he smiled victoriously. "That's precisely what I thought. There's no good reason for you to put yourself in harm's way. Mephistopheles is a potential murderer. Strolling down the promenade with him is as wise as me sticking my head in the aforementioned lion's mouth. And while that might be grand fun, it's undoubtedly a bad idea."

"I disagree."

"You're saying I should stick my head in the lion's mouth, then?"

"If you wanted to, I'd support it even if I didn't like it." I lifted my chin. "*If* Mephistopheles is the murderer, then he wouldn't be stupid enough to attack me, knowing he would be the first person you and Uncle targeted. However, staying close to him, gaining his trust, even flirting with him, allows me an opportunity to infiltrate their troupe. If he trusts me, then the others will, too. Who knows what I'll be able to observe that way?"

"There is one too many ifs involved," Thomas said, voice carefully controlled. "If something goes wrong, then *you* will also be in the direct line of fire. The risk isn't worth the reward in this instance, Wadsworth."

"Then I'm sorry to say we're at an impasse." I shook my head. "I feel quite the opposite. Some risks are worth taking, even if they seem impossible at first."

Thomas snorted, but his expression was laced with mild disgust. "You sound like him now. In fact, I dare say that you enjoy being around him, just admit it. Is that what—"

I reached over and turned his face to mine. "He will neither harm me, nor come between us, Cresswell. I don't care what sort of illusion he tries casting. My heart is yours, no sleight of hand will steal it."

Before he could argue, I leaned forward and pressed my mouth to his. He drew me closer, his hands sliding around my waist, two anchors in a sea of unknowns. We stayed like that, kissing beneath glittering constellations and sporadically falling snow, until the sounds of late-night stragglers broke us apart.

With effort, Thomas escorted me to my door and bid me good night with a chaste kiss. I looked up at the moon, thoughts as scattered as the stars. If Thomas was correct, and I'm sure he was, then who was the ringmaster and what was he either running from or hiding?

I slipped into my room and glanced at the clock. Midnight was fast approaching. After exchanging my fur for a wool overcoat, I listened at the door connecting my room to Mrs. Harvey's, relieved to hear her quiet snoring. Hopefully she'd sleep through the night and not check on me. There was no way I'd fall asleep now, so I crept along the quiet end of the promenade, hoping to find out some answers from the man in question himself.

⟨⚬⟩

"There you are, the curious Miss Wadsworth. I wondered if you'd venture out a second time. But are you here to finish our little chat, or is there something more to your meeting me?"

Mephistopheles emerged from the shadows of the rowboats, a demon rising out of the foggy mist, a wine bottle dangling from one hand. His mask now reflected the moonlight, making me shiver—I wished he'd take the horrid thing off.

"Ah. That's it." He gazed unabashedly at my form. "Come to steal back your soul? I may be feeling generous this evening, but not that much. It is mine and I do not share."

I rolled my eyes. "You fancy yourself quite a bit. Why do you care if I like you or not when you have an entire ship of passengers who are captivated by such theatrics? Shouldn't you be bothering one of them? They would appreciate your lurking about, brooding. Not to mention"—I eyed him closely—"my cousin says that trapeze artist, Cassie the Empress, is quite smitten."

He set the bottle down and leaned against the wall, a movement that was too casual and common for him somehow, and scrutinized me. Thomas was right—now that I was looking for it, he did seem to have an air of station about him. One he hadn't cultivated by observing the wealthy, but by practicing and living it since birth. There was much more to him than he let on.

"Are you in possession of so many friends that you needn't make another?" he finally asked. "What injury have I wrought upon you to deserve that barbed tongue? I'm simply getting to know you. I don't see any crime in that. Yet there you stand, ready to convict me."

"Don't think I missed that performance earlier or your intention behind it." I marched over to where he leaned against the wall of rowboats. "You're trying to create a rift between me and Thomas. I consider that to be injury enough."

"And?" he asked. "Was he so offended by my kissing your hand? If he was, then you ought to look into finding another beau. Jealousy is a disease that spreads. If anything, I've done you a considerable honor by rooting out that cancer of an emotion. You're quite welcome."

"It would take something much more inexcusable to break us, and I guarantee it is impossible, so don't even attempt it."

"There you go," he said with a toss of a hand. "If you two are unbreakable, then I might try as hard as I want to gain your affection. Where's the harm in that?"

"It is indecent and wholly unnecessary considering you and I don't even know each other, and another woman is in love with you. You are playing a game and I won't take part in it." I tried keeping myself from shouting, but my voice rose all the same. I took a moment to compose myself. "And it is unkind. If you truly want to be friends, that's hardly the way to go about it."

"I'm a showman. I am not kind. Nor am I decent." He lifted a shoulder as if he were simply commenting on something as insignificant as the weather. "If you expect me to be either, you will be disappointed."

I glared at him, hands curling at my sides. "Then why, pray tell, did you wish to meet again?"

He had the absolute *nerve* to smile at me. "Based on your experience with forensic medicine, I have a revised proposal for you. And it isn't of the marriage variety—ah, please don't look so sad." I all but bared my teeth, and he tossed his hands up in placation. "I'm only kidding, Miss Wadsworth. I require your assistance with my show."

He paused, watching to see if I had any arguments thus far, which I did not.

"I saw your face when your cousin came onstage that first night—you do not approve of the carnival or her role in it, do you?"

That was untrue. "That is none of your concern."

"Isn't it, though?" He grinned again and I thought of all the ways I might pry that smile from his face. "What if I told you I could assist you? You desire to help your cousin be free of the show and Houdini. I know a secret that would aid your cause. Only if you help me. Do we have a bargain? My assistance for the price of yours?"

I was desperately curious about the secret he knew, but had learned the price of curiosity. He must have seen something in my expression, though, something that gave him hope.

"There is one stipulation. You cannot utter *one word* of our deal. Not to Mr. Cresswell or your cousin, or anyone else aboard this ship. If they were to find out…well, I would be forced to play my hand and tell *your* secret."

"What secret?" I bristled. "I have done nothing to worry about."

"Are you certain?" he asked, all innocence and deceit at once. "I doubt Liza would ever return home if she discovered you were to blame for her inevitable heartbreak."

"I have not even agreed to this, and yet you're already blackmailing me?"

He lifted a shoulder again. "You didn't say no straightaway, did you?"

I stared at him, working out the offer and trying desperately to rein my emotions in. My initial inclination *was* to say no, slap him with a discarded glove, and walk away. To rush off in the opposite direction and not lay eyes on him again before we reached America.

It would be the wisest choice.

The safest.

It was also the choice that was selfish and would neither help my cousin nor myself. I'd been raised to use inaction as a security net, but it didn't lend itself to exploring uncharted waters.

Mephistopheles stepped closer, a wolf scenting his prey. I could see my distorted image reflected back in the filigree of his mask, and I shuddered.

"I will give you what you most want, Miss Wadsworth. Your cousin free from ruination and disgrace, all without you having to play the role of villain. And I will get what I most want in return for your help."

"What is it that you most want? Surely it cannot simply be my help with the show."

"Your cousin, if rumors are to be believed, is no longer able to assist. I do need another pretty girl to help dazzle the crowd. That's all."

"I cannot perform nightly—it's preposterous to believe my uncle would be all right with it, especially after he's the one who's forbidden Liza from that very thing."

"I don't require your help every night. Just for one show in particular." He gazed at me intently. "Do you want to free your cousin from Houdini or not?"

My palms itched. I did not want to think about Liza's tattered reputation should her romance with Houdini either end or become widely known.

"Liza will be laughed at, mocked, scorned," Mephistopheles pressed on, knowing he'd found the correct thread to tug that would unravel my resolve. "Her family destroyed. She will never host another tea, be courted by a handsome gentleman, or be invited to a lavish ball." He took another step forward. "She loves those things, doesn't she? Will you stand by, watching as she sets her entire life on fire for a man who is sure to disappear once the smoke clears?"

A cloud floated past the moon, darkening the skies for a moment. It was midnight and I'd already been warned about those types of bargains.

He leaned in, his gaze locked on to mine. "Do we have a deal?"

Late nineteenth-century circus performers

TWELVE
DEAL WITH THE DEVIL

BOW
RMS ETRURIA
3 JANUARY 1889

His gloved finger ghosted over my cheek, never directly touching it, but making my pulse speed up nonetheless. I did want my cousin to come home. I wanted her to be happy and free from judgment. But I knew I was wading in murky waters. Just because I saw how much devastation her choice would cause did not grant me the right to choose *for* her.

Love was a tricky, complicated thing—so morally gray. Both grand and terrible things were often done in its honor. But could something truly be done out of love if it had the potential to hurt the one at its heart? I wavered.

"Sounds like a fair deal, does it not?" he said. "All you have to do is participate in the finale—without telling a soul what you're doing—and everything you desire will be yours. I'll even give you those lessons in sleight of hand I'd originally promised. Since you have become somewhat of a celebrity in London society, your presence will lend credibility to my scientific work; my assistance will save your cousin. What do you stand to lose?"

His opening words came to mind immediately, *"Which will you lose before the week is through? Your heart? Your head? Perhaps you, too, will lose your life, your very soul."* The shadows near us loomed closer. My heart banged around. The bargain sounded too simple, too easy, for me to agree to. Which meant there was some hidden benefit for Mephistopheles and some detriment to me. I studied his carefully composed expression.

"I . . ."

"Yes?" Somehow he'd managed to move again without my noticing. He smelled of a sultry, spicy incense. Hints of ginger and citrus mixed with careful notes of vanilla and lavender surrounded us. I resisted the urge to breathe it in deeply. His gaze traveled across my features, openly examining me.

"All I have to do is go onstage during the finale?"

"More or less." He smiled. "I'm still working out the details."

Technically Liza would simply be learning the truth, then she'd form her own decision based on facts presented to her. Nothing would be hidden. If she still chose to stay with the carnival and Houdini, then I would not interfere again, though I'm sure Uncle would have much to say regarding that. My palms tingled. I was only bartering for information. I was not forcing her hand or making a choice for her. And all I had to do was show up onstage for his foolish grand finale; it was hardly a taxing proposition. Still . . .

"Do we have a bargain, Miss Wadsworth?"

Indecision stopped gripping my mind. I could not sit in the comfort of safety, not when the risk was too great to my cousin. That was moral obligation enough. "If I accept your offer—I'll need more details of what Harry Houdini has hidden. No lies."

Mephistopheles crossed his heart. "No lies."

I bit my lip, praying curiosity wasn't getting the better of me. "Then I accept your bargain."

Mephistopheles lifted one side of his mouth, and my heart sped in protest. His look didn't promise there wouldn't be regrets involved. Quite the contrary. It was too late of a warning, though. I'd already made a deal with the Devil and now I'd see it through.

"What information do you have on Houdini?"

"There's a woman in America he writes to. Very often." He shook his head. "I don't have to be a detective inspector to figure out how much he loves her. Every town or city we pass through, he sends off another letter." His expression turned from smug to pained. "Even after he met Liza, the letters have never ceased. I fear that, well, to be honest, I *know* he hasn't mentioned it to her."

The scoundrel! In love with another woman, sending her notes from each adventure—and all behind my dear cousin's back. I closed my eyes, hoping to dull the anger. Pretending I didn't know what a lying rogue he was would be difficult, especially when I longed to disembowel him.

"Why do you care about Liza's reputation?" I inspected the ring-master's face, searching for any hint to his true motivation. Like most everything else about him, his expression was carefully controlled, giving me nothing but a slight smirk to go on. A smirk with just the right hint of innocence to make the trouble seem worth the risk. "What does that matter to you?"

"It doesn't. I simply need to give my show a boost, and as the passengers are aware of your forensic background, you, my dear, will play along and claim my tricks are truly magical. If you, an expert in your field, are convinced, then my reputation will improve. Something I'm in desperate need of as bodies keep showing up during or after my shows. This information is strictly a bargaining chip— one I'd not use if I didn't have need to do so." A slow grin spread across his face. "Don't appear so chafed. I already told you, I'm not a decent man."

I drew in a measured breath. No, he wasn't. "You do realize how impossible it's going to be—convincing passengers that magic exists—don't you?"

Mephistopheles held a hand up. "I don't believe your job will be as difficult as all that, Miss Wadsworth. Your lovely presence at the right time in the finale is all that I'll need."

I puzzled it out for a moment. "Are you asking me to be one of your performers?"

"Only for one night. Though you'll need to practice with the others every night to catch up."

"Wonderful." I rubbed my temples. "You're forcing me to learn from the criminals you've hired."

"Entertainers," he corrected.

And possibly at least one murderer. "Well, they weren't very welcoming when I attended their practice this morning. I'm not sure they'll assist me with this bargain of yours."

He stepped forward, that dangerous smile back in place. "Which is why I'm giving you lessons in front of them. Let them see how much I favor you...then they'll do their best at gaining your attention."

"But they'll believe there's something more inappropriate happening between us." Another realization clicked in as he nodded. "You're betting on it, actually."

"Indeed, my star pupil is already learning." He beamed. "So now you understand why that...Mr. Cresswell, was it? He's not to be made aware of our bargain. We need this to appear authentic. Let them think I'm truly wooing you and winning your hand. They'll be much more likely to bring you into the fold. And I need everything to go smoothly at the finale, especially after the murders. Investors get fickle about attaching their names and money to that sort of thing."

Thomas trusted me completely; however, I couldn't imagine him not being a *little* uncomfortable with this arrangement, especially after our earlier conversation. I hesitated. "Thomas is good with keeping secrets. Plus, you might want him participating in the finale, too. He's very gifted—"

"His reaction to our alleged tryst needs to be unscripted, Miss Wadsworth. Should he fail in his performance, others will know there's nothing between us. They will never speak to you or want to know you, should they catch even a *whiff* of dishonesty. I need them all on board with working to ensure the success of this carnival. Nothing will stand in my way, especially not some sensitive lover. I've worked too hard and sacrificed much in this endeavor. I will not fail now."

I stepped toward the railing, allowing the cold breeze to clear my head. Thomas might not be happy, but the ruse would only last four days. In that time I'd be able to protect Liza from Houdini's lies, learn sleight of hand as I'd wished and apply it to my forensics, and be granted access to the secretive carnival group. The very one that might be harboring a murderer. While it had its detriments, our bargain also had its beneficial points. I needed access to the performers to solve this case, and given their aloofness toward me, this was an opportunity I could ill afford to decline.

Mephistopheles moved to where I stood, his arm nearly brushing mine as he leaned over the railing and watched the moonlight bounce across the sea. This was a business transaction, nothing more. Any warnings of losing my head or heart blew away on the next ocean gust.

"Fine." I stuck my hand out, pleased when he returned the gesture and shook. "You and I will play our game of pretend, but I require proof for Liza about Houdini. I think the news ought to come from me. When and where I choose."

He glanced down at our hands, almost appearing surprised at finding them still clasped and abruptly let go. "Any other demands?"

"You are not permitted to kiss me. No matter what. That is a part I do not wish to play."

"Interesting." His lips twitched upward. "Very well. So long as you never wish for me to do so, you have my word."

I kept my focus on his eyes, refusing to glance lower, lest he get any sordid ideas. "Good. We're all settled, then." I wrapped my cloak around me and peered down the empty deck. "I'll meet you after breakfast for—what is it? Why are you shaking your head?"

"We have four days left before the grand finale, Miss Wadsworth." He held his arm out. "Your first lesson begins tonight."

When Mephistopheles waltzed into the practice room, a swagger in his stride and a crooked curve upon his lips, chatter slowed, then promptly died down. Knife throwers paused in their target practice; trapeze artists sat upon their swings; all attention turned to their ringmaster. And me. Most truthfully, their gazes were locked upon my hand on his arm. The one I moved ever so slightly upward at his whispered insistence. I had not forgotten what Liza had said about him never showing up to these practices. It was another deliberate move on his part, one containing the most impact.

"See?" He leaned closer, the heat of his breath on my neck. "Look at the way they're sizing you up, wondering how you earned my favor and how they might wrest it away from you. You, my dear, are now a threat. And a prize." As if just noticing the quietness of the room, he tore his gaze from mine. I wondered at how authentic he made it appear when I knew it was only another act. "If you'd like a shot at performing this week, I suggest you keep practicing."

Everyone began running through their routines, well, everyone except for Cassie, the trapeze artist; the Empress. She sat high above us, watching from behind her mask as Mephistopheles guided me to a table and pulled a chair out for me. Once I'd arranged my skirts, he dragged another chair around until our legs almost touched. I batted my lashes, but dropped my voice. "Watch yourself, sir. I'd hate to kick you by accident."

"You asked me not to kiss you, Miss Wadsworth," he said, the smile growing larger, "you never mentioned touching in your stipulation. Better luck next time. Now, then. Let's run through the basics." He pulled a deck of cards from his suit and placed them in my palm, his hands lingering. "First, you'll need to hold your cards properly in order to cut them one-handed."

He adjusted them until they fit lengthwise in my palm.

"This is how dealers hold their cards. For our purposes, you'll start like this and shift them up toward your fingertips." He moved the cards from my palm to my fingertips, keeping them in the same position. With clinical efficiency, he drew my pinkie down to the bottom of the deck, securing it comfortably in my grip. "Good. This allows you enough space to cut the deck between your fingers and palm, plus you now have better command over it."

I shifted the deck around, trying to get a better feel for it. "How do I cut the deck with only one hand? It feels like I might drop a few cards if I move."

"Ah, excellent observation." Mephistopheles gently tapped my index finger and then my pinkie. "These two fingers will be what actually hold the cards in place. It takes some getting used to, but once you practice enough, you'll find that your thumb is free to flip the cards, and your ring and middle digits assist with cutting the deck in half and rotating them. Here, allow me."

Forgetting about the eyes I still felt boring into us, I leaned in. He pressed the top half of the deck with his thumb, allowing it to drop open in the middle, as if it were a yawning mouth. Next, his index finger came off the top as the bottom portion slid into a ninety-degree angle, forming an L shape with the cards. Both his middle and ring fingers loosed the upper deck as his index finger pushed the lower half forward, completing the shuffle. My eyes crossed.

"The mechanics of it are quite complicated," I said, watching as he repeated the steps much faster. "You make it appear so easy."

"Once you get the movements down, it's simple body memory." He handed me the playing cards. "You won't even have to think of what you're doing, it'll come naturally."

It wasn't dissimilar to some of my forensic practices becoming body memory. I set my attention on the cards in my hand and slowly, painfully, went through the motions. I'd gotten to the part where I cut the deck in two, permitting myself a whoop of accomplishment, when the cards dropped out of my grasp and littered the table and floor. I cursed, one of my more colorful offerings, and the ringmaster threw his head back and laughed.

I glared. "I'm glad my suffering is such a joyful experience for you."

Still laughing, he retrieved the cards and handed them over. "You're taking this quite seriously. It's only magic, Miss Wadsworth. It's supposed to be fun."

I tried a few more times, ending with mostly the same horrendous results. The cards slipped from my gloved grasp, I swore in foul ways, and Mephistopheles practically wheezed with delight. I hated him.

Just when I thought I might march over to Jian Yu and steal one of his knives to slash apart the cards, an accented voice calmly asked, "May I show you another trick?"

I twisted in my seat, eyeing up the performer brave enough to interrupt and recognized him from Liza's earlier introductions. Andreas, whose tarot card counterpart was the Fool. His hair and skin were nearly the same pale shade—a blond close to white. Constellations dotted his velvet suit jacket, another not-so-subtle ode to the Moonlight Carnival.

Mephistopheles raised a brow. "Andreas. This is Miss Wadsworth, my newest protégé. We're finding where her talents are best put to use for the grand finale. Miss Wadsworth, this meddlesome creature is Andreas." I hid my surprise when the ringmaster pushed back from the table and offered his seat. With a lingering look at me that might singe someone with its heat, he bowed. "Excuse me. I'll go find us some champagne."

Remembering my role, I sunk my teeth into my lower lip and watched the ringmaster pick his way through the performers. I hoped my expression appeared like longing and not constipation. When he'd made it halfway across the large room, he paused, as if he'd forgotten something. He pivoted slowly on one heel, halting once he faced me again. Grinning, he blew a kiss in my direction and then continued on his way.

This time the flush in my face wasn't faked.

Andreas cleared his throat, obviously uncomfortable. Which made for two of us. I shook myself out of my mortification and forced my attention on the young man before me. It was time to get to work on my part of the bargain.

"What magic do you have to show me?" I asked, trying to sound as interested as possible. "More card tricks?"

A smile twitched across his lips. Unlike Mephistopheles, there was no trouble or heat behind it. If anything, he appeared quite shy. My mind immediately churned with suspicion.

"It was the first trick I did well and it's not difficult to learn." He held a playing card up with one hand, a Queen of Hearts. With his other hand, he flicked the card, and before my very eyes, I now stared at the King of Spades. I blinked. "It's called a snap change. Mephistopheles says 'trick the eyes, convince the mind.' What you need is two cards, and you hold them right over each other."

I nearly groaned. "Every time one of you claims something is easy, I'll know you're lying. How on earth is this simple?"

His smile deepened, revealing a dimple. "My Liesel used to say something very similar. She hated card tricks, but she loved this one." He repeated it and I still couldn't identify the trick. "Place the two cards on top of each other. Then all you need to use are your thumb, index, and middle fingers. The middle finger pulls the top card under, revealing the back card. The flick is the misdirection. There's something about an audible distraction that tears attention away for that one critical moment."

He did it a few more times, moving slow enough for me to pick up on the mechanics. Basically, the front card slid underneath the other and rested between the thumb and middle finger, hidden from view by the second card. There wasn't anything simple about the trick, but it was easier for me to attempt—more like a snapping motion. Andreas handed me the cards and watched as I fumbled along. I wasn't sure how my mastering a card trick would lend authenticity to the Moonlight Carnival, but it was fun, and my true goal of learning about the performers was being met, so I continued to practice.

"What does Liesel do for the carnival?" I asked, attention straying to him. "Is that how the two of you met?"

He shuffled the deck, removed two more cards, and continued demonstrating the trick while I mimicked him. "No, she didn't work for the circus. Mephistopheles had sent me into a village in Germany one day for roses. I took one look at her and knew I was forever lost. She actually gifted me with the looking glass I use for my divinations."

"Are you two married?"

Sadness descended into his shoulders, weighing them down. "Betrothed. Were betrothed. My Liesel...she passed away."

My thoughts flashed to Thomas. I could not fathom carrying on without him and saw a different sort of strength in Andreas when I looked upon him now. "I—I'm so very sorry for your loss." I wanted to ask how, but couldn't quite bring myself to do it.

He absently flicked the cards, snapping one over the other in rapid succession. "Jian tells me it gets easier, though I'm not certain that sort of loss ever fades away."

I set my own cards down. "Has Jian lost someone he loves as well?"

Andreas glanced over at his friend, unblinking as Jian practiced his sword tricks. "His entire family. They were murdered. The swords?" He nodded as Jian hefted one and sliced through a stack of wood. "I think he imagines using them on the men who did it."

"How...do you know any details?"

Andreas's gaze darted around. "Only that soldiers stormed his village while he was away. They killed everyone and burned their houses. When he returned it was to charred bodies and smoking ashes. There are rumors that he hunted them down and slit their throats while they made camp, but I don't think that's true. He took up practicing with blades after their deaths—he didn't want to be unable to defend anyone again."

"Dear God in heaven," I said, feeling as though I'd been kicked in my center. "That's horrid. How—"

"—did it get to be so late?" Mephistopheles appeared in my line of vision, holding a pocket watch up to his masked face. "I believe it's time for us to say good night. You have an early morning lesson and you need your beauty rest."

I was too saddened by Jian's history to form annoyance at the snipe. I stole one last glance at Jian before standing. I made to leave when Andreas jumped up. "Don't forget your cards, miss. You'll need to practice as often as possible. We all do."

I smiled and accepted the playing cards. Mephistopheles paraded us out in front of all the performers, his hand never leaving the small of my back. Once we'd made it to the darkened corridor, he stopped and removed a letter from his jacket. "Here. Houdini had started writing this before the manufactured accident."

"Accident? What do you mean…" I opened it up, brows raised. "Most of it's covered in ink!"

"I know." He grinned. "You ought to have seen him carry on about how clumsy I was after I bumped into him. Thought for certain he might have gutted me right there if he could've." He leaned over my shoulder, tracing the opening line. "'To my dearest'…"

I batted him away. "I can read, thank you." I scanned what remained of the ink-splattered letter, stomach clenching.

It was as he'd said: Houdini loved another. I longed to crumple the paper but tucked it into my bodice instead. On the surface my bargain might have appeared to benefit Mephistopheles more, but I suddenly felt much better about protecting Liza from Harry Houdini and his lies.

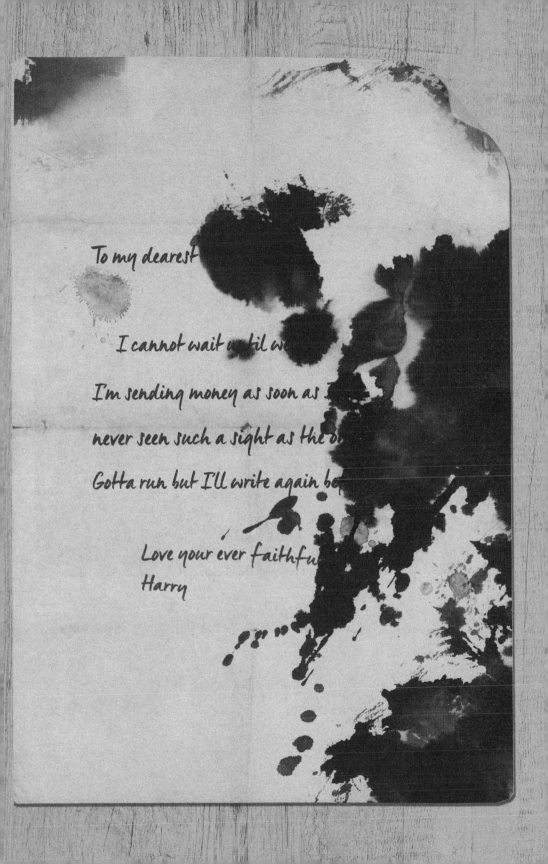

To my dearest

I cannot wait until we

I'm sending money as soon as

never seen such a sight as the o

Gotta run but I'll write again be

Love your ever faithfu
Harry

Acrobat

THIRTEEN

ACE OF WANDS

"Like this?" I asked, looping my legs over the bar. Even with the safety net below I did not feel an ounce of comfort. And I didn't think my costume—a mere boneless frost-blue corset and thick white stockings—was entirely to blame. Though I was slightly concerned the added weight of the excessive beading might ensure my death should I fall.

Cassie snorted, but didn't make fun. "You'll only swing back and forth. With your legs hooked over the bar, you'll be able to grip it tightly enough that you won't fall." She held the bar steady, brown eyes fixed to mine, not in challenge but curiosity. "Don't worry, this isn't what your role in the finale is going to be. This is just for fun."

I seriously questioned their idea of a good time. Swinging from a tiny little bar more than twenty feet in the air seemed like certain death. How she managed it in beaded costumes with long trains was either a miracle or magic or both.

Sebastián swung over from his side of the practice room, legs over the bar and arms extended outward, a wide grin on his face. As if he weren't already talented enough with his contortions, now he was doing them in the sky. "Easy, see? All you have to do is let go."

"You're all mad," I muttered under my breath. "Absolutely mad."

"Normal is overrated." Cassie nudged me toward the bar. "Extraordinary is unforgettable." I took the bar in my hand, but the Empress quickly stopped me. She clapped my hands with a strange white substance that felt both sticky and chalky. "Resin. It helps with your grip."

"I thought I was only using my legs for this?"

"Yes, well"—Cassie turned me about, placing my hands on the bar—"you need to hold on and then loop your legs through, right?"

I'd much sooner prance naked on the prow and sing a bawdy-house song.

"Everything all right up there?" Mephistopheles yelled, cupping his hands around his mouth. "Practice is almost over. Guests will be heading out for breakfast soon, and we must deposit Miss Wadsworth in her chambers before anyone notices her absence."

I shot him a dirty look that he probably missed, since I was higher than a building. "Nuisance. I'd like to see him swing on the trapeze."

Cassie laughed. "Don't challenge him. He'll do it, and if he breaks his neck, then we're all out of a job. And I need the money."

I took the bar in my hands, ignoring the dampness that seemed to seep through the resin powder. "Are you saving for something?"

She adjusted my grip and demonstrated how to bring my legs up and over, ignoring my question. My stomach flipped. "No...I..." She heaved a breath out. "I made unwise choices and may owe a bit of money to people."

I threaded one leg over the bar, heart racing for multiple reasons. "People who also work for the carnival?"

Cassie motioned for me to repeat the procedure with my other leg. I hesitated, but only for another moment, hoping she'd keep talking. This was exactly what I needed: information that might prove to be a motive for murder. She helped pull my leg over the bar and made sure it rested solidly against the backs of my knees. While I did feel secure with the grip, I felt anything but comforted while dangling upside down. The ground was very, very far away.

"No," she finally said. "The people I owe aren't in the carnival."

Before I could inquire further, she untied the trapeze from where it had been secured to two large poles for me and gave me a slight push. I couldn't control the yelp that escaped my lips as I flew across the room. I closed my eyes, fearing that I'd either be sick or panic and do something stupid and go crashing to my death.

"Open your eyes!" Mephistopheles called up. "Enjoy the view! Come on now. I didn't peg you as a coward."

The rogue was squawking like a chicken. I cracked a lid, colors and lights flashed by, much like I imagined my life to be flying away. I swung one way, then the other, each pass seeming to go on simultaneously forever and too fast to recall.

"Look at that," he shouted up. "You're flying!"

My heart thrashed and my breath came in short bursts, though fear was ebbing away to excitement. I slowly extended my arms. In this moment I understood the draw of the carnival—the magnetic pull to run away from restrictions and simply let go. To allow myself complete and utter freedom to soar.

Despite my morning trapeze practice, the late-night bargain I'd struck with Mephistopheles felt like I had, indeed, sold my soul to the Devil. I had no right to meddle with Liza's affairs, yet how could I sit back and remain inactive while Houdini destroyed her life on a romantic whim? His letter clearly indicated his love and admiration for a woman who was not my cousin. And yet imagining myself handing the evidence over and watching her heart shatter felt equally horrible.

I paced along the small rug of our cabin, dreading the next hour of performances. I was no better than those acting onstage—pretending to be a decent cousin when I was a filthy liar. Liza was content with her choice, but only because she didn't know the whole truth. Somehow having Mephistopheles intervene seemed kinder than flat out breaking her heart.

Truth was a blade I did not wish to stab her with. Perhaps he should be the one to give her the letter. Seemed like the sort of wretched thing he'd enjoy.

"Audrey Rose?" Liza hovered in the connecting-room doorway. She was resplendent in a raspberry-colored evening gown that had layers of black lace over the skirts—no one would recognize her dressed in her finery and without one of those filigree masks. I was thankful the Moonlight Carnival required such costumes; it would help keep my cousin's identity a secret and make it easy for her to return to England without society being any the wiser. Mephistopheles truly had considered everything when he'd run from his own family name, whatever that was.

"You look gorgeous, Cousin."

"It's a bit odd," she said, turning her face from side to side in my looking glass, puckering her lips. "I've not sat in on a performance since London. Though it will be nice to be a member of the audience for once. An entire evening free of the costume makeup will be delightful. It feels like plaster and dries my skin in the most wretched ways!" Liza stopped adjusting her coiffure and glanced at me in the looking glass. "Is everything all right? You seem on edge. You're not even dressed yet...are you not going to the show?"

I plopped onto my bed, the weight of my secrets pressing me down. "I'm not sure. I was up early and didn't sleep very well—perhaps I might miss this one night."

Liza dropped her hands and came to my side. "You simply

cannot miss this show! The Ace of Wands will truly be remarkable to witness. I've seen her practice and still cannot believe how brave she is, swallowing fire—you'd enjoy speaking with her, too. She's always studying new journals on engineering and science. A lot of the performers draw up ideas and give them to Mephistopheles to create."

I raised my brows at this. "He engineers the props entirely alone?"

"Oh, yes." Liza nodded. "He makes all of them. No dream is too far-fetched or out of reach. Whenever we're practicing, he sequesters himself away to craft what we need. He doesn't usually permit anyone in his cabin—he claims it distracts him, but I believe he's not keen on having anyone steal his innovative secrets. He plays everything close to his chest, that one."

"So no one ever has access to his personal room, then?" I tried sounding as nonchalant as possible.

"I'm sure the women he beds are invited in."

"Liza!" My face burned yet my blood froze. It was a crass angle I hadn't considered. Perhaps a jilted lover *did* commit the murders. Maybe she was intent on destroying his carnival the way he'd destroyed her heart. I'd never seen him without his mask, but the sharp cut of his jaw and fullness of his lips hinted at attractiveness. "Does he take many women to his chambers?"

"Why all the interest in the ringmaster?" Misunderstanding the source of my curiosity, she narrowed her eyes. "You have something real and grand and irreplaceable with Mr. Cresswell. Mephistopheles is a great showman, but that's the crux of it. He's all show. I caution you to remember that. He's inviting, but in the way the flame on a candle is. It might set ambiance, create a sense of warmth, but if you get too close, it will burn you."

"You've become quite the poet," I said, lightly. I wanted to ask if she had those same fears and concerns over Houdini, but pressed my lips together. I motioned vaguely in the direction of my trunk. "What should I wear?"

Liza jumped up, clapping her hands together. "Something breathtaking." Carefully sorting through my gowns, she lifted one up as if it were a prize. Pale sage with pink roses and ribbons that had been sewn onto one shoulder and cascaded from the right hip to the floor, it was certainly a showstopper. "This is it. You will be more dazzling than the performers in this."

Tonight the dining saloon had transformed once again. Tables were dressed in dark blue silk, the surfaces shiny enough to reflect lights, while crystal goblets twinkled like glitter. White calla lily and eucalyptus garlands spilled over each table and brushed the checkered floor—decadent and fragrant. I longed to run my fingers over the velvety softness of the petals, but managed to maintain an air of dignity. I glanced at Liza and Mrs. Harvey, who wore similar expressions of awe. I wasn't the only one who felt as if I were walking into a star-filled dream.

Thomas and Uncle were already swirling drinks, heads bent in what appeared to be a heated debate, when Mrs. Harvey, Liza, and I entered the room. I'd made excuses for not going over case details with them this afternoon, locking myself away to practice sleight of hand. It was disastrous. I mostly got a workout in picking up the cards after I'd dropped them all over the floor. Though the snap trick Andreas had taught me was slowly improving.

Always in tune with my presence, Thomas lifted his attention, and heat shot through me as our eyes met across the room. He said something to my uncle, pushed back from his seat, and was at my side a moment later, offering his arm. My pulse thrummed at his touch.

"Ladies. You are all stunning this evening." He placed a hand around one ear, tilting his head to the side. "Did you hear that? I believe it was the sound of hearts shattering across the room. Do be careful as you step over bloody shards."

I shook my head. "Honestly? 'Bloody shards'?"

"Do you blame them for being envious? I'd be riotously jealous of me, too. In fact, I might challenge myself to a duel after supper."

Thomas grinned, escorting us all to the table without further teasing. I swore sometimes his manners were so polite, so exquisitely regal, I had a hard time remembering he was the same young man who'd been called an automaton during the Ripper investigation. He leaned in, whispering so only I could hear.

"We had an interesting day. Captain Norwood called us in to discuss a rather delicate matter." He pulled my chair out, then did the same for Mrs. Harvey. A waiter had come over and assisted Liza. Thomas took a seat next to me. "Apparently, a first-class cabin was broken into last night. Sometime during supper and the show."

"How strange."

"Indeed. Murdered passengers, a missing girl, a burglary... this ship is a floating nightmare for the captain."

Chandeliers dimmed. It wouldn't be long before the show now. Waiters moved around the room with practiced ease, setting covered trays down at each table. I wasn't sure what was on the menu tonight, but whatever it was, it smelled divine. It helped cover up the slight odor of kerosene coming from the stage. My mouth watered as the scent of butter, lemon, and garlic wafted up, greeting my senses. A carafe of white wine was set at our table, indicating our entrée might be seafood. I hoped for prawns or scallops or even a nice, plump lobster.

I shook myself free from hungry thoughts, returning to the matter at hand. "How did the captain or occupants know the cabin had been broken into?"

143

"The lady's trunk had been rummaged through," Thomas said, lifting the lid of his tray. Half a lobster broiled to perfection and smothered in garlic butter with fragrant green herbs sat in the center of the plate. I nearly groaned when I lifted my own lid. "Her finest bolts of silk were missing, along with a few scarves. As you know, her maid would have taken greater care with those garments. She'd never scatter them about like that."

"Why was she traveling with bolts of fabric?" I asked.

"She was bringing them to New York to have them made into dresses by a renowned dressmaker. Apparently the pattern on it was designed for a costume ball—it had vines wrapped around trees near what would be the hem, and constellations near what would have been the bodice."

"So the fabric was stolen but the woman was accounted for, correct?"

"Yes," Thomas said, pausing to sip from his wine, "she reported it to the maids who came to clean her room."

"Hmm. Well, if it were to turn up, it would be unmistakable." It was all so strange. Missing bolts of fabric, young women who seemed to vanish under the twinkling dark skies. Two hideous murders. Surely it had to be connected, but *how* was the question of the hour. Last night we'd had a respite, though I feared it wouldn't be long before another body showed up. "What do you make of it?"

Thomas cut into his lobster, stopping to answer me before taking a bite. "Honestly? I'm not sure. There's not been much in the way of clues, making it difficult to deduce anything. Missing silk isn't that unusual. We're aboard a ship with a lot of passengers, most of whom don't need to sign their true names for the ship log. Expensive fabrics fetch decent coin—it might be the only motivation for the theft."

"Unless it's all connected. Then theft isn't entirely the motivation."

"Unfortunately, we have no way of knowing what's connected

and what isn't. Thus far we know she's got no affiliation with either victim." Thomas sipped from his goblet. "Conjecture and speculation aren't solid facts."

He sounded a lot like Uncle. While I agreed that divorcing myself from emotions was pertinent while in the laboratory, I also knew the value of trusting my gut instincts when something didn't feel right about the theft.

I took a careful bite of my dinner, relishing the savory flavors as the lights turned way down. I turned my attention to the stage, where swaths of silver and pale blue silk hung from the ceiling—stars and snowflakes knotted at their ends. It simultaneously gave the impression of shooting stars and falling snow. Glitter caught the dim light as the stars twirled in place. It was stunning—another masterpiece for the Moonlight Carnival.

I expected Mephistopheles to appear onstage amidst the smoke and cymbals explosion. I did not expect to see a petite young woman twirling twin flames at her sides stride into the room. The scent of kerosene was stronger now, burning my nose a bit with its sharpness. Perhaps they should have waited until after supper before sending her out. The delicate flavor of lobster was all but ruined.

"That's Anishaa. Her tarot is the Ace of Wands." Liza broke away from her conversation with Uncle and Mrs. Harvey, leaning in to whisper, "Her costume's supposed to represent ice."

I could see how that was true. Silver hair matched sequins sewn across her corset and was braided in thick strands about the crown of her head. Her skin was painted bluish white everywhere it was exposed—arms, hands, face and across the sweep of her collarbone. It was chilling, in a way, seeing how she appeared as a creature born of frost who played so menacingly with fire. Her top hat and corset were a white so pure they almost seemed ice blue.

In fact, upon closer inspection, I could see pale blue threads shot through with silver trimming the entire ensemble. Even her eyes—exposed by larger holes in her mask—had been edged in blue and gold and her lashes were pure white. She looked like a frozen star.

She lifted a wand of fire and exhaled, flames streaming out as if she were a dragon. Gasps went up around us as she strutted to the opposite end of the stage and repeated the trick. I couldn't help but stare as she took the same wand of fire and swallowed it as if it were a delicacy.

"It's magnificent, isn't it?" Liza asked, eyes following the fire-eater as she cartwheeled across the stage, stood tall, and swallowed another torch of flames. A stagehand ran another set of flaming wands out and she tipped her head back, spitting flames skyward. "Their acts might be a lie or an illusion, but they live honestly. They don't hide who they are, or pretend to play by society's rules. Not like the nobility, who smile to your face while sticking a dagger in your back."

I dropped my gaze to my plate—the food tonight truly was exquisite, though I found my appetite to be suddenly uncooperative. If Liza knew I was the one holding a dagger to her dreams of wedding Houdini, she'd never speak to me again. I spent the next few moments with my head half in the conversations around me, and half on the guilt that kept piling up.

It wasn't until the first screams began that I jolted back into the here and now.

FOURTEEN

THE STAR

DINING SALOON
RMS ETRURIA
4 JANUARY 1889

A fire erupted onstage, turning the fantastical winter setting into a hellscape. Flames roared at fleeing guests, jumping from one silk thread dangling from the ceiling to the next. Now instead of snowflakes and shooting stars, fire and ash rained down. Anishaa frantically shouted for assistance behind the curtains, and buckets of water appeared. As the acrid odor of smoke drifted through the air and black soot sloshed over the stage, the screaming increased. Another almost familiar scent wafted around. It smelled as if it were—

"Merciful God above...what *is* that?" Liza grabbed my arm so hard I yelped. "Up there! I think—I think I may be ill."

I dragged my focus skyward and felt the blood drain from me. Tied up in exquisite silks cocooned about each arm, a person shrouded in black gauze swayed spread-eagle above the stage, a black crown of stars fastened about its head. Flames engulfed the figure from its feet as if it were a human torch sprung to life. I stared, frozen with disbelief as chunks of roasting flesh began splattering down.

The person had been hung upright, the flames traveling from the feet toward the head at a fierce pace.

Surely this couldn't be real. It hadn't been so long since my last delusion—I'd been plagued by them while in Romania. That's what this horror was: a trick of the mind.

Only it wasn't.

"Don't look." I clutched my cousin and pulled her head to my shoulder, allowing her to sob. Thomas met my gaze and held it, offering me his strength and allowing mine to fortify him in return. I ran my hands over Liza's hair, hoping to soothe her and myself with the action. "It's all right. It's going to be all right."

"Everyone remain seated. And calm. The flames are mostly contained to the body." Uncle swept his attention over our table; his first priority was to ensure our safety, though I knew he'd want to get to the victim quickly. He looked to Thomas and nodded, silently passing along responsibility before he disappeared into the exiting crowd.

"It isn't alive," Thomas said, his voice calm despite the fiery inferno and Mrs. Harvey's wails. "Look."

The last thing I wanted to do was stare at the nightmare before us. But my brain slowly slipped into the coolness of a scientist.

"How..." I forced myself to ignore the scent of burning flesh and hair. To look beyond the clumps of Lord knew what that slopped to the ground. I rocked Liza gently, registering the lack of screams or movement while the fire turned the person into a living star. Thomas was right—whoever it was had already been dead before being set aflame.

A kindness, if one could call being murdered, then having your corpse torched, kind.

With a jolt, the body above the stage jerked downward, and those who hadn't yet made it out the door to safety screamed in horror.

"Lower the ropes again!" Mephistopheles rushed onto the stage, shouting at crew members who must be hidden in the rafters. "Cut it down! Cut it down *now!*"

Two men wielding swords ran under the burning body, hacking at the disintegrating fabric and dodging burning ashes that rained down on them. It might have been Jian and Andreas, but I was seemingly only capable of rocking Liza and trying to keep my own tears from escaping. Narrowing my world to that one comforting motion held me together.

Waiters and staff shouted for order, but the patrons were beyond their control. Tables turned over. Women swayed and men shoved. It was an absolute horror show as people fought to squeeze through the only two exit doors.

"Smother the flames!" Captain Norwood emerged into the chaos, tossing horse blankets at the people onstage. "Stamp them out!"

Mrs. Harvey held a hand over her mouth, but the lines of wetness streaking down her face betrayed her fright. I wanted to obey Uncle and remain seated and calm, though I also longed to take my loved ones from this hell and shelter them from all the horrible things the world could bring forth. I wanted to bury my face in my pillows and scream until my throat felt raw and my tears had dried up. I could stand dissecting bodies, but watching a person burn was entirely different. Whoever had done this was a monster, the likes of which even Jack the Ripper and Vlad Dracula would hesitate to emulate.

"Oh, God...that smell." Liza buried her face farther into my shoulder. My own emotions reared up, trying to overtake me, but I grabbed them and shoved them deep within. I could not succumb to them now. Possibly not ever. Everything around us became mechanical in my mind—the only way I could process what was happening and not crumble with grief.

The body finally fell to the stage, the sound like an eight-stone sack of oats crashing to the floor. Most of the damage in the room had only been done to the corpse and the silks that had tied it up. Aside from the sooty water spilling over the stage and puddling on the floor, the dining saloon escaped ruination. My macabre gaze returned to the charred remains. I did not wish to examine it up close. I did not want to believe this was real. But wishes and wants had no place in my heart.

Thomas patted Mrs. Harvey's shoulder, doing his best to be comforting, though I could see the strain in his own expression. It was hard to shift into that cold calm when the scent of burnt flesh stung your nose and eyes. "Mrs. Harvey? Are you able to bring Liza back to your chambers?" The older woman's lip trembled, but she nodded sharply. "Good. Everyone's almost gone and the fire's out now. You should be all right. I want you both to go straight to the cabin and lock the door. I'll check on you when I escort Audrey Rose in a little while. All right?"

He spoke calmly, but there was a strength in his voice that made my senses slowly come to. It seemed to have the same effect on Mrs. Harvey. She blinked a few times, then held her arms out to Liza. "Come, dear. Let's get us some water for a bath."

Liza loosened her grasp on me enough to look into my face. I'm not sure what she saw there, but she quickly blinked back fresh tears. "You ought to come with us. Please. Please don't go near that...that stage...please come with me."

I wanted to. More than anything I wanted to clutch my cousin's hand and run from this room, never looking back. I'd only ever questioned my love of forensic science once before, and this was testing my resolve again. "I'll join you in a little while. I promise."

"No! You have to—"

"There is a blade in my nightstand." I hugged her close. "I want you to get it and keep it with you until I return. Do not allow anyone in unless it's either myself, Thomas, or Uncle. Not Mephistopheles, nor anyone from the carnival. Not even Harry. Do you understand?"

I'd meant for my speech to be fortifying, but Liza's tears spilled down her face, dripping onto the collar of her bodice. "Are we unsafe? Do you believe we'll be attacked next? I—"

"It is a precaution," I said. "Nothing more." I gripped her hand tightly. "Take care of Mrs. Harvey, all right?"

Liza pressed her lips together. I could see the molten core of her harden into steel. She might have bent a little, but she was too strong to break. She gripped my hands back and nodded. "I'll do my best." She faced Mrs. Harvey and, though there were traces of fear in the way her hands shook, she straightened up. "Let's hurry."

With a final glance over her shoulder, Liza guided our chaperone out of the smoky room. I watched the door a few seconds after they'd gone, gathering up my own inner steel. A gentle touch on my arm indicated it was time to don my own mask—now I would perform the role of forensic scientist. I took one more deep breath, immediately regretting it as smoke singed my nose. I coughed, which only made it worse.

"Here. This might help a bit with the smell and the smoke." Thomas handed me a damp napkin, then dabbed one into a water goblet for himself. He held the cloth to his face, allowing it to act as a barrier. I did the same, and the itch in my throat eased. Thomas kept his attention on me while I steadied myself. "Better?"

I nodded. "Thank you."

Without uttering another word, we made our way to the stage and smoking remains. Uncle was already standing over them. "Captain, I need this stage clear of people for the rest of the evening. We must salvage what we can as far as evidence is concerned. No crew."

Norwood dragged a hand down his face. There were bags under his eyes, indicating he hadn't slept well. Which was understandable—his magical voyage had diverted from Heaven sent to Hell bound. "Anything you need, Dr. Wadsworth. But we must clean up the tables and linens and—"

"Not now. This entire room must be cleared out immediately." Uncle crouched beside the blackened corpse. He flicked his gaze up to me. "We will perform the postmortem here."

My palms tingled as I stood at the foot of the stage, eyeing our temporary laboratory. Silks that hadn't burned entirely hung in tatters, smoke rose from the body, and ashes covered much of the scene like gray snow. It seemed the most wretched of places to carve open a corpse, but was actually quite fitting given the theatrics of it all.

A crew member rushed over to Uncle, handing him his medical satchel. Uncle must have sent for it as soon as he'd left our table. I had no idea how he always remained calm during the worst of storms, and could only hope to emulate him one day. The young man backed away from the scene, his eyes wide and unblinking. A few moments later, the dining saloon was empty and we were ready to work. Mechanically, I took aprons from Uncle's bag and handed them out, then tied my own about my waist. The flowers on my gown bulged and the hem would most certainly get ruined with soot, but I didn't care. I removed my gloves and folded them neatly. They would affect my grip on the scalpels.

Thomas helped me up onto the stage, and I somehow found the will to slow my heartbeat, to clear my mind. I stood over the body, pressing the dampened cloth to my nose.

"The fire started at the feet," I said, voice cracking. Uncle and Thomas jerked their attention from the corpse to me. "The gauze melted there, but not on the face. Same with the burnt skin. It's charred on the legs, but the head isn't as bad. Thomas was correct earlier—whoever she was, she wasn't alive when the fire began."

Thomas stalked around the body, fingers tapping his lips as he glanced from the ceiling to the floor and all around. His face was a mask of ice. When he switched into this role, I understood why others were sometimes frightened of him. Except now I no longer thought their taunts of him being an automaton were correct—when he transformed into a deductive scientist, he looked more like an unforgiving god, sent to mete out justice.

A muscle in his jaw flickered. "An emerald ring. Looks to be an heirloom."

I ripped my attention off of Thomas and stared at the ring, heart pounding. A memory struck me at once.

"Miss Crenshaw," I blurted. "Her mother said she had an emerald ring. And she never took it off."

Thomas knelt beside the body. "Victim has auburn hair. Lady Crenshaw has a similar shade, though it's not definitive proof."

"No, but it's a start." Uncle twisted his mustache. "We'll need to collect physical descriptions and see if the Crenshaws can confirm height and weight. It's not impossible to identify the body, but let's not traumatize anyone by making them inspect it if we don't need to. I'd also like to know if Dr. Arden has ever treated any member of the family. Perhaps the victims are all connected to him." He nodded toward the ring. "Once we complete our investigation, we'll also see if this is indeed the ring they'd mentioned." He set his mouth into a grim line. "Hand me my scalpel, Audrey Rose."

I did as I was told. Normally, the bodies were already without clothes when I assisted Uncle in his laboratory. Removing the clothing was a bit harder in this case; Uncle had to carefully cut away what fabric he could, doing his best to not accidentally carve off burnt flesh. Instead of risking harm to the lower half of the body, he focused on cutting away material from the torso up. I noted that she'd been stripped to her underthings, and from what was left, the lace appeared to be of a fine quality. She was likely another first-class passenger, our murderer's preferred victims. Uncle moved briskly and efficiently, his years of training and practice showing.

In a few moments, he had the body ready for our inspection.

After performing a quick external examination and finding no obvious outward causes of death, he brought the scalpel to the flesh and made a Y incision, swiftly parting the skin. I handed him the rib cutters and stood back as her inner cavity was exposed. Uncle wiped his hands down the front of his apron, smearing the cream fabric with rust-colored liquid. I imagined he longed to wash in carbolic soap, but couldn't worry about contamination now. He leaned over the body, sniffing. Previous experience told me he was looking for signs of poison. Often a scent could be detected near the stomach if it had been ingested. I tried not to think about the victims of our last case in Romania.

I handed him another blade and he carefully opened the stomach, searching through its contents. He rooted around for a bit, then stepped back. "If she ate chocolate cake, sugared berries, and champagne before dying, then what does that indicate?"

"She must have had an awful stomachache," Thomas said blandly.

"Thomas!" I shot him a look of horror. "Be serious."

"I am." He held his hands up. "All of those are sweet. And are more than likely to hide poison in them. I imagine her stomach must have hurt immensely. It probably started slowly, and she'd thought it was simply from the overindulgence. Then she would have likely figured out something was wrong soon after, when the pain increased and the perspiration began in earnest." He pointed to her hands, red and splotchy from where they'd been burned. "Her nails are broken, but the cuts are on her palms, not from fighting the murderer. A fine indicator that she clutched herself, trying to dull the pain."

Uncle removed the stomach and motioned for a tray. I held it steady as he deposited the organ on it with a slick thud, doing everything in my power to not picture the broiled lobster the tray had held earlier. With forceps, he pulled a few undigested berries out. "We'll need to run tests, naturally, but these appear to be belladonna."

I mentally flipped through lessons on poisons. Belladonna was a nightshade, sometimes called the devil's berries. An uncomfortable feeling slid through my bones. She would have suffered greatly after ingesting that many berries—her heart rate likely sped up, her breathing and muscles unable to work properly. Whoever had fed this dessert of death to her was heartless. I could not fathom what it must have been like, sitting there, watching her body convulse as death claimed her. This murder was slow and deliberate, the staging of the body extreme.

I placed the berries in a vial for further inspection, watching Uncle sew the corpse together again. His stitches were neat and precise, exactly as he'd taught me.

"Have the captain show Lord and Lady Crenshaw the ring. See if they're able to identify it as their daughter's." He turned his attention on the body, his expression sad. "It's the least we can offer as far as peace goes."

Thomas went to do the gruesome task of sliding the ring off her finger, but I stopped him. I didn't want to be so cold and clinical in this moment. It felt much too solemn for that. I bent down and gently lifted her arm, taking great care as I removed what had once been a treasure to her, according to her family. I sat on my heels a second more, then laid her arm over her chest. She had been tortured, murdered, then had her body turned into a spectacle of fear.

"The Star," I said, mostly to myself. Thomas and Uncle wore similar expressions of confusion. "The tarot card most likely associated with this staged death. I've..." I didn't want to tell them I'd gotten hold of a deck of tarot cards along with my playing cards, so I shrugged. "I borrowed Liza's cards and studied them last night. This body looks like that card. We need to figure out what it means. Combined with the others, it might lead us to our murderer."

Uncle looked skeptical, but nodded assent. I pushed myself to a standing position, the ring clasped tightly in my hand. Gone were my feelings of horror and sadness. In their place a spark of anger ignited. Whoever had done this had gone too far, and I would not rest until they paid for their crimes.

"Cover her with a cloak before they take her away," I said, my voice like ice. "I'll bring this to the captain now."

I spun on my heel and strode toward the door, determination pounding through me like a second heartbeat. This ship might be turning into a floating nightmare, but I refused to give in to fear.

FIFTEEN

AN INDECENT SITUATION

LORD CRENSHAW'S CABIN
RMS ETRURIA
4 JANUARY 1889

"That's Elizabeth's." Lady Crenshaw's gaze never left the ring Captain Norwood held out. "Wh-where did you find th-this?"

Captain Norwood drew in a deep breath. "I'm so sorry to be the bearer of bad news, madam. But Miss Crenshaw's body was..." He glanced down, seemingly at a loss on how to describe it.

"No. It cannot be." Lady Crenshaw shook her head, eyes glistening. Lord Crenshaw clutched her arm and she sunk back. "Elizabeth is back in London, I'm sure of it. She must be back home by now. We'll write her and see as soon as we're in New York. There cannot be truth in this." Her voice broke.

"I'm so very sorry for your loss." Norwood's mouth snapped shut as Lady Crenshaw fell to her knees. "We are doing everything to locate her murderer—"

"Get out." Lord Crenshaw's tone was low and dangerous.

"Sir, we—"

"Leave us."

"Very well. If you need anything, come directly to m—"

"Damn you and this accursed ship!" he shouted, startling both the captain and myself back. "Forget the ringing endorsement you sought. A workhouse would be better recommended. I will see both you and that circus destroyed."

He slammed the door so hard the lifeboat hanging outside smacked the wall. Captain Norwood's shoulders heaved with breath. "I'm not fit for this sort of work. Dr. Arden didn't take the news much better. Can't blame either of them—losing a child is a pain no parent should ever suffer."

"Uncle needs to speak with Dr. Arden," I said slowly, not wishing to be insensitive. "Will you send word and have him meet with Uncle soon?"

The captain nodded, though his attention was set on the dark sea. "It was supposed to be a legendary voyage. Now it will simply become infamous. Mephistopheles promised the moon. He swore if I allowed them free passage that cruise liners with nightly entertainments would become the height of fashion. That our names would be written amongst the stars. He is nothing but a liar."

I wasn't sure how to respond. The entire evening had already spiraled into darkness and I didn't think it could all be blamed on one person. Witnessing the Crenshaws' grief and now the captain's was too much. And I had more work to do before locking myself away in my own cabin.

"There's still time to set everything right," I finally said. "We've got three more nights."

Captain Norwood moved away from the door and led me toward my cabin. "Three more opportunities for murder, Miss Wadsworth."

We walked silently after that, and I couldn't help but fear he was correct.

"Are you quite mad?" Liza exclaimed, jumping off the bed as I changed into a plainer dress. "How is it all right for you to seek Mephistopheles at this hour, yet if I go to Harry it's out of the question?"

"Must we really go over this again?" I rubbed my temples. I was exhausted and wanted to crawl under my covers and not emerge until we were pulling into New York Harbor. "Uncle has already banished you to this cabin *and* threatened the asylum. And if that isn't enough of a reason, there's always the murderer that's running about this ship."

Liza got that defiant gleam in her eye as she stood and crossed her arms. "Which is why we ought to walk down together. Their rooms aren't far apart. Isn't there safety in groups?" I opened my mouth to argue, but she'd brought up a valid point. Sensing my hesitation, she pressed on. "Not to mention, do you even know where Mephistopheles's cabin is? How do you plan on finding him? Who will go to their grave, lying to defend you, should either of us be caught?"

I gave her an exasperated look. "I have questions regarding the murder. It's hardly a clandestine affair you need to lie about. And I am not going to get caught."

"Oh? And what if Thomas finds out you've been visiting another young man? At night. Alone. To simply discuss *murder* in his chambers without either Uncle or Thomas present. He will think you're—"

"Liza," I said, interrupting before she could finish that scandalous thought. "Thomas would never be so foolish. We trust each other."

"He's human, you know. No matter how clinical and intelligent he may be, he's got human emotions. I think you forget that sometimes. He buries them, but they're there."

Part of me wished to give her the letter Houdini had written to his secret lover and see if she was as eager to visit him after seeing firsthand what a scoundrel he was. I drew in a few deep breaths.

Tonight wasn't the time to divulge that misery. With any luck he'd reveal that through his own coarse actions, and I'd never have to give her that terrible letter.

After offering an exaggerated long sigh, I threw a cloak at my cousin. "I only need to speak with Mephistopheles for a few minutes. You'll need to leave when I do."

Liza tossed the cloak about her shoulders and grinned. "This is what it's always like for you, isn't it?"

"What do you mean?"

"Always pushing forward, pursuing truth." Her smile faded, turning into something tinged with sadness. "I always imagined your work with Uncle as an adventure, but it's also quite difficult, isn't it? The things you see..."

Murder victims flashed through my memory in rapid-fire succession. Victims from Jack the Ripper, torn apart and discarded like rubbish. Bodies drained of blood from just last week while Thomas and I had been studying in Romania. Everywhere I went, death trailed behind. I hoped tonight would not follow suit. I shook those thoughts free. "Come on. It's getting late."

Ropes creaked, the sound evoking images of giants lifting their old bones and gazing at those who dared disturb their centuries-old slumber. Even traveling arm in arm with Liza, I couldn't deny the promenade was an eerie place at night.

Liza clutched me closer. "We need to go into that corridor. The stairs will take us down to the next level."

Wind whipped pieces of hair from my braid, adding to the chills that were already running rampant down my body. I truly did not wish to enter a darkened corridor at night with a murderer running about, but saw little choice. At least Liza and I were together. There was small comfort in that. I swallowed hard and followed my cousin as she pulled the door open and glanced over her shoulder at me.

The corridor lights flickered, the buzz from the bulbs like a swarm of bees defending their hive. Liza moved swiftly down the metal stairs, and I plunged after her, trying to ignore the rapid beat of my heart or the third set of footsteps I was certain I'd invented in my imagination.

We descended for what felt like an entire century, but in reality was only a moment or two. Without hesitation, Liza pushed the door open and peeked out onto the deck of second class.

"Everything is empty," she said, grabbing my hand. "Let's move quickly, though."

She didn't need to tell me again. We raced down the deck, stopping only periodically to glance over our shoulders. Though I still swore we were being followed, no figure appeared. I was certain I wasn't the only passenger aboard this ship who was starting to invent midnight monsters. We hadn't encountered anyone since supper, and the rooms all appeared to be shut up tight, as if they could barricade the evil away.

"There's Mephistopheles's chambers." Liza halted a few doors down from them. "Harry's room is three away. Fetch me as soon as you're ready to leave."

She kissed my cheek quickly and hurried off. I watched her sneak down to Houdini's cabin and slip inside before bringing my fist to the ringmaster's door. I heard something that sounded like papers rustling. I counted off five beats of my heart and knocked again. The door flung open, revealing a masked woman in a robe. Cassie. Judging from the way the fabric clung to her slim frame, I didn't believe she had on anything beneath it. Her unwelcoming expression more than hinted I'd interrupted something. My face burned when I put together what.

"I-I'm so very sorry, I—"

Mephistopheles moved into the doorframe, a lazy grin upon

his face. I noticed he was completely dressed, not a wrinkle in his clothing, and his cursed mask was still in place. I almost sagged with relief. "Come to profess your undying love?"

"However did you know?" I asked, loud enough for Cassie to hear. I leaned in indecently close and whispered, "Perhaps when you're dreaming."

"At least it's not in my nightmares." He winked. "That would be most unfortunate for you."

I stood back and stole a glance over his shoulder, noting bolts of fabrics and an odd assortment of netting, pearls, and more sequins than I imagined the world contained. A suit jacket with tassels hanging from the shoulders lay on a table with more embellishments ready to be added. It seemed Mephistopheles had quite the sewing hobby— yet another piece to add to the puzzle of him.

"Cassie?" he asked, not sounding at all patient. "Unless there's anything else, we're done for tonight."

Cassie scrutinized me before slipping out of sight. I recalled what Liza had said—Cassie was . . . close with the ringmaster. I suddenly wished to pull a disappearing act of my own. No wonder she was so annoyed; I'd ruined her romantic plans. As if reading my thoughts, Mephistopheles tilted his head. "Cassie was just finishing up her final fitting. Her new costume is a real showstopper—you ought to see it."

"It's not any of my business what you're doing," I said. "And I didn't ask."

"No, you didn't." His lopsided grin was back in place. If he was disturbed by the earlier murder or having the remainder of his evening tryst ruined, he didn't show it. "But you appear awfully relieved for someone who doesn't care." Before I could argue, he stepped back inside and reemerged with a heavy coat. "See yourself out, Cassie. I'll have someone drop the costume off before the show tomorrow."

I stood there, mouth agape. "You cannot be serious."

"Not often, but I do have my moments."

"You're going to put on another show tomorrow? That's madness!"

"Which is good business, Miss Wadsworth."

"Of course it is, how silly of me to think having another show after a body *burned onstage* tonight was anything other than a tremendous idea."

The ringmaster raised a brow above his mask. It truly was a remarkable feat. "It is wise because it will serve as a distraction for those who seek it. Beats the alternative of locking everyone away for three nights, jumping at every creak and groan the ship makes. That, my dear, is madness inducing. Lock a man up and cracks begin to show."

"Is that something you know firsthand?"

He motioned for us to move down the deck, far enough to remain unheard when Cassie left. We kept a respectable distance, but it still felt as if we were too close.

Once we'd reached the end of the ship, I leaned against the railing and kept my focus off of the ringmaster. I needed to think clearly, and he made it difficult with his brash flirting. Wind nipped at my ears and neck. The coldness helped snap my thoughts into place.

"Well? To what do I truly owe the honor and delight of your presence? Are you ready for your next lesson? Or have you mastered your card trick already and have come to boast?"

I stared out at the churning sea. Waves rolled and tossed themselves back and forth, much the same way my mind waded through new information.

"It's been two days," I said, still not looking at him. "Do you honestly expect me to master tricks when bodies keep appearing?"

Mephistopheles barked out surprised laughter. "I don't deal in honesty, but you're a sharp delight, Miss Wadsworth. Shame you won't allow me the honor of cutting my heart in half."

I turned, finally meeting his stare. "I'm not sure I know what you mean."

"Well, *I'm* not sure I believe you," he said, regarding me carefully. "Which means you're doing much better than I'd anticipated with your lessons."

"Sleight of hand can hardly be applied in a situation such as this."

"Can't it, though? Words themselves are tricky, wicked things." He grinned as if he'd uncovered some truth I hadn't hidden particularly well. "Anyway, what I mean is every rose can draw blood as much as delight. Yet we do not hesitate to inhale their fragrance, do we? Danger does not detract from appeal; it increases it."

He bent near enough that his breath was a whisper of warmth on my skin. Gooseflesh rose. In fear or excitement, I couldn't discern.

"I am unafraid of being pricked when the reward is so sweet. You, however...what is it that you're afraid of?"

For some reason Thomas's face flashed across my mind.

Mephistopheles stepped closer. "What do you fear the most? Certainly not death. That you're intrigued by." He placed his arms on either side of me and I involuntarily tensed. "Ah. Bars caging you in? Now that's something you're terrified of. If you want a life of freedom, simply take it for yourself. What's stopping you?"

My heart beat so quickly I feared it might cease. "Is this part of tonight's lesson?"

"This?" He angled his face near my ear. "This is a bit of friendly advice. You cannot live your life following someone else's rules. Would you like to explore other avenues of science? Perhaps forensics aren't the only thing you're passionate about. You might enjoy putting your skills into engineering."

I tried to keep my breathing steady. He might be acting interested for show, but he saw the truth of me. A truth I didn't even think Thomas had discovered. It made me want to simultaneously hug him as well as kick him. I *was* intrigued by mechanical things, my father had crafted toys and I'd always wished to learn how to make them myself. Father had taught my brother, but never indulged me, since I was a girl and it wasn't a "proper feminine pursuit." I'd been given more dolls than I knew what to do with, but gears and bolts…that had been what I'd truly wished for.

"I want to speak with Jian," I said, breaking the strange moment. "Take me to wherever the performers are and let's make up whatever ruse you'd like."

"I'm not sure it's a wise decision after tonight's events." All the teasing in his face disappeared. "The performers have decided to deal with their stress in their own special way. It might get a bit sloppy." He pulled out his pocket watch. "Likely it's already beyond sloppy."

"Cassie's not with the other performers," I pointed out. "Perhaps Jian is not engaged in whatever debauchery you're suggesting the others are doing."

"Actually, I'm fairly certain he's the one passing out the liquor." He stared off into the dark water. "I hope Andreas hides his swords again. Things got quite interesting last time he drank his mood away. The Green Fairy is a tricksy mistress." He leaned against the railing next to me and glanced in my direction. "Do you believe he's capable of murder?"

"How can I possibly answer that when I haven't been able to speak with him more? If you're serious about solving these murders, then bring me there now."

"Of course I'm serious about that. If this carnival fails, I have to go back to my old life. And I'd rather jump into the sea than find my way into another gilded cage."

I searched his face. Perhaps he and I weren't so different. "Where are the performers?"

He raked his gaze over me, though it wasn't in his normal roguish way. There was something swift and almost analytical about it.

He pushed himself off of the railing. "If you insist on attending this gathering, you'll need to dress the part."

I brushed down the front of my velvet cloak. The dress underneath was a bit plainer than the evening gown I'd worn earlier, but there wasn't anything wrong with it. I frowned. "I want to blend in."

"Which is exactly why you need to get rid of that boring thing. You'll be a ragweed in a bed of wildflowers." He crinkled his nose. "Sometimes you need to stand out in order to blend in."

"That makes absolutely no sense."

"But it soon will." He pulled out his pocket watch seemingly from thin air again, grinning as I shook my head. "Lesson number two begins now."

Vintage absinthe posters and labels

SIXTEEN
LA FÉE VERTE

PERFORMERS' PRACTICE AREA
RMS ETRURIA
4 JANUARY 1889

"Tug at that neckline all you wish," Mephistopheles whispered as we stood outside the door to the performers' practice area, "but I promise it won't suddenly sprout leaves and grow. It would defeat the purpose of décolletage."

I shot him my most scathing glare, though it was hard to tell if it had the same effect, as I was also wearing a filigree mask. "I cannot believe I allowed you to dress me in this. I look like a cancan dancer. My aunt would have heart failure if she knew."

"I can see the redness in Mother's face now." Liza smiled from behind her own mask. "Perhaps I ought to suggest this theme for my coming-out ball."

Despite how exposed I felt, I smiled. Aunt Amelia would most certainly collapse onto a fainting couch should she see us in our current states. Liza's costume was similar to mine; we both wore red-and-black-striped corsets—cinched tightly to show off our *décolletage*, as Mephistopheles had pointed out—and black tights, but somehow the ringmaster had managed to make me into his gaudy equivalent by adding extra embellishments.

Sequins covered my risqué bustle and drew the eye to parts of my physique that were desperately close to being bare. My white undergarments had ruffles and lace edged in silver, the only part of my costume that hinted at the Moonlight Carnival. Which no one would ever witness as I refused to lift my skirts and show off my limbs. My silk top hat was black with red bullion—nearly identical to the hat he'd worn on opening night.

Harry gave Liza an amused grin. "I can't wait to meet your old lady."

"'Mother' would suffice," Mephistopheles said primly. "'Old lady' is crassly American of you."

Liza waved off the correction. "Can't we go in already? If we're only staying for an hour, I want to make it count." She batted her lashes at me. "Please? You look stunning, Audrey Rose. Let yourself go a little bit tonight. Have some fun. We could all do with some lightness."

I didn't think "fun" was the most appropriate thing to focus on, what with the burnt corpse we'd seen earlier, but I let it slide. I needed to figure out which performer might be taking his—or her—theatrics to a murderous level, and a drunken soirée might be the perfect venue to garner information. Though judging from the vibration of the music, the party might be a bad idea. I glanced down at my exposed bosom and exhaled. Thomas would certainly be mad he missed this little act of mine, especially since he was always teasing about drunken debauchery.

"Behold." Mephistopheles pushed the doors open. Unlike the organized practice session from the night before, the room was in utter chaos. Music thumped off the walls, masked performers danced to the hedonistic beat, lines of women in cancan clothing similar to mine kicked their legs high, exposing their frilly underthings.

"Is this the mischief you warned patrons about?" I asked, trying to gain control over my racing thoughts. Lights pulsed overhead, dangerously close to flickering out.

Milky green drinks sloshed onto the floor and down people's chins, but they either didn't notice or didn't care. My attention moved from one scene to the next, heart pounding along to the drums. I'd never seen so many bodies in motion before; so many people dancing against each other in shocking ways. Clowns jumped over barrels, then tumbled to the ground, clutching their stomachs and laughing until their makeup smeared. Cigar smoke went up in different intervals throughout the cavernous room, the scent heavy and thick in the air. I had walked directly into the Devil's Lounge.

This had been a terrible mistake. I took a step backward, right into the ringmaster's waiting arms. He leaned close, raising his voice above the clamor and, despite the heat of the crowded room, chills wound their way down my body.

"This, Miss Wadsworth, is the mayhem portion of the show." We stood so close I felt his chest rise and fall with breath. "This is also a time to remember the first rule of thumb—do *not* lose your head."

"Don't worry. I don't—"

Jian, performing a cartwheel, landed close to us, and I jumped back, nearly knocking Mephistopheles over in my haste to get out of harm's way. Jian was equally impressive as the women who were doing the cancan. Instead of the usual glare he wore for me, he fixed us both with a sloppy grin. "Welcome to the *real* show!"

He tossed an arm about my shoulders as if we were the best of friends, pulling me away from the ringmaster. I glanced behind me to where Mephistopheles still stood, trying not to laugh. So much for relying on him to help. My attention darted around, but Liza and Houdini had already slunk into the fray. It seemed no assistance would be coming.

"Let's see what you can do," Jian slurred. "Dance with me!"

"Oh, I-I don't think..."

"Exactly!" he shouted over the drums. "Don't think. Just dance."

Before I could politely decline his offer, he spun me around, skirts flying upward as I twirled out and bumped into another dancer. She tossed her head back and laughed, spinning into her partner. I practically fell over myself, trying to shove my petticoats back down. Jian dropped to the ground, his legs split to either side of him.

"Are you all right?" I yelled. Dear heaven above, that had to have hurt. He hopped back onto his feet, then kicked one limb up and clapped his hands below the knee, his grin wicked and wild and...free.

"Come on! Try it out—you'll like it!"

I'd much sooner enjoy stabbing my hand with a fork. I shook my head and pointed to a table lined with fountains of what appeared to be ice water. A refreshment was a much better idea, and the cold water might help alleviate some of his drunkenness. "I'm thirsty."

His gaze stumbled over to the general direction I'd indicated, his brows tugged close. He squinted a bit, then smiled. "Ah. Excellent idea. I'm starting to understand Mephistopheles's admiration."

I could barely hear him over the music and decided it wasn't worth pursuing. If he believed the ringmaster was truly infatuated with me, it simply meant our act was working. We made our way through the crowd, most of whom parted as Jian cut his way through. I stayed close behind him, both out of necessity and worry that I'd get swept up in another lurid dance.

He marched right over to the first spigot and prepared a drink. I subtly shifted, taking in the people kissing in dark corners. My brows shot to my hairline when I noticed Cassie wrapped around a young man who most decidedly wasn't Mephistopheles. In fact, I believed it might be the contortionist, though it was hard to be sure since they were so entwined.

Jian handed me a cloudy drink and followed my gaze. "Don't worry about her, there's nothing going on with her and Mephistopheles. Not for a while now."

I accepted the drink and sniffed. It didn't smell very strong, but I didn't want to chance impairing my own deductive abilities. "Was she upset when she—"

"—found out he was actually interested in you?" He laughed. "I've never seen someone so small throw such a fit. She trashed her costume, and nearly tossed a shoe through Andreas's magic mirror." His attention turned to my untouched drink. I handed it over and he gulped it down in one greedy drab. "Now that would've been something to see."

"Would Andreas get violent?"

Behind his mask, I could have sworn his eyes dilated. "I mean it would have broken his heart." He fixed another drink and swayed in place. "Anyway, Cassie's not mad at you. If she's angry at anyone it's Mephistopheles. He'd better watch himself—she's the type to teach lessons. You should have seen that last guy." He shook his head. "He'd have been better off with the lions."

I tried not to watch her too closely. She was now backing the same young man against the wall, kissing down his neck. It was much too intimate a moment to intrude upon, even though she had no qualms of making a show of it.

"That's Sebastián."

"The contortionist?"

"That and he's her husband." Jian chuckled at my stunned expression.

Someone chose that moment to shoot a light out. I threw myself to the ground, hands over my head as glass rained down and the room got that much darker. Performers whooped at the dimmer lighting. My pulse thrashed about as I slowly stood. This was madness.

Completely unfazed by the growing debauchery, Jian tossed his next drink back, then staggered over to the fountain. I feared if he drank anything else, I'd not get any useful information from him. Shoving my own nervousness aside, I hurried after him.

"Cassie and Sebastián are married?" I asked. "He must have been furious about Mephistopheles."

A motive to destroy the carnival if ever there was one. Might they be a murderous duo? I stared as they clawed at each other's clothing. Jealousy was a powerful motive for anyone. And each of them might be suffering from it. Sebastián because his wife had so openly pursued another man, and Cassie for so openly being cast aside. I wanted to rush to Thomas and tell him every last theory sprouting up in my mind, but the cursed bargain prevented me from doing that.

"They both do as they please and it works for them." Jian looked at me through half-lidded eyes. "Hey... you haven't finished your drink." I didn't bother pointing out that he'd done that for me twice. "Lesss make a toasss."

"Maybe we ought to hold off until next time," I suggested. His slurring was much worse. He waved me off and went about making two more drinks, concentrating as if the fate of the world depended on this potion. I would have been more amused if I wasn't worried the persons responsible for three deaths were passionately embracing in the corner.

Jian poured a knuckle of green liquid into each glass, then managed to place slotted spoons over them without knocking the glasses over. A miracle, considering the state he was in. Next he placed sugar cubes on the spoons, set them ablaze, and maneuvered everything over to the water fountain after the flame extinguished.

Lining the spigots up with the sugar, he twisted them on. Ice water dripped slowly, disintegrating the sugar as it fell into the awaiting liquor. The pale green color shifted to an opaque smoke, reminding me of a forbidden brew. It finally clicked what it was. Absinthe.

Intrigued, I accepted the glass, holding it up to the dim light. It was all the rage in both upper-class houses and bawdy clubs; some claimed it offered hallucinations, but that was only true if extra wormwood had been added to it. I bit my lip. I wanted to try it very badly, but I also needed to act responsibly and gather clues.

Someone stepped up beside me, but a lot of people jostled about. I didn't pay them any mind. "Are you going to pretend to drink that?" I snapped my attention around. Cassie raised her brows. "Or do you need some help?"

"I haven't pretended to drink anything."

"Maybe not." She studied me. "But there are other things you're pretending, aren't there?" Her attention left me briefly and I didn't have to follow her gaze to know she was speaking of the ringmaster. "You might be acting at infatuation, but he's not."

I swallowed hard. I couldn't detect any malice in her words—if anything, there was almost a sense of camaraderie, like we were sisters in battle, fighting against wicked men. I lifted the glass to my lips. "I appreciate your advice," I said, "but I really am enjoying my time here."

I went to toss back the drink as I'd seen Jian do several times when a hand shot out and covered the rim. My lips pressed against the crescent moon–stitched glove and I drew back as if I'd been burned. Mephistopheles shook his head. "This might be a little too magical for you, Miss Wadsworth. I'd like to return you to your chambers in one piece. Heaven forbid Thomas Cresswell comes challenging me to a duel."

He held my stare and I could have sworn there was true concern in his face. I politely removed his hand from my glass, aware of our audience. I had no doubt he was, too. Which was precisely why he shouldn't have mentioned Thomas. "Have a drink with me."

"It's late."

I lifted a shoulder. "Suit yourself."

Before he could utter another word, I gulped my drink down. It was most unladylike and barbarous. I loved it. It tasted of licorice and burned pleasantly on the way down, different from wine in the sense of the warmth that spread from my stomach to my limbs. My body felt as if it was as light as air. Muffled sounds grew louder. Colors richer. Someone laughed close by and I giggled along with them for no good reason at all.

"Come, let's get you to bed." Mephistopheles gently took my arm, his brow creased. He really was quite good at all this pretend stuff. He almost had me convinced he cared.

I wriggled out of his grasp, grabbing a handful of my petticoats as I darted away. The coarse material felt amazing beneath my touch and I suddenly wanted to prance around the room, kicking my legs up. No wonder everyone appeared so happy—this elixir was pure magic. A woman wearing a full mask stuck her hand out, waving me over. Several women had their arms linked, throwing kicks in unison. Suddenly, it was the most logical thing to do.

Without hesitation, I hooked my arm around hers and joined in the fun. My heart thundered in my chest, alive and boisterous. I'd never felt so untethered before, so free from judgment and restraint. My entire family would balk at my behavior; for all I knew Thomas would even be puzzled. But I didn't care. Not about any of that darkness. Murder. Crime. Sadness. Loss. I pretended each emotion was a balloon that needed to be released into the universe, and I let it all go.

I kicked my legs higher each time I switched feet, ignoring the fact I was exposing more skin than I'd ever shown in public before. I closed my eyes, becoming one with the rhythm around me. This was how it felt to truly be free.

Two large hands clasped my waist, lifting me in the air. I laughed and shook my skirts, a thrill going through me. Liza had been right—having a bit of fun didn't detract from the seriousness of the evening, but it was a fantastic way of coping with it. Death surrounded me, but life did, too. In these stolen moments, I appreciated just how alive I was.

Lips pressed close to my ear and I instinctively arched into the touch, momentarily forgetting where I was and who I was with. I was lowered to the ground and I spun the second my slippers touched down, grinning. Mephistopheles's eyes widened in shock and he abruptly stumbled back. I was having too much fun to be disappointed he wasn't who I imagined.

"Would you please do that again?" I asked. He hesitated briefly, then brought me near and twirled me away, his cockiness returning as he lifted me above the dance floor. I held my hands out to either side as he spun us around. "I feel like I'm in a fairy tale."

He placed me back down, eyes filled with mirth. "If a fairy tale is what you're after, I'll put a curse on you and lock you in a coffin or tower of your choosing. Then I'll kiss you awake and we'll live happily ever after. That's how those things work, you know."

I shook my head. "You're really charming, aren't you?"

"That would be *Prince* Charming to you, Miss Wadsworth."

We didn't speak again for what felt like hours, but I danced and laughed and had almost convinced myself that a future in a carnival wouldn't be the worst fate after all.

SEVENTEEN
SOMETHING IN THE CARDS

I was up before the sun, peering out the porthole in my cabin, watching the nearly black waters turn gold as it rose and stretched across the horizon. The sea was choppy, promising a winter storm in the next day or so. I turned around and couldn't stop a smile from forming. Liza slept soundly, her limbs tangled up in the covers and her hair spilling around her like drizzled caramel. I still could not believe we'd sneaked into the carnival's party, and that I'd actually danced the cancan. It was reckless and the memory provoked worry. Not over what I'd done, but rather how much I'd enjoyed it. I only wished Thomas could have joined us.

Pushing that out of my mind, I quietly moved to the small vanity in my room, leafing through the notes of parchment I'd written out sometime after we'd returned to our cabin. I included every last odd occurrence that had happened since we'd boarded the *Etruria*.

On one scrap of parchment I had "Miss Arden murdered, likely poisoned, though evidence was indeterminable. Playing card found prior to body onstage: Ace of Spades. Connected? Father a physician. Tarot card enactment: Seven of Swords."

On another, "Stolen bolts of silk, scarves."

On a third sheet I'd written, "Miss Crenshaw murdered by poison. No playing card found. Tarot card enactment: the Star."

From my meager attempt at sorting out the tarot card meanings, the best I could come up with for the Star was "transformation." How that fit in with the case and murder was beyond me.

The next piece of paper said, "Miss Prescott—first to be murdered, stabbed. Playing card found: Ace of Clubs. Father a chief magistrate. Tarot card enactment: Ten of Swords. Betrayal. Quite literally, stabbed in the back."

I sat back, fingers tapping over the papers. There had to be something there, something that tied them all together. Or perhaps there were two separate mysteries coexisting. One person was committing petty burglaries; another was murdering women as if they were tarot cards sprung to life. My skin crawled like beetles in a grave. I knew Thomas was correct about criminals using the ships for anonymous passage between continents, but could there truly be two criminals aboard our vessel? I supposed it wasn't out of the question—two out of a few hundred passengers wasn't that high a number at all.

What I wanted to do next was gain entry to Miss Crenshaw's cabin. After the discovery of chocolate cake in her stomach, I wanted to compare a sample from her room.

Someone knocked lightly on my door and, assuming it was either a tea service or an attendant, I opened it. I clutched my dressing gown closed, narrowing my eyes. A quick glance over my shoulder found my cousin still lightly snoring, her breaths deep and even.

"It's a bit early to be calling on me, Cresswell." I tugged him inside, peering down the deck to be sure he hadn't been seen. "People will think you've spent the night here." I studied the curve of his lips and the widening of his eyes. Fiend. "Which is precisely what you're hoping for."

"You injure me with that accusation, Wadsworth. Must I always have ulterior motives?" He lifted his hand to his heart, staggering a bit. "Perhaps I was simply bringing you tea."

"Oh? Is that what you were doing?" I stared pointedly at his empty hands. "Forget it. You're here and that's actually perfect. Come look at these. But be quiet." I indicated the random clues, trying to ignore the fact I was in a dressing robe and we were in a bedchamber. At least we weren't alone. If he started kissing me, I'm not sure I'd wish to stop. I'd missed him immensely last night. "Do you see any pattern or formula with these?"

Thomas removed his top hat and was across the room in a few short, long-limbed strides. He pushed the papers around the desk, frowning a bit at one. "Miss Prescott was murdered on night one, but Miss Crenshaw went missing before we set sail. The order in which we find the bodies doesn't necessarily indicate the order in which they were murdered."

"Thomas," I said, a new idea sprouting, "will you teach me how to place myself in the mind-set of a murderer? Like how you did the first time we met?"

He strummed his fingers against his thighs. "In your uncle's class?"

"Yes," I said, attention shooting over to my still-sleeping cousin, "when you pretended as if you were Jack the Ripper and had gutted the first victim. I want to learn to do that. It's not much different than all of the magic in the carnival, is it?"

Thomas looked at me strangely. "I suppose they both include a certain level of playacting, but I'd like to think my method is a bit more scientific than the man swinging swords about."

"Still, I'd like—" Another knock came at the door and I

181

swallowed my words as quickly as Anishaa had gulped down those flames. I started shoving Thomas toward my trunk, not knowing where else to stash him. Liza stirred, but didn't wake. "Get in there . . . quickly!"

Without much argument, Thomas folded himself into the trunk—an impressive feat given his tall stature—and I tossed one of my gowns over the top, hoping to hide him under the tentlike skirts. I smoothed down the front of my dressing gown, cracking the door an inch.

Mephistopheles leaned against the doorjamb, gaze dropping to my robe. I felt my breath leave my body in a whoosh as if I'd been punched. This was the worst possible situation. I could not let Thomas overhear our conversation because of the bargain, and I could not admit to the ringmaster that a young man was already in my chambers. If Mephistopheles said anything about the cancan last night, I was certain Thomas wouldn't let the subject drop until I fessed up.

"Hello, Miss Wadsworth. Were you expecting someone else? You seem like you've swallowed an egg."

He made to invite himself in, but I held my arm out stiffly. "What are you doing here?"

"Good day to you, as well," he said. "It's amazing—you have no issue with our meeting in darkened nooks on the ship, or coming to my cabin at indecent hours, but heaven forbid I initiate a private meeting. The shame."

"If you wish to speak with me," I said, keeping my voice low, "then we shall pick a place to meet. In public. Preferably when I am decently dressed and have a chaperone."

"Was Liza acting as your chaperone last night?" He peered around me, making a show of inspecting my quarters. "Are you hiding a secret lover I ought to be aware of?"

"I'm in the process of buffing my scalpels," I said, indicating the medical bag on my nightstand. "If you're not careful, I might use those blades on your sparkly suits."

"Threats are unbecoming and don't suit you." He sniffed, feigning hurt. He turned to leave, then pivoted back. Even at dawn he wore a mask, reflecting the orangey reds of the rising sun.

"Oh, and you ought to tell Mr. Cresswell to remember his hat. I see it's sitting out on that vanity of yours. Wouldn't want anyone to have the wrong impression, now, would you? Thank goodness your cousin is pretending to sleep, else people might really start talking."

Before I could deny or claim it as my own, the ringmaster stuck his hands in his pockets and walked swiftly down the promenade. The sound of his sullen whistling added to the chorus of wind and waves. I curled my hands into fists, wishing I could muster up loathing him. Having two young men around who felt the compulsion to share each annoying observation they made was enough to drive anyone mad.

Once the door clicked shut, Thomas pushed the dress aside, brows raised. "Now might be a good time to discuss Mephistopheles, especially since your uncle has asked me to watch after you. What's so important that he needs to call on you at this hour? Doesn't he know that level of impropriety is strictly my area of expertise?"

I walked over to him, bent down, and cupped his face in my hands, relishing the feel of his warm skin without a layer of silk between us. "We will discuss everything soon, I promise. But right now I need to get dressed and you need to leave before someone finds you here."

After sneaking another glance at my "slumbering" cousin, I pressed my lips to his, soft and gentle at first, then let go of polite restraint. Thomas didn't seem to mind the distraction; he pulled me near as our kiss deepened. With great effort, I kissed him gently, then sat back on my heels. It was most decidedly my favorite form of sleight of hand.

"We wouldn't want anyone to have the wrong impression," I said, unable to hide my smile. "They'd assume we were in here kissing."

"We wouldn't want that, now." Thomas shook his head, and somehow we were kissing again. "It would be highly indecent. Being almost alone. In the room of the girl I want to marry. The one who keeps refusing me."

"Thomas...I...you know I'm not refusing you," I said. "I want to do this the correct way. My father deserves to be included. Please don't think it indicates hesitation on my part, I'd—"

"A wedding?" Liza popped up from the covers, eyes wide with delight. "I *must* help plan it! What season are you thinking? Spring would be divine. The flowers, pastels! Winter is also breathtaking in the right application. Your black hair would look gorgeous against ice blues and whites."

"A wedding, elopement. I am in favor of any season or occasion." He hopped out of the trunk, then helped me stand, giving me a chaste kiss. After he plucked his top hat up from the vanity, he smiled. "We will worry about the details later." He glanced back at the table of clues I'd laid out. "In the interim, I'll see what I can figure out about those. Maybe some connection will make itself known. Oh, and Liza?" He turned a grin on her. "I look rather breathtaking in pale colors. Spring is just around the corner, too. Perhaps you might start there."

With a tip of his hat, he slipped out of my cabin. Listening as Liza prattled on about wedding ideas, I went back over to my trunk and rummaged through the silks and velvets.

"Your father is going to be so pleased," she said, that dreamy look still on her face. "I cannot believe you've not mentioned his intentions sooner. I do hope that Harry will propose—we make a decent match as well, don't we?"

The letter Mephistopheles had supplied seemed to catch fire in my nightstand. Once Liza read it, her heart was going to shatter. I offered a tight smile, unable to break the news to her just yet. "I have no doubt you'll marry a man who makes you very happy."

There were only so many secrets I could keep before I started to unravel.

The Fool tarot

EIGHTEEN

THE FOOL

I tucked my hand into the crook of Thomas's arm and tried not to gawk at the transformation of the ship as we made our way down the now-crowded promenade. The public rooms and long covered deck of first class had been re-dressed as if they were private carnival tents in a floating bazaar.

The gentlemen's smoke room was filled with warped looking glasses; the dining saloon boasted tightrope walkers and acrobats and...clowns. I shuddered at their garish face paint, deciding I'd much rather splice open a bloated corpse than be locked in a room with a single clown. I sped up, not wishing to linger anywhere near them, and Thomas chuckled. I flashed him my finest scowl, which only made him laugh harder.

"Removing intestines before luncheon is all right, but clowns are where your limits end?" he asked. "You never cease to amaze me, Wadsworth. What if I dressed up like one and knocked at your door later? Do you think you'd faint into my ruffle-sleeved arms? Reviving you might be worth the makeup and silly costume."

"Don't make me sneak spiders into your cabin," I said. "I am not above dirty warfare."

"You delightfully cruel woman." His eyes practically danced with mischief. "What does it say about me that I find myself even more attracted to you after that threat?"

"It means you are as darkly twisted as I am, my friend."

We continued down the promenade and paused to watch Sebastián, the contortionist, twist his body in ways that boggled my anatomy-centered mind. He lifted his chin in hello and scuttled across the deck as if *he* were an arachnid. I laughed aloud as Thomas hurried us away.

I couldn't stop the double beat of my heart when we came upon the newly transformed music room. An ornately lettered sign sat propped out front that promised secrets of the past, present, and future to be divined by THE AMAZING ANDREAS; MYSTIC AND SEER OF ALL FORTUNES.

He hadn't included his tarot namesake, the Fool, in his title—a smart choice considering I doubted that would attract many believers. I stopped walking, forcing Thomas to come to a halt, as I recalled another time I'd encountered someone with claims of seeing into the future. During the Ripper investigation a man named Robert James Lees had offered his assistance to Scotland Yard, claiming he'd had direct communication with one of the victims. Not wanting to miss a potential clue, Thomas and I had traveled to his home, taking him up on his offer to divine secrets of the recently deceased.

Chills meandered down my spine—I had a feeling it wasn't due to the cold ocean breeze snaking down the open-air corridors. Mr. Lees had claimed to have spoken with my mother—and as much as I disbelieved such nonfactual nonsense, I'd found what I'd been looking for just as my mother's spirit had told him. Whether it was luck or pure coincidence, there was something to it. Or at least something worth investigating. Perhaps I might unearth a clue for this investigation, one that might end these murders for good.

On a ship filled with devilish debauchery, hope seemed to be the deadliest sin of them all. I felt it tugging me forward, taunting and teasing me with the promise of something I knew to be impossible. Andreas was a showman, not a diviner. He could no more tell me who killed those women than he could bring forth my mother. Thomas inspected the sign I was transfixed by and then my face. He smiled sadly, dissecting my emotions and deducing their root. In times like this, I was grateful for his uncanny ability to read my moods.

"Would you like to have your future read by the Amazing Andreas?" he asked.

"You don't believe in fate or fortunes."

"No, I don't." He grinned at my exasperated expression. How one man could be utterly charming in one instant and sharp as a blade in the next was utterly maddening. "I'll meet you back here in a little while."

I peered into the black-and-white-striped curtains that hung in place of a door, biting my lip. "Is that a polite way of saying you'll not be joining me? What about Uncle's proclamation that you must escort me everywhere? A leash only extends so far, you know."

"I will never be your keeper, Audrey Rose." Any traces of humor vanished. Thomas lifted my hand to his lips and pressed a kiss to it, causing my heart to race for a new reason. "Plus, it's a magnanimous gesture to not distract either yourself or the Amazing Andreas with my own exemplary skills at divining the future." He laughed when I rolled my eyes. "That and I saw a stand on the main deck selling pastry fried in melted butter and doused in sugar."

"You're abandoning me for sweets," I said with a slight shake of my head. "How magnanimous indeed."

"Don't be jealous of pastry, my love. Its golden crust and buttery taste cannot compare to your delectable personality. Much." Thomas eyed the sign once more, lips twitching upward. "All right...let's

189

make a bargain, since those things seem to be all the craze here. I'll give you five minutes to get settled and another ten for the Amazing Andreas to call forth the ghosties and convince them to stay for a spot of tea and a chat. Then I'll return."

"How is that a bargain?" I asked.

"It's not, really. I was seeing if you were paying attention." I leveled a severe look at him, and he held his hands up in mock surrender. "A joke. You know…those things I'm horrid at but am practicing nonetheless?" When he leaned in, his lips grazing my ear, there wasn't anything humorous about the desire that shot through me. "Perhaps I'll bring you back a treat, too."

I smiled sweetly. "Here I thought simply being in your presence was treat enough." Before he could entertain himself with another of his witticisms, I swept open the striped drapes and stepped inside the fortune-teller's lair.

Inside, a crystal chandelier hung from a ceiling that seemed to reach forever. Layers of lush black-and-white silk gathered around the light fixture, pinned back in a way to give the appearance of being under a huge tent. Silver candles dripped wax onto wrought-iron candelabras evenly spaced throughout the interior of the room.

From the shadows Andreas emerged. I took a sharp breath. His mask was the color of fresh blood and reminded me of a skull that had been recently boiled of its flesh. He stood there a moment, not moving at all, allowing me an opportunity to drink him in. He wore a navy tailcoat embroidered with silver constellations and black trousers and gloves.

He bent at the waist, blond hair pale enough that it was almost white. "Pardon my entrance, Miss Wadsworth. My soul travels the in-between, restless and wandering," he said in accented English. "In constant search of the past, present, and future, I find time to be an idle wave." I tried puzzling that out and failed. "I am the Amazing Andreas. Welcome to my chamber of divination."

"It's good to see you again." I bobbed my head in greeting and fully entered the room. Pillows edged in silver fringe sat piled in clusters, though there were also stools and chairs and tables. Elaborate incense burners hung in tiered layers in one corner, filling the room with a spicy and enticing scent. It reminded me of Mephistopheles. I bit my lip, unsure of where to go. Lounging on the floor felt too indecent, though I supposed being alone with a masked man was debasing enough.

"Sit, please."

The Amazing Andreas gestured to a rather large looking glass. It leaned against the wall, tall and somehow slightly foreboding for such an unassuming piece of furniture.

"The looking glass is infused with magic from Bavaria," he said. "It is no ordinary glass—this has the ability to show your future." He ran his hands down the front of his very nice waistcoat, puffing out his chest a bit. "To my knowledge, it has near one hundred percent accuracy with showing who your husband shall be. Most young women leave here quite satisfied."

How extraordinarily disappointing.

"Is that all it does?" I asked. "I thought it showed one's future. What if there is no marriage in mine? Will it not show my career or any other part of my life, then? There are those who prefer to not marry anyone. What does the looking glass show them?"

Andreas gave me the sort of look one made when passing a foul chamber pot. To his credit, his tone was still quite cordial when he spoke. "In order for me to work the spell properly, I'll need to secure your hands with a bit of ribbon behind your back." He produced a thick, black satiny ribbon from his coat, allowing its end to flutter down in dramatic fashion. "And place a cover across your eyes. Spellwork is very fickle, you see."

I pursed my lips, hoping to contain the unpleasant retort that had sprung to mind. Now I understood why they called him the

Fool. He'd have to be one to think I'd agree to being tied up and blindfolded while alone with him. Was there any young man in this carnival who wasn't a miscreant? After a minute, I said, "Indeed, I imagine it is fickle."

He sighed, the first unscripted sound that he'd uttered. "Mephistopheles thinks it will be good practice for the finale. He said the blindfold provides the right amount of flair."

I stared at the foggy-looking glass, unconvinced such a dingy thing could possess any flair. "Well, since Mephistopheles isn't here, I think we're safe from listening to his demands." I glanced around, focus falling to a deck of cards. I pointed them out. "I'd prefer to have a tarot reading. It might be useful in our investigation."

Andreas didn't seem very keen on disobeying the ringmaster, but smiled. "As you wish."

Without further comment, I situated myself on the cushioned stool and kept my attention fastened on the cards he shuffled. I only saw the backs of them, but they were beautifully done—painted by a skilled artist. They were darker than night and had silver filigree flourishes at each corner and a black full moon with a pearly crescent on one side. Silver stars were placed above, below, and to each side of the moon within a moon.

Andreas caught me admiring them and held one up. "May I present the one and only *Cirque d'Eclipse tarot*." He smiled shyly at my raised brows and added, "Mephistopheles wishes for the Moonlight Carnival's theme to be present in every detail, even something as small and insignificant as tarot cards."

He turned the card one way, then the next, showing off the magnificent shine of the silver lines, but never revealing the image on the front. Two interlocking eights lay at the top and bottom of the cards, reminding me of something else I couldn't quite place.

"Did you paint those?" I asked, doing my best to keep my hands to myself. I longed to flip them over and see the fine artwork I knew had to be present on the other side. "They are absolutely magnificent. I've never seen paint shimmer like that before."

"I did not," he said, shaking his head. "Mephistopheles made these himself. He prefers to—Mephistopheles teaches everyone cartomancy and tarot. We're unable to join the carnival until we're proficient." He chuckled and continued shuffling the cards, leaving me to wonder at what he didn't say.

"So every performer is well versed on both playing cards and tarot?"

Andreas nodded, but didn't elaborate. "Is this your first experience with tarot?"

Aside from the bodies that were being staged, though I didn't feel it was the appropriate response. Instead I nodded absently, as a new thought wedged itself into my brain. I watched the fortune-teller shuffle the cards, thoughts spinning. If Mephistopheles was into crafting cards, could he be the person leaving them with the bodies? I shook myself out of that nonsensical thought. He was no murderer. I watched Andreas again; he obviously was proficient with tarot and the various meanings. But so was every other performer, thanks to Mephistopheles.

"If you're the fortune-teller, why does everyone need to know the card meanings?"

Andreas scratched the back of his neck. "People pay a decent sum for their futures. When we're in a new town, we often set up multiple tents that feature tarot readings or go to different pubs. Sometimes Sebastián plays the role, sometimes even Jian. We can triple our income. It's good business. Now." Andreas set the cards facedown before me. "It is your turn. Shuffle the deck until you feel the first one speak to you. Beware—it might only be a whisper, so listen closely."

I reached for the deck, then drew my hand back. "What if the cards don't say anything?"

"They will. Closing your eyes and focusing on a single question helps," Andreas said. "How do you feel about yourself and your path? Think of only that and close your eyes and shuffle. The answer will make itself known."

I did as I was bid, unable to help feeling ridiculous as I shuffled one card to the next, concentrating on a multitude of emotions. That the cards could possibly tell me something about myself that I didn't already know was foolish. How I'd been taken with the idea of visiting the fortune-teller was a testament to how much this silly carnival was affecting my best judgment. Maybe Andreas was called the Fool after the people he attracted to his tent, like myself.

Suddenly, I felt a slight pull in my center…a strange bit of resistance to shuffling to the next card. My eyes flew open, how in the—

"See? Spirits speak in whispers and tugs." Andreas smiled his patient smile and tapped the table in front of him. He certainly didn't look like a killer when he wore that expression, but I'd not rule him out based on that. "Place the first one here, lay it facedown. We'll do a six-card spread and then flip them over once they've all been pulled. All right?"

"All right." I inhaled deeply, unsure of the validity of it, but the alternative was watching Uncle spear his vegetables and bicker with Mrs. Harvey over the dessert course.

"This time I want you to focus on your heart's deepest desire. What is a truth you hide even from yourself?"

I closed my eyes tightly, unsure of how I'd find something hidden from me. Once I felt that same odd resistance I pulled another card. The next four questions I needed to concentrate on were my fears, what was working with me in life, what forces were conspiring against me, and what the outcome of it all would be. Satisfied that I'd taken my part seriously, Andreas flipped the first card over, revealing a gnarled, bearded man standing alone at the top of a frozen mountain peak, the sky a swirling black and gray behind him.

"Ah. The Hermit. Since this card indicates how you feel about yourself, I'd wager you're struggling with an internal conflict. You likely have many questions, are feeling alone, and perhaps have run out of patience. Now is the time to retreat until you find answers to what troubles you."

"Hmm." I blinked down at the card, disbelief dragging my mouth into a frown. It was luck. Stupid luck that the first card held a shred of truth. I *was* feeling alone and in need of answers. I had to figure out so many mysteries, and because of my bargain with Mephistopheles, I couldn't even recruit Thomas for some of the problems I had. Things would be so much easier with my partner—I hated retreating on my own.

Unwilling to give anything away, I flipped over the next card. A young masked man danced in a disjointed manner, his outfit crude and clownlike. Clearly my inner spirit was feeling like a court jester. Fabulous. According to this card, the thing I longed for most was to be a fool. Though I supposed it was also accurate. This entire evening was a foolish distraction I could ill afford, and yet here I sat, having my cards read like a gullible mark.

"The Fool. An interesting choice. It is the only card in the tarot that indicates infinity." Andreas steepled his fingers and stared unabashedly into my eyes. "Is there someone in your life you're unsure of? Perhaps a beau or potential suitor? This card indicates you might have conflicting feelings for someone…Mephistopheles or—"

I turned the next card over. I did not wish to even step onto that path. "The World. What does this one mean?"

It was another magnificent piece of artwork—a young woman swung two batons, the train of her lavender dress floating on an invisible breeze. In each corner of the card there was a different beast— man, eagle, bull, and a winged lion.

Andreas tapped the card. "This represents your fears. You're close to giving up because you're afraid of failure." I turned over the next two cards—the Empress and the Sun. What was going for and against me. "The Empress is a time of harvesting. It's a wonderful time to start a family or pursue your passion. The Sun, on the other hand, is causing a few delays. If you can persevere, you'll achieve what you seek in a blaze of flame and glory."

I exhaled through my nose. It was all rubbish, but I had to admit it was disturbingly accurate for my current predicament.

"Andreas?" I began, not quite ready to see my last card. "What does the Star card mean?"

He blinked at my change in focus, but then drew his brows together in thought. "The Star is an interesting card. It relates to personal transformation…hope…and being blessed in your endeavors. Though there are many, many other ways it can be incorporated into a reading. Why the interest?"

"Simple curiosity." Not wanting to get into a discussion regarding the last murder victim, I turned the final card over and scowled down at it. There was no need for me to read the name at the bottom, the artist had done a fine job indeed of painting a self-portrait. Mephistopheles's likeness smirked up at me, the wicked glint in his eyes a near-perfect replica of the young man in reality.

"The Magician," Andreas said, never taking his attention off the card, "is the outcome most likely in your future. Beware of making bargains you cannot keep, though. The Devil is a trickster in us all. He often makes you believe one thing, while covering the truth in plain sight." Chills caressed my body at those words, so similar to my earlier thoughts. Andreas bit his lip, seeming to weigh his next words carefully. "Be cautious with who you give your heart to. And be even more wary of those who seek to steal it."

NINETEEN
A SEVERED CONNECTION

Thomas leaned against the wall opposite the music room, finishing off the last bit of his fried pastry. He grinned when he spied me lingering outside the fortune-teller's makeshift "tent" and held up a second sugar-coated pastry.

"I swear I was going to rescue you from the Amazing Andreas... once I finished my sweet dough. Here"—he handed my treat over— "tell me this isn't the most delicious thing you've ever tasted. Aside from me, naturally."

I huffed a laugh. Thomas was a scoundrel and a horrendous flirt, but I couldn't deny enjoying it. Despite the unease swirling through my system at the sight of the Magician card and the revelation of how many performers were skilled with tarot, I popped a piece of fried dough into my mouth and nearly groaned. It truly was one of the most delicious things I'd ever eaten.

"Do I even want to know how much butter they used to make it taste that good?"

"Hmm." Thomas pretended to think on it a moment. "Probably

not, Wadsworth. And you most certainly don't wish to know how much sugar they sprinkled onto it once it came out of its butter bath." He offered his arm and we slowly made our way toward the saloon. "Did Andreas gift you with an amazing glimpse at your future? I hear his magic looking glass is all the rage. A young woman was speaking very loudly about her future husband. Apparently she saw his reflection in the glass and wasn't pleased."

I offered him a bemused look, but didn't comment.

"I'm taking it that you're stunned into silence by how adorable our children are. I bet they take after me the most. My Cresswell genes are quite impressive. Though you will make fine little ones yourself." He patted my hand lovingly. "Try not to be too hard on yourself, though. We cannot help who is the fairest of us."

I stopped walking, mouth dropping open. "Our children?"

Thomas cocked his head. "You know...smaller-sized humans who spit up on things and require an indecent amount of attention until they're grown? I imagine we'll have an entire brood of them."

"You can't be serious, I—"

Mephistopheles strode down the corridor with Jian and Anishaa, lips twitching into his signature smirk when he glanced up and noticed us. He broke away from the performers and shook a few eager hands of passengers as he drew near. I silently prayed he wouldn't mention our dancing last night.

"What a fortunate surprise, Miss Wadsworth." He took my hand in his, pretending to kiss it, and pulled an ink-blue rose from the air. "A rose for the lovely Audrey Rose."

"Oh, wonderful," Thomas said. "Satan has decided to claw his way out of Hell and join us. I had no idea he did subpar tricks, though."

The ringmaster turned his attention on my companion as if noticing him for the first time. "Satan. The Devil. Prince of the Underworld. Let's not forget that Lucifer was a fallen angel—I imagine he was quite handsome. If the role fits..." Mephistopheles shrugged. "Anyway, it's always interesting to see you again, Mr. Cresswell, but if you'll excuse us, I need to speak with your"—he purposely stared down at my empty ring finger—"friend, isn't it?" Mephistopheles didn't smile again, but satisfaction oozed off him when Thomas clenched his jaw. "Don't worry. I'll return her to you shortly. If she cares to return, that is."

Thomas stood there, fingers tapping his sides. I wasn't sure if he was waiting for my refusal or considering how angry Uncle would be if he discovered I'd wandered off unchaperoned with someone he didn't approve of. I glanced at Mephistopheles and bit my lip. I didn't wish to abandon Thomas, but something large must have happened for the ringmaster to want to talk before our scheduled meeting. I took a step in his direction, then stopped.

Thomas inhaled deeply. "If I come across your uncle, I'll tell him you needed a bit more time to get ready. Meet me outside your cabin in half an hour."

"Thomas." I made to reach for him, but dropped my arm. "Thank you."

"Thanking me is unnecessary." He leaned in and kissed my cheek, unconcerned with our scowling audience. "You are *always* free to do as you please. Even if you choose to follow a strange man in a gaudy suit into the bowels of a steam cruiser while someone in his show is murdering women." Delight flashed in his eyes when the ringmaster exhaled loudly. "I'll see you in a bit."

"If my suit is so gaudy then why are you staring at it like it's your one true love?"

"Thomas," I warned. "Do not comment on his jacket. He missed his evening nap and is cranky."

"Yes, well, there was only one spot available in the nursery and I thought Mr. Cresswell should take it."

I hid my smile as Thomas stared down the ringmaster like he was a reanimated corpse.

"Miss Wadsworth?" Mephistopheles asked, tone lacking any decorum or patience. "Shall we?"

He offered his arm, but I ignored it and hauled off toward the promenade deck without assistance. I was already in a rotten mood thanks to the tarot reading, and now the sudden appearance of Mephistopheles, the Devil himself, turned my disposition even more sour. Confused over my feelings indeed. I'd show Andreas how faulty his cards were.

Once we made it to the end of the deck free from passengers and performers alike, I whirled on him. "You're trying to irk Thomas and it's not fair to me. When I agreed to help you it was also supposed to benefit *me*, remember? This"—I motioned between us—"is not beneficial. What is so important that you require my assistance *this* moment? You seemed to be having fun with Jian and Anishaa, not searching for me."

"Not here." Mephistopheles pointed toward the corridor leading a few floors below. I tried to hide my shiver as we entered the dimly lit hall and walked swiftly down the flight of narrow stairs. Our footsteps echoed along the metal stairs, alerting anyone below of our arrival. I wanted to ask about the playing cards and how cartomancy might play into the killings, but didn't wish to do so when we were so far from other people.

We came to the end of the stairwell, and I was amazed when it opened into a vast storage space that must have taken up at least a quarter of the entire hull. Cage after cage of iron bars and exotic animals lined each side of the cavernous room. Monkeys and tigers, lions, elephants, and wolves whiter than snow. I paused near the zebras, admiring their contrasting colors.

"Well?" I faced the ringmaster, hands on my hips. "What urgent matter do you have?"

Standing there alone with him, I tried not to think about last evening, his hands on my waist, laughing like I was some other person as he twirled me around. How free I'd felt for a moment.

"I've noticed you haven't given Liza the letter yet." He ran his gloved hands down the side of one cage, inspecting them before brushing them off. "Would you prefer if I did it? Then you might act as if your hands aren't stained in the nastiness of the matter."

"Is this why you wanted to talk?" I bristled at his tone. "How is opening someone's eyes to the truth a terrible thing?"

He stopped walking down the line of cages, facing me. "Sometimes we choose not to see things we know are true, simply because we wish to keep the fantasy of what could have been alive. To see the realness of a thing, well, sometimes that removes hope. An unfortunate side effect. As a scientist you must know that. You cannot always remove a tumor without taking a bit of the surrounding healthy tissues, can you?"

I crossed my arms over my chest. "No, I do not require your assistance. And I don't wish to wax poetic on how speaking the truth is like removing a tumor, or any other such nonsense. Was there anything else you needed, or did you only intend to irritate me?"

"You anger rather quickly," he said. "I enjoy chaos, remember? I like studying reactions. You weren't so quick to be rid of me last night."

A flush crept along my skin.

"Any other parting words of wisdom, or might I go back to the carnival?"

Mephistopheles marched up to the lion's cage, a muscle in his jaw twitching in annoyance. "Apologies for interrupting your romantic evening, Miss Wadsworth. But I thought you might want to see what I discovered before I alert the overbearing captain." He jerked his chin toward the back of the cage. Judging from the strong earthy scent hanging in the air, the hay had been freshly changed.

I doubted he'd dragged me down here to see that, so I carefully leaned closer and jerked back. There were splatters of blood on the floor of the cage. But that couldn't be right. I inhaled deeply, and exhaled. There was a logical explanation waiting, I simply needed to think like a scientist.

"Don't you feed the lions fresh meat?" I asked. My brain refused to acknowledge what my eyes were reporting as truth—the basis for all good illusions. "I'm sure it's simply—"

"The severed limb that's to blame?" He pointed to something I'd not noticed at first; it was stiff and protruding from the hay. I closed my eyes briefly and cursed.

A pale arm gnawed to the bone at one end.

Unless it was a *very* detailed prop for the carnival, it was all too real. No illusion or trick. "Yes, I'm quite sure that does explain all the blood. How silly of me to require your assistance with sorting that out."

I shot him an irritated look. "Don't be cross with me. I'm not the one trying to destroy your carnival. Perhaps you should have thought of these consequences before carrying on a flirtation with a married woman."

"My carnival is in peril and there's a severed arm in front of you, yet you'd like to discuss my sleeping arrangements?"

"When they might be the *cause* of said issues? Yes."

I pushed past him, noting the shock on his face, and edged around the back of the cage, trying to get a better view of the arm. With the freshly laid hay, it was difficult to tell if someone had been killed *in* the cage or if the arm had simply been tossed in after.

"You need to have the lion removed from there immediately," I said. "This whole cage needs to be secured and scoured for clues."

I inspected the lion. It was impossible to tell how much of the body he'd consumed—perhaps it was just the one arm, meant to distract us. The large cat lazily washed himself, licking his paws, then dragging them behind his ears in a contented way only a full belly could provide. My own stomach flipped at the implication of such actions. Tonight had been so close to ending without another death.

"Shouldn't this animal be with the others for the show?"

Mephistopheles stepped closer. "It appears he's too full to be of use. Which is probably why he was left behind."

"That means this was deposited prior to the show."

I swallowed my revulsion down. I could not allow my emotions to surface now—perhaps not ever. I'd witnessed a lot in my uncle's laboratory—cruelty almost too violent to be believed. But this? This was an entirely new level of horrific. To toss someone to an animal to feed upon... it was monstrous.

"You need to summon my uncle," I added, noting Mephistopheles hadn't yet moved. "And Thomas. We need them. Someone is dead. Whoever did this is out to ruin your show—you better hope we can prove it's Cassie and her husband, or you might be the one held responsible."

"*That* is your best deduction?" Mephistopheles crossed his arms and scowled. It was hardly the sort of reaction I expected from anyone who'd stumbled across a dismembered piece of a body. If he was free of guilt, he was doing a terrible job of proving it. "Cassie and I, handsome though we might be together, were never lovers. She wanted to, but I declined. Mixing business with pleasure is never a good idea. Though I cannot tell if you're simply curious for your own reasons. Perhaps you're jealous."

"Are you entirely mad? You wish I were jealous."

He seemed to think on it. "Yes, actually, I do. Regardless of that, if I wanted to involve your uncle or that arrogant assistant of his immediately, I would have done so. What I want is for *you* to investigate first. *Then* I will fetch those two. I need discretion—the carnival cannot keep withstanding these blows. I'm doing everything I can to keep the acts going, to distract patrons, but even I cannot produce miracles. I need you to help me."

"Thomas is my partner," I argued. "We each have skills that complement the other's."

"And? Are you incapable of simply *looking* at something without either of them?"

We stared at each other, each holding our ground for an exaggerated moment. It was a battle of wills, and if I was selfish, I'd not surrender simply to spite him. Since there was a slain person involved, I took the higher ground.

"Fine," I spat. "But someone needs to get that lion out of the cage *now*. I cannot properly investigate the scene *and* worry about being mauled by that beast."

"Fine," Mephistopheles echoed, brushing past me and snatching the ring of keys from a hook on the wall. "Glad to see there are things you're able to do without assistance."

He stuck the key in the lock and yanked the door open with a screech that made the big cat growl, low and dangerous. Apparently he wasn't as full and docile as I'd thought.

"What are you doing?" I asked.

Mephistopheles swiped a leash from the inside of the cage and held it up as if it were the most obvious thing in the world. "Removing the lion from the cage like you asked. Have you been drinking the Green Fairy again this evening? I thought that was *our* special thing."

"Why are *you* the one getting the lion?" I ground out. "Shouldn't you fetch an expert?"

With a disgusted grunt, the ringmaster turned his back on me and marched toward the lion. Now that I was looking closely, I could see bits of blood stained around its pale muzzle and fleshy parts near its whiskers. Mephistopheles either didn't notice the gore or pretended it wasn't there as he made his way toward the animal. I didn't know whether to be impressed or horrified as the large cat slowly put his paw down and eyed the intruder.

No matter how well trained the lion was, there was a part of him that would forever remain wild. The intelligent gleam in his golden eyes sent gooseflesh skittering along my body. The effect seemed lost on Mephistopheles entirely. He was moving a bit too boldly for his own good.

"Have a care, would you? You're going to get yourself killed," I said, drifting forward, "then I'll have to sort out your blood and entrails from the victim's."

"If that happens, then consider it a test of your immeasurable skill."

I took a steadying breath. "I will not watch this madness."

"Sometimes, for the greater good," he said over his shoulder, "it's necessary to get your hands dirty. Do you trust me, Miss Wadsworth?"

Only a fool would put their faith in someone they didn't know and who prided themselves on illusions. "What on earth is that supposed to mean?"

Instead of responding, Mephistopheles snapped the leash like a whip, setting the other animals chittering in their cages. My gaze fell to the severed arm once more and I quickly looked away. The time would come soon enough to dissect that bloody fragment.

I moved forward, gripping the bars to give myself something to do other than fret as the ringmaster drew within reach of the lion. Unlike the quiet calm of the cat, my pulse was a constant roar I couldn't settle. Dealing with the dismembered arm was horrendous, but bearing witness to an animal attack would be even worse.

Sensing the growing tension, the lion sniffed the air, tufted tail twitching across the blood-splattered hay behind him. He was a coil ready to spring an attack at any moment. I clutched the bars until my knuckles ached.

"Be careful. Please."

I'd whispered barely loud enough for me to hear, so I was surprised when the ringmaster stumbled over a clump of hay and glanced at me. Everything happened too quickly after that. The lion, already suspicious of the masked gentleman inside the cage, sprang up from its hindquarters. Mephistopheles jumped back, but he wasn't fast enough. The lion swiped the front of his waistcoat, tearing the material with no effort. I could only imagine what those claws could do to bare flesh. If he didn't escape soon, I was going to find out.

"Run!" I yelled. "Hurry!"

Mephistopheles fell, scrambling backward like a crab scuttling away. Without a doubt, he was going to die. My heart pounded a battle cry. I scanned the dimly lit chamber, searching for something to use against the lion. My attention fell on a cane—without thought, I grabbed it and raced for the side opposite Mephistopheles, running the cane across the bars, creating the most dreadful racket.

In my mind I fancied it a fabulous distraction, but reality was not my friend. The lion paid me no attention; he plodded forward, eyes never leaving his prey.

"Hey!" I smacked the bars now as if I were a cricket player. The result was a metallic clang that nearly rattled my teeth. This made the lion pause at least. I used all my strength to hit the bars again and again, the sound so loud it refused to be ignored. Finally, the lion turned its head, annoyance plain in the twitch of its tail. Both the big cat and the ringmaster stared dully at me, as if waiting for the next bang on the rungs. "Run, you bloody fool!"

Mephistopheles shook himself out of his stupor and got to his feet; he turned his back on the big cat and was nearly to the cage door when the animal whirled around and struck him a second time. I screamed, convinced I was going to see him torn limb from limb. The unexpected shrillness startled the lion—it wasn't much, but it was enough for Mephistopheles to tumble out of the cage and kick the door shut.

I darted around the cage, fastened the lock, and dragged the ringmaster to safety. He cringed at my rough handling, but didn't cry out. I had no idea if that was a good sign or not. Perhaps he'd been injured so badly he was going into shock. Corpses were one thing; nursing a living body back to health was not my area of expertise.

"Are you hurt?" I ripped my gloves off, running swift hands over the front of him, searching for any obvious wounds. His clothing was tattered in the front, but I didn't see any blood. Yet. "Any pain you're aware of at all? How many fingers am I holding up?"

I couldn't remember much else to ask, the dead didn't usually tell me what had hurt until I cut them open and rooted around for clues.

He blinked slowly from behind his signature mask, seeming to consider this. I had no idea if he was thinking about potential pain or if he was about to pass out. "It's...difficult...to tell. Perhaps my back?"

He struggled to sit up, then winced. With swift medical efficiency, I propped him up against the wall and wrestled his coat and waistcoat off. I knelt beside him and tugged his cravat away in a brisk motion even I was impressed by. My bare fingers were already undoing the buttons at his collar when I paused, suddenly aware of our position and what I was doing—if anyone caught us alone down here with his clothes half off, I'd be in a world of scandal.

Mephistopheles blinked at me. "This isn't the first time you've removed a cravat, is it?"

"It would be the first time I used it to strangle someone, though."

"So violent." His eyes fluttered shut and he groaned. I shoved my worries aside. If anyone came down here they'd see an injured man and someone capable of offering medical assistance. Nothing more.

I finished unbuttoning his shirt and pulled it open, quickly inspecting his torso for any signs of damage. There was nothing but unblemished bronze skin. I ran my eyes over him twice to be certain, ignoring the sense of wrongness at his state of undress. I shook my head. He might have internal injuries that would be more worrisome than if his flesh had been torn. Prodding his torso for tenderness might be the best thing to do, though I wasn't sure if it would hurt.

"You haven't sustained any outward injuries to your person." I lifted my gaze to his; we now were very close. Too close. He stared at me, unblinking. "Perhaps you have a concussion. You appear a bit—"

He toppled forward, nearly burying his head in my chest. "Please." The word was a plea in itself. Arms gently came around my waist. "Please accept my apology."

"You have nothing to apologize for." I embraced him back a moment, worried over how hard he'd hit his head. "Come. Let's stand up, shall we?"

After a wobbly attempt, I finally managed to get him on his feet. I held on to him, afraid he'd stumble back down and do more damage to his brain. I was about to offer him his jacket when he staggered into me, pressing us both into the wall as he stopped himself from falling. At this rate, it would take a lifetime to get him to a real physician. Dr. Arden had refused to leave his chambers, and I wasn't sure if there was another doctor aboard the ship.

"Are you all right?" I asked. "If we're moving too fast, then you ought to sit."

His hands slowly came up to cradle my face and he leaned his forehead against mine. Clearly he was having a delusion. "Remember."

"Remember what?"

208

"Our bargain, Miss Wadsworth." He slumped against me and I worried there was some injury to his back that I'd missed. Before I could help stand him upright again, the sound of shoes hitting the stairs two at a time reached us. My first thought was elation that someone else would be able to help with the disoriented ringmaster in my arms. But when I saw it was Thomas who skidded around the corner and stopped short, I could have sworn my heart sank down to my toes.

The ringmaster leisurely pushed himself back, attention torn between me and Thomas. His odd insistence that I remember our bargain suddenly made sense. He'd manufactured this. All of it. I gripped my fists as he stood straighter and began buttoning up his shirt, completely and utterly stable on his feet.

"Mr. Cresswell, I assure you things aren't what they appear," he said, not sounding at all convincing as he donned his tattered jacket. He indicated the tears. "I was under attack and Miss Wadsworth rescued me. It was terribly valiant on her part and quite embarrassing on mine."

Thomas didn't so much as breathe from what I could see, but his sharp gaze was falling all over the room, likely reconstructing the scenario in that astounding way of his. With sadness, I realized he'd looked at everything in the room except for *me*. My uncle and the captain rounded the doorway a moment later with Cassie and halted.

"What on earth is going on?" the captain asked. "You have a performance to give. And this one"—he jabbed a thumb in Cassie's direction—"wouldn't say what the urgency was about. Only that you needed us straightaway."

Mephistopheles stepped away from me and nodded toward the cage. "Miss Wadsworth and I were investigating the mystery of the severed arm. But you're right—the show must go on. At least this murder won't be the main attraction tonight."

With that, he offered a mock bow, signaled to Cassie to follow, and disappeared up the stairs, leaving me alone to deal with the chaos he'd unleashed. I took a deep breath and met Uncle's furious glare. Facing the lion in its cage would be mildly less intimidating, even after its attack.

"I can explain everything, Uncle."

TWENTY
A FINE DEDUCTION

ANIMAL CARGO HOLD
RMS ETRURIA
5 JANUARY 1889

"What in ten hells does he mean by 'mystery of the severed arm'?" Captain Norwood's voice was a boom of thunder in the tense quiet. A monkey near the end of the cargo hold screeched, and I did my best not to flinch from either outburst. The captain was as temperamental as the sea he navigated. "Tell me it's not an *actual* human arm."

"I'm afraid there is a human specimen in the lion's cage," I said, never imagining I'd be stringing those words together. I tore my gaze from the captain and focused on Thomas, hoping to do my best to explain to him—as well as the captain and my uncle—what had just transpired...aside from me wrapped in the arms of an undressed man.

"Mephistopheles was trying to remove the lion when it attacked him," I said. "I haven't been able to fully inspect the scene yet, so I've no further details. From first glance, however, someone has changed out the hay. It's possible it was done in an attempt to tidy up the murder scene, but I won't know for certain until I'm able to get into the cage and have a proper look."

Thomas strode toward the cage and severed limb in question, his focus moving from the large cat to the gnawed arm to God only knew what. He strummed his fingers along the metal bars, the sound dulled thanks to the leather gloves he wore. The captain opened his mouth, but my uncle silenced him with a raised hand. No one ought to interrupt Thomas while he lost himself in those equations only he could see. Not for the first time did I wish to possess a fragment of that particular skill of his.

"This isn't the murder scene," he said, and I knew him enough by this point to not doubt his deduction. "This is simply where the body was left. In fact, I don't believe the rest of the body was ever here. It's likely overboard by now, or the murderer is planning on dumping it soon. Robbery or theft wasn't the motive—see the ring? This crime was either premeditated or done out of convenience."

"You seem mighty confident," the captain muttered. "Perhaps you ought to let Dr. Wadsworth speak, boy."

Thomas closed his eyes, and I could only imagine the sort of things he might be stopping himself from saying aloud. It was incredible, truly, that he'd harnessed himself. A breath later, he pulled his shoulders back and affected a tone that brooked no arguments to his authority on the matter. Despite the current circumstances, I couldn't help but feel a sense of pride. Thomas was magnificent when he used his talents on a case, his confidence well earned. He was maturing from the arrogant young man I'd met last summer.

"Thomas?" Uncle asked. "Care to elaborate for the captain?"

He nodded. "Note the shade of the blood smear on the padlock and the bit of rust color on the keys."

"Get on with it, then," the captain said. Clearly he was in no mood for pleasantries this evening. "Why should I care about the color of blood?"

"Mephistopheles wasn't bleeding, so the smearing on the padlock and the keys did not come from him." Thomas paused a moment and walked around the cage, but I swore I heard an accusation in the silence.

"From that alone it's safe to assume that the blood is either the murderer's or victim's," he continued. His tone was professional, cool, perhaps I'd imagined the tinge of agitation. "It's dark, indicating it wasn't fresh when it was transferred to the lock. I imagine it was almost dried when the murderer touched those things. If this had been the scene of the crime, then there would be blood splatter and massive stains present on the floor. A limb was removed from a person—it would have been a nasty affair. Even with the straw changed, there would be blood on the floors, walls, and ceiling. Have you been to a slaughterhouse, Captain? Messy business, that is. As for the ring? If that was the motive behind the attack, then that would have been the first thing to go."

"Maybe he couldn't get it off her finger," the captain said.

"Then he would have cut it off," I said, earning a disgusted look from the man. As if I were the one who'd shorn the arm off. "And it's not a woman's arm. Our victim is a male. And the ring is a wedding band."

Thomas wound his way between each cage, kicking stray bits of hay as he went. He knelt down, then gazed up, searching the ceiling for blood splatter, I assumed. I followed where his attention landed and blinked. A torn bit of cobalt fabric was caught on something in the low ceiling. It appeared to be silk. I squinted and just made out the outline of a panel. An idea clicked at once. "Where does that access panel lead, Captain?"

"It's simply a maintenance portal connecting this room to the crew corridors." The captain waved it off. "No one aside from select members of the crew has access. And they must first ask me for the key."

"What's it used for?" Thomas prodded. "How large is the compartment?"

"It's mostly for electrical matters," Captain Norwood said. "A man would need to crouch and fold himself over to pass through it. Not an ideal way to transport a body, if that's what you're getting at with this *theory* of yours."

I mulled that information over. Given our experience with murderers as of late, I was only too aware that a killer didn't have to be a man. "A woman wouldn't have much trouble. It would be unwise to discredit anyone at this point, sir." Another more obvious suspect leapt out at me. "Sebastián might also be capable of fitting through there." When they all stared at me blankly, I added, "The contortionist. I've seen him fold himself into knots."

Thomas's expression was carefully blank. I would have much to explain once we were off the ship.

"Miss Wadsworth, I beg your pardon, but allow me to speak plainly—there's no possible way it was used," the captain argued. "As I have just stated, the only set of keys is in *my* possession in *my* quarters. No one has been in there for two days. I'm sure of it. Unless you'd like to accuse me of depositing this limb, that panel is out of the question. You must come up with a better theory of how it came to be here."

I mentally counted to ten. Keys could be lifted, locks picked, and with an entire ship full of carnival performers who made the impossible possible, I felt the captain wasn't being realistic. Houdini was known in both England and America as the King of Handcuffs. He *alone* was gifted with lock picking, squeezing into tight spaces, and making a swift escape.

That thought froze all others, my heart icing over with it. I would need to make it my business to seek Houdini out next to inquire after his whereabouts all afternoon. Preferably before Uncle beat me to the task and set Liza off in a cold fury.

"Mmm." Uncle twisted his mustache, purposely not glancing in my direction. I couldn't deny the sting I felt. He'd been upset with me plenty of times before, but he'd never ignored me while we were investigating a crime scene. "Why do you believe it was the access point for our murderer, Thomas?"

I pressed my lips together, annoyed to be overlooked when I was the first on the scene. Thomas turned his attention to me. There was only a serious steadiness in his gaze when he replied. "Wadsworth? What are your thoughts?"

For a moment, I said nothing. I appreciated Thomas redirecting their attention back to me, but was perturbed I required assistance in the matter at all. Setting those emotions aside for the sake of staying on task, I pointed to the bit of silk.

"The torn silk is one indication that someone passed through there," I said. "The second is the promenade deck has been a flurry of activity all afternoon and evening. Between the crew setting the tents up, and the performers and passengers milling about all night, I don't see how anyone might have smuggled a body or body parts down here without drawing some attention. *Unless* they used a means other than the main stairwell to come down here."

"Good." Uncle motioned to the lion, which had taken to pacing around his enclosure. "Once the cage is empty, we'll know more." He faced the captain, gaze hard. "It's your boat, Captain, but I suggest posting crew members on every deck overnight. If the murderer is still in possession of the rest of the body, he'll be desperate to rid himself of it. I wouldn't be surprised if he tried tossing it overboard in the hours before sunrise."

The captain rubbed his temples with enough force to probably give himself a headache if he wasn't already suffering from one. "I cannot have men stationed outside the first-class promenade. How will that look to well-paying passengers? This is not a workhouse and I will not treat my passengers like prisoners. They're not being terror-ized with a theatrical murder tonight and I intend to keep it that way. I will not make them suffer."

I physically had to check to see if my head had exploded from such a ridiculous statement. Gentle prodding of my hair proved my skull was still intact, miracle of all miracles.

"You cannot be serious." Thomas tossed his hands in the air. "It would seem an awful lot better to have crew members posted along the decks than to see dismembered body parts floating about while first-class patrons made their way to breakfast and tea. 'Oh, look, Miss Eldridge, there's a mauled torso. Won't you pass the cream and sugar?'"

"Don't be absurd," the captain said, aghast.

"Apologies," Thomas said, not sounding at all sorry, "I'm only following your lead."

Uncle took his spectacles off and rubbed out imaginary smudges. "I beg your pardon, Captain. My assistants and I mean no disrespect, but you cannot pretend as if something sinister isn't happening. Sta-tion crew outside as a precaution, or this won't be the last time we're having this conversation before reaching New York. How many bod-ies must we discover before some safety measures are enacted?"

Captain Norwood gripped his hands tightly at his sides. "You are one of the most sought-after men in your field, Doctor. Show me what you and your assistants can do. I will post crew on the second- and third-class decks. You want to put your fellow gentlemen and ladies under the microscope? Then do so on your own. I will not give the command to insult them, especially not after the horrors they've been subjected to this week. There are only two days left at sea."

The captain turned to go, then glared over his shoulder. "After midnight—once the carnival is closed—I'll have the lion removed. Then you'll be free to investigate as you see fit. Until I send word, which may be after midnight or in the morning, you're to do as you like. So long as you don't mention this unfortunate event to anyone. I will have an evening free of murder and terror, and I will send each of you to the brig should you incite any panic."

Captain Norwood ushered us back up to the carnival and posted a guard outside the stairwell, allowing no one entry to the animal cargo. We were to wait until the show was over, heaven forbid we disrupt the entertainment of the rich and powerful. At least I hoped he'd send word for us after midnight; there was still a possibility he'd change his mind and not allow us back down in the crime scene until the early morning hours.

"You and I will be having a serious discussion," Uncle said, expression icy as the arctic wind blasting around us. "Until then, you are to remain with Thomas. Do we understand one another?"

I swallowed hard. "Yes, sir."

Without acknowledging me further, Uncle marched off toward his chambers.

Thomas remained silent beside me, though I could tell he was battling his own feelings. I rubbed my arms, watching a crew member hoist a carrying bag up and hold it to his chest. He'd been the lucky one tasked with transporting the severed limb to the icebox. I tried not to cringe as I thought of all the ways the scene and limb had now been contaminated. Our job had just gotten that much harder.

"I cannot fathom why Captain Norwood is so opposed to setting out a few night watchmen in first class," I said as we stood at the far end of the promenade. Revelers were still enchanted by the carnival tents that had been set up bazaar-style down the deck, laughing and milling about from one billowing striped stall to the next. Though I also noticed quite a few people who glanced over their shoulders or didn't quite laugh as hard or smile as widely as their companions. The atmosphere was muted, almost as if it was the calm before the storm. "You don't believe he's covering up for someone, do you? It's quite odd that he's less concerned over another murder."

Thomas stood near me, careful not to touch my arm as he stared out at the midnight ocean. I tried telling myself I was unaffected by his rigid stance, but knew it was yet another lie I could add to the tally. Finally, he lifted a shoulder. "I must admit that I'm struggling here, Audrey Rose."

I swallowed my immediate response, knowing instantly by his use of my Christian name that we weren't speaking of the captain. A breeze whipped sea mist into my face—stinging my eyes almost as much as the sadness in Thomas's tone. "I swear things will be back to normal soon. I need you to trust me, Thomas."

"I do." He sighed, then scrubbed a hand over his face. It was very un-Thomas-like. His dark hair was tousled in a way that hinted at his inner turmoil. "Which is part of the issue, I believe. What sort of bargain did you make with Mephistopheles?"

I tensed, glancing around to be sure we were alone. A stilt walker in ghostly shades of white and gray tottered down the promenade, her disjointed movements an eerie sight against the darkness of the ocean. We were straying too close to the terms of my agreement, and issues with Thomas or not, I could not jeopardize Liza's welfare.

"I'm not sure I understand your accusation," I said, finding a spot on the railing to buff with my sleeve. "I haven't accepted any deal with the ringmaster. You're losing your touch with deductions, Cresswell."

A moment of silence stretched between us, heavy and uncomfortable. "Would you care to know something interesting about my deductions?" Thomas finally asked, turning to me. "Your gaze drops ever so slightly, then rises when you lie. It's your signal—I've seen you do it to Moldoveanu and to your father." He searched my face, his own shuttering so I could no longer read the hurt in his expression. "We promised we'd never lie to each other." He inhaled deeply as if giving himself a moment to collect his thoughts or perhaps utter something he didn't wish to get wrong. "I'm sure you can find a way to be truthful to me *and* adhere to the terms of your bargain. We're partners. Equals. Let me in so I may help."

I wanted that more than anything and racked my brain for the thousandth time. But I saw no way around Mephistopheles's terms. If I admitted to any collusion, it would be the end of our agreement. Liza would never give up Harry Houdini on her own, and we were running out of time. We arrived in America in two days, and if I lost her there, she'd be gone to us forever.

I gripped my own fists, hoping the pain of my nails sinking into my flesh would keep my resolve strong. I hadn't put my gloves back on and could feel the phantom sensation of Mephistopheles's warm skin beneath my touch.

"I swear that I've done nothing immoral." It was the truth, though by the way Thomas's gaze grew distant, I knew it had been another horridly wrong thing to say.

"I see." He took a careful step away, the chasm splitting my chest in half. "I hope you have a good evening."

"Thomas...please," I said, stomach twisting. He shook his head, then started walking away. "I—wait!"

Without turning, he paused. "I'm—I need to get some rest before we're called back to investigate the scene. A cluttered mind makes for messy investigating. Good night, Wadsworth."

I took a few steps and forced myself to let him go. I wasn't surprised that he'd studied me so closely while we were at the Academy of Forensic Medicine and Science. Headmaster Moldoveanu was a wretched man whom I'd had to stretch the truth to from time to time. And my father...prior to his acceptance of my passion for forensic medicine, I'd had to hide my apprenticeship with my uncle. Lying had been a necessary evil, one I was not proud of.

I buried my face in my hands. Warranted or not, the fact remained I had lied. Thomas had every reason to question me, though I wished more than anything he could see the truth: I'd never hurt him.

"Ah, the dark prince flees on the midnight breeze." Mephistopheles held a glass of champagne high before sipping it. "He's right, you know. You do glance down when you lie."

TWENTY-ONE

BLACK AS HIS SOUL

PROMENADE
RMS ETRURIA
5 JANUARY 1889

I spun around. "Have you any honor at all? Not to mention, it's creepy and not endearing when you suddenly appear like that."

Mephistopheles's mask was black as the night around us. Black as his devilish soul. And perhaps as black as his eye would be if he ever sneaked up on me again while a confirmed murderer was roaming about.

He tossed back the rest of his drink and pointed to his seat where a box of half-eaten popcorn lay next to an empty champagne bottle. "I've *been* sitting here, it's not my fault you're both so unobservant."

I gritted my teeth. "How long have you been listening to us, then?"

"Long enough to congratulate you on maintaining that illusion of innocence," he said. "Paltry an attempt though it may be. Let's both agree that acting is not where your true talents lie. Though from what I've seen thus far, your sleuthing hasn't been much better. At least you are fairly pleasant on the eyes. And your dancing is surprisingly decent."

"Are you here for any real purpose or are you bored with playing parlor tricks for people?" I asked, face heating. "Or—most likely—are you simply enjoying the trouble you've caused between me and Thomas?"

"I never tire of tricks." He smiled. "Much like you never tire of inspecting cadavers."

"That hardly gives us something in common," I said.

"If you say so." He shrugged. "I disagree, though."

"By the by," I said, anger from his lion cage stunt blazing fresh, "I don't know what the point of your demonstration was earlier, but my uncle will send me back to London if I'm caught alone with you again. If you endanger my future with forensics, I will break our agreement."

"Perhaps I simply wanted to see if you cared for me or if *everything* is an act. You're becoming quite the accomplished show-woman, even if you do look down when you lie."

I opened my mouth, then shut it. He gave me a knowing look. "If your uncle would send you home because of that, perhaps studying under someone else would benefit you. You might consider studying my brand of science for a while." He waved off any further rebuttals with a flick of his wrist. "While we could chatter on endlessly over our personal dramas, I have news. Your cousin is meeting Houdini onstage after midnight. Alone. Quite scandalous for a runaway society girl traveling with a troupe of misfits."

I rolled my eyes. "She's been traveling with you for more than a week, and now you're concerned about the scandal?"

"I recall mention of your uncle threatening to commit her should she be alone with Houdini again. See? I've been sitting here, patiently waiting for you to finish with your investigation, so I might pass the news on to you immediately."

I nearly groaned. At the rate Liza and I were going, we'd both end up in adjacent cells in the asylum. "What are they doing?"

"They're working on Harry's new performance for tomorrow's show, very secretive but I've seen a preview. Now *that* one is tricky. And death defying. If he gets the timing down. Might just be death for whoever enters the milk can, though."

If ever there was a time to consider swimming back to England, this was it. Not only was Liza meeting with Houdini, but now she planned on assisting with another stage act after she'd sworn to Uncle she'd never do so again.

"The milk can?" I finally asked, knowing he was baiting me into inquiring further. "That doesn't sound very death defying. What about the handcuff act? Seems he ought to focus on being the king of one thing at a time."

"You didn't expect Harry Houdini to sit back, content with wearing one crown, did you?" Mephistopheles narrowed his dark eyes as if I might have honestly hit my head on something. "Why simply be good when you can be great? If he's going to claim the name 'the Great Houdini,' he'd better put on a show to match. People don't remember mediocre shows. To truly win the minds and memories of the audience, *greatness* is needed. That's what turns stories into legends and builds empires."

"Finding new ways of barely escaping with one's life isn't greatness. It's foolhardy and dangerous," I said. "Involving someone else in such stupidity is reckless and ought to be a criminal offense. If anything happens to my cousin, it will be his fault. Then he'll discover that kings fall like anyone else."

"Ah. I must disagree with you on one thing. Greatness lies in being driven, in not settling simply because you've reached one goal. It's a state of perpetual climbing and striving to best yourself. He will be the Great Houdini one day because he worked to earn that title, doing one impossible task after the other, never settling for simply being *good.*"

"Seems he doesn't enjoy being content with what he's accomplished."

"Contentment is the root of complacency. Your cousin chooses to follow him because he is not content to sit back and be just mediocre. Does 'the Good Houdini' or 'the Adequate Houdini' have the same ring to it?" He shook his head. "I think not. Just like a good tailcoat is not as eye-catching as a *great* one."

"Is that why you abandoned your family name?" I asked, fishing. "You weren't all right with living in contentment and luxury—it was just good, not great."

Mephistopheles turned his attention on the well-dressed men and women walking through the carnival stalls on the promenade. There were far fewer of them, and they appeared to have lost that earlier glamour. "Why live in a cage when you can make a show of escaping from it?"

"I—"

"Tell me that life doesn't sound appealing to you."

I opened my mouth, but no words came out. Mephistopheles gave me another knowing look, but didn't press the issue.

"Shall we go check on Liza and Harry?" He pulled a pocket watch out, swinging it back and forth as if he hoped to hypnotize me from prying into his past. "In a few minutes the curtain will drop for the public, but the private show will begin."

I glanced at the thinning crowd, hoping I'd spy one tall gentleman in particular. One to whom I'd reconcile all this as soon as I could. Unlike the wonder-worker before me, Thomas seemed to have disappeared for good this evening. I gave up searching and let go. I'd see him soon enough when we investigated the lion's cage.

A star shot across the sky and I prayed it wasn't a sign of how fleeting love or friendship could be.

Eerie silence greeted us in the dining saloon now that the Moonlight Carnival had taken its leave of the night. My cousin and her dashing escape artist beau huddled together onstage, their heads bent in whispered conversation. My steps faltered as I watched them work out the details of the act. There was no doubt that conspiring against Liza was treacherous, conniving behavior, and I was the ringleader of the sideshow of my own creating. I hoped she'd forgive me once all was said and done. Though I wasn't sure how long it would take to forgive myself.

Houdini's affections might be an illusion, but she seemed perfectly content with the act.

Mephistopheles whistled to Houdini, lifting a hand in greeting. A look flashed between the two young men—there and gone too fast to decipher its meaning. Perhaps it was simply a warning from the ringmaster to not fail at this new and dangerous stunt. With women murdered almost every night and the discovery of the severed arm, his carnival was teetering on a tightrope of its own. One slip and the entire life Mephistopheles had constructed for himself would be gone.

Liza smiled and hopped off the stage, dashing up to my side in a way that made me feel all the more terrible for going behind her back.

"Cousin! What a lovely surprise." She kissed both my cheeks and gathered me into the sort of hug that lifts a person's spirits as much as their feet from the ground. "I wasn't expecting you out so late. Is Mr. Cresswell coming along, too?"

"He's off brooding," Mephistopheles said as he moved toward the stage. "He's jealous of my suit. Not everyone can get away with decadent patterns and silver fringe."

She craned her neck around, searching the dark shadows of the saloon as if not believing the ringmaster. I shook my head. "He wasn't feeling quite himself and went to bed. We've had a bit of an intense evening."

"Oh."

Liza subtly flicked her attention between myself and Mephistopheles. I could see questions brewing behind her gaze and knew I'd have much to answer for once we were alone. She blinked and the suspicion disappeared. Liza read the living as well as I read the dead.

"I'm sorry he'll miss this"—she motioned to the stage—"but I'm sure he'll be charmed tomorrow evening when he sees it. It's truly magical—I swear there are forces at hand here, guiding Harry in an otherworldly way."

I released a breath, relieved to have the conversation shift to Houdini. Captain Norwood had made it quite clear that we weren't to discuss the severed limb, and even though I trusted my cousin, I didn't want to burden her. "You know magic is simply the union of science and trickery. It's just dressed-up lies."

"And there ain't no such thing as ghosts!" Harry called from the stage. "Spiritualism is a hoax."

"So you keep telling me. Again and again." Liza sighed in the way of the long-suffering and looped her arm through mine, leaning in as to not be overheard by the escape artist. "But it's also *fun*. Being caught up in make-believe is grand and romantic and you cannot *honestly* say you aren't a little intrigued by the impossibility of it all. Hope is the true magic—it's the spark and draw. I know ghosts aren't real, but should I ever wish to speak to a loved one who's no longer here, I *hope* they are."

"Hope is a strong force," I agreed.

"Indeed. I swear I'd clutch that feeling like a tether, never letting go. Same for every one of these acts. The crowd hopes for the impossible to become possible. It shows them dreams don't belong only in our heads—with hope those fantasies can become real. Taking hope away is like taking life from someone. We all need to believe we can achieve the impossible."

I felt a smile coming on. It was a good thing Liza had so much hope; she certainly needed to hope Uncle didn't discover she was the second young woman to disobey him this evening, else we were both doomed. "You're not planning on actually assisting Harry onstage tomorrow, are you?"

Liza flashed a mischievous grin. "Of course not. I wouldn't dream—"

Harry clapped his hands a few times, stalling our conversation. I managed to tear my focus from my cousin and faced the young man. "Ladies! Time's the only boss I obey and he's gettin' impatient." He beckoned to Liza. "I need your help now. I've got to prove it to Mephisto that this ain't a death trap. I got the timin' down good."

I offered a startled glance at my cousin. "Death trap? What does he mean?"

"You'll see."

With a final squeeze of my hand, Liza bounded back up the stage stairs and offered a dramatic bow before disappearing behind the inky curtains. My stomach twisted. Liza had never interfered in my passions, no matter how much society looked down upon me for my scientific pursuits.

During the Ripper investigation she had been the one who'd stood by my side, needling our friends at tea when they'd made fun of Thomas, accusing him of the violent crimes because of his love of science and lack of outward emotion. She was also the one who played the role of perfect daughter, pretending to take me out to dress shops so I might actually sneak about London with Thomas to investigate. And this was how I thought to repay her. Lies and manipulation and midnight bargains with a devilish young man.

Suddenly I was unsure I could go through with my agreement.

Somehow on this voyage, I'd turned into my father—caging those I loved instead of setting them free. It was a terrible truth to swallow, and I nearly choked on its bitter taste.

"Deviousness doesn't suit you, you know. Much to my dismay." Mephistopheles flashed a smug grin. "It might be a fun mask to try on from time to time, but I suggest staying true to yourself. Honesty is best for a reason. If you'd like to revisit the terms of our agreement, say the word."

"I—" Before I answered, Liza rolled a large milk can onstage, shifting so it was dead center. Harry hopped off the stage and ran backward, a feat in itself as he didn't plow into any tables or chairs as he peered at the contraption.

"A little more to the left...another inch...stop! Ain't that perfect?" He crossed his arms and studied the room. "Mark an *X* at each corner—make sure it's small enough to be missed from the seats. Go on and grab the portable curtain. Everything needs to be in working order—we ain't gonna have another chance to make our first impression. This one's gotta be great."

"'Please,'" Mephistopheles added. When Harry raised a dark brow, the ringmaster elaborated. "If you bid your assistant to do something, have the courtesy of using manners. And have a care about using 'ain't'—it's atrocious and distracts from your skill."

"I ain't worried about it," he said. "You shouldn't be, neither. Who else can do the stunts I pull off?" He exaggeratedly glanced around. "No one, that's who."

"You might yank rainbow-colored unicorns from purple clouds and I'd be distracted by your horrible grammar." Mephistopheles smiled. "If not for me, do it for the poor unicorns. Magical creatures deserve proper speech."

Harry rolled his eyes. "Last I checked, this arrangement worked because we stay out of each other's methods. I don't critique your magic or engineering, you don't comment on mine."

"Let's call it a bit of friendly advice from one wonder-worker to the next, then," Mephistopheles said, drifting forward to take a seat. He spilled onto a chair and propped his feet up as if he were lounging in his private quarters and hadn't staged an attack by the lion only an hour before. "You won't win many admirers in this setting if you're rude to young ladies. Do you think Prince Albert ever addressed a crowd like that? If you're going to dress in a tuxedo and starched collar and call yourself a king, complete the gentleman act convincingly. Your New York street vernacular belongs where you picked it up, like a bad case of lice."

An awful smile twitched across the escape artist's lips. "I won't be wearing a tuxedo for this act, boss. But I'll see about adding some pleasantries for the gentry." He turned to Liza with a deep bow. "Will you *please* fetch the portable curtain? We *aren't* going to have another chance at our milk-can debut. We need to show them something with some razzle-dazzle."

Mephistopheles looked faintly amused by Houdini's proper use of manners and grammar, but didn't rise to the bait. While Houdini and Liza set up the rest of the stage to his exact measurements and demands, I allowed my mind the freedom to drift over the evening's events. I couldn't stop imagining the horror the man had endured, leading up to his death. I hoped he hadn't suffered much.

As I took a seat beside Mephistopheles, I did my best to not recall how uncomfortably similar the arm in the icebox was to Jack the Ripper's laboratory and the organs he'd harvested. The ringmaster looked me over, a frown tugging his signature smirk away.

"Have you been in the woman's room, the one who was burned?" he asked, suddenly serious.

Not quite what I thought he was about to say, but I nodded slowly. "Once. When we initially got word she was missing."

He tugged a square of fabric from an inner pocket of his coat. "Anything familiar about it?"

My blood seemed to freeze as I took in the rich scarlet. I recalled the beautiful dress that had been discarded on Miss Crenshaw's floor. I hadn't inspected it closely, but I had been near certain it hadn't been cut up. "Where did you get this?"

"It was left in my cabin two nights ago. No note, no reason why." He took it back, folded it, and secured it into his coat once more. "I thought an attendant must have dropped it while cleaning my room, but now I'm not sure." From a second pocket he flourished another bit of red fabric; this one had spots of rust. Blood. "Same silk. This was delivered last night."

"It appears to be the same silk from Miss Crenshaw."

"'Appears to be'?" Mephistopheles huffed. "Why not say with confidence that it is fabric from her dress? I might play at sleight of hand, but you, Miss Wadsworth, are quite adept at sleight of word."

"As a scientist it's imprudent to say something with certainty when I cannot be sure from first glance," I said coolly. "Therefore, it *appears* to be the same fabric. Unless I had her dress to inspect, I cannot say with absolute authority it *is* the same. Similar, definitely. Exact?" I lifted a shoulder. A muscle in his jaw ticked. "Be annoyed as much as you will, but memory is an even-better illusion worker than yourself. What of your notions regarding 'trick the eyes, convince the mind.' Isn't that the same concept at work?"

"Fine. Will you accompany me to Miss Crenshaw's cabin?" he asked. "We might as well look for scientific evidence that this bit of cut fabric, which *appears* to be hers, is actually from her dress."

"Breaking into her cabin isn't the most sound idea, especially as it's a crime scene."

"Which makes it all the more appealing." He stood and offered a hand. "Let's get on with it. I'm sure the captain will come looking for you soon enough."

"That was hardly a yes."

"True. But it definitely wasn't a no, either." One corner of his mouth lifted. "I know you're as hungry to solve this as I am, Miss Wadsworth. I've started receiving complaints from patrons that aren't very promising for the Moonlight Carnival's future. Now, will you help me break into her chambers or not? As you said, she's dead. I doubt she'll mind our investigating."

I pointed half-heartedly at the stage. "What about the milk-can act?"

"You'll simply have to wait until tomorrow night and experience it with the rest of the passengers." He held his hand out again. "Ready for some mild criminal activity?"

I most certainly was not. With a sinking feeling dragging me down, I stood and followed the illusionist to the empty chamber of the murdered woman, already regretting my foolishness.

TWENTY-TWO
CAKE AND MASKS

PROMENADE
RMS ETRURIA
5 JANUARY 1889

We exited onto the promenade deck, discovering a different type of chaos from the one we'd walked through only half an hour before.

Like a swarm of ants, the crew and performers disassembled tents, folding striped canvas of black, white, and silver, packing it away for another moonlit revelry. Gone were the passengers indulging in all manner of wickedness beyond candy and treats. Scantily clad stilt walkers no longer danced like ghostly snakes in baskets, swaying to the rhythm of both the sea and seductive music. Clowns and fancy ladies smeared their waxy makeup until it looked like torn flesh over their own skin. However, no matter how tired and bedraggled the performers appeared, none of them had removed their masks.

"Why do they all keep their masks on after the show?"

Mephistopheles jerked his chin forward. "They earn twenty dollars a week plus cake with one stipulation: they are never to be seen unmasked. Ever."

"All you offer to feed them is cake?" I raised a brow. "And they agree to such things?"

"Hardly." He snorted. "It means food is included in their wage."

I frowned at the carnival jargon *and* stipulation; there were an awful lot of rules for a band of people who wished to live without them. "You don't hold Harry Houdini to the mask clause," I pointed out. "Doesn't that cause internal strife? I should think the rules ought to apply to everyone or none at all."

With a nod to detour around the opposite side of the ship, the ringmaster guided me forward, along the empty starboard deck. Here we were alone with the creaking of rope and slumbering passengers. I tried not to shudder as the wind snapped at my collar, violent and threatening as any disturbed beast.

"Harry is different," Mephistopheles finally said. "He's going to be a legend one day, mark my words. A man like him already wears a mask—he's creating himself from the ashes of what he once was. Why make him wear a disguise when he becomes a new person each night, shedding a bit more of the old Harry?"

"Who is the old Harry?"

I didn't truly expect an answer, but Mephistopheles was full of surprises.

"He's a Hungarian immigrant, but you know where he tells people he's from? Appleton, Wisconsin. Harry's got so many invisible masks, a physical one would never be as authentic."

"Is Harry even his real name?" I asked, jesting.

"Nope. It's Ehrich."

"Ehrich?"

"Ehrich Weiss. If that's even true. No one but his mother can really be sure." He counted off the cabins and slowed. "Here we are."

We halted outside a cabin two doors down from the stern of the ship. Remembering Uncle's insistence that murderers often revisit their crime scenes, I spun in place, taking in the surrounding area. Across from us there was the railing and endless sea. On either side of the cabin, rowboats were mounted on the wall like prized animal specimens. There wasn't much in the way of hiding places, so I wondered how her body had been removed.

"How do you know which cabin is Miss Crenshaw's?" I asked, suddenly. He hadn't been present when we'd investigated her room. "Have you been here before? How did you recognize that scrap belonged to her dress?" Another thought crashed into me and I narrowed my eyes. "Were you lovers?"

"Is that jealousy I detect? There's plenty of me for everyone, Miss Wadsworth. Though if you'd like to be my one and only, we might need to address the Cresswell situation. Once I've committed myself, I do not enjoy sharing."

I didn't deign to respond to such idiocy. Though it did add another layer to the mystery of Miss Crenshaw's last hours. If she'd been with the ringmaster, might someone have been watching his movements? It made me think of Cassie again—had she been jealous of his late-night escapades? Or did her husband follow him here, hoping to set him up for the crimes?

Mephistopheles patted down the front of his waistcoat, frowning. He turned out his pockets, felt along the rim of his top hat, and then bent down to fumble around the soles of his boots. "Just... another... moment."

"Honestly?" I asked, rolling my eyes skyward once I figured out what he was searching for. "How do you of all people not have a lockpick?"

"Do I look like Houdini to you?" He bristled. "*He's* the King of Cuffs."

"Obviously, else we'd be inside investigating by now instead of dawdling."

I removed one of my hatpins and nudged the ringmaster out of the way with my hip. He whistled in appreciation when I stuck the pin into the lock, jiggling it around until I heard the faint sound of tumblers clicking. Houdini wasn't the only one blessed with that skill. Perhaps if I did run off with the circus, I might practice and call myself the Queen of Cuffs. Saying a silent thank you to my father for the trick, I took one quick breath and pushed the door open.

"Look who's a wonder-worker now," I called over my shoulder. "Perhaps I'll assist Mr. Houdini with his next daring escape."

"How—"

I swept into the cabin and stopped short. Though the cabin was unlit, moonlight spilled from the open doorway across the threshold, and I was able to make out a silhouette sitting upright in the bed. Either someone had stacked their pillows into a human shape, or we'd broken into an occupied room by mistake.

Mephistopheles bumped into me and cursed. "We ought to close the door—"

"Good idea. It's a bit drafty otherwise," the silhouette said, then unfolded itself to a standing position. "Perhaps you ought to lock it, too. Wouldn't want to give anyone the wrong impression of what you're both doing here. Unchaperoned. After midnight. Doesn't look very good."

It had taken a few seconds to register that the voice was not at all who I'd expected it might be. "Thomas." My heart nearly leapt from my chest in its haste to escape this dreadful situation. "What in the name of the queen are you doing sitting here in the dark?"

In answer, a light flared to life on a bedside table. Thomas held his lantern up and motioned to the room. It was perfectly intact—not a thing out of place. Corners of the bedsheets were pulled taut, the vanity carefully arranged with jewels and makeup. All seemed perfectly ordinary, with the exception of the three of us. Someone had obviously cleaned up the room since the last time we'd been here.

I opened my mouth, but words failed. His behavior was always somewhat peculiar; however, this was strange even by his standards.

"Sometimes I find it helps to place myself in the victim's last known location. If I sit quietly, I can re-create a scene." Thomas cocked his head. "What, exactly, brings you both here? Did you discover something about Miss Crenshaw or..."

His tone was composed and cordial enough, but the flash of whatever *that* was in his expression immediately set my teeth on edge.

"We were out for a romantic stroll and decided to cap off the evening with a visit to a dead woman's room. Stolen kisses around rotting carcasses are all the rage. I'm surprised you haven't given it a go yourself." Before he schooled his features, I saw the hurt in his expression. "Honestly. What sort of question is that, Cresswell?"

Thomas drew back so suddenly I forgot my ire. He crinkled his nose. "What in God's name is that foul scent?" he asked. "It's awful." He swatted the air in front of his nose. "Putrid, even."

"What?" I leaned forward, annoyance forgotten. Last time we'd smelled something terrible it was back at the academy, and the discovery of a decomposing body had been close behind. I shoved that memory away, not wanting to think about the bats in that wretched chamber. I sniffed around, expecting the worst. "I don't smell anything unusual."

"Oh. Never mind." Thomas leaned back. "It's simply your attitude, Miss Wadsworth. It stinks."

Mephistopheles actually bent over, wheezing with laughter, and I flashed him a glare that promised sudden death should he utter one more sound. He straightened and slowly backed away, hands up in surrender, though his chest shook with suppressed laughter.

"Well, now. This has taken quite a dramatic turn." Mephistopheles pulled out his pocket watch as if he was only now remembering an appointment with Satan. "Miss Wadsworth?" I glanced at the ring-master as he strode toward the door and wrenched it open. "Truth is poison. Beware how much you ingest at once."

"Would you cease with the fortune-telling advice, already?"

"Be even more careful with how much you dispense." He looked pointedly at Thomas, ignoring my jibe. "Good evening to you both."

TWENTY-THREE

DEDUCTIONS AND DECEIT

MISS CRENSHAW'S CABIN
RMS ETRURIA
5 JANUARY 1889

I cringed. The ringmaster certainly hadn't done me any favors by uttering that as a parting gift. Once the door clicked shut, Thomas sat back on the bed, the tension seeming to go out of him at once.

"It was a simple question, Wadsworth. Not an accusation. I've said it before—I will *always* respect your wishes on whomever you choose to spend your time or your life with."

I sighed. "I understand why you're upset, I do. And I believe you're entitled to being angry—"

"I'm not angry."

His response came a little too quickly for it to be the truth. I let it go. It was something we could address once we made it to America. "Another person is dead, Thomas. Our work must come first."

"Technically, we don't know that he's *dead*. Perhaps his arm was properly amputated." He tapped his fingers along his thighs, drawing my attention. "Until we examine the limb in detail, we cannot be sure he's not alive somewhere."

"Do you truly believe that?" I asked. "If his arm hadn't been amputated properly, he'd have bled out."

"It's unlikely he's living, given the three other murders, but it remains possible." He ticked off reasons like numbers to add up or subtract. "We're aboard a ship with a traveling carnival. The engineering equipment they have is dangerous—he might have been trying to operate something and mangled his arm. Perhaps whoever had been showing him a demonstration panicked. The ship itself has any number of places where a person might be injured. Do I believe any of those to be the actual events that occurred?" He shook his head. "Unfortunately, I do not. Which is why I'm trying to piece the puzzle together. I believe this is the scene of the first *actual* murder. Logically, first crimes ought to hold the potential for the most mistakes made. It's where a murderer puts his dark fantasies into practice, though it rarely goes as planned. I'm hoping to find a clue to how this all began."

"In the dark?"

"I'd just sneaked in myself. I heard someone coming and shut off the lights." He narrowed his eyes. "You thought I was sitting here in the dark, staring at a wall? Is *that* why you appeared so surprised?" He gave me a dry look. "That's a bit eccentric, even for me."

"Thomas, I . . . we weren't—"

"Please"—he patted the bed next to him, no trace of impropriety on his face—"let's sit here a moment. There's something I've been meaning to—" He shifted uncomfortably. "Would you still like me to walk you through my method?"

I had an inkling he'd changed his mind halfway through his sentence, but didn't press the issue. What he was offering now was an olive branch—an extension of peace for both of us to move past the things that didn't matter to the case.

I walked to the bed and sat beside him. "I'd enjoy that very much. Tell me, how does Mr. Thomas James Dorin Cresswell apply his deductions to a scene such as this?"

"The incredibly *handsome* and talented Thomas James Dorin Cresswell, you mean." A faint smile ghosted across his face. "Start with obvious scenarios. Basic truths. What do we already know about the scene?"

"Well," I started, trying to recall the room as it had been. "There were two champagne flutes. A half-eaten cake and a discarded dress. The poisonous berries weren't found, so they must have been eaten before the cake."

Thomas nodded. "And yet, I'm beginning to wonder if that's what actually killed her, or if they had only rendered her incapable of fighting someone off. Which might mean . . ."

"Which might mean there was more than one person involved."

My pulse sped up with this theory. It was another strong indication that, perhaps, a husband-and-wife team had been working together to commit these acts. But then . . . "Mephistopheles claimed to have spent time with her before the ship left. Someone sent him pieces of her cut dress."

Thomas considered this. If I expected to read any emotions on his face after learning of the ringmaster's prowling, I was sorely disappointed. He was as cold and analytical as ever. "He might be lying. There's a strong possibility that he cut pieces of the dress himself, hoping to use it as sleight of hand."

"But what would be the point?" I asked, unconvinced. "Wouldn't it only throw suspicion on him? He just as easily could have pretended to not know her or have been in her room. Who would have known?"

"Secrets never stay buried for long. Someone could have seen him and he might be covering for that potential."

I sighed, hoping his personal dislike of the ringmaster didn't interfere with his normal deductions. We sat in silence, each mulling over our thoughts.

Finally, I broke the quiet. "All right. Let's start somewhere else. Say Mephistopheles did simply come over, have some champagne, and they..." I blushed, not wanting to go into detail of what might have transpired after that drink. "Then he left. Maybe someone had the cake and berries sent to her, pretending it was a token of love from him. There was only one plate and one fork. Then, after enough time had gone by and she'd gotten ill, the murderer made his move."

"Interesting." A spark of intrigue lit in Thomas's gaze. "Where would the point of entry be for the potential murderer?"

"That's quite easy," I said, motioning in front of us. "The door. It's the only way in or out of this room."

"Precisely. We ought to check it for any pry marks or"—he went rigid—"look."

I stared toward the closed door. At first I didn't see anything at all—then I squinted. Tiny spots of blood arced over the back of it. "That's an odd pattern, don't you think?"

In two long strides Thomas was examining the door with me right behind him. He rubbed his chin, probably to keep himself from touching potential evidence. His eyes darted over everything, calculating and deducing in ways I wished to bear witness to from the inside.

"Let's playact a murder, Wadsworth."

Despite the dire circumstances and the horrid story the blood splatter told, I smiled, and Thomas did the same. Perhaps we were both as devilish as the performers of the Moonlight Carnival. "I'll play the part of the victim," I said. "You're a much-better murderer."

"True." He opened the door and stepped outside. "I haven't been caught yet."

"Heathen." I rolled my eyes, but shut the door after him, waiting.

A moment later he knocked and I pushed all distracting thoughts aside. It wasn't hard to imagine how Miss Crenshaw felt as a soft knock came at her private chambers. Had the effects of the poison already begun? Did she stumble to the door, hoping to find help?

Heart racing as quick as a mouse, I cracked the door. Had she been expecting her visitor or was it a surprise caller? That would likely remain a mystery.

Thomas stood with his top hat tilted forward, casting his sharp features in shadow. Even though I knew it was him, a shudder crept along my spine. He lifted his head, but I couldn't make out his eyes. This part of the promenade was exceptionally dark even with the moon near full capacity.

"Listen," I whispered.

Waves lapped at the hull, the noise rhythmic and dulling. Steam churned and hissed from one of the nearby funnels. White noise. It might have assisted with covering up the muffled sounds of a struggle, should anyone have been awake in neighboring cabins.

"I imagine she must have known her attacker," he said, running his hands along the doorframe. "There are no scratches or marks outside the door to prove it's been pried open."

"I agree. Or she might have been too sick to refuse any assistance."

I opened the door wider, granting him entry. Once he'd stepped back inside, I remained close, studying the blood splatter. There were only a few inches between us and I could feel the heat of his body. I wondered if Miss Crenshaw had felt the same way before she'd been attacked. Did she stand as close to her murderer? Did she feel the warmth of him before he'd struck that fatal blow?

"There's no sign of a struggle in here, either," I continued, "so the attack must have happened shortly after she'd let the person in."

Thomas nodded. "Her ring was still on her finger, so it wasn't a theft. And if I recall correctly, though it was only a brief inspection, there weren't any defensive wounds on her hands. Aside from the cuts she made while clenching them. Why might that be?"

I thought on it a moment, staring directly at Thomas's chest as an idea unfurled in my mind. "Because, as you said, he struck her almost as quickly as she'd invited him in. If she was ill, her reflexes wouldn't have been quick enough to react."

For once I knew what Thomas experienced while he transported himself during our forensic cases. Instead of being prey, I became predator. My own darkness glittered like the eyes of a starving mutt at a feast, and I didn't try to stop or control its every ravenous whim.

It was both glorious and terrifying, knowing how the mind of a murderer worked, what it desired, and how it felt to hold someone's life in your hands. Sure and steady as my scalpel, I had the power to choose how to end it all with a swift flick of my blade. How to end *him*.

Power was as heady and intoxicating a feeling as the champagne Thomas and I had drunk together at the Christmas ball a fortnight ago. One teeny movement and I decided his fate. Thomas's destiny was no longer written in the stars or by any god the heavens might possess; it was my judgment to make.

I was neither merciful nor kind.

I was justice and my blade was cold and swift.

I clutched that persona, forcing it to lend knowledge I could use to our benefit. I grabbed Thomas and swung him around, making him the victim and me the murderer now.

"I'm sorry, Cresswell," I whispered, "but this is going to hurt."

Before he could protest, I jabbed him twice in the chest in rapid succession. I didn't feel as sorry as I'd pictured—more worrisome was the hollow joy spreading like darkness through my core. I was a gifted forensic student, but I was an even-more-talented murderess.

All I needed to do was surrender to that undulating dark, get swept up and away in its vicious pull.

As I'd imagined, his hands automatically shot up to his wound. I held my pretend knife at the ready, watching him press his hands to his chest where I imagined a bruise was forming. In a matter of thirty seconds I'd incapacitated him. If Miss Crenshaw had been struck with a knife, she'd be easy to handle from there. I couldn't recall any stab wounds, but then again, her postmortem was inconclusive because of how badly she'd been burned. Which might be another reason, aside from theatrics, that her corpse had been set ablaze.

Unblinking, I noted every detail as Thomas staggered back. He did not raise his hands to ward off my attack because he was too busy trying to stop the flow of blood. Miss Crenshaw's lack of defensive wounds thus far were the same.

I lifted my fist and Thomas pivoted away, avoiding the next strike. If he were truly bleeding, it would have sprayed in an arc across the door. Exactly like the evidence left there.

"That's it . . . I've figured it out!" I nearly jumped in place. Thomas rubbed his chest, eyes fastened to my improvised weapon. I stopped making a fist and tenderly reached over and held a hand to his heart, biting my lip at his grimace. "I truly am sorry for striking you. I got a bit carried away in the moment. Does it hurt?"

"Not much. You may feel free to put your hands on me anytime you please." He winked, then winced. "Though I'd prefer the touch to be a bit more gentle in the future."

"Noted." I led him back toward the bed, where he flopped down. "While it doesn't lessen the bruise, I do believe I figured out how the blood splatter was caused. The arc and slight smear are indicative of a chest wound. She would have spun slowly, maybe she even fell against the wall a moment after clutching her chest—from there I'm not sure what. But the blood pattern would arc as she turned, then smear if she stumbled against the wall, that much I know for certain. It's exactly what you did. It's not too much to assume Miss Crenshaw was struck with a knife."

Thomas offered me the sort of appraising look that set my blood aflame. There was no greater feeling than being admired for my brain. "Which means there is no doubt that whoever committed this act meant to dispatch her. She'd been targeted, but why?"

"I wonder if it's—look." I picked up a playing card that had fallen between the nightstand and bed, holding it up. "Six of Diamonds."

He took the card and flipped it over, carefully inspecting each inch of it. He handed it to me, frowning. "Perhaps the cards are literal calling cards."

I stared at the intricate design on the back—a raven with iridescent wings opened against a full moon, and thorns edged in silver around the rim. I traced the double eights near the bottom. "Or maybe it just means this is all part of a larger game. One that's the ultimate form of sleight of hand."

TWENTY-FOUR

DISSECTION OF THE LIMB

TEMPORARY LABORATORY
RMS ETRURIA
5 JANUARY 1889

Uncle peered through a magnifying glass, his nose mere inches away from the severed limb. I knew he remained angry with me over being caught alone with the shirtless ringmaster, but he required my assistance, and nothing else mattered once forensics were involved.

Thank goodness for small blessings.

Thomas grabbed the journal he'd set down while donning an apron, and resumed his note-taking. I couldn't shake a twinge of sickness when I thought of other notebooks he'd packed along for the journey—some of which contained notes written from Jack the Ripper. I was unready to read in great detail about his crimes, and Thomas kept whatever mysteries he uncovered there to himself. At least for now. I had a feeling we'd need to talk about them soon.

"The toothed forceps, Audrey Rose." Uncle held out his hand, palm up, waiting. "Quickly now."

"Yes, Uncle."

I gathered the medical instruments needed for this dissection—toothed forceps, scalpel, scissors, Hagedorn needle, string—and carried a silver tray over.

"Here." I swiftly wiped down the forceps with carbolic acid, handing them over to my uncle with efficiency. He grunted, not quite a thank you but not weighted silence, either. I watched him peel back bits of skin near where the elbow should have been, had it not been either cut or bitten off at that joint.

Flesh hung in thin strips, tattered like an old gown left to molder in a forgotten trunk. I rolled my shoulders, allowing the coolness of a scientist to settle over me. I would neither be disgusted nor feel softness. Neither of those emotions would save the victim from his fate.

Determination and a hardened heart would bring justice, though.

Uncle waved me closer, brows creased. He pried away a bit of torn flesh, exposing a familiar streak of off-white. "Do you see the radius and ulna?" he asked. I nodded, doing my best to focus only on those bones and not the outer layer of graying meat surrounding them. "While I peel back the muscle and tendons, describe what you see. Thomas, write down everything."

I bent until I was eye level with the limb, taking note of every detail. "There's splintering on the radius, but not on the ulna. On that I see a nick in the bone—I'd wager it was made by a sharp instrument. Likely a knife." I swallowed my revulsion down. "Splintering on the radius is most probably from the lion gnawing on the arm and is unrelated to how the limb was severed."

"Good, very good." Uncle pushed the skin back farther, hands steady. "Were the wounds received postmortem?"

"I—"

I bit my lip. There were no marks on the skin of the forearm, no signs of trauma sustained during a struggle. I glanced up at Thomas, but he was focused on writing. I took a moment to appreciate that I was trusted—by both of these men—to locate forensic information on my own. Pulling my shoulders back and standing taller, I allowed confidence to fall about me like a cloak.

"I believe the wounds were created postmortem. They're most likely the result of the limb being severed." I pointed to the rest of the arm. "There are no abrasions or cuts, both of which would be present in a victim who was fighting back against a knife attack."

Uncle turned the arm over, inspecting the underside of it. The flesh was paler than most cadavers, having lost so much blood, but not as pale as the more recent bodies I'd studied at the academy. Postmortem lividity was present—the slight staining visible on the underside where blood had pooled due to gravity. It indicated where a body had lain after death, and could not be altered after several hours even when the cadaver was moved into a new position. Except in a strange case when all the blood had been removed... there had been no staining then.

"Lividity is present," I added, noting the flash of surprise and pride in my uncle's eyes. I'd learned much at the academy. "I imagine he was already positioned on his back, lying down, when the murderer began hacking him apart. The evidence aligns with it."

"So it does." Uncle sounded pleased as he inspected the lividity on his own, his former annoyance with me erased. We were an odd family.

Thomas crinkled his nose. "Even without arterial splattering, wherever this dismemberment took place must be saturated in blood. I'm not sure anyone would be able to clean all of it away without leaving evidence behind."

"Very good point."

Uncle picked up a scalpel, using it to neatly cut away more of the mauled flesh. I swallowed hard. No matter how often I witnessed it, it was always a gruesome sight to behold. Carving flesh as if it were fine meat was repulsive.

"The bones were cut cleanly," Uncle continued. "Whoever removed this limb didn't use a saw or serrated blade." He set the scalpel down, then walked over to the water basin. Neither Thomas nor I speculated while he washed his hands with carbolic soap. Once he finished, he turned to us, face drawn. I had an inkling it wasn't the late hour that made him weary. "We need to concentrate on those who have access to strong, smooth blades. Kitchen staff. Crew members."

Dread, heavy and unyielding, clunked into my empty stomach. "Or most likely, based on their skill and proximity to such weapons, carnival performers who specialize in blades."

For a moment, no one spoke. There were a few obvious choices— though any one of the performers could stab someone.

"You believe Jian did this?" Thomas dragged his attention away from the severed limb. "A wonder it didn't make it as part of the stage act. Tossing melons, pineapples, severed arms. Seems quite fitting for the other theatrical murders."

"I believe he's someone we should at least consider," I said, ignoring his forced light commentary. "We also need to thoroughly research who else has access to his blades once the show is over. Does he lock them in a trunk at night, or sleep on them?" I lifted a shoulder. "If they're locked away, then we could expand the search to those who are gifted with picking locks."

I met both Uncle's and Thomas's gazes, seeing their worry mixed with my own. It was all speculation, of course, but if those swords were locked up, then there was only one young man on this ship who'd crowned himself king of escaping any cuff and picking any lock.

I ignored the scuttle of fear as it moved across my spine. If Harry Houdini kept reinventing himself, wearing new invisible masks in each city, I supposed it was possible that he wore the most convincing disguise of all: an innocent man, incapable of committing such heinous acts of murder. Maybe Cassie and her husband weren't exacting revenge. Perhaps it had been someone obvious yet not. If Houdini had a secret lover in America Liza didn't know of, there was no telling how many other secrets he had.

"Let's go make some inquiries," Thomas said, closing his notebook. "We'll start with Mephistopheles and Jian."

"If we march into the performers' practice area now, demanding to question everyone, we're going to be met with a wall as dense as London fog," I said.

"What method do you suggest, then?" Uncle asked. He'd not seen the growth I'd undergone while studying at the academy until this moment. I felt much more confident in exerting my hypothesis, less worried about being wrong or mocked if I was. Thomas had once told me he wasn't afraid of being proven wrong; he only feared not trying.

"We will simply need to craft illusions of our own," I said, already well into my own deceit act. "We'll use misdirection with our inquiries. Let them be suspicious of something unrelated. If they make their livings using that art form, there's no reason why we can't use that very method ourselves."

A slow, wicked grin lifted the edges of Thomas's mouth. "If they're the Moonlight Carnival, we ought to come up with our own fancy name. Marauders of Truth. Maidens of Mischief. Well," he amended, taking in my uncle's heavy sigh, "that doesn't necessarily apply to *all* of us. I'll keep thinking up names."

"While you occupy yourself with that monumentally important task," I said, "Liza invited Anishaa for tea in the morning. I'll see what I can uncover about her and anyone who might be a secret swordsman." I chanced a look at my uncle and smiled. "Let's plan on going over our findings before supper tomorrow."

Thomas pulled his pocket watch out, clicking it open with a grand flourish. "That gives us thirteen hours to sleep, infiltrate their ranks, create a bit of smoke to distract them, come up with our group name, and be dressed in our supper best." He ran a hand through his carefully styled brown locks. "Thank goodness it doesn't take much to make this"—he swept his arm across his person—"blindingly handsome. Unlike Mephistopheles."

"Seems the two of you learned extra skills while at the academy." Uncle took the limb on its tray and placed it in a refrigerated box loaned to us by the captain. "Though I'm not sure how sarcasm and banter will benefit this case. We need to focus on identifying who this limb belongs to."

"It's called *charm,* Professor. And I do believe it'll get us far." Thomas inhaled deeply, eyes dancing with mirth. "No one can resist a well-timed quip."

Uncle turned from the refrigerated box, looking less than amused. "Both of you are dismissed. Go to bed, then enchant or annoy information out of the carnival performers in the morning." He waved off Thomas's next remark. "Try not to aggravate any of them too much. A little of your *charm* goes a long way."

No one told *me* to be careful, which I took as a positive sign. An idea was forming that I wasn't sure either of them would like, but it was always preferable to beg for forgiveness after the fact than ask for permission beforehand. I just hoped Thomas wouldn't be too upset about me doing this next act on my own.

Morning arrived much sooner than night had left, and I awoke to the sound of knocking at my door. I scrubbed at my face and found a tarot card stuck to my cheek. I must have fallen asleep on the deck. Liza rolled her eyes, but said nothing as she shoved me toward my trunk.

"One moment!" she called out, purchasing a bit of time for me to get ready.

I cursed in the most impolite of ways, running around to pull on a decent yet simple receiving dress. A few minutes later my cousin opened the door with a grand flourish.

"I'd like to introduce Anishaa, also known as the Ace of Wands," Liza said graciously. "This is my cousin Audrey Rose."

We curtsied to each other and arranged ourselves on chairs and stools while a maid entered and set down a samovar and tray filled with breakfast sweets. I filled my cup, wincing as the first sip scorched my tongue. I peeked over at Liza. Of course, being the perennial hostess, she'd been up early, calling for refreshments. I could embrace her for her attention to detail in times like this.

Anishaa, the fire-swallowing goddess, was nearly unrecognizable out of her ice-inspired costume. Instead of the thickly braided silver wig, her hair was chin-length bluish black that hung in a smooth sheet. Her skin, now that it wasn't painted ice-blue white, was a shade between golden brown and fawn.

She gave up trying to balance her teacup on her lap and sat cross-legged on the floor where Liza was already seated. I watched, wide-eyed, as she sipped the same tea that had scalded my tongue, and offered an amused grin. "After swallowing fire every night, tea never seems as hot," she said with a wink.

At my unladylike snicker, Liza lovingly smiled before sipping from her own cup. Not wanting to be rude, I joined them on the thick carpet.

"I dare say that's true." I set my teacup and saucer down, watching the steam rise like a snake striking the air. "How did you first start eating flames? I cannot imagine attempting it for the first time. You're very brave."

"Most would say very foolish," she said, narrowing her eyes.

I offered my most innocent, benign expression. Liza huffed in exasperation, but didn't chide me for my inquisitiveness as her mother would have done. She was well versed in sensing a scheme and knew I was up to something. Instead of commenting, she passed a tray of biscuits around, probably hoping the sweets would distract from my social awkwardness.

Anishaa snatched a biscuit, eyeing up bits of chocolate before responding to my question. "A pair of wonder-workers, *fakirs,* taught me how to swallow flames. They said my name—which roughly means 'one whose life knows no darkness'—meant I was born to wield fire." She snorted. "Flames were mine to command. To swallow whole." She lifted her tea back up, taking a long pull. "I was very young and very impressionable when they first lured me away from my home, fooled by the promise of riches. I am embarrassed that I fell for their sweet words. Once I agreed to leave, they dropped me off, took their coin, and left to find another person for another carnival."

"They were the ones who ought to be ashamed. You did nothing wrong." Liza reached over and clutched the girl's hand, reminding me how talented she was at sensing what people needed and innately offering support.

"Liza's right," I added. "Tricking you into joining a traveling troupe was a terrible thing for them to do."

Anishaa lifted a shoulder and tore off chunks of her biscuit. "They brought me here and life has been good with the Moonlight Carnival. I have money, food, friends. It turned out to be all right."

"Mephistopheles was the one who did that to you?" I asked, trying very hard to not have my china rattle as my hands shook. "He tricked you from your home and family?"

"He—" Anishaa briefly dropped her gaze to her lap before continuing. "He hires people in countries he visits to seek out talent.

Anyone who's been through a...difficult time...he invites into the carnival and trains. The choice is ultimately ours to make, but he makes the deal hard to pass on."

"So is everyone in the carnival from a different country?"

"Mostly. Jian is from China. Sebastián, Spain. Andreas is from Bavaria, Cassie is French, though she speaks in an English accent. And I'm from India."

"You mentioned he seeks those who've had a difficult time; what exactly do you mean?" I asked, though Liza gave me a look that said I was an idiot for prying.

"We all have reasons to leave our lives behind." She inhaled deeply. "Now, would you like to know *how* I swallow flames? That's what everyone wants, though most don't really want the magic or illusion destroyed."

I studied her for another moment, knowing the inquiry into her past and the carnival was now over. I didn't quite know what to make of Mephistopheles. He didn't necessarily save anyone, but I couldn't quite say he'd harmed or tricked them, either. Though maybe they didn't see it that way, perhaps resentment started as a small cut and became infected over time. Perhaps someone wanted the Moonlight Carnival to be destroyed as revenge for taking them from their homes.

"Well?" Anishaa asked. "Would you like to know?"

"Please," I said, shaking thoughts of potential motives away. "How do you swallow the flames and not get burnt?"

She pushed herself up, gracefully trekking across the floor as if it were the stage. I wondered if the performers ever dropped their acts, or if their entire existence was given over to their craft.

"Observe this taper." Anishaa removed a candlestick from its holder on my nightstand, lit the end, then turned it nearly upside down. Wax beaded, slipping toward the floor. "Where does the flame go when I hold it this way?"

Understanding dawned. "Away from the bottom, or," I added, "if it were during one of your performances, the flame would be reaching away from your mouth."

"See?" Anishaa smiled warmly. "You're a natural." She cupped her palm around the candle, snuffing the flame out, and set it back in its holder. "Same principle is applied when I 'swallow the fire.' All I'm doing is removing the heat from my face, then carefully exhaling as I put the torch in my mouth. Most living things need oxygen to breathe, even fire. Deny it of that? And it dies like anything would." She folded herself back on the floor where Liza and I remained seated. "The real trick is using the laws of physics. Like that scientist... Newton? Mephistopheles taught me all about him. He was right, it helped hone my performances."

Her voice changed a bit while speaking of the ringmaster, admiration tinged with a bit of longing. I wondered if there was a person aboard this ship who hadn't fallen under his spell. Well, besides Thomas.

"Does Mephistopheles help all the performers?" I asked, eyes fixed on my teacup. I imagined he charmed young men and women in each city or town they'd passed through. If she'd harbored feelings for him that he didn't return, perhaps it might prove to be motive. That mixed with resentment would be a powerful reason. "He seems as smart as he is handsome."

Liza shot me an incredulous look, but pressed her lips together. Apparently, I was in for a good scolding once we were alone. Despite what everyone in London thought of Thomas and his odd behavior, Liza liked him very much, and my interest in the ringmaster was not right in her romantic book, no matter what my reasons were.

"Mephistopheles is..." Anishaa seemed to formulate her answer carefully. "He's very gifted at what he does. Many benefit from the lessons he chooses to give. We're all very grateful to him."

I sat back, fiddling with the buttons on the side of my gloves. "Did he give such lessons to Cassie?"

Liza suddenly found her tea infinitely intriguing, and Anishaa seemed at a loss for words.

"Would you like to see him as no one aside from his performers do?" Anishaa finally asked. I hoped she didn't mean naked as the day he'd come into this world. I nodded slowly. "Meet me on the second-class promenade in one hour. Then you'll understand why we'd all do anything for him."

Plague doctor

TWENTY-FIVE
GEARS AND GADGETS

AUDREY ROSE'S CABIN
RMS ETRURIA
6 JANUARY 1889

"Would you care to explain what that was about, Cousin?"

Liza's cheeks were splotchy pink, a great indication of how upset she was. Any moment steam might shoot from her ears. I swallowed nervous laughter, knowing she wouldn't appreciate being told she was her mother's daughter in this moment.

"I am not one to judge, but you seem awfully intrigued by Mephistopheles," she continued. "Emphasis on 'awful.' What about Mr. Cresswell? Have your feelings for him changed that quickly? Your letters from the academy seemed to indicate some grand romance, though you were upset with him at the time." She inspected me with sharp-eyed focus, similar to how I'd dissect a specimen with my scalpel. "Has Mephistopheles won your heart so easily? I thought you would see through his lies."

I pinched the skin between my thumb and forefinger, using it to focus.

"Where is the scandal in speaking with someone?" I asked. "It's not as if Mephistopheles has declared himself to me. Perhaps I simply enjoy hearing about his use of science. I've always been intrigued with engineering. We're not so different, you know."

"Is that what he's told you?" Liza gave me a long, measured look. "That you're both similar in nature? That you belong together?"

Her tone was drenched in disapproval, though I could see the concern in her face.

"What if he has said those things?" I lifted my chin, doing my best imitation of being indignant and hating myself a little more for it. How many lies would I be forced to tell before this charade was over? "It's true. We both love science. His is just a bit more flashy. There's much I could learn from him, though. Things that might help me figure out where, exactly, I belong."

"Dissecting the dead *is* much less showy," she said drily. "Maybe you should borrow one of his masks. Or ask his costumer for a new autopsy gown. I'm sure he could sew something up that would restart any heart. Where you belong is with Uncle and Thomas, solving crimes for those who could not do it on their own. Not dressed up and prancing around a stage in a different city each night on the arm of a man who will always love the show more."

"Don't be sour, Cousin," I said, trying hard not to read too much into her last sentence. "I simply enjoy learning how he engineers his tricks. He is quite…the machines and mechanisms he builds are incredible. If he would focus on creating medical tools…" I trailed off, suddenly not speaking any more half-truths. If Mephistopheles used his brain to craft machines used in surgeries, there were endless possibilities for healing.

Liza searched my face for a moment, not quite convinced. I fought to keep my expression frozen into the mask I'd donned.

"Be careful of giving your heart to men like that," she finally said, shoulders slumping.

"Men like what?" I reached over and gripped her hand. "Scientists and engineers?"

"Liars."

"He's an illusionist," I said, not missing the venom she'd injected into that single word. "A wonder-worker."

"Exactly." Liza took her hand from mine and crossed her arms. "A liar. In a fancy frock coat."

For a heart-grabbing moment I feared that Mephistopheles had acted on our bargain against my wishes, leaving Liza an anonymous letter with information on Houdini. I swallowed hard, feeling the wall of lies crumble in on me. It was time to come clean about one secret. "Is...is everything all right between you and Harry?"

"Of course. Why wouldn't it be?" She examined my face, her lips turning down. There was something in her eyes, though. Something that indicated all wasn't as well as she'd like me to believe. "What is it? What aren't you telling me?"

This was it; the moment I'd been dreading. Suddenly, looking into my cousin's pleading eyes, I couldn't bring myself to break her heart. She gripped my hand. If she was having doubts about Houdini, I needed to give her all the information I had. We made land in only one more day. Still, I couldn't seem to make myself take that last step.

"Please. Whatever it is, I need to know."

I dropped onto the bed, heart thudding slow enough to toll the hour of dread. Without saying a word, I reached over and removed the half-ruined letter from my nightstand. I gave it to Liza, keeping my eyes averted as she sank down beside me.

"That lying scoundrel!" She crumpled the paper, voice trembling when she spoke. "I'll toss him overboard like the piece of rubbish he is! Where's my cloak?"

Fearing her temper might lead her to such extremes, I gathered my courage and faced her. "Liza...you cannot confront him."

"Are you mad?" she cried. "Of course I must confront him!"

"At least wait until we've reached port. There's already so much to contend with, please, I beg of you. Wait. It's only for one more day, and then, if you still wish to do so, I will help you toss him into the harbor. I swear it."

Liza marched in a circle around the room, shaking her head. "You want me to act as if nothing is wrong? Would you do the same thing if you were in my shoes?"

"I would do whatever needed to be done," I said truthfully. "Especially if it came down to putting an investigation first."

Liza stared at me and I couldn't quite pick out the emotions that shifted across her face. "Tell me this much, where did you get the letter? Did Anishaa give it to you?"

"Mephistopheles did. I've—I haven't wanted to ruin your trip."

"This wasn't simply a trip for me." Her lips trembled. "He was supposed to be my future. I gave up so much." She swallowed whatever she was about to say, her voice as hard as diamonds when she spoke next. "Never, ever, give up yourself for someone else, Audrey Rose. The right person will want you just as you are. And if they don't?" She sniffled, and shook her head. "Forget them. Tipping the scales too far in either direction is nothing but trouble. I gave up my home and family for kisses, playing cards, and empty promises of a future. Houdini is a liar, and I'm glad to be done with him."

"Liza, I wanted to tell you, I just—"

"I promise I will not say anything to him for now. I'll act as though everything is well. Heaven forbid the King of Cards have any distractions before his next stunt." Liza purposely glanced at the clock on my nightstand. "You'd better hurry or you'll be late for your meeting with Anishaa and Mephistopheles. He's never alone for long, Harry often meets with him after breakfast. Which will only give you a few minutes with him. Here." She pulled out the stool by my vanity. "Sit and I'll braid your hair."

I stared at my cousin a beat more, wanting to crack the wall she'd suddenly built around herself, but sat instead. She ran a silver-handled brush through my hair, twisting and pulling it into shape. I pretended not to notice the single tear that streaked down her cheek as she fastened tiny red buds into my hair, or the way her eyes purposely refused to meet mine in the looking glass. It seemed I wasn't the only member of my family keeping secrets on this voyage now.

Ocean mist sprayed over the railing of the boat, forcing me to walk closer to the cabin side of the promenade to avoid catching a worse chill. With Liza's assistance I'd changed into a more elaborate day dress—a long-sleeved deep burgundy velvet overlaid with delicate black lace. I'd added kidskin gloves and a dark cloak. I looked like a splatter of dried blood. Which was quite fitting, considering what I was about to do. Sacrifice was messy business.

What Liza hadn't seen me add was the leather belt fastened at my thigh and the scalpel I'd stuck in it. The weapon belt was a design I'd had crafted in Romania for myself, the best Christmas gift to date. My fingers brushed down the front of my bodice, comforted by the knowledge of my blade, though the plan formulating in my head was much less soothing.

It was brash and risky, but the reward would outweigh the peril. I hoped. I hadn't had an opportunity to speak with Thomas, so I was depending on his ability to glean truth from subtle clues. Hopefully he wouldn't be hindered by Mephistopheles's jibes. And hopefully I wouldn't be distracted by how sick I felt over Liza's despair.

A young couple passed by, their eyes darting around the deck as they clutched each other a bit too tightly. They were the first people

263

I'd encountered, and their stroll did not appear to be as relaxing as they were attempting to make it. In fact, most of the ship felt too quiet. Passengers were taking more of their meals in their cabins and only venturing out when absolutely necessary. A pretty prison was what this ship had become.

I continued on, thoughts tumbling over one another.

Out this far in the water there were no gulls calling overhead, singing their own songs of woe. Instead there were snippets of conversation that rolled down the wooden deck toward me, too muffled to make out. Women and men in less fine suits and dresses than those of first class, but still quite fashionable, peered out from their cabins as I made my way toward Anishaa. My heart thumped against my chest in warning, but it was too late to turn back now. I was here, and the plan needed to unfold now.

Mephistopheles had his back to me, but I recognized him by his scarlet tailcoat, gleaming knee-high boots, and narrow-hipped swagger. From this direction he resembled a pirate king. I wouldn't be surprised to discover that he added an aquatic act once they landed in New York.

"Next time, twirl the torches as if they were a pocket watch on a chain," he was saying, swinging his watch in a wide circle. "The velocity will keep the flames from spreading along the metal rod and look impressive from the audience. But do it quickly—it's still metal and will burn your lips if they accidentally touch it."

Anishaa peered up at him through lowered lashes, and I was surprised the ringmaster hadn't noticed her crush. She seemed to balance on the edge of each word and idea he offered.

"A fine scientific deduction," I said. Mephistopheles whirled, looking startled by my unannounced visit, yet pleased. He clutched the watch, then pocketed it. "Metal getting hot with fire. Who would've guessed? Next you might tell her that ice will be cold to the touch."

"Miss Wadsworth. Always a pleasure." His mouth quirked as he gave a slight bow. "I have it on good authority that falling in love is like toying with fire. Warm, crackling with heated passion..." Anishaa snorted and he motioned for her to practice.

"Well, if one is foolish enough to play with flames, they shouldn't be surprised when they get burned."

Anishaa's expression was bemused while she twirled the flames, allowing us a bit of privacy, though I noticed her attention kept darting over to the object of her secret affection.

"Would you care to see my work space?" Mephistopheles asked, all gentlemanly manners belied by the cunning gleam in his eye. "It's just around the bend." He smiled behind his mask—a wolf inviting Red Riding Hood into the darkened forest. What he didn't know was that this particular girl carried a weapon beneath her hood and had an assortment of wolf hides mounted in her chambers. "I promise no immoral behavior. Just gears and gadgets. Maybe a bit of grease. Nothing too romantic."

"You certainly know how to charm a girl," I said. "Next you'll show me your mask collection." I peered close to this newest work of art, a pale gray with cloudlike swirls of white, noticing the slight hitch in his breath as I drew near. "How many do you own, one thousand?"

"Closer to one million." He grinned, regaining his composure. "Practice twirling one, then the other, like we discussed," he called over to Anishaa. "We've got to work on when you spit the flames next. I'm almost ready with the new tonic."

She nodded, then continued her work. He folded my hand over his arm, escorting me down the promenade to his lair. I'd only been half jesting about the masks, but it wouldn't surprise me if he did have that many. He probably needed an entire trunk to transport them.

"Spitting fire?" I asked. "That sounds a bit dangerous. And a little crass."

"It's not as if she'll be spewing flames onto the crowd like chewing tobacco. Danger can be found in everything, even the mundane. And that's quite boring," he said. "To what do I owe the pleasure of your company this early? It's not time for a lesson. Did Mr. Cresswell send you here to break off our romantic entanglement? I thought he might throttle me in Miss Crenshaw's cabin. I bet he hated sharing toys as a child."

"First, I am not anyone's toy, sir. And second, if Thomas was upset, don't you believe he would be the one standing here, challenging you for my affections?"

Mephistopheles snorted. "Well, he *does* seem the type to run his enemies through." He squinted at me. "Is that the sort of thing that attracts you? Perhaps I'll start challenging your other suitors to duels. I may even remove my mask once I've won. Let them gaze upon the true face of their victor."

"You mean the face of their mortal enemy?"

"I doubt they'd call me their friend after being introduced to Nightsblade."

"Nightsblade?" I asked, stopping. "Is that the name of your imaginary friend?"

"Close." He chuckled. "You've heard of nightshade, correct? Tantalizing plants, but deadly. Like my sword. Nightsblade."

"Clever." Unease ran its icy fingers down my back. Belladonna—a type of nightshade—had been found in Miss Crenshaw's system. "Does everyone in your carnival need to be in possession of a weapon to be accepted? Like a secret mask-wearing society of sword wielders?"

He laughed again, only this time I wished to withdraw my arm from his.

"Hardly. Jian and I are the only ones who've got swords," he said.

"His are for his tricks; mine is from my past. Alas, we have more important things to discuss. Time is one law I cannot seem to break, no matter how much I beg, borrow, or steal, I cannot produce more of it. Any news on who has been murdering passengers? Investors are not happy, and I fear what the future will bring for the carnival. No other cruise liner will hire us if they think we're harboring a murderer."

I considered asking him about the tarot cards and why have each performer learn them, but didn't want him to be suspicious of my motives. Nor did I wish to give away the fact I suspected both the tarot and playing cards were a cipher of sorts—their meanings clearly detailing the story of the crimes for anyone capable of reading it. If he was the murderer, then he might alter his methods of killing.

"Not yet, but I do have a theory I'm working on." I wet my lips, hoping to not raise his suspicion by being too curious about his passing comment. "Whose sword is bigger? Yours or Jian's?"

He stopped short, staring at me as if I'd disrobed in front of him and everyone else on this promenade. From the appraising glint in his expression, I didn't think he'd mind if that happened. It took a moment for my brain to catch up with the innuendo I'd accidentally made.

"I—I mean," I stuttered, "which is more finely crafted?"

"Hmm." He started walking again, though that devious smile still curled his lips. "If I'm being honest? I'd say his. Nightsblade is a gorgeous sword, but Jian's are works of art."

Now I was the one who halted our procession. I hadn't expected him to be anything other than cocky. "I thought men like you lied for sport."

"Which makes it all the more fun for you to sort out the truth from my lies."

He kept walking, not in a hurry or appearing suspicious. If

anything, he seemed relaxed, his stride confident. We were nothing more than a young couple, strolling along the promenade. Except he wore a ridiculous mask and I wore a concealed blade, and most of the ship wore fear like a new overcoat.

A few times I caught him lifting his face as if to feel the sunshine, though the sun was hidden behind a thick layer of clouds. A storm was brewing.

"Jian had his swords crafted by an expert bladesmith from the Ottoman Empire during his travels," he continued, though I hadn't inquired. "The metal practically sings as it cuts through the air. You'll have to come to one of his practices—you can hear it best when there's not a crowd."

"Does he sleep with his swords near? It sounds as if they're worth a great amount."

"Why all the curiosity about Jian?" He paused near a cabin in the middle of the deck. "Do you believe he's keeping bodies in his sword bin?"

His question was light, but there was an edge in his expression that pricked my pulse.

"Can I not inquire over a singing sword without a motive?" I asked. "Not everything revolves around you, you insufferable thing."

"Yes, but—"

"You know? I just had a tremendous idea! You ought to rename his show 'Jian, the Sultan of Singing Swords.' I'd wager people would love to hear that symphony. Perhaps you can engineer a way to enhance the sword song. Have you tried using the methods of an ear trumpet to amplify sound?"

Mephistopheles raised both brows. A feat I was always impressed by, since he never took off his mask. "Are you interested in turning your scientific mind into profit?" He held a hand to his heart. "Have I convinced you to join show business after only a few nights? I'm even better than I thought. And I thought quite highly of my wooing skills before, mind you."

" 'Show business'?" I asked, relieved to have distracted him. "Is that what you're calling the carnival today?"

"It's what P. T. Barnum calls the circus, has a nice ring to it, doesn't it?"

I scoffed. "I've heard rumors of him being unkind and a scoundrel. I'm not sure basing anything off of him is a wise idea."

"He's an opportunist, as are most businessmen, which doesn't require respectability."

Mephistopheles inserted a key, then pushed open the door, revealing a cabin unoccupied by anything other than tools and props. There was a faint scent of metal in the air, and, for once, it wasn't due to spilled blood.

He flipped the light on, revealing ordinary-enough-looking things mixed with the improbable. Top hats with metal parts on the inside, bird cages with mechanical doves covered in real feathers that appeared so lifelike I had to touch them to be sure they were toys. I spied a tailcoat hanging on a hook, the entire inside of it stitched with metal and gearshifts. Raven feathers perched along the shoulders, sleek and shiny as oil.

Scattered across the vanity were screws and bolts and plague-doctor masks. I shuddered as I drew closer to one, its leather beak a cream so rich it appeared to be carved from bone.

"These are..."

"Terrifying?" he supplied, picking one up and running a gloved finger over the large beak. I imagined his expression as thoughtful, though it was hard to tell. "Did you know that during medieval times, when plague doctors wore these, they placed aromatic scents at the tip of the beak? Rose petals, juniper berries, lemon balm, and mint. They helped keep putrid scents of death away." He set it

269

down. "They were also allowed to perform postmortems on the dead, though it was forbidden to others during those days. Someone such as yourself would have faced grave charges."

"How does it relate to your carnival?"

Instead of answering straightaway, he turned and removed a black caped overcoat from a peg and donned it along with circular glass goggles and finally the plague mask. He slowly faced me, standing there, unmoving, dressed solidly in black except the bone-white mask. He reached for a small top hat, adding it to complete his look of a gentleman plague doctor come to call on the nearly dead.

Shivers ran along my limbs. His silence was as creepy as the costume, if not more so.

"Well?" I asked, stuffing my nerves deep down. "What do you plan on doing in those costumes?"

He slowly moved forward, circling me as a vulture might do to a fresh carcass.

"By now your pulse is likely pounding." Mephistopheles drew close. "Your breath catching the tiniest bit. I have your full attention, your full fear and excitement. I promised three things in my opening sequence, Miss Wadsworth. Do you recall them?"

I refused to be afraid. He'd said his carnival was filled with magic, mischief, and mayhem. "I do."

I couldn't see it behind this new mask, but I pictured the devilish grin he'd worn countless times before. "When the finale stage is filled with an army of plague doctors, I believe it will cause a bit of mayhem in the saloon. Wouldn't you agree?"

A terrifyingly gothic scene indeed.

"Perhaps in light of the fact young women are being murdered and at least one man has been dismembered," I said coolly, "you ought to rethink that. I know I won't be wearing it." I nodded toward another costume laid out on the bed. It was somewhere between lavender and moonbeam gray—another fanciful outfit for the Moonlight Carnival. Silver fish scales lay over the shoulders like armor, the corset of the bodice composed of deep charcoal and black scales. "Who is that for?"

Mephistopheles turned around while he removed his terrible costume, put his old mask on, then pointed at his workbench. On it was the most elaborate mask I'd ever seen. I wasn't sure how I'd missed it during my first scan of the room, but there *were* a lot of objects. This mask was more like a Roman war helmet, complete with open jaws that contained fangs. A dragon skull, I realized upon closer inspection.

"Anishaa asked to redefine her act—to come up with something more memorable." He fingered the fine fabrics of the costume. "She wants to be known as the Dragon Queen instead of a plain old fire-eater. So I obliged. Now, with the aid of a special tonic I'm crafting, she'll not only swallow the flames, she'll breathe them."

"But that sounds—"

"Dangerous?" he asked. "No more so than following a young man into his room, alone, with masks and machinery. Tell me," he said, shutting the door, "when did you start believing I had anything to do with the murders?"

TWENTY-SIX

A BEAUTIFULLY DRESSED SPY

MEPHISTOPHELES'S ENGINEERING CABIN
RMS ETRURIA
6 JANUARY 1889

My hand ghosted over the hidden blade sheathed on my thigh. "Who said anything about guilt?" I asked. "Unless there's something more you haven't told me. Have you news to share?"

To either his or my own credit, he seemed impressed that I hadn't shrunk away from him. He leaned against the door, arms crossed. "My issue is with you parading about this ship, pretending as if you're interested in me in front of my performers, when in reality you're just a beautifully dressed spy for your uncle."

"You're the one who wanted them to believe there was something more between us! And I take great offense to that." I drew myself up. "I am no one's spy." Liar, definitely. But he hadn't accused me of that. Yet. "I'm doing exactly what you asked as per our bargain. If you're that upset, perhaps it's time to change the terms."

"Do not insult my intelligence," he said. "Yes, I may have wanted them to see us together, to work a bit harder to teach you tricks for the finale, but nowhere in our agreement did I mention flirting or staring at me when you think I'm not looking. Or, would you have me believe between our midnight rendezvous and your predawn dissection, you've found yourself thinking of the softness of my hair, the sharp angle of my jaw, the—"

"—the arrogance of your demeanor." I rolled my eyes. "Perhaps, despite good judgment, I enjoy your company. If you're that confident of yourself, why is it so hard to believe?"

"So those looks are real?" He examined me closely, attention falling to my lips and remaining there. Half a breath later, he turned the lights off, then slowly moved toward me. My heart, the only thing *not* playing along with my false bravado, stuttered at his growing proximity.

Uncle had not mentioned my rebellion earlier, but if he were to find out I'd flouted his rules once again... I held my ground. Mephistopheles cocked his head, inspecting every steady breath I took and every slow blink of my eyes, searching for a lie he wouldn't find. I held an image of Thomas's crooked smile in my mind, projecting it onto the young man before me.

Reaching a hand out, Mephistopheles tenderly pushed a stray lock over my ear.

"Are you certain that's what you'd like me to believe, Miss Wadsworth? That you're here, in this cabin alone with me, because you choose to be... of your own free will... with no motive? You simply wish to spend the morning with me?"

I nodded, not trusting my voice to remain strong when the rest of my nerves were ready to crack. I saw the hunger in his gaze then, the longing he couldn't cover with any mask. I knew he wanted to kiss me, though I wasn't conceited enough to believe he wouldn't gaze at most any young woman the same way. He was an opportunist. And this was a perfect opportunity. His fingers reached out once more, his touch barely anything at all, while he waited for permission.

Up this close I could smell his cologne—it reminded me of the aromatics used in the plague mask, but was heady instead of frightening. Perhaps he was a true mage—because here, in a cabin below the world I knew upstairs, I couldn't help but fall under his spell.

In the dark it was easy to forget he wasn't the boy I kept thinking about. The one whose lips were becoming as familiar as my own. My heart surged when he leaned toward me, his face so close to mine. I noticed subtle dark growth over his skin, as if he hadn't had time for a proper shave this morning.

Curse me, but I almost longed to feel its roughness against my own skin, so similar and yet so different from Thomas. Something in my expression must have shifted, unleashing him. He slipped his hands into my hair, gently pulling me closer. I did not resist.

I lifted my chin, knowing it was the most dangerous deception of all, pretending he was someone else, yearning for what his lips might feel like, how cool the filigree of his mask might be under my fingertips. His mouth hovered over mine, sharing breath but not touching. Not yet...

"I've thought about doing this all week," he whispered against my lips. "A-are you certain—"

The door banged open. "Have you got those new cuffs ready yet? Liza's in a mood and I ain't got anything better to do than—"

I jerked away from the ringmaster, face flaming as Houdini's mouth snapped shut. The escape artist appeared as if he was about to do just that. He stood for a full breath, frozen with indecision.

"Uh...sorry to interrupt. Anishaa didn't mention—" Houdini motioned toward the two of us, not meeting either of our eyes. "I'll come back for the cuffs."

He slipped out from the room before Mephistopheles could regain his composure. I collected my breath, grateful for the interruption, though I hadn't been surprised. Liza *had* mentioned that Houdini met with the ringmaster around this time, something I'd been counting on. My plan had been hastily constructed on the walk here, but with any luck, I'd played my part convincingly. Gossip was a currency most couldn't help spending.

For better or worse, performers would hopefully be whispering about the clandestine meeting between me and their ringmaster. They might have suspected it before, but there would be "proof" now of our feelings. A sleight of hand to keep their attention where I wanted it.

I stepped away from Mephistopheles, giving us both space to breathe as I smoothed down the front of my skirts. Had Houdini been a moment later, I might have fallen into my own trap.

Mephistopheles rubbed the back of his neck, seeming at a loss on how to proceed. "I must apologize for my forwardness, Miss Wadsworth. I didn't mean to be so untoward—"

"Please, let's not worry over what could have happened." I waved a hand in the air, not feeling half as bold as I sounded. My knees wobbled and my heart stuttered frantically. I loved Thomas, but I couldn't deny the appeal of the ringmaster. Was it possible to pretend to be someone else so thoroughly that you actually stepped into that life? "Right now, I need to examine Jian's swords. I know we were only joking before, but does Jian keep them locked up? Are they near yours?"

The ringmaster appeared reluctant to turn the conversation away from our almost-kiss, but relented. "Next to and below the animal cargo is where we keep the trunks for the show. Tents, tightropes, most every prop we use is there, including the trunks containing Jian's swords. They're painted lapis blue and encrusted with bits of mosaic tiles. You can't miss them."

It did not go unnoticed that he hadn't confirmed where Nightsblade was. "Would it be all right if I had a look down there?"

He didn't answer at first, expression calculating. "What does this have to do with the murdered women?"

"It has to do with the severed limb, actually." I had the impression that if I strayed too far from the truth, he'd unravel each of my lies. "I have a suspicion that they're connected."

"Very well." He sat on a stool in front of his makeshift workbench, picking up a few bottles filled with clear liquid and dark powders and setting them in a row. "You may investigate anything having to do with the carnival. Though I warn you, not all the performers will take kindly to having their things snooped through. You may want to go alone and not get caught." He smiled shyly. "I'd offer to accompany you, but I have a bit of work to do before tonight's show. If I can sneak away for a moment, I will." At my raised brow he motioned to the corked bottles. "Dragon fire. Though it's not for tonight's performance. I'll tend to that once you're gone."

"Is it the new Houdini act you were going to show me last night?" I tried not to let my relief show that I'd be alone in my search. I wasn't sure we'd have another interruption should he lean in for a kiss. "Any hints about what you're working on?"

His grin was full and wide. "Something spectacular."

I wound my way down and around labyrinthine halls of twisted metal and matte bolts, noticing how empty certain parts of the ship were compared to others. Silence was never complete, though. Some vibration or dull movement could always be heard as well as felt, whether by my fingers trailing over the walls or through the soles of my silken shoes. The ship was alive with constant movement, its engines guzzling energy to exhale steam or its auxiliary sails throwing their arms wide to tame the wind. It was like a metal dragon, flying low over the sea. I shoved those thoughts away and focused on my surroundings.

These narrow corridors were used by the crew, hidden and dark, wedged into the heart of the *Etruria*. Doors were spaced fairly evenly, leading to servant cabins or storage, I wasn't sure. My skirts swished as loudly as the blood pulsing through my veins while I turned into another dimly lit corridor. I hoped to avoid running into anyone— though the captain had informed the staff of our investigation, I did not wish to be seen.

Hollow sounds of dishes clinking and smothered voices bounced around the hallway. I hurried along, not pausing to listen. According to the directions Mephistopheles had given me, I was almost upon the room where the swords were kept. Footsteps suddenly clomped from around the corner, slow and steady. Whoever marched toward me was unlikely to be one of the rushing crew. Which meant it was probably a carnival performer.

I glanced around, heart near bursting as I took in few hiding options, then rushed to the nearest door. I rattled the handle, but it was locked. I raced to the next, keeping one ear turned to the footsteps that were getting closer. Another locked door.

"Merciful God above," I cursed. Of all the rotten luck in the world. I tried the handle on a third door and nearly dropped to my knees in supplication as it opened. A shadow bent around the corner, and right before its owner followed, I slipped into the darkened room, sealing the door shut with a subtle click.

"Room" was a generous term. I'd had either the luck or sheer misfortune of ending up in a very tiny, very crowded broom closet. Sticks and poles poked my back, bruised my limbs, and fought to regain their space. I stood very still, praying that nothing would clatter to the ground. The sharp scent of cleanser bit at my nose, dust motes joining in the brawl. A bucket filled with liquid sloshed over the sides, the astringent dampening my shoes.

I felt a sneeze coming on and vowed to every saint I'd ever heard of to defuse the blasted thing before it gave my position away. Aunt

Amelia would quirk a brow, claiming it was the sinner's curse and attending services a bit more would prevent things such as this.

I pinched my lips together, as if I could keep the sneeze in by force of will alone, my eyes pricking with tears. Whoever had been coming down the hall had slowed. I pressed my ear to the door, listening. Someone was testing the handles of doors.

I fought the urge to bang my head against the metal. The sneeze seemed to release me from its imminent arrival, allowing my shoulders to sag. Relief was short-lived. Before I could hold it in, I sneezed, the sound loud and unmistakable.

"Gesundheit."

I began to say thank you, then froze. The person who I'd been hiding from wrenched the door open, stepped inside, and closed it as swiftly. For a moment I was stunned; the closet was barely large enough for me, and now with . . .

"Cresswell? What in the name of the queen are you doing?"

Though I couldn't see it, I swore I could feel him smile. "Following you into dark, abandoned corners, of course. What else ought I be doing? Your uncle's inspecting the severed limb. Again. After calling on Dr. Arden without luck, I stopped by your cabin, but Liza told me you'd gone to walk the third-class decks." I felt him shrug. "I tried to get your attention, but you practically ran into the stairwell."

I rolled my eyes. "Following me into the closet doesn't seem like your best idea."

"Isn't it, though?" he asked. Before I could respond, he gently pressed his lips to mine. An ember of desire caught flame. Suddenly, being alone with him in a dark, forgotten place was much more appealing. I pushed my near kiss with the ringmaster from my mind. Nothing could ever compare to this. Mephistopheles was simply an illusion. Thomas was the real thing. "See? It was a brilliant plan."

I sighed. He was correct, but wanting to kiss him and needing to use our time wisely were two things that needed to remain separate for now. Then there was the matter of my almost-kiss with Mephistopheles that we needed to discuss. Eventually. Thomas might not be so eager for stolen embraces after I told him about that.

I laid a hand against his chest, stalling any more kissing. "Jian's swords are kept in the next room. I'm hoping if they were used in any of the attacks there will be evidence on them. The severed arm was nicked quite badly, there must be signs of it still on the weapon used. If we want to investigate, we need to hurry. The performers will be getting ready to practice for the finale soon."

"You've been busy this morning." Thomas opened the door, then rubbed his hands together. "How do you know when they practice? Have you managed to single-handedly charm the carnival?"

A twinge of regret twisted my core. I wanted to tell him about my excursion with the ringmaster and of our wretched bargain, but that required time to reveal my whole plan. And time was something we were woefully short on. Instead of opening more avenues of discussion, I smiled demurely. "Perhaps."

"Swords, secrets, and stolen kisses." His eyes flashed with delight. "You speak the language of my complicated heart, Wadsworth. I am a very lucky man."

I hoped he would still believe that once I'd confessed my morning activities in full. "Come on, Cresswell. We've got a chamber to investigate."

TWENTY-SEVEN
WEB OF ILLUSIONS

Thomas and I entered the storage chamber with great caution—not uttering a single word or breathing too deeply until we were certain of being alone. The room was large—cavernous, really—and painted the steel gray of a battleship. Edison bulbs hung from intervals in the ceiling, buzzing with power when Thomas flicked them on.

There was no denying how eerie it was. No animals paced in cages, but I could have sworn I felt eyes on my back as I slowly crept down aisles of stacked trunks, all various shapes and sizes and colors. I didn't see any indication of which trunk belonged to which performer or act, and was grateful for the description Mephistopheles had given me. If not for that, we could spend the remainder of our trip opening each one.

"We're looking for a trunk that's lapis with mosaic tiles," I whispered over my shoulder. "There will be more than one." Thomas was quiet a moment. I turned, expecting to find him distracted by something, surprised when I saw he was no longer following me. "What is it?"

He shook himself out of whatever thoughts had grasped him. "Look around, Wadsworth. There are trunks upon trunks upon trunks."

I worried that the lack of sleep was making him a bit dull. "Yes, not completely unexpected in a storage unit."

"I mean there are numerous places to hide evidence…and bodies." He ran his hand over the closest trunk. A lacquered black so shiny I could almost see our reflections in it. "And this is simply one room. Think of how many more there are on this ship. If the murderer has begun dismembering bodies, then he or she doesn't have to be tossing them overboard. They can be safely tucked away, then discarded along the road to their next destination." He patted the side of the trunk. "The bodies wouldn't even need to be placed in large coffin-sized trunks, either. If in pieces, they could fit anywhere. For all we know, we might be standing in a veritable graveyard this very moment. The captain claims to have had the upper decks thoroughly scoured, and we've yet to find the rest of the body the arm belongs to."

Chills dragged their nails down my back and over my arms. A light bulb above flickered, attracting a stowaway moth that repeatedly thrashed itself against the light. Corpses did not trouble me; the men who made them did. "Let's hurry. We don't have much time."

We rushed down one aisle, then the next, scanning each trunk. At the end of one wide passage I noticed a rather large upright box, covered with a dark cloth. It was much larger than a coffin, perhaps double the size—it was something to investigate another time.

"We ought to split up," I said. "We'll cover more ground that way, and faster, too."

Thomas nodded and veered off to the aisle next to mine. I hated being this far at the back of the room—it made it nearly impossible to hear if someone had entered. Anyone might be lurking in one of the aisles, waiting to spring a trap. I was just starting down the next aisle when Thomas called out.

"I believe I've found it," he said. "Come have a look."

I ran around to where he was hunched over a long trunk. It was even more beautiful than I'd pictured. The blue was striking against the tiles that reflected like broken bits of looking glass. I bent down, noticing the locks on either end. I reached for my hatpin, then halted when Thomas clicked it open. He caught my stare and grinned. "Mephistopheles and Houdini aren't the only ones in possession of tricks. You ought to see what I can do with my—"

"Miss Wadsworth," Mephistopheles said from the end of the aisle, startling me away from Thomas. "I see you missed me so much you've brought a stand-in." He turned to Thomas, frowning. His attention dropped to the open trunk at our feet. "This chamber is off-limits to outsiders. I was just making sure she'd found her way safely here."

"Is that how you knew what time the performers were practicing?" Thomas asked, his tone neutral. "You were with him this morning?"

My voice suddenly seemed to disappear. I wet my lips, pulse speeding. "Yes…"

"One should always honor a lady's choice." Mephistopheles grinned. "You may run along now, Mr. Cresswell. I'll escort our lady back to her cabin soon enough."

Thomas was the picture of restraint as he ignored the ringmaster and instead met my gaze. I did not want him to go, nor did I want him to feel brushed aside for the ringmaster again. But if we were to solve this crime, I'd need to listen to my head and hope my heart would withstand the pain.

Caught between the two, I did what needed to be done for the greater good of our investigation.

Though it pained me to do so, I took a step toward Mephistopheles. I'd hoped Thomas would've deduced the truth, but a look of hurt flashed in his eyes. He jerked his head in an imitation of a nod. My heart wrenched.

"Very well. We'll finish our discussion later, Wadsworth."

He eyed the ringmaster another moment, then strode out the door, shoulders stiff and hands clenched. I stood there, unmoving, wondering if I'd just unintentionally changed my future. Fate was a fickle thing.

"Such a pity," Mephistopheles said. "You're going to break his heart. Though it will be amusing to watch him cut himself against the blade of your indecision."

I counted to five, hoping to regain my composure. "Is that so? Would you like to know what I think of you?"

"Enlighten me." He nodded. "It ought to be amusing."

"You're arrogant, deceitful, and think too highly of your own wit." I ticked off each detriment on my fingers. "Shall I go on?"

He drew his brows together, looking genuinely baffled. "You forgot the most important attributes: handsome and well dressed. When was the last time you saw a tailcoat this sharp?"

"You're ridiculous."

"I'm honest." He smiled. "You're simply annoyed that you *do* enjoy my company. I make you think, broaden your scientific theories and ideas. I get under your skin and you loathe it."

"Yes," I agreed, nodding, "you do get under my skin. Like a scalpel."

"Which means I'm smooth and cool as a blade." Mephistopheles lifted a shoulder. "Should we grab some tea and discuss more of my appealing qualities? Or should we skip straight to the kissing?

I must admit, I've been dreaming of our almost-kiss nonstop. Next time I see Houdini, I'm going to drown him. Though maybe you've found other ways of occupying yourself. I'll grant you this: Cresswell is handsome, though I still edge him out there. It's my dark, brooding looks. He also can't compete with the mask."

"Honestly?" I rubbed my temples. "You're the most maddening person I've ever encountered."

"Another distinguished honor." He bowed deeply. "I'm sure Mr. Cresswell will be vexed by that declaration as well. Second place is, well, not first, is it? Though it's something he'll have to get used to, especially the more he's around me. He might need some coddling to make it through. Poor chap. I'll have to see if Isabella is up to the task. She's mentioned him a few times now."

He watched me like a hawk might eye a potential meal. I silently counted to ten, but said nothing. Mephistopheles was trying to rile the truth out of me. But he'd need to do more than that. "You're distracting me."

"A problem shared by most every woman—and some men— I meet." The humor flicked out of his gaze as if a candle had been suddenly snuffed out. "I warned you about being caught down here, didn't I? Do you have any idea what sort of trouble you'd have caused if—*damn* it."

I glanced over my shoulder to see what had ruffled him enough to swear. Andreas and Jian walked down the aisle, heads bent in hushed conversation. It was odd seeing them in regular trousers and shirts, their glittering costumes saved for the stage alone.

Before I could take in any other details, Mephistopheles hurriedly wrapped an arm around me, dragged me close, then pressed a chaste kiss to my lips. I heard the scrape of wood against metal and realized the ringmaster was slowly moving the trunk of swords back into place, using our kiss as the sleight of hand.

I shut my eyes and tried not to think of how pleasant his lips were—how soft and gentle, so at odds with his sharp-tongued swagger. A moment later Mephistopheles pulled back, his expression a combination of wicked delight along with a smattering of apology. I wondered if I appeared as startled and confused as the thoughts rushing through my head.

He gave his performers a lazy grin, never taking his arm from my waist. Which was a good thing; I wasn't sure I wouldn't stumble away. He gently squeezed in warning. "A bit early for you two. As you can tell, I wasn't expecting anyone down here for a while. Or shall I say *we* weren't expecting anyone. I was giving Miss Wadsworth the grand tour."

"Is that what you were doing?" Jian asked, not bothering to hide the amusement in his tone. "*Touring* the supplies? I bet next time you'll tour the toilets."

My cheeks flamed, but I didn't dare to contradict him. Jian let his dark gaze fall to mine, and I could only guess at what he saw. Another foolish young thing caught up in Mephistopheles's web of illusions? Or was he sizing me up as another victim to add to his list? My attention slid to Andreas, whose face was nearly as splotchy with color as Liza's had been earlier. I couldn't tell if he was embarrassed for me or for the indecent show the ringmaster and I had put on. Perhaps he was disappointed I'd ignored his tarot reading and hadn't stayed away from the Magician.

"Semantics." Mephistopheles took my hand, making a grand show of escorting me out of there. "I expect you both in the saloon by eleven. Tonight's show requires extra hands. And keep practicing what I showed you for the finale. We need to help these people forget murders and simply remember the Moonlight Carnival."

Without saying more, we left the performers to gather their things. As we entered the corridor, I thought about both young men, deciding that either one of them could be the murderer we sought. Andreas appeared quiet and shy, but in a group filled with wonder-workers, that might be his own illusion.

"Well?" Mephistopheles said once we were well into the next cor-ridor. "Did you at least find anything worthwhile, or was that a giant waste of time? Not that our kiss wasn't worth the trouble. That was quite nice. Wouldn't you agree?"

"Depends on whether or not this belongs to you." Thomas appeared from around the corner, holding a signet ring in his palm. A lion's head surrounded by thorns with bloodred rubies set in its eyes. It was stunning. And its arrival certainly seemed to stun the ringmas-ter; he went very still. I didn't believe his reaction was from the sur-prise appearance of my friend. "Strange that your swordsman would keep this in his trunk. Stranger still that you sent Miss Wadsworth directly to it, then followed her there." Mephistopheles appeared as if he would tackle Thomas to the ground in order to retrieve it, but managed to remain in place. "This is your family crest, it is not? Or is it another stolen identity that you've taken on?"

"It's mine," he ground out. "And I've not stolen anything, Mr. Cresswell."

I removed my arm from Mephistopheles's. I didn't question how Thomas had sorted out whose ring it was; I knew if he was certain, then I was as well. "Did you place your signet there for me to find? What sort of game are you playing?"

"I may play the role of villain," he said quietly, "but that does not make me one. Perhaps you ought to ask yourselves this: If not me, then who? Who else would wish to set suspicion on me? Who might benefit from the carnival being cast under scrutiny?" He shook his head, light glinting off the mask. "Making up your mind about a person before getting to know them makes you susceptible to true evil. I am not the villain of this story, no matter how hard you try to cast me as such. My signet was stolen at the start of the week. I didn't wish to share the information."

He was right, regardless of how much I wished to dispute him. We were quick to blame him, think the worst of him, based on our emotions, not facts. It was the first rule of being a decent scientist and investigator, and we'd broken it.

"Can either of you think of someone who might seek revenge?" he pressed. "I certainly can. But then I'm not the one wasting time crafting a narrative to explain away evil deeds. I'd suggest you turn your critical lens on the upper class. Where is Dr. Arden? He disappears for the majority of the voyage, and yet all you do is knock on his door a few times? And what of Miss Crenshaw's father? Would a man that powerful simply accept his daughter's fate? Would a lord sit politely back, knowing his precious girl had chosen a lowly carnival performer over her family and paid the ultimate price for it? Or would he destroy that which had destroyed him?"

"So you did carry on a secret affair with her?" I asked, troubled by the uncomfortable feeling in my center.

"She was a lonely girl in want of a friend, and I, too, was tired of being alone," he said. "I listened to her fears. But that's all that passed between us."

He eyed his signet but didn't make a move to take it back. Another surprise. Without saying another word, Mephistopheles brushed past Thomas, leaving us both to silently rethink our list of suspects. It was a passionate speech. The sharp words chosen with the eye of an expert marksman, one who knew how to both aim and strike his target. Whether it was a shot meant to distract or disarm, I couldn't be sure.

Harry Houdini with wife, Bess

TWENTY-EIGHT

MILK-CAN ESCAPE

DINING SALOON
RMS ETRURIA
6 JANUARY 1889

Chandeliers flared brightly, then dimmed, our not-so-subtle clue the show was about to begin. Most of the chatter in the saloon halted, though the din of conversation never fully stopped. My heartbeat nearly tripled, though I couldn't tell if it was fear of what might happen. The murderer hadn't announced his last victim in a grand way, and I knew deep within my bones it was only a matter of time before horrific carnage was unleashed in sinister fashion.

One glance around the noticeably smaller crowd confirmed I wasn't the only guest who worried about what might happen next. Empty seats stuck out like missing teeth in a forced grimace. One more night of terror and the audience might disappear altogether.

"I can't believe your uncle insisted we spy on this show," Thomas whispered. "Not that I'm complaining. This entrée is infinitely more pleasant than spending an evening with my nose in a severed limb. Or listening to Norwood bark at crew members."

I sighed. Leave it to Thomas to break the heaviness of the night by comparing our supper to a postmortem. He hadn't mentioned a word about my morning activities, and I decided to let it go for the moment. I was also grateful Uncle would miss possibly seeing Liza onstage again. Once she'd discovered he'd be sitting dinner out, she'd quickly made plans to assist with Harry's act. Worry wedged itself between my shoulder blades. I hoped she wasn't planning on creating her own theatrics tonight. Thomas cleared his throat, and I shook myself free of thoughts.

"Yes, well, when one must choose between herbed squab and putrid flesh," I said, "it's such a difficult decision."

"Don't worry." Thomas flashed a mischievous grin. "There'll be plenty of time for rotting flesh after dessert. I promised your uncle I'd assist directly after the show. You're more than welcome to join, unless you've got more nefarious plans to attend to."

Thomas's tone was light, but I still saw shadows of doubt creeping across his expression. I did my best to smile, though I suddenly felt as if I were drowning. I had to practice for the finale and meet with the ringmaster for yet another lesson. Hopefully I'd gather more information regarding the murderer to make it all worthwhile. "Of course I'll assist tonight."

Uncle seemed to have forgiven me for rebelling against his one rule, his focus now entirely on the mystery of this ship. He believed—though others in his profession scoffed at the idea—that murderers frequented their crime scenes. Since someone was targeting members of the first-class passengers, he'd instructed us to continue being social. Take note of anything even slightly amiss. We were to be spies and apprentices and detectives in one—a challenge we were both eager to accept.

Mrs. Harvey cut into her roasted squab, either purposely not listening to our less-than-savory dinner talk or happily lost in her own thoughts. I sipped from my water goblet, focus straying to the stage as the lights dimmed and stayed that way. A moment later

Mephistopheles appeared, rising from the dark pit beneath center stage, surrounded by the usual cloud of smoke. Against my better judgment, my heart gave an excited jump.

For the first time I realized he was similar to a phoenix rising from the ashes. While I'd been working to unravel the mystery surrounding the murders, I was no closer to unearthing any clues about him or who he'd truly been before taking his stage persona. Perhaps he had burned his old life to the ground and emerged into something untouchable.

"Welcome to the sixth evening of the greatest show from sea to sea," Mephistopheles said. "Tonight you will bear witness to the most magnificent escape of our time. Or perhaps...perhaps you will see a young man's life ended before your very eyes. I make no guarantee that the next performer will survive. Victory will make him a legend, but failure means a drowning death."

The silence that followed his opening statement was palpable. No one wanted to witness a man drown, especially after the last few nights. I knew the importance of carrying on after death, but this seemed a bit crude considering the circumstances.

Mephistopheles clapped his hands twice, and assistants rolled something onto the stage hidden by a velvety curtain. It took a great effort by my cousin and Isabella to push the massive object to the center of the floor. Trepidation wound its way through my body.

"What you see here is a galvanized-iron vessel filled to the brim with water." Mephistopheles nodded toward Isabella and Liza. They yanked the curtain off, revealing the large milk can. "Not only will Houdini submerge himself in this milk can, we will secure it with massive locks, ensuring that not even he can escape."

Murmurs broke out, and the room seemed to take a collective breath. Climbing into a can full of water was dangerous enough, but locking it was a new level of madness. Mephistopheles allowed worry to simmer, enjoying the bubbling torment of the carnival's patrons. I could have sworn his eyes twinkled a bit more at their distress.

"There, there, everyone," he said in a soothing tone. "I'll allow Houdini the honor of announcing the rest." Mephistopheles threw his hands out to either side, welcoming his star to the night stage. "Behold the incredible, the impossible, the intoxicatingly terrifying escape artist of the nineteenth century! Ladies and gentlemen, I present to you the Great Houdini!"

The crowd was mostly quiet whenever Mephistopheles took the stage, but when Houdini entered the room this evening, the hush that descended was a living, breathing thing. Darkness and density and the throbbing beat of one's own blood pumping in the void of outward noise. I'd heard people remark on being able to hear a pin drop, but the truth of Houdini's presence was so much more than that. I could have sworn I heard each contraction of my heart, each molecule of oxygen I barely breathed in, all of it so loud within my head it had to be heard across the sea to London.

Mephistopheles was correct once again: Harry Houdini was destined to become a legend, if only for the magnitude of his presence. He was a man of modest stature and extraordinary might. At least on this night, after we'd all seen death made into a spectacle.

"A bit dramatic for my taste," Thomas whispered, leaning in. "How many adjectives can one use in a sentence? Mephisto might be in want of a thesaurus. Perhaps I'll gift one to him."

"Hush," Mrs. Harvey scolded, her attention riveted on the dark-haired young man wrapped in a plush robe. Without preamble, Houdini dropped the robe. Heat flooded my cheeks; women and men gasped around the room. I'd never seen a man in his small-clothes, and Houdini was practically naked.

"Oh, my," Mrs. Harvey said, then took a long pull of ice water.

"It's been a moment since I've seen a man in his underthings. Poor Mr. Harvey, Lord rest his soul. He—"

"Please, I beg of you, do not elaborate," Thomas interrupted, giving her a look of pure dread. "Some things are better left to our imaginations. And even then we might not wish to go down that creative route."

"Humph." Mrs. Harvey picked up her fan, waving it steadily about. I'm sure it had nothing to do with being upset and everything to do with being once again riveted by the young man parading around in his smallclothes. He seemed to soak up the attention.

Liza, ever the daring assistant, kept the smile on her face, though I could see the strain. I hadn't yet spoken to her to see how she was faring, interacting with Houdini after the love letter revelation, and would do so immediately following the show. If she made it through this act without letting on how upset she was, she might make it to New York without dunking him in the ocean yet.

"The clock, if you *please*!" Houdini's voice boomed out with the command. The assistants rolled a massive timepiece a few feet from the milk can. His gaze strayed to Liza, then quickly moved on. "Now," he addressed the audience, "I need a volunteer. Who will come up and inspect my prison for any defect?"

Thomas's arm shot into the air. I kicked at him under the table but missed, judging from the way he waved his arm around. The escape artist passed over my friend in favor of a robust man of around forty-five years. The man banged a cane on the side of the can, the clang proving it was no fake. He did a thorough job of walking around, tapping each side of the milk can. He even lifted the lid, inspecting it for who knew what. Satisfied, he gave a curt nod, then returned to his table.

"As you have witnessed, there are no tricks involved," Houdini called out, voice clear and loud. "I want you all to hold your breath and watch the seconds tick by." He motioned toward the stopwatch. "Begin the count...now!"

Mephistopheles hit a button on the side of the clock, setting the second hand in motion. He'd never remained onstage to assist before, and I wondered if he was only here tonight to watch for anything amiss.

Tick. Tick. Tick.

Everyone inhaled deeply, then held their breath for as long as they could. Most exhaled by thirty seconds.

Tick. Tick. Tick. A few more after forty. Almost all were dragging in breaths before a minute had passed.

Tick. Tick. Tick. Thomas's cheeks remained puffed out, and he seemed no more distressed over the lack of oxygen than he did by the sight of the half-naked young man onstage. Houdini grinned when my friend finally released his breath.

"Now, I ask that you all hold your breath once more. But first..." He strode across the stage, completely unconcerned about the death trap lurking behind him. Without further discussion, he climbed into the milk can. Water sloshed over the sides, forcing his assistants to back up or stand in the growing puddle. "I wouldn't feel right being called the King of Cuffs without my bracelets, now, would I? Liza, please bring my handcuffs."

His use of proper manners brought on the ghost of a smile to Mephistopheles's otherwise blank expression. He was a quick learner, something highly valued in this business.

Liza, smile still in place, stepped forward, cuffs in hand. At this the crowd turned indignant. Someone yelled out, "This is madness! No one wants to see a man drown. Where's the fire act? Bring out the fortune-teller!"

Mephistopheles, still posted near the giant stopwatch, cocked his head. "If you're afraid of death, you ought to leave now. Neither Houdini nor I can guarantee his survival. Smelling salts are available to any and all who may require them."

"People have died! This is unacceptable." The man shook his head at his table and stormed from the room. No one else protested the idea of witnessing a man possibly drown before their eyes. Which was unnerving. Any one of these passengers, eager for death, might be involved with the murders. Or become the next victim.

My gaze drifted back to my cousin, who was still smiling behind her mask. Angry though she might be with Houdini, if there was even a hint of this act going wrong, she wouldn't be able to maintain her cool stance. I hoped.

Unease crawled along my thoughts. If anything were to go wrong, it would be easy to claim faulty equipment. However, would that be too quiet of a murder for a killer who enjoyed theatrics? Or would the thrill of taking out a legend in the making be enough of a draw?

Houdini held his arms up, waiting for the cuffs. Liza clapped them onto his wrists a bit too exuberantly, the sound near echoing in the quiet. He glanced at her from the corner of his eye, but lifted the cuffs up proudly.

"These are regulation police handcuffs." He tugged on them, proving how real they were. "Once I submerge myself underwater and my assistants have replaced the lid, I ask that you all hold your breath along with the clock."

A long look passed between Houdini and Mephistopheles, and the ringmaster finally nodded. Despite logic telling me all would be well, my palms tingled when Houdini maneuvered himself into the vessel. Either for our benefit or his own, he took a large breath before submerging himself. Liza and Isabella were on the can in an instant, securing the lid in place. At the same moment the lid clanked down,

Mephistopheles started the clock. It seemed they'd practiced quite well. This was one science experiment they could not get wrong. Not only for Houdini's sake, but for the fate of the carnival.

Tick. Tick. Tick.

Once more, I dragged in my breath along with the crowd, holding it until I convinced myself my eyes would burst from my skull if I didn't release it.

Tick. Tick. Tick.

The second hand echoed like a gong, all the while Houdini remained below water.

Tick. Tick. Tick. More gasps burst forth from people in the dining saloon. Forty-eight seconds had now passed with the escape artist still submerged. Liza and Isabella shifted, their pretty smiles frozen in place.

Tick. Tick. Tick. Mephistopheles called out, "One minute."

Thomas tapped along to the ticking of the clock, the sound setting my nerves into more of a tizzy. I clamped my jaw together until it ached. At the minute-and-a-half mark, Liza and Isabella casually lifted the domed lid. Houdini burst upward, hands still shackled, and drew in a ragged breath. Water splashed onto the stage, the sound not even close to as lulling as the waves outside.

Houdini drew in a few more deep breaths, eyes twinkling. "This time, instead of just a demonstration, my assistants will also padlock the lid, making escape nearly impossible. I'll either set myself free..."

Mephistopheles walked over and patted his shoulder. "Or we shall set your corpse out to sea."

A few patrons stood and quietly left the room. Light from the corridor flashed each time the door opened and closed, the illumination adding to my twisting worry. Houdini dunked underwater, and Liza and Isabella secured the lid, this time padlocking it in two places. While they did that, the ringmaster started the ticking of the clock—it took nearly thirty seconds for the lid to be locked. Surely Houdini would be exhausted after already demonstrating the act. It was beyond madness to do it again so soon; this was a death wish.

My heart knocked frantically, searching for a way out. There had to be an explanation for the trick, but I couldn't locate one. This time, Liza and Isabella covered the milk can with a curtained screen. It was midnight-blue velvet with a thousand silver stars embroidered onto it.

Tick. Tick. Tick.

Tap. Tap. Tap.

I couldn't decide if Thomas's tapping or the incessant ticking was worse. Mrs. Harvey twisted her napkin in her lap, eyes fastened to the starry curtain.

Tick. Tick. Tick.

Tap. Tap. Tap.

I moved about my seat; there were so many more-pressing things to be concerned with. The severed limb. The slain women. The identity of the murderer who might be in this very room . . . yet my pulse roared at the possibility of what was happening behind that curtain.

Tick. Tick. Tick.

"One minute, thirty seconds," Mephistopheles said. I had no idea if I'd imagined the strain in his tone. Passengers grumbled as the clock ticked on. What had started as good fun was turning into panic. A few people pushed back from their seats, fists clenched at their sides.

Tick. Tick. Tick.

"Two minutes." Mephistopheles's foot tapped faster than the clock. Both Liza's and Isabella's arms began trembling, the curtain wavering with them. "Two minutes thirty seconds."

"Help him!" a man cried, followed by another. "Release him!"

"Something must be wrong!" another passenger yelled. The crowd grew uneasy. More pleas cropped up. Still, the ringmaster kept his focus stuck to the ticking second hands.

"Three minutes!" he nearly shouted. Sweat beaded his hairline. Either he was the most talented actor the world had ever known, or something was going dreadfully wrong.

I stared at my cousin, noting the way her eyes kept darting to the clock. By now almost everyone in the crowd was on their feet, yelling, demanding action. I was about to jump onstage and open the bloody can myself when Mephistopheles yelled, "Check him now!"

The curtain dropped in an instant, revealing a soaking wet, unshackled Houdini. He bowed deeply as the crowd went utterly wild with applause and whistling.

"I don't believe it," I muttered. "How on earth did he manage to get the padlocks back onto the can?"

Thomas opened his mouth, but Mrs. Harvey silenced him with a look. "Not a word out of you, dear. Or I swear I'll finish my story about poor Mr. Harvey and his underthings."

I'd never seen Thomas snap his jaws together faster. I wanted to smile, but found it nearly impossible as my gaze caught on Houdini's. There was something in the gleam of his eyes that made all the hair on my arms stand at attention. I'd thought for certain he'd be the next victim, and I had a troubling feeling he knew it.

TWENTY-NINE

A FRIGHTFUL DISCOVERY

THIRD-CLASS PROMENADE
RMS ETRURIA
7 JANUARY 1889

Wind bit at my face, stinging my eyes and making them water as I hurried along the abandoned deck of third class. At this hour, the sun was a mere gash on the horizon, tinging the water a crimson black as it spilled across the waves. I shut images of bloodbaths from my mind, moving as quickly as I could to the temporary laboratory. A noticeably pale servant had delivered a note from Uncle that had stated "You're needed in the laboratory. Straightaway."

I'd thrown on a simple muslin dress and stuffed my feet into the first shoes I could find—dainty little silk things that would have to do, though Thomas would certainly raise a brow at them as he'd done in the past. His teasing didn't matter; swiftness did.

There was an aura of urgency in the air, and I couldn't help but inhale it in great gasps, setting my limbs in motion. I didn't need to possess Thomas's skill in deductions to know a body had been found. Uncle wouldn't send for me this early if it were about the severed limb. A thorough dissection had already been completed, and in truth, there wasn't much else we could do with it.

This was something worse. Much worse.

Another blast of arctic air barreled through the corridor, forcing me to bury my nose into my fur collar. The storm that had been threatening was almost ready to wage its assault. My steps rushed over the deck, the wooden slats cold as the winter air frosting the railings. A prickling sensation between my shoulder blades brought me to a halt, glancing back down the empty deck. At least I believed it remained vacant. This early in the morning, before the sun actually rose and the sky was somewhere between blood and shadow, it was hard to tell who might be lurking against the wall.

I stared a beat more, then turned and continued on. When I came to the entry to the stairs, I paused again, listening for any sound of pursuit. Waves steadily lapped the side of the ship. Wind howled low through the tunnel-like deck as it gusted. Steam hissed far above from the funnels, or smokestacks, as Thomas called them. No footsteps, though. I was alone with my conjurer of an imagination.

Without thinking, I touched the blade hidden on my thigh. No matter how tired or in a hurry I'd been to forgo finding proper shoes, I'd made sure to not leave without a means of protecting myself. One fact remained: a person on this ship was snatching victims as if they were pearls plucked from oysters and stringing them up in horrific ways.

I'd not be taken without a fight.

Satisfied I was alone, I plunged into the dim lighting of the narrow stairs, beads of perspiration already beginning as I descended deeper into the overly warm belly of the ship. New sounds emerged. The loud machinery of the boiler, constantly being refilled to power our journey across the sea. A horribly familiar scent also unfurled its fingers, beckoning me to the source the closer I drew. The sweet stench of human rot permeated the space, made worse by the heat of the boilers. I thought of Mephistopheles's plague masks, wishing I had some herbs to smell now.

Anything would be better than a nose full of decomposition.

I finally reached the bottom of the stairs and nearly ran down the corridor, slipping as I swung into the laboratory. Uncle glanced up, his face grim. As I'd suspected, a shrouded body lay on the examination table before him.

"Uncle," I said by way of greeting. I took a breath to steady myself and entered the room. Thomas hadn't arrived yet, though I imagined he'd be joining us soon enough. It took a moment, but the strong odor of death settled into an uncomfortable backdrop, hardly occupying space in my thoughts.

"Prepare for the postmortem. I want to examine the heart, stomach, intestines. Or what's left of them, at least." Uncle handed me an apron. "We'll begin soon."

"Yes, sir."

I strode over to Uncle's medical bag, removing the tools needed for this full examination one by one and laying them out in a row on a tray. Bone saw, toothed forceps, rib cutters, scalpel, enterotome, skull chisel, just in case, and a Hagedorn needle to sew the corpse together.

"The hammer with hook is in the side pouch," Uncle said, tying his own apron and rolling up his shirtsleeves. I nodded, setting about retrieving it while he scrubbed his hands and arms with carbolic soap. We were creatures of habit, he and I, both finding peace in our postmortem rituals.

A set of hurried footsteps brought my attention up as Thomas practically leapt into the room. He hadn't bothered with a jacket, and his white shirt was rumpled and mostly untucked as if he'd fallen asleep in his clothes. Even when we'd been investigating the secret tunnels below Bran Castle, I hadn't seen him so disheveled. From the look of him, it didn't appear that he'd been in bed for too long before being roused. I wasn't sure I wanted to know what had kept him preoccupied.

A muscle in his jaw ticked as his eyes lifted from the covered corpse and met mine across the room. We'd known it was only a matter of time before another body turned up, but it didn't make it easier to deal with. I offered him an encouraging nod, hoping he'd read the sadness in my own expression. Our chosen field of study showed the dark side of life; it was difficult to not be pulled into its void. The day death became easy to accept was the day I needed to set down my blades. Judging from the expression on his face, Thomas felt the same.

"I apologize for the delay, Professor." He produced a notebook and pen, situating himself near the examining table. "Miss Wadsworth." He tipped his chin in formal greeting. "What have I missed?"

"We're just getting started," Uncle replied, moving to stand over the cadaver. "They found the body in the cargo hold approximately thirty-five minutes ago. It had been stuffed into a wooden crate." He removed his spectacles and pinched the bridge of his nose. "The smell drew the attention of a crew member, and he alerted the chief officer. This one is a bit different from the others. Prepare yourselves."

I swallowed the bile searing up my throat.

Uncle had been taking meticulous notes for more years than I'd been alive, adding to theories and scientific findings of other doctors, such as Dr. Rudolf Virchow, who'd developed standardized postmortem protocols. Both men had found putrefaction in the air occurring two or three days after death. Intense odors, such as that from the corpse in this room, would be present by the fifth day. Meaning Miss Crenshaw might not have been the first to die after all.

"Let's begin." Uncle pulled the shroud down, revealing a discolored female body, naked except where he'd covered her with strips of cloth. It was one of the last decencies she'd been shown; her murderer certainly hadn't been kind or careful with her person.

My gaze swiftly traveled down in assessment, then froze. Slashes were apparent on her throat, and her torso had been split open. More precisely, she'd been *ripped* open. I held in a gasp at the brutal state of the victim. Uncle was right—this murder was unlike the others. The previous victims, while horrid in their own right, had been slain quickly. Their bodies sustained the most damage post mortem. This woman had been stabbed and slashed while she was still breathing. It almost seemed as if an entirely different person had attacked her. Which couldn't be.

Everything in the warm room suddenly became too hot to bear. I took a few breaths, hoping to steady the erratic beat of my heart. Jack the Ripper was dead. There was no way this crime was done by his hand, yet the similarity of the wounds was striking. Part of me wished to toss the medical tools on the table and run. Run far away from this corpse and these violent murders that never seemed to end.

But on this ship, in the middle of the great Atlantic Ocean, there was nowhere to escape.

Death didn't disturb me; memories of the Ripper case were a different matter altogether, though. Thomas bent near. "It's an equation, Wadsworth. Find the clues and add them together."

I jerked my head in response, emotions cooling. I set the tray back on the table and gave my uncle the measuring tape. Outside I was as sturdy as the ship, while inside I churned with emotion like the waters we sailed through. I wasn't sure the Ripper case would ever leave me in peace.

Uncle measured the body from foot to crown with efficiency, then reported to Thomas. "Deceased is approximately one hundred and sixty-two-and-a-half centimeters. Shoulder-length brown hair. Caucasian. Estimated weight is between eight and eight-and-one-half stone." I wiped down the scalpel and handed it to my uncle before he asked for it, then prepared the toothed forceps. "Greenish discoloration is present in the middle of the abdomen."

He gently prodded the closed eye, checking to see if it yielded, and I tried not to wince as he pried the lids open. For some reason, the examination of the eyes was my least favorite part.

"Eyes are milky and slightly protruded," he said. "Conditions in the cargo hold are moderately warm to cool. From outward examination, I'd place the death between seventy-two and ninety-six hours."

Our external examination was complete. Now it was time to unearth clues left by the murderer. Uncle pulled the skin taut on the collarbone, pressing his scalpel until the skin split in its wake. He repeated the movement on the opposite side before dragging the blade down the center, completing the Y incision. Though with the torso ripped open, he didn't have much to slice into below the ribs.

Once Uncle cracked the sternum, I clamped the rib cage open without being asked. He grunted approval, high praise considering his attention never wavered once the postmortem began. Up this close the odor was strong enough to cause a few stray tears to slide down my face. I rubbed my cheek against my shoulder, then collected a specimen jar in case Uncle needed it.

"Lacerations are present over the intestines. Both large and small." He leaned closer, until his nose was a mere hand space away from the exposed cavity. He took the scalpel and carefully moved the muscles away. "Ribs show marks from knife blades. Victim was stabbed repeatedly before being partially eviscerated."

A strong indication that whoever had committed this murder had been enraged. This was no random crime—there was too much passion and anger involved.

Uncle drew back, dabbing at the sweat on his brow. "The nicks in the bone are similar in appearance to those found in the severed limb. Though closer inspection with a microscope will be needed to be conclusive. They're also reminiscent of wounds left by Jack the Ripper. Strikingly so." We all paused for a moment, not wanting to utter the impossibility of that aloud. "Thomas, is there a problem?"

"Apologies, Professor." Thomas's pen rushed across the journal, capturing each word and detail with the same precision Uncle used to carve the dead. I forced myself to focus on his quick, sure movements.

I came back into the procedure as Uncle sliced into the stomach, revealing more clues as to time of death. "Contents are mostly digested." He removed his rust-colored hands and peered at me over his spectacles. "What might that mean, Audrey Rose?"

"Time of death would have occurred between meals." I leaned over the cavity to get a better look. Uncle stepped aside, ever the professor of forensic medicine. "If I had to guess, I'd say it indicated she'd been murdered very late at night, or in the early morning hours before her first meal."

"Good." Uncle poked around the empty stomach, making sure we'd missed nothing. "Now we'll just need to find out who else has been reported missing to the captain. Her clothing is folded up there. Someone ought to recognize it."

I followed his gaze to a pile of tattered and worn garments. Judging from the tears and patches, she wasn't a first-class passenger. Her life had likely been hard and she did not deserve to have it ended in such a callous manner. Dread pulled my shoulders down. Dissecting a cadaver on a slab of cool metal was hard, but not impossible. Attaching names and a life to a victim, however, was impossible *not* to feel.

"Shall I say what we're all thinking?" Thomas asked. "Or does this crime not seem disconnected from the others to you?"

Uncle glanced back at the body, expression shuttered. "We will treat this as we treat all cases and make no assumptions either way. What else have you deduced?"

"Since this corpse is female and is in possession of all her limbs, we have another problem." Thomas closed his notebook, then stood beside me. "There is still another body out there. Have all the crates been searched in the cargo hold?"

Uncle shook his head. "Captain Norwood felt uncomfortable with that."

I rubbed my temples, doing my best to ignore the pulsing anger. "So our captain would rather wait until the next victim's stench coats the corridors of the ship? It's bad enough that he refuses to ask Lord Crenshaw to comply with our investigation and he is very sensitive to Dr. Arden's need to remain locked up in his rooms, but when will he worry about the victims? Unless he doesn't want these crimes to be solved. Perhaps he's the man we're searching for."

Thomas paced the perimeter of the small room, tugging at his collar. I'd been so consumed with the postmortem, I'd forgotten how warm it was down here. He moved one way, then the other, constantly in motion, much like his thoughts.

"His arrogance is an ugly quality, though I don't believe he'll hang for that." He stilled. "The ringmaster is charming, brash. Utterly full of himself and has excessive taste in dramatics."

"Those traits, while annoying, don't mean Mephistopheles is our murderer," I said. "If not the captain, or ringmaster, then who else?"

Thomas stuffed his hands into his pockets. "I'd say Jian is too obvious, though still a decent suspect. And the Amazing Andreas is quiet enough to be terrifying. His type is the one that taxidermies animals and secretes them away in hidey-holes. Though maybe we've been focused on men when we should consider our murderer might be a murderess."

"A Knight of Swords, a Fool, a Hierophant, an escape artist, a ringmaster, and now either an Empress or an Ace of Wands," I said, prattling off each of the performers' stage names. It was truly remarkable that we could all maintain straight faces while naming potential murderers. "Out of those, you believe a woman is our killer?"

Thomas pulled his pocket watch out. "Whoever is responsible, we need to figure it out quickly. Once we reach American shores, our murderer—or murderers—will slip from our grasp."

THIRTY

GREATEST TRICK OF ALL

MEPHISTOPHELES'S WORKSHOP
RMS ETRURIA
7 JANUARY 1889

I lifted my hand to knock when the door to Mephistopheles's work-shop swung open, startling both myself and the unsuspecting Andreas as he walked into me. The fortune-teller took one look into my face, then threw his hands up, stumbling backward. "Don't hit me, miss. Please. I told you the magic looking glass was better than the tarot. *You* didn't listen!"

"I—what?" I asked, unsure if I ought to be offended. "Have that many people smacked you after a reading? I thought we were friends… I've been practicing that card trick. The snap-change one? Remember?"

Mephistopheles chuckled from somewhere in the cabin behind him, and Andreas's face scrunched up.

"Take heart, my friend. If you'd brought out that wretched look-ing glass, she'd have kicked you." The ringmaster appeared in the doorway, clapping a hand on the fortune-teller's shoulder. "One glance at that filthy glass sends all the wise girls running for maids and cleaning supplies. Now then"—he turned on his performer—"give her back her brooch and be on your way."

"My..." I felt around my cloak, realizing the pin was missing. "How?"

"Here." Andreas thrust the brooch at me and snatched his cloak from the hook near the door and huffed. "The looking glass divines the future. And there is nothing wrong with it. It's an antique—the patina gives it character. The spirits enjoy it."

"Whatever you do," Mephistopheles said, "do not repeat that rubbish to Harry. You know how he feels about those who claim to speak to spirits or tell the future. And how many times do I have to tell you to not steal from patrons? It's bad for business."

"Harry Houdini is a fool. And she is not technically a patron anymore, is she?" Andreas gave the ringmaster a haughty look before dashing into the morning light.

"He gets a bit sensitive about his Bavarian portending relic." Mephistopheles motioned for me to step inside before shutting the door. Dust motes moved like glitter in the shafts of thick morning sunshine. "I bet he stole the thing from some tiny shop in a nameless German town."

"That's what you want to comment on? What about my brooch?" I swung around, head cocked. "Does Andreas have a habit of thievery?"

"No, he makes a living at it." He walked over to his worktable and fiddled with some pieces of mechanical cage he'd been making. "Before you ask, I've already checked his chambers for clues or knives or other murder ephemera. Everything was a mess, but no blood or bodies."

"Well, I don't trust him."

"A wise deduction on your part. For that matter, you ought to be terrified of me." From his tone, I didn't think he was entirely joking. "Rumor has it that another body was discovered this morning. Is that why you're blessing me with your presence?"

"How do you know about it?" I asked. "Have you made other midnight bargains with spies?"

"Jealous?" He glanced at me over his shoulder, a smile tugging one side of his mouth up. "Your cousin told me when I saw her this morning. She'd found a note you'd left in your room."

"Oh." It was a simple-enough explanation, though I didn't know quite what to make of it. "Why did you need to speak with my cousin so early?"

"I take it you finally gave her Harry's letter." He turned fully in his chair, eyeing me. "She was quite touchy. Hardly the mark of a girl blissfully in love with her suitor. I also apparently annoyed her by knocking on your cabin door like a...how did she phrase it? 'A stray cat in heat,' I believe was the charming term." He smiled. "She threatened to have me neutered. Imagine that."

For some silly reason my cheeks warmed at the thought. "Why were you calling on *me* so indecently early, then?"

He looked at me like I might be a bit dull. "To invite you to breakfast. Though I thought better of it once I'd discovered where you were. Dissection and tea don't sound all that appealing, though maybe your tastes are a bit more depraved than my own." I rolled my eyes. "Tell me"—his tone was suddenly serious—"what did you discover?"

I hesitated, unsure of how much information might be too much to share. For all I knew I was standing in the room with the very man who'd murdered all those women. "How well do you know the people who are part of your carnival?"

"How well do we truly know anyone, Miss Wadsworth?"

"Don't start equivocating." I crossed my arms. "If you'd like to hear my theories, you need to participate in being helpful. Tell me who you trust and who you don't. We need to narrow down the suspects. Any information you have might be of use."

"I do not have the luxury of trusting anyone." He pointed at the mask he wore. "If I did, I would not keep myself hidden like a common thief. Do I believe in the people who work for me? I do. I believe they are all unique and wondrous. And horridly misunderstood. I also know that they all have a past, most of them criminal."

"Even Anishaa?" I asked, skeptically. "She was lied to and taken from her home and family. I have it on good authority that you were the one who made that bargain."

"Is that all she said about her past? Interesting."

He motioned for me to take a seat on a settee that was piled high with bolts of fabrics and costumes. Reluctantly, I did.

"Would you care to hear a story, Miss Wadsworth?"

I did my best to not show my impatience. Everything was a riddle with him. "Will it be beneficial to the case?"

"Eventually," he said. "But it may take a moment to arrive there."

"All right, then. Tell me."

"My grandfather taught me his best trick," Mephistopheles said, surprising me with an actual family detail. There was a wistful expression in his gaze that made him seem like any other young gentleman. Except for the cursed mask. He shook his head. "Though I doubt my father would be pleased to hear it."

"What did your grandfather teach you?"

He offered a smile tinged in sadness. "To dream."

I drew my brows together. That wasn't at all what I'd been expecting, which should have been expected coming from Mephistopheles. "Yes, but was he also good at engineering? Did he show you how to craft trick hats and boxes that saw people in half? Surely that's more valuable in your business than a simple dream."

"The greatest trick of all is dreaming without limits."

"Everyone dreams, Mephistopheles," I said. "There's no trick to it."

The ringmaster stood and picked up a toy-sized hot-air balloon. He beckoned me to come near and lifted it into the air, watching it hang prettily between us, all pale blue stripes, crescent moons, and tiny pearls. Up close, I could see the little wicker basket had been woven through with silver thread.

"Dreams are strange curiosities," he said, eyes still on the balloon. "Sure, everyone possesses the ability to lay their heads down and imagine, but to do so without limitations or doubt? That is something else entirely. Dreams are boundless, shapeless things. Given strength and form from individual imaginations. They're wishes." He looked at me, then reached out and removed my hatpin. "All it takes is one shard of doubt to wedge itself into them"—he swiftly stuck the balloon with my pin, and the air whooshed out as it descended to the ground—"and they deflate. If you can dream without limits, you can soar to great heights. Let the magic of your imagination set you free."

"Does your grandfather approve of your carnival?" I asked, hoping it wasn't too rude of a question. "Or is that why you wear a mask? To hide."

Mephistopheles stared down at the ruined balloon. "My family does not desire to know a thing about my show. They purposely act as if neither it nor I exist. As the spare heir, I was never required to be the good or decent one. I simply needed to be there in case the unthinkable happened to their favored son."

There was no trace of bitterness that I could detect, though his words were brutally harsh in their honesty. Part of me longed to reach over and comfort him, while the more sensible side refrained from acting on the impulse.

"My grandfather passed away and my father withered. He's still alive," he amended, "but my brother mostly runs the estate. It was best, they said, if I didn't displease my father with my useless dreams while he recovered. My follies were for swindlers and other lowborn thieves—things I supposedly needed to be extra wary of, since my mother is from Constantinople. They worried about society speaking even more poorly of me than they already did."

"I'm sorry." My heart clenched. My mother, being half Indian, had occasionally faced similar prejudices from small-minded people. "I know how hard it is to desire approval from your parents, even if it's the last thing you truly want."

Mephistopheles rubbed at his mask, but didn't take it off. "Yes, well"—his voice was a bit rough—"now you see why that signet is so important to me. I might have been a disappointment to my family, but I'm not quite ready to give them up. My grandfather insisted I have it once he passed on, and it's my last link to him."

My hand went to the heart locket around my throat. I would go mad if anything happened to my mother's necklace. I recalled the longing in Mephistopheles's eyes when Thomas had produced his signet. If it were me, I'd have throttled someone until I got it back.

"Why didn't you tell anyone your family ring was missing?"

He smiled, but it was more fierce than sweet. "I do not need anyone learning my true identity. Who knows what sort of blackmail might be used, should my name be discovered. The carnival folk are brilliant, but they're also practical. They need coin and earn it anyway they can."

"You believe Jian or Andreas stole your signet, then?"

"I'm not certain who stole it. They are all dear to me, but I have no idea how deep some of their own scars go."

"That's terrible."

"That's life, my dear." He lifted a shoulder. "They are the dregs of society—the throwaways and so-called freaks. When that's beaten into you by others, you tend to stick to yourself and live by your own code. Who can you trust when the whole world turns so savagely on you? And in the name of what? Because we choose to live by our own rules? Because a young woman would prefer to cover herself in ink instead of silk? Or because there's a person who enjoys swallowing flames in place of mucking out alleys in the East End?" His hands clenched at his sides. "I can no more blame them for biting the hand that feeds them than I can ignore the fact that society kicked them until they learned to strike back at anyone who dared to get close. We might band together, but we will always be apart, too. This carnival is home for now, but it won't be forever for some. There's always a grander dream, or larger goal, to achieve. This is the cost of dreaming without limits. This is the dark side of show business."

I thought of one act in particular. "Like Houdini?"

Mephistopheles retrieved the broken balloon and tossed it into a rubbish bin. "Like him. Like Jian. Like Anishaa. Andreas. Cassie. And even Sebastián. We are all together—brothers and sisters— in this madness, until we're not. I don't relish thinking of them as thieves or scoundrels or even murderers, as you might suggest, not when that's how so many others view them. But the fact remains I do not have the luxury of casting anyone aside. Though I am more inclined to believe it's someone who's not part of my troupe. I don't know much about the captain, but he is . . . I'm not sure. He seems out for glory. I don't know what he'd do with my signet or why he'd murder his own passengers, but I also can't say he wouldn't have stolen it or killed those people. Or had one of his crew members do the deeds for him. Perhaps he dreams of owning his own ship. My signet would fetch a decent price. And if he ends up 'saving the day' by finding the 'true' murderer, well, then, he'd be called a hero, wouldn't he?"

"I thought dreams were good things," I said, thinking to the start of our conversation.

"Ah, yes, but you cannot forget nightmares often begin as dreams."

"If this dream has become such a burden, why not quit? You have the ability to walk away. I'm sure your family would gladly welcome you back."

He gave me a sad smile and I thought perhaps it might be the truest thing I'd ever seen from the illusionist.

"If only it were so easy. You see, you create an escape for someone else, realizing at the last minute that you've trapped yourself in a cage of your own design. By then it's too late—the show has taken on a legend of its own, and you are powerless to overcome those bars, so you submit to your art and allow the world to consume you, knowing the cost. Each performance siphons a bit more of your soul."

"Sounds...pleasant. But do you still enjoy it?"

"You want me to remove my mask for you, Miss Wadsworth? You want the truth, then it shall be yours." He stepped close to me, but I didn't back away. "You both love and hate it, this ravenous beast that feeds until you're nearly spent and never thinks of giving back. But you cannot fault it, you understand its selfishness—you were once selfish, too. So you make excuses for it, nourish it, love it, coax it into a monster so large it will never be satiated with what you give. You either must end it entirely—at the risk of yourself—or carry on until the last curtain falls and you take that final bow."

A tear slipped down my cheek. "That's incredibly sad, Mephistopheles."

"That is the nature of the show—it never truly ends, only slumbers until it wakes and does it again. The performers you see out there?" He gestured toward the door. "They do not belong anywhere else. They have no home other than the one under the stage lights and striped tents. The show is home. And we are all much too indebted to its shelter to leave it behind."

"All of you feel that way?"

"The fire-eater? The swordsman? The gentleman who nearly drowns each night...do you believe they'd be welcomed into the circles you belong to?" He shook his head. "Society scorned them, turned them into freak shows and curiosities, and now they are only interested in cheering because of the glamour of those velvet curtains. The allure of magic and mysticism. Should they encounter those same performers on the street, they would not be so kind or accepting. It is a sad truth that we do not live in a world where differences are accepted. And until such a time, Miss Wadsworth, I will provide a home to the misfits and unwanteds, even if it means losing bits of my soul to that hungry, unsatisfied beast Mr. Barnum has called show business."

I wasn't sure what to say. There was so much more at stake for Mephistopheles than I'd have thought—so much each and every person involved with the carnival stood to lose. They were a family of discarded souls, lost until they'd found a home with each other. It would destroy them if one of their own was the monster they so desperately tried to keep out of their reality. A chosen family who dealt in dreams and was living a nightmare. My chest ached. I did not want to break any of their hearts, but I couldn't turn away from the crimes.

"If the murderer is a performer..." I sighed. "It would be better if the carnival didn't hinder the investigation. And I don't mean better for me or my uncle," I added at the flash of incredulity in his face. "I know you take care of your own, but if word spread of you harboring a murderer—it will destroy everything you've built. Beast or not. This show will come to an end."

Mephistopheles took a shuddering breath. "If I tell them to turn on each other, it will end badly no matter what." He shook his head. "Enough of all that. Is Mr. Cresswell planning on returning my signet anytime soon, or is he prancing around at night wearing it, wishing he were as handsome as me?"

I blinked at the abrupt change in subject, but didn't press the issue. "I will make sure you have your ring back."

"I knew I liked you with good reason." With that, he offered his arm. "Come. It's almost time for breakfast. I'm sure Mr. Cresswell would enjoy spending time with you before the show tonight."

I hesitated before taking his arm. "I was under the impression you'd want to keep me from Thomas as often as possible."

"Don't think I've gone and done the valiant thing, now, Miss Wadsworth. I'm still the same scoundrel you met a few days ago." A bit of mischief was back in his eyes. "I simply want to steal you right out from before him."

I didn't bother responding. Let Mephistopheles believe he could pull off the biggest sleight of hand. I knew there was no one who possessed enough magic to spell me away from Thomas Cresswell. At least, I believed that to still be the truth. But in a world where illusions were hard to distinguish from reality, it was getting harder to tell.

THIRTY-ONE
METHOD OF DISTRACTION

BOW
RMS ETRURIA
7 JANUARY 1889

Jian tossed jewel-encrusted daggers into the air, handle over blade, in rapid-fire succession, juggling them as if they were no more dangerous than apples or oranges. It seemed far too early to be so cavalier with a weapon like that. He watched my reaction from the corner of his eye, mouth pressed into a flat line. He'd made it perfectly clear he did not care for me or my presence in his carnival, though my only crime thus far had been to exist. As far as he knew, anyway.

"Is that what you'll be teaching me this morning?" I asked, hoping I sounded as unaffected as he looked. "Or will I be playing a different role in the finale? No one's told me what, exactly, I have to do."

Andreas glanced between us, sinking his teeth into his lower lip. "Actually"—he held a long, thick ribbon up, his expression a bit sheepish—"you'll be standing against that board, wearing this for now. I'm not sure about the finale. Mephistopheles hasn't told anyone what we're doing yet."

I followed where he pointed and shook my head. "No. Learning how to throw a knife or wield a sword is one thing, standing *blindfolded* against a board as a target is quite another. That's sheer madness."

Jian quirked a brow. "Are you scared?"

I whipped around to glare at him. Clearly he was either under the influence of the Green Fairy again or he was utterly insane. "Of course I'm scared! Any person with an ounce of logic would be. You want to throw daggers at my person. And you don't like me."

"I have very good aim."

I pointed to myself to accentuate the point. "And I ought to simply trust that you won't miss on purpose?"

Andreas shifted beside me. "Would you like me to go first?"

"You're going to blindfold yourself and let him throw knives at you?" I shook my head. "You're all mad. Absolutely, uncaringly mad."

As crazy as the idea was, however, it was hard not to recall the precise way Miss Prescott had been slain. How the knife had unerringly found its target and severed her spinal column and pierced her internal organs. If Jian was as good as both he and Andreas claimed, then there was truly no way I'd stand there and offer myself up like a sacrificial lamb.

I blew a breath out. Logic told me it was dangerous and to run from the room, but I needed to do this. If not for me, for Miss Prescott. Time was running out and I had to gather as much information as I could—if we didn't discover who was behind these murders, he or she would slip into the bustling New York streets and get lost within the cacophony forever. Witnessing Jian's throwing abilities firsthand would benefit my research. "Fine. But if you miss, Mephistopheles won't be pleased."

Jian's stony expression didn't change, but I could have sworn there was an added sparkle in his gaze. Without further comment, I turned on my heel with as much dignity as I could inject into the movement and marched up to the target board.

Andreas tied the blindfold around my head, then bent to whisper, "I'm sorry for stealing your brooch earlier…it's a trick I'm still working on. I swear I would have returned it to you."

"Make sure Jian doesn't slip, and all will be forgiven."

He patted my arm and adjusted me so I was standing in profile against the wooden board. I didn't so much as breathe too deeply when he stepped back and Jian yelled out, "Get ready!"

My palms tingled. I swore I suddenly needed to either use the loo or sneeze or scratch some phantom itch on my arm. My muscles were so tightly locked I started to think maybe they weren't still at all, but shaking from the effort of not moving. Before I could work myself into true hysterics, I felt the swish of air near my ankles followed by a *thwack* as the blade drove into the wood.

I exhaled and nearly sagged with relief. It was a good thing I hadn't had time to take a deep breath; in rapid-fire succession, three more blades whizzed by my body, embedding themselves into the wood with splintering efficiency. One near my knee, the next just below my hip, and the last one near my ribs.

"Fire!" Jian shouted. I sincerely hoped he was throwing the last of his blades and that I hadn't magically found a way to self-combust from fright.

Thwack. Thwack.

Two more blades flew by, the slight breeze of them startlingly close to my sleeves. Grateful this so-called lesson was over, I made to remove my blindfold when another knife sailed through the air, pinning itself into the ribbon I held. Warmth dripped down the side of my face, and I ripped the rest of the blindfold off, eyes wide as I lifted a hand to my ear and it came back wet with blood.

Jian shook his head. "I warned you not to move."

Without so much as an apology, he gathered up his knives and left the practice room, leaving Andreas to fuss over my superficial cut. As he raced around the trunks, searching for a bit of cloth to dab the remaining blood, I couldn't help but wonder what other messes he might clean up for Jian.

⟿⟿

I crossed my arms over my chest and planted my feet solidly. "There is no good reason for you to hold his signet hostage, Cresswell."

"I disagree. Respectfully so, Wadsworth." Thomas lifted his chin, stubborn as a mule. "It may be useful as evidence. We cannot simply give it back because he asked nicely."

I gritted my teeth. "You're being immature and you know it. This has nothing to do with the case and everything to do with your dislike of Mephistopheles."

Something that appeared close to annoyance flashed in his eyes. "Is that what you think of me now? That I'd withhold someone's possessions out of *jealousy*?"

I lifted a shoulder. "You haven't given a better reason for keeping the ring."

"You're getting too close to this case," he said, inspecting me. "Whatever bargain you've made, it's time to break it. We'll solve the murders another way—you needn't be so involved."

"I'm sorry, Thomas, but I have to see this through."

He shook his head. Before he could say anything more, Uncle and Liza hurried around the bend, spotting us near the bow and increasing their pace. Tear streaks glistened down my cousin's cheeks in the late-morning sun, setting my emotions in a flurry. Abandoning my disagreement with Thomas, I rushed forward, clutching her hands in mine. "What happened? What's wrong?"

"It's M-Mrs. Harvey," she half sobbed. "She's missing."

"What?" Thomas's voice rose before he reined it back in. "Have you checked her cabin? She's always napping."

Uncle shook his head. "It was the first place we'd looked. We also checked the breakfast room, saloon, women's parlor, and the starboard promenade."

Chills whipped down my spine with the breeze. "Surely she must be somewhere."

"We've searched *everywhere*." Liza's lower lip trembled. "She's simply gone."

Without a parting word, Thomas took off running down the deck, a hand clutching his hat as he raced toward his chaperone's cabin. It took every bit of restraint I possessed to not go charging after him. I could not fathom what his emotions were—he'd never said so, but Mrs. Harvey was the closest thing to a mother he'd had, and he would be broken if anything happened to her. My own heart ached at the thought of her meeting a wretched end. I quite loved Mrs. Harvey and her traveling tonic and kindness.

A dark feeling slithered through my core. If Mrs. Harvey was missing... that could mean the murderer had specifically chosen her to inflict the most damage on my friend. If Thomas was rendered unfit to use his skills, whoever killed those young women might go free. While I didn't want to think Mephistopheles was to blame, it was the sort of cunning plan he'd come up with. He'd already manufactured a lion attack for reasons I still didn't understand—for all I knew he might have also left his signet in the sword container, hoping Thomas would take it. Was each odd detail something painstakingly thought out, wished for, all leading to emotional entanglements and missed connections?

I held my cloak tighter, and looked around. Hardly anyone was out today—either too afraid of the bodies that kept being found or of the impending storm.

"Let's hurry." I clutched Liza's hand and moved quickly down the promenade, hoping I didn't sound as scared as I felt. Uncle was two steps behind. "Tell me everything from the beginning. How did you discover she was missing?"

"We were to eat breakfast together." Liza sniffled. "I promised to give her a tour of Harry's equipment and introduce them afterward..." Her voice trailed off almost subtly, making me wonder what she wasn't saying about Houdini. "She was so excited, I cannot imagine her missing it. For some reason she kept asking if he'd be practicing for another aquatic act."

That certainly sounded like Mrs. Harvey. I patted Liza's arm, trying to steady her without causing further distress. The motion also helped keep me calm and focused. I needed to remain in control if Thomas fell apart. "Were you to meet her at our cabin or hers?"

"We were supposed to meet outside the breakfast room at quarter past eight." Liza drew in a ragged breath. "I was running a little late myself, but by quarter to nine, I decided to check on her rooms. I wasn't sure if she'd overslept. When I got to her room and knocked, no one answered."

"You weren't in our cabin?" I asked. Liza shot me a look but didn't elaborate.

Uncle kept pace behind us, remaining silent but watchful. It was impossible to discern what his feelings were—unsurprising, since he was the man who'd taught both Thomas and myself the importance of divorcing emotions from both murder scenes and investigations.

"I went to fetch you, but you were out, so I ran to Uncle." She glanced over her shoulder, either assuring herself he was still with us or hoping he'd not overheard my earlier question of where she'd been. "I found him en route to the captain and we started searching everywhere."

I tried not to let my own fear show. It would have taken something extraordinary to keep Mrs. Harvey from being introduced to Harry Houdini. "She's probably chatting with one of the other ladies. You know how distracted she gets."

I could no longer tell who was pulling the other down the promenade faster, Liza or myself. We rounded the corner and practically ran to Mrs. Harvey's cabin. The door was ajar, and Thomas was standing in the center of the room, fists clenched at his sides.

"Have you—"

He held a hand up. "One more moment, please. I'm almost…" He abruptly walked over to her trunk and popped the lid open. "Her cloak is missing, as are her gloves. There's nothing out of place, which means she was likely interrupted on her way to breakfast."

"How did you know where she was going?" I asked. He hadn't been present when Liza offered that information.

"There. The tea in the cup on her nightstand is ice cold to the touch." He pointed it out. "Under the saucer is a paper with this morning's date on it, meaning she'd had the tea delivered when she woke up. Since there's no sign of a meal, it's not a stretch to assume she was heading to breakfast with your cousin. She is acting as a chaperone, so another easy deduction. Now then"—he spun on his heel, eyes darting over everything once more—"who would have enticed her enough to not send word of her being late?"

I felt Liza's awe fill the space. Uncle's was there as well but was a bit more tempered, as he'd witnessed Thomas's deductions firsthand several times. For Liza it might be akin to seeing a circus monkey speak English. Or perhaps watching a magician who truly could make miracles happen. Thomas was every bit as incredible as the ringmaster, if not more so. Mephistopheles was amazing at engineering tricks, but Thomas unearthed truth by using his intellect.

"Come," Thomas said, abruptly moving out the door, "let's pay a visit to Mephisto. Wadsworth? Lead the way to his lair."

We rushed past third-class passengers who crowded the deck, my pulse galloping faster than any racehorse the closer we drew to the workshop.

There were many more people out than I'd seen on our way to Mrs. Harvey's cabin. Some of them appeared stricken, faces pale as the frost creeping up the ship's railing. My body thrummed with warning— something had happened. Something that created an uncomfortable buzz and a glazed-over look of worry. Or was I simply imagining things? I slipped over a section of slick walkway, and Thomas's hand shot out, steadying me. I gripped his arm, noticing Uncle had also taken Liza's as we picked up speed. Each step forward filled me with more dread.

Once at the workshop, I dropped Thomas's arm and banged on Mephistopheles's door, the pounding more frantic than my heart. I waited a breath, then knocked again, this time louder. The vibration reverberated up my arm and I felt it deep within my bones, but I couldn't stop myself from banging again and again. We had to find Mrs. Harvey. I couldn't imagine—

Thomas carefully wrapped his hand over mine, stilling me. "He's not here, Audrey Rose. It's all right."

I stared at the closed door, jaw clenched against the tears that were threatening. Mrs. Harvey *needed* to be all right. I sucked in a deep breath, composing myself once again. The cool air helped soothe the rising panic.

"All right," I said. "Let's head down to the carnival cargo area, Mephistopheles—"

"Dr. Wadsworth!" We all jerked our attention toward the sound of the ringmaster's voice. I wasn't comforted by the expression on his face—it was more wild and frenzied than I'd ever before seen, even half hidden by a mask. "Please, come quickly."

Mephistopheles skidded to a halt, then swung back in the direction he'd come from, not waiting to see if we followed. Thomas looked half mad with worry, but kept whatever he was thinking to himself, guiding me into the stairwell after Mephistopheles as quickly as my bulky skirts allowed. Instead of descending into the belly of the ship, we climbed the stairs up and up, the sounds of our shoes clomping over the metal and ringing both above and below.

Uncle and Liza brought up the rear, while Thomas and I practically clutched at Mephistopheles's scarlet coattails. I'd ceased to be surprised when we reemerged on the first-class promenade and headed straight toward the music room. Mephistopheles had addressed my uncle rather than me, which wasn't promising.

Without preamble, he threw the door open, thankfully revealing a sobbing Mrs. Harvey in the corner, hanging tightly to a very pale Andreas. Jian loomed behind them, his expression as stormy as the churning sea. If he were a god, he'd be wrath incarnate.

"Mrs. Harvey." Thomas rushed to her side, dropping down to his knees, examining her for any wounds or trauma. Liza let go of our uncle and assisted Thomas.

My own emotions calmed at seeing Mrs. Harvey alive, though terribly shaken, her whole body vibrating with tremors and her lips moving silently in either prayer or comfort.

I immediately switched into scientist mode, attention falling over every object in the room while Thomas tended to his chaperone. The tarot cards Mephistopheles had painted, the *Cirque d'Eclipse,* were scattered across the floor. The magic looking glass lay propped against the wall where I'd seen it last, appearing no worse for the wear.

"There." Mephistopheles told my uncle and me. "In the trunk."

Uncle pushed his spectacles up his nose, his expression harder than the polished wooden planks we stood upon. I steeled myself as well; coming upon a body any place other than in a sterile laboratory was always a challenge. We were scientists, not monsters. I crept over to where the trunk sat alone behind a tower of tasseled pillows, fine silks and scarves spilling from its sides as if it'd been disemboweled. Andreas shut his eyes tightly, looking as though he wished he could conjure up another fate.

Uncle reached the trunk first, halting ever so slightly before bending in for a closer look. My pulse quickened with each step I took; I knew there was a body, but the discovery of *who* was a wretched thing. Finally, I stood over the trunk and peered down, stomach churning.

"Mrs. Prescott." I clapped a hand over my mouth, shaking my head. The mother who had seemed so devastated and lost after her daughter had been killed at our table, always staring out at the endless sea. Part of me longed to sink to my knees, trying to search for a pulse that I knew had long since ceased. I could not fathom telling the chief magistrate that not only had this cruise ship taken his daughter but now his wife. The invitation he'd received swam through the forefront of my mind. The murderer clearly wanted the Prescott women aboard this ship in order to kill them. Though why he'd kill Mrs. Prescott quietly and leave her in a trunk seemed to differ from his normal theatrics. Perhaps he was desperate to lay the blame on someone else. Maybe planting her body here would lead us to investigate Andreas—he was, after all, well versed in tarot meanings.

Instead of falling apart, I inhaled deeply. "We need to notify her husband at once." I barely recognized my voice—it was cool and unwavering. So unlike my churning emotions. Mephistopheles stared at me a moment before nodding. I faced my uncle. "Let's get her decent for his identification. You take her arms; I'll get her legs. We'll place her on that settee in the corner."

Ten phunny phools

THIRTY-TWO

FIVE OF HEARTS

MUSIC ROOM
RMS ETRURIA
7 JANUARY 1889

"Come. Let's get you settled with some brandy." Captain Norwood extended an arm toward the chief magistrate. "If there's anything else you need..."

Chief Magistrate Prescott stared, unblinking, at his wife. I could not fathom his thoughts.

"With all due respect, Captain," Uncle said, "I have a few questions for Cheif Magistrate Prescott first."

The captain's face turned crimson. "Not now, Doctor. Can't you see he's a wreck?"

Chief Magistrate Prescott didn't even respond to his name. He was most decidedly in shock, but Uncle was correct. We needed to press him for information that would be useful immediately. Time had a strange way of distorting facts.

However, Uncle relented. "All right. We'll call on him later."

Once the captain had led the stricken man out of the room, I turned back to the body of Mrs. Prescott, doing my best to divorce myself from memories of her in life. We'd laid her across a settee and propped her head up on an embroidered pillow, giving her the appearance of a peaceful rest, albeit an eternal one.

"Close and latch the door," Uncle said, directing his attention to Thomas, then inspected Mephistopheles as if he were a new brand of mold that we needed to be rid of. "Take your fortune-teller and swordsman and leave us. We'll speak more later."

Jian's eyes flashed. "What else is there to say? Andreas came here to divine Mrs. Harvey's future with the magic looking glass. That's when he—" He shook his head. "Forget it. I'll be in my cabin. Come on, Andreas."

The fortune-teller glanced toward the looking glass, biting his lip. "No harm will come to—"

"I'll make sure none of your belongings are ruined," I said. I knew how valuable the looking glass was, and not simply because of its supposed ability to see into the future.

With that, both he and Jian left, the ringmaster giving us a curt nod before following them out.

"I'll escort Mrs. Harvey back to her rooms," Liza offered. "Don't worry," she added when Thomas looked ready to protest, "I'll stay with her until you return."

I clutched my cousin's hands once. "Thank you."

"Of course."

As Liza guided a still-muttering Mrs. Harvey out the door, the first mate came in with Uncle's medical bag. Uncle motioned to the foot of the settee. "There is fine. Now, then. Audrey Rose, come inspect the body. Tell me what you notice. Thomas, are you ready?"

My friend removed the journal and pen from his inner jacket pocket, a grim set to his lips. "Yes, Professor."

"Good. Audrey Rose? Do as we've practiced."

I swallowed the growing lump in my throat, forcing myself to see only this new case. I walked around the body, trying to locate any clue before picking up the measuring tape as Uncle had done earlier. "Victim is one hundred and fifty-seven centimeters. Reddish-brown hair, neatly maintained. Though there are some bits of gray near her temples." I steeled myself and peeled back her eyelid. "Eye color is brown." I held in my gasp. "Petechial hemorrhaging is present in the whites of her eyes."

At this Uncle stepped forward and peered into her unseeing eyes. "Excellent, Niece. We have the likely cause of death—suffocation."

I nodded, slowly seeing her last moments unfold in my mind. There were no signs of strangulation on her throat, no abrasions or contusions on her flesh; however, her lipstick was smeared, leading me to believe she'd been smothered by something. A glance around the room showed plenty of potential murder weapons. Pillows, silks, and fabrics—any one of them could have been the object that ended her life. I leaned over and lifted her hand, noting the body was warm to the touch. She'd been slain very recently. Andreas had apparently entered the cabin with Mrs. Harvey, but I'd no idea when Jian had arrived. I'd need to investigate his whereabouts more.

I pointed out the pillows and fabrics to Uncle. "If this is the murder scene—which I believe it is, since I cannot imagine someone dragging her body here without witnesses—then I'd wager we'll find a bit of her lipstick on whatever was used to smother her."

"Yes. What else?"

I slowly walked from her feet to her head and back again, taking in every outer detail I could. "Part of her skirts were cut... there. See? The fabric was snipped away in a line—too neat to have been torn in a struggle. I believe it happened after she'd been murdered."

Thomas stood, lifting the edge of her outer skirts to better inspect the missing fabric length. It was a beautiful garment—pale as freshly fallen snow with bits of silver threaded through. The contrast of the purity of color against her sudden death seemed gruesome. She appeared ready for a wedding, not a funeral.

"Whoever committed this particular murder seems to have an obsession with pretty fabrics. Despite how odd that may sound," he said, straightening up, "I believe that's at least part of our motive, though not likely the main reason."

The three of us looked at one another, minds seemingly racing in new directions. There was one person who immediately sprang to mind while thinking of nice fabrics; the same young ringmaster that I kept defending. I glanced back down at the missing length of silk. I could no longer deny that it was becoming harder to clear Mephistopheles from at least some guilt. Though I could also not deny that something about the motive didn't quite sit right in my center. Uncle had taught us the importance of trusting our instincts, but I no longer could. At least not where the ringmaster was concerned.

Dozens of costumed performers emerged from each corner of the room, picking their way around tables, silent and ironically frightening in their joker's hats with dangling bells. Their full masks were white with tarry black diamonds painted around their eyes that dripped down to crimson lips. It seemed no matter what horror the afternoons brought, the evening shows would go on. A symphony composed of Renaissance instruments fiddled an old tune, the violins and harps sounding mournful, giving the impression of having gone back a few centuries in time.

Against my best efforts, I shuddered at the puppetlike performers. If these Venetian jesters were terrifying, I hated to see the plaguemask act come to life. Mephistopheles's imagination was a dark and treacherous place.

Stiff white tulle ruffles around their collars and hips evoked images of ballerinas who'd broken free from Hades, but at a great cost. Black and gold triangles of fabric completed the collar and skirts, and also made up the waistcoat and sleeves. I didn't know how these hellions could ever be considered humorous—they certainly didn't invoke any feelings of levity as they danced and hopped from one nimble foot to the next in quiet procession through the room.

I couldn't help imagining their costumes being pieced together from a collection of fabrics stolen from victims—a macabre trophy that the killer could secretly admire each night. I knew it wasn't probable or likely, but it didn't prevent gooseflesh from rising on my arms.

Thomas eyed them the way one might stare at a horrid accident, his lip curled. I wanted to laugh, but couldn't find the will to do so after our somber afternoon studying Mrs. Prescott's corpse. I also couldn't ignore the tension from our earlier argument—it had been stuffed away in light of the larger issue, but the uncomfortable feeling persisted.

"The flame-tossing jugglers I understand," he said, "but this? What exactly is their purpose? They're simply peculiar. Mephisto is losing his touch. Perhaps he's finally made a bad bargain—which isn't unexpected. No one's as perfect as me."

"This entire carnival is peculiar," Uncle muttered. "I'll be glad to be done with it all. One more night after this now."

Liza lifted a delicate shoulder. She was unable to participate in the show, since Uncle was in attendance this evening, but didn't appear too upset by it. Her gown was exceptionally gorgeous tonight— beaded crystals sewn onto a rose-petal pink. "That's precisely the point. Their peculiarity is the draw—you're so focused on them, I bet you haven't noticed what's being hauled out onto the stage."

My attention snapped to the next act that had quietly come in when all eyes were focused elsewhere. Liza sat back, a smug look on her face. Even Uncle appeared surprised for a brief moment before tucking into his meal again.

"Love or loathe him—you have to admit Mephistopheles is remarkable. He knows exactly what distractions to use." My cousin's gaze landed on me for emphasis, and I wished to slowly crawl under the table—she was most decidedly not helping my cause. "Harry has learned so much in just a few short weeks. Mephistopheles is quite the teacher."

"And," Uncle said under his breath, "possibly quite the murderous fiend as well."

Deciding to don bravery like it was my most exquisite accessory, I glanced at Thomas. He looked like he'd swallowed a toad. I politely coughed a laugh away. At that he offered a tentative smile and I did, too—it was good to be back on the same side.

"Yes," Thomas said blandly, "next we'll be hearing that he's walked across the sea."

"If he attempts that, then I'm sure a Siren or whale will swallow him whole," I said. Thomas perked up at the thought. I turned to my cousin and leaned close to avoid being overheard by the diners at the nearest table. "Would Harry use theatrics as a distraction to something more serious? What—what if one of his experiments went terribly wrong? Would he tell anyone, or simply try and make the bodies disappear? You have to admit, the trunk is a very Houdini way of disposing of something."

Liza stared at me as if I'd gone mad. "Missing and murdered women are not the best way of having his performances end up in the papers, Cousin. Harry wants fame, not infamy. Same goes for Mephistopheles. You can't honestly believe they're to blame?"

"What if that's what he wants you to believe?" Thomas asked. "Perhaps fame is the misdirection. Do you really know what he's after?"

Liza opened her mouth, then shut it. I imagined she was taking her mother's advice to count to ten before speaking when a kind word couldn't easily be found. "Harry would not be involved with anyone who was—what? Do you both think Mephistopheles is actually a murderer?" She snorted, forgetting about manners. "If you want to throw accusations around, you ought to investigate Captain Nor-wood. Have you seen the way he treats his crew? I wouldn't doubt he'd be capable of tossing people overboard if they displeased him. The man is an absolute nightmare."

On that much we were agreed. I could see the captain shoving someone over the railing in a fit of rage. He was an odd character—at once completely pleasant and docile and, when angered, fierce and nasty as they came. But I did not believe he had an ounce of theatri-cal violence in that well-structured suit of his.

Mrs. Harvey leaned across the table, lips still trembling from the shock she'd received earlier. I wished to reach over and embrace her. Shaken though she was, she refused to sit alone in her chambers. Thomas had offered to stay and dine in with her, but she'd have none of it. I had an inkling it had to do with the rumor of Houdini sport-ing his underthings once again that gave her an extra push to attend the show.

Though most other passengers must not have felt the same—the dining saloon was even more empty tonight than it had been yester-day. The ship was slowly turning into a ghost vessel, places once filled with life now seemed haunted and silent.

"What do you think is behind that curtain?" she asked. "I hope it's not another milk can. I didn't care for that act one bit. Too much tension isn't good for your constitution. I don't think I can handle another fright so soon."

"Cousin? What secrets can you offer?" I turned to Liza, ready to lighten the mood with a joke when the lights flashed, then went out, leaving us in darkness broken only by candles flickering on our tables. Uncle muttered something about not being able to see his entrée, but I decided not to comment.

"Esteemed guests." Mephistopheles's disembodied voice hung in the air like fog. "Tonight we ask you to turn your attention skyward, as the Empress puts on her most heavenly show. Note there are no nets, and should she fall, well, let's not worry on that now."

A single light illuminated Cassie as she sat on her trapeze, staring out at the crowd. On her head was a crown with twelve glittering stars at the points; her bodice had pomegranate seeds sewn across it—to represent her ruling over the earth, according to Mephistopheles's lesson on tarot card meanings—she was regal and elegant, haughty and proud. With her hair in golden ringlets cascading down her back tonight, I could see how she embodied an ideal angelic figure. Though I knew better than to be fooled by her innocent appearance.

Her act started off slowly; she swayed from one end of the room to the other. Swinging from one trapeze to the next, seeming to delight whenever her fingertips left the safety of one and grabbed onto the other. I recalled longing for that sense of freedom when my brother and I had attended a circus during the Ripper murders. There was something beautiful about letting go.

A second floodlight announced another performer joining her ranks. The young man twisted and flipped, crisscrossing over Cassie as their tricks became more intricate.

"That's Sebastián," Liza whispered. "He uses the contortion angle quite well for this act."

I watched the contortionist with renewed interest. Was he capable of killing the women aboard this ship and staging their bodies so horridly? I hadn't gotten to speak with him and noticed he'd shy away each time I'd get close. As he flew back and forth above us, tumbling across the sky, I could certainly imagine the hidden strength in his lithe body.

What remained of the dining saloon politely enjoyed the show, though there was a considerable feeling of subdued awe present. I wondered if it was fear of things turning deadly, or the lack of that very essence. These passengers were the most unaffected by the crimes. Though they might be putting on an act of their own until this nightmare ceased.

"Ladies and gentlemen." Mephistopheles's voice echoed, though he was nowhere to be seen. "Prepare to be enthralled. Our stage has been set, and this next act is sure to dazzle and stun. Please contain yourselves as the great Houdini attempts to escape death once more in his infamous torture cell!"

Thomas made to open his mouth when a third light suddenly flashed on, and the curtain hiding the object onstage was lifted away by invisible hands. I shouldn't have been surprised by the intake of breath or the subsequent screams as people began piecing together what they were looking at.

Suspended inside the torture cell—a glass tank filled with water—a woman stared out at us with milky-white eyes. I would believe her to be a mermaid of legends if not for the obvious fact she was very real and very dead. What appeared to be five anatomical hearts were skewered with long rods through her limbs, discolored from being submerged. On the front of the glass, a playing card was posted, too small to make out from where I sat.

Someone vomited near us, but I couldn't tear my gaze from the tank. It took a few moments to snap myself free of my own terror and realize this victim was familiar to me.

The woman in the tank was none other than Lady Crenshaw.

THIRTY-THREE

MOTIVE

DINING SALOON
RMS ETRURIA
7 JANUARY 1889

Venetian jesters near the stage faltered, their disjointed steps no longer part of their roles but from their fear that felt thick as tar perme-
ating the room. They stood still, openly gaping at the dead woman,
their silence more frightening than it had been while they pranced
about from foot to foot.

If there had been any hope left of this being some horrid part of
the show, it withered immediately. A heartbeat later, the audience
fully grasped what had startled our entertainers enough to cease their
creepy procession.

Knives clattered to plates, gasps went around the room, and,
judging from the sound of a body slamming into a surface, at least
one passenger had passed out. I could hardly blame them; the sight of
Lady Crenshaw floating in that tank with her whitish eyes and long
hair winding through the water was straight out of a penny dreadful.
A tale almost too wretched to be real.

As if they were star performers accepting their own roles in this
horror show, Uncle and Thomas sprang from their seats and rushed

to the tank. I tossed my napkin on the table and half stood, ready to run after them, but didn't wish to leave Liza and Mrs. Harvey unattended. Even with the steady hum of terror pounding through my body, one truth calmed me: I didn't believe anyone else was in immediate danger. At least, not yet.

Uncle shouted at the frozen carnival crew, "Draw the curtains!"

Almost instantly, the demand was obeyed, and the inky curtains quickly fluttered shut, taking with them the view of the submerged corpse. I stared at the velvet drapery, thoughts churning. If Thomas and Uncle hadn't acted so quickly, I might have been able to convince myself I'd invented such a morbid sight. Another staged body. It was almost unfathomable.

Last month I'd studied the insides of a drowning victim. I could not shake the image of those blue lips and bloated belly from my mind no matter how hard I tried. Only that man had died as the result of a horrid accident—Lady Crenshaw likely had not.

Captain Norwood appeared from somewhere near the stage and began ordering staff and crew about like a general commanding his army. Within seconds of his arrival, passengers were rushed through the doors. Regardless of how many bizarre murders we'd borne witness to, the patrons didn't make the evacuation task an easy one.

Chaos and discord raced about the room, dragging people to the floor, crushing them under the fleeing crowd. I blinked, unmoving, at the scene as if I were a mere apparition spying on the goings-on in Hell. Surely if such a place existed, it would appear exactly like this. A small fire flared up near the back of the room—the result of candles falling onto the table linens.

"Go." Liza clutched my hands in hers, eyes wide but determined. "Uncle needs you up there. I'll take Mrs. Harvey to our room. Again." I blinked back a sudden prickling in my eyes and Liza tugged me into a crushing embrace. "Everything is going to be all right.

We'll be in New York by midnight tomorrow. We just need to make it through one more day."

I nodded, unable to do more, and stepped back. Once they'd made their way toward the exit, I gathered my skirts and ran as swiftly as I could up the stairs and ducked behind the velvet curtains. Mephistopheles stood, hands on his hips, staring at the dead woman.

"I'm telling you, it's simply not possible for her to have done this alone," he said. His tone implied it wasn't the first time he'd shared this information, and he was trying to remain calm despite the floating body in his show's prop. He pointed to the top of the contraption. "See those locks? Someone slid them into place. It takes two of my men to fit the tank together. Once she'd gone in the water, there's no possible way for her to maneuver the lid and then lock it. And do you honestly believe she skewered five hearts and then posted the playing card of the same name on the glass?"

"What does the Five of Hearts mean?" I asked, no longer worried about what suspicions I might raise. "You know cartomancy, right?"

Mephistopheles rubbed his brow. "Jealousy. It means ill will of the people surrounding you."

"It makes sense, given her letter," Thomas said.

"Letter?" I moved to Thomas's side and noticed a square of paper in his hand. He glanced over and handed me the note while Uncle moved around the tank, taking in the details. I quickly scanned the paper, pulse galloping as I read the hurried script.

My actions led to the death of that girl. I purposely overpaid her in the name of charity after my husband admired her beauty, then claimed she'd stolen from us when my husband inquired about the missing coin. I wanted her to know that while she might have been pretty for a street wretch, likely earning more than just compliments from married men, she survived because of upstanding citizens such as myself. I was envious. And that flaw has cost me my most precious gift — my daughter. I cannot live with the guilt. I'm truly sorry for all that I've done.

I reread the letter, brows drawn together. "Which girl is she speaking of?"

"That's the question of the hour, Wadsworth." Thomas lifted a shoulder. "Perhaps she's discussing something that occurred off the boat. In fact"—he pointed to the second line—"I guarantee that whatever this refers to happened before any of them boarded this craft. I believe this is our murderer's motive."

Understanding dawned bright as the sunrise. "All we have to do is figure out who this refers to and then we'll have our murderer."

Mephistopheles sidled up to my other side and snorted. "Oh, is that all? That shouldn't be difficult in the slightest."

Thomas eyed him in a way that had me already shaking my head. "Perhaps not to someone such as yourself," he said. "However, someone with a bit more wit and intelligence can make connections. Observe." Thomas gently took the letter back and cleared his throat. "*'While she might have been pretty for a street wretch...'* Based on this line, one, with a semi-intelligent slant, might deduce that the 'girl' in question worked a profession that would be below Lady Crenshaw's station, but not so low as to prevent them from interacting. Which leads one to consider a few possibilities."

"You're unbearable," Mephistopheles muttered.

I smiled. "He's only just beginning."

Thomas ignored the commentary and ticked off probable jobs on his fingers. "Selling food. Selling trinkets. Selling ribbons or silks. Given Lady Crenshaw's status, I doubt she'd be the one doing any shopping for food supply. It would be too far beneath her. That task would be left to the kitchen staff. Next, I cannot picture her buying a trinket that didn't come from a more 'suitable' shop. *Exempli gratia,* she would not bother with anything that didn't cost a significant coin to boast about with the ladies at her weekly tea. Flowers, ribbons, or silks might be the key. It would show her wealth and ability to spend money on frivolous things."

Mephistopheles shook his head. "You're quite smart, aren't you?"

"Of course I am," Thomas said. "Is that supposed to be insulting? Whatever will you comment on next; the golden flecks in my eyes? The sharpness of my jaw?"

"The extraordinary size of your ego?"

An impish grin slowly spread across Thomas's face. "It's not the only prodigious thing I can boast about."

"Ignoring that sentiment, you're saying if this were a story, you'd be the hero, correct?"

"Don't be ridiculous," Thomas said, appearing truly offended. "I'm dark and mysterious. And as likely to kiss or kill you on a whim. Does that sound heroic to you? Not many heroes are good-looking masterminds. I, however, have harnessed my dark talents for the greater good."

"Ah. I understand now." Mephistopheles's lips twitched. "You're a lunatic."

"I prefer 'unpredictable.' It's got a nicer ring to it."

I cleared my throat. "Honestly, you're both infantile. Can we please focus on the poor woman in the tank?"

Blessedly, Jian, Houdini, and Andreas picked that moment to come backstage. Each of them blanched at the sight of the corpse but, to their immense credit, managed to tear their gazes away and not be sick. I noticed Anishaa huddling just behind the curtain with Sebastián and Cassie, on their faces matching expressions of shock and terror.

Harry gave Mephistopheles a steady look. "Everyone's talkin' about layin' low until New York, then leavin' for good."

The ringmaster's face set into a grim expression. He seemed almost resigned to the fact that his dreams were beyond salvaging.

Something tugged deep within my center, longing to fix this whole situation. Before Mephistopheles could comment, I stepped forward.

"We're close to solving the murders," I said, raising my voice so they'd hear, hoping I sounded much more confident about that fact than I felt. "We've already discovered the profession of the girl Lady Crenshaw described in her letter. It shouldn't take too much longer to connect more pieces."

I glanced at each performer, then flicked my gaze to Mephistopheles. It was hard to discern anything for certain behind his mask, but I could have sworn I saw gratitude in his eyes.

"The show must go on," I said. "It's what you all do. Give the passengers a bit of hope and distraction—they need it, and you—more than ever. Let's make the finale something worth remembering."

THIRTY-FOUR
SPECTACULAR SUSPECT

FIRST-CLASS PROMENADE
RMS ETRURIA
7 JANUARY 1889

"No, no, no." Anishaa shifted my ungloved hand down several inches. "If you hold the baton too close to the flame, you'll set yourself on fire. The skirts of our costumes are highly flammable with all the tulle. You need to hold it near the end. Good. Now just move it around slowly, pretend you're painting the sky with flames."

I quirked a brow. " 'Painting the sky with flames'? Sounds like a dramatic canvas indeed."

Anishaa slowly cracked a smile. It had only been a few hours since the discovery of Lady Crenshaw's body, and tensions were still high. "I used to paint back before my life became this." The grin faded. "My family encouraged my creativity, though they never approved of the circus."

A few moments of silence passed between us, broken only by the soft crackling of the fire. If I wasn't holding a torch, I'd give her a hug. "Well, now you're a living bit of artwork. And that's an incredible—"

"I read the letter! How are you going to deny it?" Liza's piercing voice rang out. I briefly closed my eyes, not surprised but dreading the fact my cousin was unleashing herself now. We were so close to New York, if only she could have held off for a bit longer. "This is over, *we* are over! I do not wish to see or speak to you again!"

"I ain't been writin' to no one!"

Liza, her face near burgundy, stomped through the dining saloon, ignoring each attempt Houdini made to halt her procession. Anishaa and I exchanged nervous glances, but kept our mouths shut. I wished to be back on the trapeze with Cassie and Sebastián, far from the fireworks that were happening offstage. One more look in Anishaa's direction proved she felt the same; the flame eater stared longingly toward the curtains, probably wishing she possessed the escape skills Houdini did.

"Liza, the only woman I write to is my mother! You gotta believe me—"

"No, Harry, I don't 'gotta' do anything!" She marched through the room and threw her mask at his feet. "Take your lies and sell them to someone else. This conversation is over!"

"I swear—"

Mephistopheles strolled into the room with Jian and Andreas, halting when he saw Anishaa and me holding on to our flaming batons and Liza and Harry storming around. "Lovers' quarrels are not permitted during practice. Please save the added drama for a private show only."

Liza offered her most withering glare to the ringmaster and lifted her chin. "We're through here. Make sure he stays far away from me, or you'll have an entirely new spectacle on your hands."

With that she slammed the door, rattling the glassware that had already been set up for tomorrow night's dinner. Harry made to follow after her, but Mephistopheles stopped him with a hand to the chest. "Let her collect herself. It's never wise to push a person who's upset."

"But I ain't doing anything wrong!"

"Let's go get ourselves a nice drink." Mephistopheles wrapped an arm around the escape artist and escorted him around the tables and through to the other side of the room. "We've got to stick together now. The show needs you at your best."

With one look over his shoulder at me, he led the distraught Houdini out.

Anishaa shook her head. "We should probably put these out. I've got to get some rest and you need to do the same." She leaned in and sniffed my hair. "You might want to bathe before morning, your hair smells a little like kerosene now. It'll be hard to hide that from Thomas or your uncle."

I absently nodded and followed Anishaa to a bucket of water that had been set up for us, extinguishing my flaming baton with a hiss of steam. Something about Houdini's insistence of innocence bothered me. He appeared genuine, his face screwed up in pain. Either he was an expert liar, or he'd been telling the truth. Or a version of it.

Which meant there was a strong possibility the ringmaster had crafted yet another illusion. One more lie to add to a list I feared was never-ending with him. Perhaps Houdini wasn't the one Liza needed to escape from after all.

A few hours later, I slipped from my chamber, hoping that enough time had passed for me to find who I was looking for. He wasn't lurking near the prow, which meant there were only two more places he'd be at this hour.

I checked over my shoulder, ensuring I was alone, then headed toward the stairwell. I flew down the stairs, the metal biting into the soles of my feet, reminding me of how alive I was, and how fleeting that could be.

I burst into the animal cargo and Mephistopheles jumped a little but quickly recovered. He studied me from the shadows and I replied in kind. His mask was firmly in place, though his shirt was wrinkled and damp. He appeared as horrible as I felt.

"You lied to me." I watched him closely, searching for any crack in the armor he wore as often as his masks. "About Houdini's letter. He was writing to his mother, wasn't he?"

Mephistopheles didn't so much as blink, his gaze traveling from my eyes to my mouth, smirking a bit when he elicited a scowl. "I didn't lie, my dear. If you recall that night, I never claimed he'd been writing to a secret lover. Did I?"

"Oh? You didn't?" I scoffed. "Then I suppose I produced the half-destroyed letter myself and crafted a story to go along with it all on my own."

He held my gaze, expression wiped clean of humor. "Consider it your first true lesson in sleight of hand, Miss Wadsworth. Sleight of word is also a valuable tool for any magician or showman. Our minds are magnificent conjurers, capable of endless magic. What I said and showed you that night was simply a half-ruined letter. Your mind fabricated a story—it jumped to its own conclusion. I never said he had a secret lover. I never claimed anything other than he writes to someone and sends a letter from each city."

I shook my head, wishing I could shake the man before me. "But you said he loved her."

Mephistopheles nodded. "I did. I imagine he loves his mother very much."

"You claimed that Liza was unaware of the letters or woman. You made me think there was something more going on—you..." I went back to the night of our bargain, stomach sinking with each new memory of our conversation. He hadn't lied. He just hadn't been entirely truthful.

"I, what?" he asked. "I laid facts out for you, Miss Wadsworth. You *assumed* I meant lover. You *assumed* he was untrustworthy, simply because of our professions. Your prejudice interfered with your ability to inquire further, to ask more specific questions, to separate fact from the fiction of your mind. You had the opportunity to clear everything up; I would not have lied to you. That was a choice *you* made, and did I benefit from it? Of course I did. I make no denial of the fact I've used this method on people before, and I will most certainly do so in the future. If you're angry with anyone, it ought to be yourself as well. You created an illusion of the truth you wanted to see."

"You're a terrible person."

"I'm terribly accurate at reading humanity. Change human behavior, Miss Wadsworth, and I'll change my tactics."

"You made me break Liza's heart for no good reason."

"Really? Can you think of not one reason that's positive?" He cocked his head. "Do you truly believe that she belongs with an escape artist in a traveling carnival? Or is it a whim that has dire consequences? You did your cousin a favor, Miss Wadsworth. But sometimes they don't come in sweet-smelling bouquets. Houdini would have broken her heart eventually, or she would have broken his. The right choice isn't always the easy one." He offered a slight bow. "I hope one day you'll understand that. Good night."

"Oh, no," I said, marching after him and tugging him around to face me. "You don't get to do that."

"Do what, exactly?"

"Pour kerosene, set it aflame, and walk away when the fire is too hot for your tastes."

He leaned against the lion's cage, expression thoughtful. I hoped the lion would decide to have a midnight snack. A foul and wretched thought after knowing the animal had consumed at least part of one victim. A victim we'd yet to identify. I shuddered. Mephistopheles shrugged out of his tailcoat and draped it over my shoulders—the embroidered scarlet velvet reminding me a little too much of blood.

"I use science and study the human mind the same way you do," he replied calmly. "Don't be angry you took the boring, traditional route. You could still choose differently, you know. You want to set your world on fire, I'll give you a matchbox."

" 'Boring'?" I parroted back. "Pardon me if I do not find amusement in the idea of potentially destroying a life on a whim. Perhaps you ought to stick to crafting pretty costumes."

"If you'd like to join my midnight carnival permanently and offer up more stellar ideas, you simply need ask."

"You are completely mad if you think I'd care to join you or your depraved use of 'science' and engineering for good. Your acts are violent, savage things. All they show us is how horrid the world can be." I tossed my hands up when he smiled. "Why is this amusing?"

"I find your vehemence endearing."

"I find your lack of compassion appalling," I said. "Are you ever serious?"

"Of course I am. I am seriously the most honest person I know," he said, his voice frustratingly calm. "Truth is a blade. Brutal and ice cold. It cuts. Sometimes when spoken carelessly it even scars. Our performances expose that fact and make no apology for it. Once again, if you're upset with anyone, it's yourself. What truth did you discover while that tank was unveiled tonight?"

"Aside from the body? I discovered that you're all willing to go too far for a stupid carnival."

"Is that all?" He smirked. "Did you enjoy it? I'd wager your heart beat a little faster. Your palms dampened with dread and expectation. We are all fascinated by death—it's the one thing each and every one of us has in common. No matter our station in life, we all must die. And we never know when it's coming for us. Seeing someone nearly drown in itself isn't scary or intimidating. It's the truth and realization of *what* truly excites us that is most disturbing."

"I'm not sure I know what you're getting at."

"Don't you, though?" He tilted his head. "Tell me, Miss Wadsworth. Imagine this: When that curtain drops around the tank and the clock starts counting, those seconds ticking loud enough to cause arrhythmia, what is the whisper in your mind between heartbeats? Are you secretly praying that Houdini will make it through? Hoping against seemingly insurmountable odds that he will defeat death? Or are you sitting there, fists clenched below the table, both dreading and anticipating the possibility that you're about to witness something we all fear? What is most exciting? Most terrifying?"

I swallowed hard, and didn't answer; I didn't need to. Even though we'd not gotten a chance to witness the act he spoke of, Mephistopheles already knew what I'd say, anyway.

"That is the truth we offer," he said. "We are, all of us, desperate for a way to overcome the biggest threat of all: death. At the same time, we're all hungry when it comes for someone else. You may hate the truth, deny it, curse it, but the fact remains you are equally enchanted by it. Knowing the flames are hot isn't always a deterrent from playing with fire."

When I said nothing, he lifted a shoulder, but there was a tightness around his mouth that belied his nonchalance. "Life, like the show, goes on whether we agree with it or not. If we stopped living, ceased to celebrate our existences in the face of death or tragedy, then we might as well tumble into our own graves."

A thought struck me. "Whose idea was it for the torture cell tonight... yours, Houdini's, or the captain's?"

"Let's call it a mutual agreement." The lion growled, startling Mephistopheles away from the cage. He straightened his waistcoat. "What did you learn regarding Mrs. Prescott's death?"

That anyone, including him, might have placed her in that trunk. I shuddered—two women, stuffed into a trunk and a tank. Both horrendous resting places. "We're going to do a postmortem in the morning. Her husband wished for one night to say goodbye."

"You're confident you'll identify the cause of death, though?" he pressed. I nodded, not ready to admit we'd already discovered that she'd likely been smothered. "Interesting."

"It's not really that interesting or hard, once you've practiced enough."

"Some would say the work you do is impossible. Think on it a moment, if you will. You take a body, carve it open, and read clues left behind. Sounds impossible to anyone untrained in your field. Reading the dead? Identifying cause of death by sight, by determining which organ wasn't functioning properly?" He walked in a circle, hands behind his back. "You have to get your hands messy, though, don't you? To do something others think is impossible—no matter what the arena or circumstance—your hands will get stained in the process."

I took an unsteady step backward, nearly losing my footing by the tiger's cage. There was an air of confession to his words, ones that made the little hairs along my arm stand at attention. I knew nothing of this young man, save for his ability at misdirection.

My heart thundered. Was Mephistopheles using me as a sleight of hand this entire time? These midnight meetings might be his way of distracting Thomas—making him believe there was something clandestine happening between us, forcing him to overlook any other sinister acts he could be committing. Thomas might trust me, but no matter how hard he denied it, he was human. His emotions could be toyed with like any other's. Just as Liza had warned.

And I'd been equally blinded by Mephistopheles. I was doing exactly what he'd asked because I wanted to help my cousin at all costs. A fact he had noticed straightaway. Magicians were trained to find marks in a crowd, and Mephistopheles was among the best.

He watched me from the shadows, the caged lion prowling back and forth behind him. There was something dark and cunning to Mephistopheles—a cat with a full belly who was deciding if the mouse was worth killing yet. Or saving for another day when he truly hungered for it. I never quite knew which he desired more and which thrilled me most. Perhaps I was as twisted and gnarled on the inside as he was.

He didn't move closer but managed to fill the space between us anyway. I longed for a clever retort, something to prove how unafraid I was to win at his games, but he glanced down at my hands pointedly. "If you wish to accomplish great things, sometimes you must get your hands dirty on the climb up. But you've already done that for your pursuits. It's a bit odd you don't allow me the same courtesy."

I noticed the smudge of dirt on my palms. I rubbed my hands together, but the stain refused to lighten. I must have grabbed onto the bars at some point, though the image of stained hands unnerved me; I'd dipped my hands into blood more times than I could count.

"Thanks to rough water, the captain said we won't make land for one day now, Miss Wadsworth." Mephistopheles turned to go, then paused, fingers tapping the doorjamb. "I sincerely hope you solve these murders for both our sakes. I'm not sure the carnival will survive another hit. There's more than one way to make a man drown."

THIRTY-FIVE

EIGHT OF SWORDS

I slipped into my room, relieved to find it unoccupied. Liza must have stayed out with the other performers to work out her annoyance, and Mrs. Harvey was likely asleep. No one would be any the wiser about my midnight meeting with the Devil.

"Maddening fool." I sat on the edge of the bed, absently tracing the orchids stitched onto my silk skirts, Mephistopheles's words tumbling through my mind. There was most certainly more than one way of killing a man—whoever had been terrorizing the ship was acquainted with that sentiment.

I pulled the playing cards out from my nightstand and set them on top of the blankets. Half were found with bodies, and the other half were found near the crime scenes. Ace of Clubs. Six of Diamonds. Ace of Spades. Five of Hearts. Yet the murders themselves were fashioned after tarot cards and their meanings.

Five of Hearts correlated to jealousy. Ace of Clubs, wealth. Lady Crenshaw was most certainly jealous over some unidentified young woman. The Ace of Clubs had been staked through Miss Prescott on opening night—perhaps her father had been bribed.

I rubbed my temples. None of it made sense. Unless, perhaps, whoever was perpetrating these crimes was indicating he or she was laying their cards out for all to see. It was a stretch, but it might be a good place to start.

I leafed through the other notes I'd jotted down and spread them next to the cards. Uncle believed sometimes a pattern might emerge or our brains might pick up on something after having written it down. His methods rarely failed me. I added a few new notes.

Tarot card found in Jian's act— Justice.

Body impaled with seven swords. (Dr. Arden's daughter, tarot Seven of Swords)

I paused, recalling that Mephistopheles had said it was called a reversed Seven of Swords. And its meaning…its meaning was… something about a person who believed they'd gotten away with something. Or so he'd said. So did that indicate that Dr. Arden's daughter had been in trouble? Might she have believed herself to be free from whatever crime she might have committed? I hadn't a clue where to go about locating that answer—Dr. Arden still refused to leave his chambers or answer the door, and the captain was growing antsier the closer to America we got. Moving along, I added the next bit of information.

The Star tarot (body burned onstage)—emerald ring found, confirming Miss Crenshaw as deceased. Tarot meaning "transformation"?

Six of Diamonds found in her cabin. Meaning to be determined.

Poisonous belladonna found in stomach contents—cause of death.

Severed arm found in lion's cage—still unidentified, likely male based on examination. Wedding band left untouched.

Mrs. Prescott found suffocated in a trunk, no tarot. Connected how?

Lady Crenshaw deceased in a tank, Five of Hearts instead of tarot. Note left detailing her perceived crimes. She could not have placed herself in that tank, however. Card meaning: jealousy.

I sat back and rolled my head one way and the other, stretching out my muscles. There was most certainly a consistency with the crimes, with the exception of the severed limb and the body found in the cargo hold. They did not appear to be connected with the other murders. Unless they had been unfortunate victims who happened upon the crimes and could report them to someone. And potentially identify the murderer…

"What am I missing?" I asked aloud. "What connects you all? What story do these cards tell with their meanings?"

I thought of Dr. Arden's odd behavior, of how he'd kept us from speaking with Chief Magistrate Prescott, how he openly lied to us. What might he be hiding both the Prescotts and himself from? And after his daughter's murder, why was he still unwilling to talk with us?

A chief magistrate and a physician. A noblewoman with a guilty conscience. Two possible witnesses. Two different styles of cards, both holding secret meanings to be deciphered. I nibbled on my lower lip, concentrating hard as an idea slowly niggled around the edges of my brain. If Thomas was correct, then Lady Crenshaw had likely encountered a girl who sold something worthy of the Lady Crenshaw's attention. Ribbons didn't quite seem to have boasting factor over tea, though. Were I hosting a lavish party, or one that I'd like to seem as such, I'd purchase as many flowers as I could afford. That would make quite a statement of wealth, especially if the flowers were from a hothouse. My pulse picked up. It was the most plausible scenario.

The Crenshaws and the Prescotts each received free passage on the *Etruria* and knew each other before setting sail. If Lady Crenshaw upset her husband enough, it might stand to reason that he'd gone to his friend, the chief magistrate, and filed a complaint against the flower girl. Did they not offer her a fair trial, instead sending her off to the workhouse, whose conditions were likely more deplorable than the streets she fought to survive on?

But how did Dr. Arden fit into this theory? I pulled a tarot deck out that Mephistopheles had given me, tracing the filigree edges of the Death card, thoughts churning. A man of medicine would be tasked with seeing patients, even those who'd committed crimes. Perhaps he'd been the prison physician and had administered a tonic that killed instead of saved. Maybe it was no accident. Maybe one of his powerful and rich friends asked him for this favor and he obliged. Might each of them be involved in some larger plot to cover their own crimes? It would explain why Dr. Arden wished to keep everyone from talking. The less they said, the less they could implicate themselves in a murder of their own doing.

I glanced around the cabin. It was starting to get late enough that Liza ought to return soon, and the last thing she needed was to be surrounded by more trauma. I straightened the mess of evidence I'd collected and swept it into the nightstand, saving my tarot deck for last. My cousin had been through quite enough and—as I went to close the drawer, a small box with a ribbon closure caught my eye.

My blood felt as if it cooled several degrees when I noticed the Eight of Swords tarot card that sat tucked beneath it. My initial reaction was to pick the box up and toss it across the room, screaming until someone was alerted. But my logical and curious self couldn't bear the thought of destroying any clues. Someone had purposely left this inside my nightstand and I didn't believe it was out of kindness.

Pulse speeding, I reached over and tentatively pulled the box onto my lap. It wasn't very large, though I still hesitated to open it. A dark, wretched feeling settled around me. Whatever this box contained, it was not going to be pleasant. I stared at the tarot card, allowing a moment to pass to steal myself against this new task. A blindfolded woman stood prisoner in a cage of swords. Her entire body had been tied with silks, indicating there was no escape. Seemed like a good metaphor for this ship.

I jerked my attention back to the box, breathing harder. I ought to run to Uncle's cabin and open it there, but it was late and what could he do other than offer moral assistance? Surely, if he or Thomas received the box, they'd not wait to tear into it. Still, I gave myself another moment to focus on breathing steadily, and slowly, carefully, pulled the ribbon apart. Before I lost my nerve, I removed the lid.

Inside, on a bed of crushed velvet, lay a finger.

I blinked as the sounds in the room amplified. Suddenly I could hear every last tick of the clock. Each ocean wave that quietly lapped against the hull of the ship. I even heard creaks coming from next door where Mrs. Harvey seemed to have awoken. All of it was too loud. I focused on inhaling and exhaling. I wanted to throw the box out of my room, but it would be both careless and extreme. A severed finger couldn't hurt me.

A folded scrap of paper was wedged beneath the finger, a bit of blood splattered across the creamy card stock. If I'd been disturbed by the finger, a whole new wave of trepidation crashed through me. A note from a killer was never a jolly good time.

My own hands shook as I plucked it from the box, careful to avoid touching the new bit of evidence. I unfolded the note and was thankful I'd already been seated. Had I been standing, I was certain I'd have collapsed on the spot.

Miss Wadsworth,

This ought to be considered your first
and last warning. Halt your investigation
or the next piece of your cousin you
receive will be her head. My performance
is nearly over, and should you play your
new role of the obedient young woman, I
will release Liza alive at port. Should you
choose differently, your fate won't be the
only one affected.

I reread the threat, heart pounding faster than my thoughts.

Liza.

Liza was in danger.

The murderer had her and I knew with every last fiber of my being that he meant every word. He'd already mutilated her poor, innocent hand. He would kill her and turn her body into another spectacle. And it was all my fault. I pressed my hands against my eyes until all I saw were white flashes behind my closed lids. I could not simply sit and wait for Liza to be returned, unharmed. It went against everything I held dear. But I also could not make it obvious that I was searching for her.

I stood, pacing around the small cabin, never feeling more as if I had been a bird trapped in a metal cage. How a ship could contain so many nooks and crannies and darkened places to commit nefarious deeds was beyond comprehension. I rushed over to the service wall and rang for an attendant. I needed to send for the one person who could help in this situation.

I scribbled a note with instructions on where to meet and had already donned my overcoat and pulled on thick gloves by the time the maid arrived.

"Take this straightaway. Please let him know it's urgent."

She nodded and left as swiftly as she'd arrived. Unable to wait any longer, I slipped into the night and ran toward the only place left where I felt free from the metal walls closing in.

THIRTY-SIX

MIDNIGHT RENDEZVOUS

FIRST-CLASS PROMENADE
RMS ETRURIA
8 JANUARY 1889

I examined the vast expanse of ocean, watching as its nothingness grew into a monster so large I had no hope of ever evading it. My heart rate jumped into a full-on trot. It was hard to fathom that I'd thought this voyage would be fit for daydreams at the start of the week.

Now Liza was taken, her finger sitting in a velvet box, and there was an entire ship full of mysterious people who each possessed opportunity and motive. Surely the answer had to be there, glinting like a shard of broken glass reflecting moonlight, waiting to be discovered. If only I could grasp it before something unthinkable happened to my cousin.

I felt his presence before he spoke, and faced him. In the dark he was nothing more than a silhouette before he stepped closer. "H-have you found anything out?" I stammered.

Thomas wrapped his coat around my shoulders and gazed out at the sea. "Captain Norwood has the entire crew searching the ship. They're combing every inch—your uncle's wrath is more motivating than anything, I believe. If Liza..." He drew in a sharp breath and exhaled loudly. "They won't stop searching for her."

He held me close, though it didn't stop the internal shudders from racking my body. Liza was being tortured. I had done that to her. My wretched affinity for getting involved with crimes now placed her into the heart of one. Father had been correct all those months ago. Decent people didn't expose themselves to the underbelly of the world.

I looked out at the undulating black waves, tucked beneath Thomas's arms. We stayed that way for a few moments, though the majority of me was buzzing with a need for action. I wanted to rush from room to room, screaming, until Liza was found. If I didn't gain control of my emotions and clear my mind, I'd be of no use to my cousin. They'd likely haul me off to the brig and that would only complicate things.

Liza. My heart contracted. I longed to shatter myself against the ship and sink to the ocean floor. Instead I set my jaw. "I cannot shake the feeling of a connection we're missing. What do the cards have to do with everything?"

Thomas glanced at me from the corner of his eye. "At this point, I'm not sure it matters."

"Everything matters and you know it." I sighed. "Jack the Ripper chose women who were forced to sell themselves, the Dracula case targeted mostly members of the House of Basarab. What of these women? There has to be some tie that binds them together in the murderer's mind. How do these puzzle pieces fit? Better yet...who knew them before they set foot on the *Etruria*? And why take Liza? What does she have to do with it?"

"Well, they seem to have known each other prior to boarding the ship. That is a fact between Dr. Arden and the Prescotts, at least. As for your cousin?" Thomas inhaled deeply. "She's likely only a bartering piece. We're gaining ground on the murderer, and he isn't pleased. A nerve has been struck and he or she is lashing out."

I huddled into Thomas's overcoat as a particularly icy blast of air whipped along the promenade. "There's something about the cards that bothers me and I can't quite figure out why."

He raised a brow, eyes sparkling. "You've got an idea, don't you?"

"Come," I said, tugging him toward the cabins, finally able to put my energy into action. "I know just who might have an answer for us."

Houdini opened his door and cast a weary glance at us. I was surprised to find him alone—no Jian or Andreas or even Mephistopheles.

On a small table near his bed lay a book with drawings and diagrams. Most of which appeared to be contraptions that would make Death shudder.

"Are you going to go through with the torture cell trick?" I asked, moving fully into the rather large space as he swept his arm in welcome. Several trunks and tables were stacked around in messy piles. Cards and cuffs and chains all spilling from them.

"I ain't quitting this business. No matter how many bodies show up, I won't be intimidated by nothin'." He narrowed his eyes. "Did Liza send you here?"

Hearing her name sent needles spiking through my system. He hadn't yet heard she was the newest victim. I couldn't bring myself to respond. Thomas moved forward.

"No"—Thomas's voice was cordial enough to be a warning— "but Miss Wadsworth will gladly send you overboard if you keep that tone up." At Houdini's confused expression, he added, "She's the muscle. I'm clearly the charm."

Houdini shook his head as if to free himself of the absurdity of the idea and moved over to the bed. "If Liza didn't send you, then why are you here?"

"I have questions about playing cards." I interrupted Thomas before he could provide any more *charm*. "As the King of Cards, I figured you'd be the perfect person to answer them."

He eyed me warily but finally nodded. "What do you wanna know?"

I pulled out the cards found with—or near—the victims and laid them on the table, feeling only marginally terrible at having kept them. Normally, I'd never consider tampering with evidence. I hadn't a clue if the order in which they were found mattered, but I did my best to set them down in the time period they were first discovered.

"Five of Hearts, Ace of Clubs, Ace of Spades, Six of Diamonds," he said, glancing up. "Where's the rest of the deck?"

"That's all there is," I said, pointing to the first card. "Do they mean anything?"

If he noticed the slight hesitation in my statement, he didn't let on. He picked up the cards, inspecting them carefully on each side. "For starters, these are Mephistopheles's personal set."

Thomas went very still beside me. "How can you be sure?"

Houdini flicked something on the card with his pointer finger. "See that?" I leaned in for a better look at the thorns woven around the edges of each card. "And these?" Houdini showed us tiny cursive making up the circular shapes on the back of the cards. *"Vincere Vel Mori."*

" 'Conquer or die'?" I asked, silently thanking Headmaster Moldoveanu for forcing us to freshen up on our Latin.

"If you say so." Houdini lifted a shoulder. "What it means doesn't matter to me."

"Why does this lead you to believe Mephistopheles is the owner of these cards?"

"He's got the thorns and Latin all over most of his things. Surely you noticed it all over the practice rooms." Houdini grinned. "It was also etched onto the fountains the night you danced with the Green Fairy. You might not recall that, though, seeing as you'd partaken in spirits."

I felt Thomas's attention on me, and realized he was slowly piecing the puzzle together of what that statement meant. Clearly, I had been keeping things from him, and he was not looking pleased. Knowing him though, he was likely more annoyed that he'd not deduced it first.

"What else can you tell us about these cards?" I asked. "Why might they be significant?"

Houdini stared at them again, focus turning inward. "Six of Diamonds is known for romantic problems, arguments, and basic lovers' quarrels, according to your cousin."

"Liza told you that?" I asked, frowning. I knew my cousin enjoyed the idea of séances and convening with spirits, but I hadn't known of her talent with reading cards. I could have been seeking her advice on cartomancy this entire time.

"I told her it was a load of crap. She said, 'So's flirting with other girls,' then stormed out." He picked up the Ace of Spades, turning it one way, then the other. "This one means misfortune. Sometimes it's also a difficult ending." He moved the Ace of Clubs and Five of Hearts around. "Not sure about these. If anyone can figure it out, Sebastián, Andreas, or even Anishaa can probably help you, if Liza won't. But don't get your hopes up—this stuff don't really mean nothing. They're just cards."

"Anishaa is also talented with cartomancy?" I asked. "I thought she only knew tarot."

Houdini gave me a strange look. "She's the one who told Mephistopheles everyone needed to learn—that we could expand our business if we had more fortune-tellers. Andreas was only doin' that Bavarian magic lookin' glass bit before her. And to be honest? It wasn't all that good."

My thoughts whirled with new possibilities. If Anishaa was that talented with both kinds of cards, then she might be the very person we were looking for. Perhaps her feelings for Mephistopheles weren't as I'd suspected. I supposed it was possible that he'd entered into some bargain with the families that had been targeted, and she didn't approve.

Houdini raised his brows, probably wondering at the look of excitement I was sure was showing on my face.

"Thank you," I said, "you've been very helpful."

Thomas motioned for me to exit the room, then halted, fingers strumming along the doorframe while he studied Houdini. "Why were you initially arguing with Liza?"

Houdini's gaze strayed to mine, and I hoped he didn't say to ask me about it. I would have a hard time explaining how I witnessed their fight at one of my secret practices. I was already dreading the Green Fairy explanation I knew was coming. The moment passed and he lifted a shoulder.

"A dead woman's floating in my tank and all she wants to ask about is who the lady I'm writing to in America is." Houdini exhaled dramatically. "I told her it was nothing—I ain't got no sweetheart nowhere. Only woman I love—or write to—in America is my mother. Liza didn't believe it."

Thomas was silent a moment, focus drifting over the room. Lord only knew what he'd divined from it and the young escape artist. "No, I suppose she didn't. Good night."

It took everything in me to keep from asking a dozen questions as we made our way through the empty corridors and climbed the stairs. When we'd reached the second floor, I stopped. We were secreted away in a stairwell; hopefully no one would overhear us.

"Well?" I asked. "Do you believe him?"

"Yes. Whether or not I believe every word out of his mouth is another matter entirely." Thomas inhaled deeply. "I know you don't want to see the truth behind Mephistopheles's illusion, Wadsworth, but as of this moment, he's dangerous. He's secretive, and his playing cards were left with almost every victim."

"Which seems awfully convenient as far as evidence piling up," I argued. "You must admit, it sounds as if someone's going out of their way to make him the obvious suspect. And what of Anishaa? She's someone who we've not fully looked into, but clearly is a valid option."

"Undoubtedly," Thomas said, lowering his voice. He looked down, fiddling with a button on his sleeve, and my stomach clenched. "We need to talk."

I couldn't deny that I figured a serious conversation was coming, though part of me longed to run off and hide. There were some things I'd rather not face. "All right."

Thomas folded his arms against his chest and watched me very closely. "You've been meeting with Mephistopheles at night?" It wasn't really a question, though he had the courtesy to frame it as such. I swallowed hard and nodded. I was a coward. "You drank absinthe and danced...with him?"

I closed my eyes and drew in a deep breath. "Yes."

When Thomas didn't answer straightaway, I finally managed to sneak a peek at him. I expected to see anger and betrayal written across his expression. What I actually found was much worse. Before his face shuttered, I saw a glimpse of the boy who never truly believed he could be loved. The one I had promised to never hurt; a promise I'd just broken along with his tender heart. His eyes were void of emotion when he met my stare.

"I meant what I said about you being free," he said, voice barely above a whisper. "If there's a chance you might be...if you think your heart—" He blinked quickly enough that any hint of wetness was gone before I could be certain. He cleared his throat. "I won't ever tell you who to choose or which path to take. But I would ask that you tell me one thing; do you have feelings for him?"

"I..." My heart thudded against my ribs. I wanted to cry out that that was an absurd question, but for some reason the words failed to rally past my lips. Thomas could spot a lie as easily as one could spot the sun on the horizon. And I had no intention of lying to him. The truth was complicated and messy, but he deserved to know every doubt lurking inside me. I held my hands out, palms up. "I-I'm not certain what I feel."

He scrubbed his hands over his face. I reached out, hating myself for the conflict bashing about within me. I clasped his hands and drew them away, searching for some way to comfort him, to quell his fears, but anything I said now would ring false.

The truth I hadn't been wanting to face was simple. Somehow— I wouldn't remotely call it love, it had been far too soon for that—but somehow I'd realized that my heart might be capable of finding *interest* in another. I could deny it, try pretending it away, but I was starting to care for Mephistopheles. It was like a small, fragile bud. Given enough care and attention it might bloom into something beautiful. I didn't know what that meant for Thomas and myself. He deserved to have someone love him wholly and without doubt.

Neither of us had ever formally courted anyone, what did we

know of ourselves or relationships, let alone marriage? I could not in good conscience relieve him of his doubts when mine could not be reasoned away. This might simply be a momentary lapse in judgment—a reaction based on fear, or it might be an indication I wasn't quite ready for that sort of commitment. At least not until I could slay my doubts.

"Thomas...I—"

"Please. Don't." He held a hand up. "I never really—" He shook his head. "For all of my bravado and ability to read a situation, I never could calculate what you saw in me."

"Thomas, you mustn't—I do love you, I just—"

"If you wish to go, I'll never make you stay. I might not do and say the proper thing all the time, but I do know that I love you enough to set you free."

I was about to argue that I didn't want to be free, but that wasn't true. All my life I'd longed for freedom—freedom to pick and choose every detail of my life. To make good decisions and horrible ones. Decisions that would break my heart and remake it ten times over. I just never knew having choices could be so hard, or hurt so much. A tear slipped down my face.

"I love you, Wadsworth. No matter what or who you choose, I always will." He leaned in and pressed his lips to my cheek. "If you'll excuse me, I must try and sort out the playing cards."

With that, he turned and hurried down the corridor. The blast of cold wind that blew in when he pushed the door open finally snapped me from my daze. Whatever strength I'd had vanished and my knees gave out. I put my head in my hands and sobbed, not bothering to hide the sounds of my despair. My life was a tattered mess. Liza was in mortal danger. Thomas was heartbroken. A murderer made our ship his deadly playground. And I was filled with more turbulence than the ocean we traveled through.

I permitted myself another moment to cry, allowing the tears to freely slip down my face, dripping onto the floor. It felt as if something in my chest had permanently cracked. I gripped my fists until the pain was all I could focus on. Then I pushed myself up, brushed down my bodice, and took a deep, shuddering breath. Liza was missing. A murderer was taunting me. No matter how much it pained me to think it, I could not focus on Thomas and our relationship now.

Not wanting to waste another moment stunted by my emotions, I exited onto the first-class deck and almost ran down the darkened promenade on the starboard side of the grand ship.

Wind howled, the sound reminding me of a man who'd lost the world in a game of cards. I clutched at my hat, keeping my face turned down against the breeze. Winter was reminding us that there were more fearsome things to worry over than simply men with agendas, or girls with broken hearts on this boat.

I gave up on walking swiftly and ran as fast as I could, my mind focused on the pattering drum of my feet, the beat of my pulse, the fear clawing its way down my spine. I needed to hurry—to scour the ship until I found my cousin...

Movement toward the bow caught my attention and I paused outside my cabin door, listening for any signs of struggle. Visions of bodies being tossed into the hungry ocean crawled their way into my sensibilities. I stared into the shadows, waiting for the darkness to lazily blink back at me, bringing all of my fears to life. Sounds of sails snapping in the wind drew my attention upward and I staggered back. Someone was standing up on the icy railing, his tailcoat a whip snapping behind him. All it would take was one slip and he'd be plunged into the deadly waters.

Moonlight broke through the cloud cover, offering a glimpse at the young man. He stared over the edge into the ocean, and before I knew what I was doing, I ran for him.

Whether it was to save him or make him pay for his crime of confusing my heart, I couldn't tell. I simply raced until my arms were around him and we both crashed to the deck, the air whooshing out as I wrestled him to the ground.

THIRTY-SEVEN

UNMASKED

FIRST-CLASS PROMENADE
RMS ETRURIA
8 JANUARY 1889

Mephistopheles rolled away from me, clutching his stomach and moaning. "I think you've broken one of my ribs. Was that really necessary? Next time you tackle me, be sure it's in one of our bedchambers."

I jumped to my feet, dragging the ringmaster with me. I clutched the collar of his shirt until he sputtered, hands fumbling to remove my fingers. I didn't care if I strangled him. "Are you quite mad? You almost fell overboard!"

"No." He dropped to his knees, wheezing, but kept his focus on the deck, refusing to meet my glare. "I'm quite sane. And I was only checking on something."

"Care to enlighten me?"

"No. Not particularly." He squinted as he stood. "Have you been crying?"

I stepped back. "Liza has been..." My voice cracked and I nearly lost my hold over myself once again.

"Liza has been...drinking? Knitting children's socks? Strangling

Houdini with his chains, or better yet, his cuffs?" He rubbed my arms, voice softening. "Tell me. Liza's been..."

I swiped at the tears that had managed to slip out. "Taken."

"What do you mean, 'taken'? Has Houdini done something to her?" He glared down the promenade and squared his shoulders as if he'd go marching into battle this second.

I shuddered, though I was no longer sure if it was due to the frosty air. Houdini was talented with cards himself. He might very well have taken my cousin and tortured her because of their fight. Perhaps he was acting back in his cabin; I trusted no one on this cursed vessel. "Someone sent her finger to my chambers."

Mephistopheles stared at me a moment, then unleashed a horde of curse words that weren't all in English. If I didn't feel so ill, I would have been impressed. He pressed his hands over his eyes and then dropped them to his sides. "All right. Start from the beginning. How do you know it's Liza's finger?"

"How is this helping?" I tossed my hands up. "Whether or not it's *actually* her finger is not the issue. The issue is someone who has murdered several people aboard this ship has taken her."

The ringmaster reached over and wrapped me in his arms. I was so surprised, I didn't protest. "There's more, isn't there? Why else were you crying?"

I laid my head against his chest, listening to the quick thrum of his heart before pushing back. "I don't even know who you truly are, and yet you'd like to have my innermost thoughts laid bare."

"Very well. You want the truth of me?" He sighed, reached up, and—quick enough for him to not change his mind—took his mask off. I stood there, mouth practically agape and held in my gasp. After all this time and his insistence that he remain anonymous, he'd just thrown it all away. His dark eyes were lined in darker lashes, his brows generous and bold, like him. A flop of black hair curled over his forehead and around his ears.

I searched his face, seeking any flash of recognition. I would have sworn we'd known each other from some other life. But he was just a young man, ordinary and charming with a dimple in his cheek. Was this truly who he was, or was it another mask to use to his advantage? His earlier words of not having the luxury of trusting anyone came back, haunting me like specters.

"You've been murdering these girls, haven't you?"

"Not quite the reaction I was hoping for, Miss Wadsworth." Mephistopheles jerked back and shook his head. "I suppose that's what keeps things interesting." He ran a hand through his dark hair, tousling the already unruly locks. "But no. If it's a confession you're after, I'm afraid you won't find it here. I've not killed anyone or anything. Except a few mosquitoes. And I don't feel too apologetic about that, especially after they took off with a hefty amount of blood and left wicked itching."

"Honestly . . ." I paused, noting how close we'd gotten again, my attention straying to his upturned lips, the longing in his eyes catching me completely off guard. "I—"

He leaned in and gently pressed his mouth to mine, his touch shocking but not unpleasant. For a moment I didn't think about every cursed thing that had happened in the last hour, focusing instead on his lips as they slowly parted. He clutched me close, hands gripping the material of my dress as if convincing himself I was no illusion. I thought about running my hand through his curls, they were so lovely, yet . . . a flash of Thomas's face snapped me into my senses, I broke away. "You swore you'd not kiss me!"

"You're partially correct," he said, breathing hard and holding his palms out in surrender. "I said if you appeared as if you never wanted me to. But sometimes the way you gaze at me—I shouldn't have done it, Miss Wadsworth. I've told you from the start I'm not honorable or good."

"Liar. Fiend. Second son. Thief." I stared down at my slippers. "Who are you really, Mephistopheles?" He opened his mouth and I silenced him with a raised hand. "No games. Tell me who you are and why I ought to believe anything more you say."

He inched forward, hands still up where I could see them and sighed. "My name is Ayden Samir Baxter Thorne. My father is an earl, and my mother is an angel from Constantinople. As is evident by my exquisitely good looks."

When I didn't return his smile, he lowered his hands.

"As you just kindly noted, I am the second son—the spare heir. I could either stay in England and spend money frivolously, or I could give it all up and pursue my dreams. Debaucherous and lowly though they may be. I needn't get into which I chose. I put my engineering skills to use and my flare for theatrics—and thus the Moonlight Carnival was born. A safe haven or sanctuary for other unwanteds. Ones who've had it much worse than I have."

Something about his name kept dragging my attention back to it...then I recalled the cards in Houdini's room. *"Vincere Vel Mori."*

" 'Conquer or die.' Our family motto for generations. My great-great-great—I'm not sure how many times over, but one-of-many-greats grandfather was granted knighthood by King Richard the Lionhearted. That's where the crest and motto come from, though I don't think we conquer much other than hearts and card games these days." Mephistopheles's eyes grew reminiscent before he collected himself. "It seems you've been much better at your sleuthing than I've given you credit for."

Chills erupted like the undead from their graves and raced along my spine. I pulled out the card I'd taken from Houdini, watching the ringmaster's expression carefully. "Your calling cards, I believe. Very crass, but certainly a showy way of leaving a signature mark at the crime scenes."

Mephistopheles looked more confused than guilty. "Those cards, my love, might have been left at the crime scenes. But it wasn't done by me. They were stolen around the time my signet went missing." He raised his brows. "Speaking of priceless family heirlooms, where is my signet now, still with Cresswell?"

"It's in a safe place until I sort out all the truth from lies." I flipped the card over, ignoring the twinge of guilt. "Is there anything special about these cards? Anything at all that might contain a hidden clue or meaning? No matter how obscure, anything might help."

"Let's see." He took the card. "You see these?" I nodded. The little flourishes were lovely, but judging from the annoying slant of the ringmaster's lips, they held meaning. "This is an infinity symbol."

"What does a double infinity mean?"

"Oh, some romantic nonsense about two fates being forever tied together." He shrugged, then took in my expression, the levity leaving his voice. "What's wrong?"

"I think that... I believe that might mean something to the murderer. How do they all fit?" I took the card back from him, turning it over and over while fragmented thoughts slowly pieced themselves together. "Nobility. A doctor. A justice of the peace. What is the common link? Two fates, forever combined. Each playing card has an infinity symbol and each tarot a deeper meaning of the same." I paced near the railing, ignoring the clapping of waves against the hull. "Ace of Spades. The Ace of Spades and the reversed Seven of Swords. What ties them together, two fates, two stories, coming together as one?"

"Perhaps you need to sit for a moment," Mephistopheles said, no longer sounding like the tease he was. "All this talk of romance has taken its toll." He held a hand to his forehead, expression serious. "I feel the same."

"In cartomancy, what does the Ace of Spades mean?"

Mephistopheles searched my eyes, likely believing me to be as mad as the murderer. He rubbed his temple. "From what I can recall off the top of my head, it means misfortune or a difficult ending. Are you sure you're feeling quite well?"

Exactly what Houdini had said. I waved him off, knowing I was onto something, and yet it was still slightly out of reach.

"Lady Crenshaw was the catalyst. She set this whole thing into motion." I tapped the card. "Six of Diamonds. Houdini said this card indicates arguments. Lord and Lady Crenshaw fought about something—an attractive girl. The cards that have been left are telling us exactly what sin the victim committed. The tarots are their fates, the ones they brought upon themselves."

Mephistopheles scrubbed a hand across his face. "This is a bit far-fetched. And if I'm saying that, you can be certain it's a stretch. If they had some lovers' quarrel or fight, why would it have been left with their daughter?"

"It's not about romance," I said with sudden certainty. "It's always been about revenge." I flipped the card over and traced the double infinity symbol. "Two paths. Two different types of cards. Two fates. One infinite, everlasting loop for justice."

"And who might the murderer be, then?"

I thought of Jian and his short temper—Andreas had mentioned his entire family had been slain. The details of that crime had been impossible to wrench from either of them. Then there was Cassie and Sebastián and the people they owed money to. Might those people be the Ardens, Crenshaws, and Prescotts? Did they find some means of extorting money from the performers, and they stood to lose everything? Anishaa and Andreas also couldn't be taken from the list of suspects—each of them had reason for vengeance and knew the cards' meanings. Though from everything I'd gathered, most every performer had a base knowledge in tarot. Even I had been instructed to learn and practice with both tarot and the playing cards. Harry Houdini didn't strike me as a criminal, but then again the murderers I'd encountered hadn't, either.

Then there was the ringmaster, the person who'd created an entire carnival that hid behind new masks each night. The young man who'd taught me everything about sleight of hand and sleight of word—and could not ever be fully trusted to reveal his true hand.

I gazed out at the sliver of moon, appearing more like a scythe ready to strike than anything else, unable to stop seeing it as a portent of new horrors to come.

"Tonight is the last night," I finally said, shifting my attention back to the ringmaster. He was free from a mask right now, but that, much like the sudden stillness of the sea, wouldn't last. A flash of Liza's finger lying in the velvet box crossed my mind. I squeezed my eyes shut, then opened them. Clouds slowly crept across the sky, lining up in formation. A storm would break by morning, but hopefully I'd have my cousin back before then. "One more performance."

If only there was just one suspect left before the finale.

Hanging from his ankles from the cornice of a building, the escape king strips off a straitjacket while crowds below cheer him on. From HOUDINI by William L. Gresham. Holt. (This picture is from file of Brown Brothers for use with reviews only.)

Harry Houdini

THIRTY-EIGHT

GRAND FINALE

Captain Norwood twisted in his overstuffed leather chair, his gaze stubbornly fixed on the glass half filled with amber liquid sitting on his mahogany desk. It was hardly past sunrise, though judging from the whiskers on his face, he hadn't yet been to bed.

"Chief Magistrate Prescott hasn't heard from Dr. Arden in days, and mentioned arguing over whether to come forward with certain...information they'd received, so I told the chief mate to enter the doctor's chambers." Norwood sipped from his glass, then winced. "There wasn't any blood, but the room was a mess. I don't think his is a story that's going to end well. Especially given that note."

At my raised brow, Uncle walked over to where I stood and handed the crumpled paper to me. I recognized the handwriting as the same from the note I'd received regarding Liza, and my heart picked up its beat.

Dear Doctor Arden,

I have a riddle I cannot solve. Perhaps your skill with sums will prove better than mine.

One wretched lord, one corrupted magistrate, and one cowardly doctor . . .

Equals one innocent life stolen.

Which of the three is most responsible?

Every night this goes unanswered, another life will be forfeited. Choose selflessness and I'll show mercy you do not deserve. Choose selfishness and you will see my wrath.

P.S.: Show this note to anyone and I will feed your limbs to the lions.

I swallowed the sudden lump in my throat and discreetly handed the note to Thomas, stomach churning. The postmark was the first of January, the very day we'd set sail. If Dr. Arden had only brought this to the captain then, perhaps he might have secured the passengers before anyone had lost her life.

I exhaled. "If only" and "what could have been" had no place here now. Although, if Prescott and Arden were arguing over this very thing the day after Miss Prescott was murdered, they were likely too frightened to say anything else, lest the murderer make good on his threats. Which he did anyway.

"It's highly possible, given the threat laid out in that note, that his arm is the one that had been severed." Uncle walked over to the porthole and inspected the water running down the glass in thick, frantic rivulets. The storm broke just prior to daybreak, and the rest of our journey would not be an easy one. "It was male and had a wedding band. Though without a body, it's all conjecture. He might very well be holed up in another cabin. Have you contacted his wife?"

Norwood swirled his drink. "He was a widower."

Thomas and I exchanged glances from our post near the wall, our problems from the night before pushed aside in light of our work. We were to be present, but Uncle had wanted us to remain silent and study the captain. Everyone was suspect at this point.

A sharp rap on the door finally drew the captain's gaze upward. "Yes?"

A wiry man in uniform stepped in and promptly removed his cap, nodding to us before addressing the captain. "We checked all the performers and their trunks and didn't find anything unusual, Captain. Seems like everything is ready for the show."

Thomas pressed his mouth into a flat line. He needn't say so out loud, but there was no way the crew could be certain what was and what wasn't a murder weapon. The performers had swords and daggers and ropes and handcuffs, and countless other oddities that might be used.

Uncle looked at me and Thomas, then turned his attention back on the captain, twisting his mustache in the way that set my nerves on edge. "With all due respect, you ought to cancel the finale altogether. There's no way this is going to end well for anyone."

Norwood tossed back the rest of his drink, the rain now pelting the side of the ship. It sounded like hail. "I'm afraid it can't get much worse, Dr. Wadsworth."

A tingle raced down my spine. I knew by now that no amount of arguing would alter the captain's abysmal decisions. I wish I possessed the same sentiments, but knew this finale would be the spectacle the murderer had been waiting for, his epic ending of revenge.

Tonight's stage reflected the overall feeling of the ship—the inky curtains were overlaid with tattered gray gauze, giving the appearance of a moldering tomb. Even the roses, which had been painted black, seemed foreboding and on the brink of decay.

Passengers sat so quietly at their tables they might as well have been corpses in a grave. Food remained mostly untouched, though it appeared to be edible artwork the way the lobster claws reached toward the heavens and the filets were sliced to perfection.

I pushed English peas around my plate, unable to eat, either. Tonight was the last of our treacherous voyage, and everyone seemed as if they were perched upon needles, waiting for the final celebration or funeral. It would be another sort of death, in a way, one that determined the fate of the Moonlight Carnival. Mephistopheles was determined to make it memorable, though I could not shake the sense that the murderer had the same sentiments. This was the moment he'd been waiting for—the grandest unveiling of all. He'd carefully plotted his revenge, and I feared nothing would prevent him from seeing it through. I prayed that Liza was all right, that she would not be the star of our show.

I felt Thomas's gaze on me, calculating and methodical. He hadn't attempted to continue our talk from last night, and it both relieved and worried me.

"Are you all right, Wadsworth?"

"Of course." I flicked my attention to him, then back to the doors. The plague doctors would be entering any moment now. Shortly after that, I'd be called up to the stage. A lucky volunteer, chosen to brave Andreas's magical looking glass and then stand against Jian's daggers. It seemed as if my random training sessions would be useful after all.

"You're not planning anything scandalous without me, are you?" Thomas asked, voice low enough to avoid Mrs. Harvey hearing. Uncle had excused himself to direct the search for Liza, and it had taken every ounce of self-control I had to not chase after him and forgo the finale. "That would be unfair, you know. I'm quite good at improvising, especially after some wine."

He held his glass of white wine up, a crooked smile easing onto his face. The calculation remained in his gaze, however, telling me he wasn't about to believe the next lie that spilled from my mouth no matter how well its delivery was. Things were still tense between us after our midnight conversation, and would likely remain that way until we could truly talk. Though I was not convinced it would go any differently—perhaps I wasn't the marrying kind. Maybe I'd always seek freedom from any perceived cage, real or imagined, no matter how often Thomas assured me otherwise. He deserved someone who could banish their doubts. Perhaps he and I were only meant to be work partners.

I sighed. "I'm to participate in the finale, and *no*," I whispered as his face partially lit up, "you are not permitted to assist me. I didn't interfere when you volunteered to be cut in half."

He drew back as if I'd slapped him. "Is this what you've been doing at night with Mephistopheles?"

"Thomas," I warned. He sounded so hopeful, but a flash of my kiss with the ringmaster reminded me how tired of lies I was becoming. I hadn't initiated it, and it might have only lasted a second, but the kiss still happened. I would not tell him that was all we'd been doing when it wasn't the entire truth.

He swallowed hard and stared down at his plate. Apparently he'd lost his appetite now, too.

A string quartet entered the room, their violins and violas playing a soft and dangerous tune. Suddenly lights fell upon two cellists sitting with their instruments near the edge of the stage, their half masks glinting in the blue hue that washed over them.

"Ah. Brahms's String Sextet number one in B-flat Major." Thomas closed his eyes as if soaking in the deliciously played string music. "Opus eighteen is one of my favorites. And a fine choice for the finale. It's slow to start, then listen to that there...the melody goes faster, more frantic, the piece builds to a crescendo, and then"—he sat back—"and then it goes back to a sweet warning. Danger is on the horizon."

"Yes, well," I began, when the doors burst open and the truly macabre and bizarre entered the dining saloon. Audible gasps went up around the room as rows of plague doctors made their silent procession, filing in one after the other, their birdlike white masks even more disturbing against the backdrop of the woeful cellos and violins.

Choreographed to perfection, once they'd invaded the space between the tables, they all stopped, pivoted, and began waltzing around, holding their sleek black cloaks out with one arm. They looked like birds with broken wings. Herbal scents wafted around, no doubt from the fragrant bits placed in their masks. Mephistopheles had gone the authentic route, sparing no detail. I hoped it didn't mean we'd need the aroma to cover up the scent of decay.

The music took a darker turn, the strings more melancholy and deep in tone, raising gooseflesh down my arms.

"String Sextet number two," Thomas murmured, brows tugged together. "Another appropriate choice. Though it seems—"

Mephistopheles nearly exploded onto the stage. He appeared behind a wall of igniting fireworks, the white sparkling flares shooting high to the ceiling and remaining that way for several beats of my heart. Smoke lingered before him, grayish tendrils curling about before disappearing. The room now stank of sulfur.

"Ladies. Gentlemen." He swept his arms out, and instead of simply appearing like wings, his cloak actually had black feathers sewn onto it, so inky and dark it almost looked iridescent. "Welcome to the grand finale. I promised magic, mischief, and mayhem. And this..." He walked around in a wide circle, lights clicking on and illuminating different acts already set up in rings on the stage. "This evening is devoted to mayhem. Prepare to be swept into the space between dreams and nightmares. Welcome to the final night of the Moonlight Carnival."

Resplendent in her dragon costume, Anishaa stepped into a ring onstage. The pearly lavender scales practically glowed as she blew fire out in long bursts. The audience in front screeched, moving their chairs swiftly back and away, hoping to avoid being burnt.

Another bright flood lamp clicked on, drawing the crowd's attention skyward, where Cassie shot across the room like a shooting star, tumbling from one trapeze to the next. My heart thrummed. Clowns juggling colorful balls hopped from side to side, making faces. A tattooed woman with a large snake picked her way through the saloon, sashaying as she went, her pet hissing whenever anyone stared too hard. Once everyone was in their spots, it would be my turn. I gripped my napkin beneath the table, focusing on my breath.

Finally, Andreas and Jian made their way into the room, hoisting Houdini upside down on a large wooden scaffold as they went. He was wearing a straitjacket, over which his entire body was woven in chains. I hadn't seen him practice this trick, and I imagined it was yet another secret the ringmaster had kept to himself.

Once Houdini was strung up like a fish that had been caught, wriggling on the line, Mephistopheles stomped his feet three times, and rings of fire went up around each act. This was it. I sunk my teeth into my bottom lip, watching each performer for any hints as to who might be plotting murder this very moment. Everyone seemed suspicious. And nearly each of them had motive. My pulse sped up—any moment now...

"A volunteer is needed from the audience tonight." Mephistopheles walked from one end of the stage to the other, gloved hand shielding his eyes from both the flames and blaring lights. "Who amongst you is brave enough to stand before the knight's blades of fury? Who has the strength to stare into the magical Bavarian looking glass and witness their future?"

The room seemed to hold its breath; not one person moved, lest they were called up to the stage. Understanding dawned brightly. Here was yet another reason Mephistopheles had asked me to participate in the finale—he'd feared this very thing would happen. After the first murder, he'd purchased a bit of insurance for his carnival. The show would go on, and he would have audience participation even if that was an illusion as well.

I slowly stood, my red-and-black-striped evening gown suddenly feeling two sizes too small.

"Audrey Rose, wait," Thomas's voice was low and urgent. "Don't. Something is wrong...where is the contortionist?"

I gestured up to the ceiling as Cassie vaulted from one trapeze to the next, where I knew Sebastián was waiting for his cue to join her in flight.

"You!" Mephistopheles jumped from the stage, his cloak wings spread out intimidatingly. Diners at the nearest table quickly shot up from their seats and rushed to the doors, dodging around the plague doctors who continued to waltz to the same two songs that were being replayed. Apparently the costumes were a bit too frightening, and the sudden movement of the ringmaster wasn't helping to quell their fears. "Come, sweet lady"—he offered his arm—"let us see what fate has in store for you this evening."

I squeezed Thomas's shoulder lightly and accepted the ringmaster's arm. Once we were onstage, waiting for the target board to be rolled out, the gravity of the night finally struck me. Someone was either about to die, or their corpse was about to be displayed. Of that much I was near certain. Neither of those scenarios would be welcome, especially if my cousin was harmed.

Or if the someone was me.

I wiped my palms down the front of my bodice. The stage lights were hotter than I'd thought. Or perhaps standing before the crowd—though it was a fraction of what it once had been at the start of the week—was more unnerving than I'd imagined it to be.

I subtly glanced from Jian's blades—glinting each time he swung them around—to Anishaa spitting fire to Houdini already half freed from his constraints. He'd escape these new bonds and make yet another legendary story of himself. Andreas, in full plague-doctor costume, stood before his looking glass as if standing guard over the future. All I needed to do was step up to the target board, and the true finale would start. I hoped it would not be my death march.

"Ladies and gentlemen," Mephistopheles crooned, "let the mayhem... *begin!*"

Fireworks burst off in the corners of the saloon like fountains of sparkling water. It might not have been the best idea, considering how jumpy everyone already was. One woman collapsed onto her table, squishing the lobster and sauce across her bosom. Another man shoved back from his seat so quickly, he fell over. Plague doctors nearby assisted them, which might have been more frightening than the loud noise.

Even amongst the stirring crowd Thomas drew my attention as he always did, his sharp gaze stuck to something behind me, brows knit. I half turned, but only saw the looking glass. No one was lurking behind it. No bodies hanging, set ablaze, or submerged. It was just as it always had been, except it appeared as if the ringmaster had finally convinced Andreas to clean it up a bit.

"Miss Wadsworth?" Mephistopheles whispered. "It's time."

I took a deep breath and picked my way around the rings of fire until I stood before Jian's target board. A woman's silhouette had been painted onto it, allowing the audience a hint as to what was to come. I went to reach for a blindfold, but Jian gave one jerk of his head. "Not tonight. Here." He handed me an apple, his taunting smile softening into something that almost looked like respect as I took it without so much as a tremor in my hands. "Place this on your head. And don't. Move."

I swallowed hard, eyes darting around the saloon in search of a bit of strength. A nod of support. What I needed was my best friend. Except Thomas was nowhere to be seen. "I…"

"Miss Wadsworth," Mephistopheles said, briefly taking my hand in his and squeezing it in comfort, "be brave."

In a haze, I slowly walked to the target board, mind moving faster than the silver-clad stilt walkers who'd just entered the room, spinning teacups on sticks. For Thomas to have left…

I reached the board and brought the bloodred apple to the top of my head, only half thinking about my safety. Liza. He had to have figured something out about my cousin, or was he too angry to sit and watch me onstage? Perhaps he worried Mephistopheles and I might have been practicing our own act and the thought made him ill.

Jian barked commands at the audience, but all I felt was the heat from the lights, the sound of the crackling flames nearly drowning out the string sextet as it lurched into the next melody, and the general cacophony ringing in both my ears and my chest. A bead of sweat rolled between my shoulder blades. Something was wrong.

I stared unseeingly at Jian's waistcoat—it was unusual for the Moonlight Carnival. It was made of cloth stitched with an enchanted forest from a fairy tale, complete with vines and trees and constellations. I'd seen it before...

A knife sailed through the air, landing near my ear. Another rapidly followed, sinking deep into the wood on the opposite side. My pulse roared. I'd missed something. Something that had caught Thomas's attention. I could have sworn my makeup was melting down my face under the burning lights. Another knife struck near my skull. Thomas had been staring at the looking glass, but Andreas couldn't be the one who'd stolen my cousin and severed her finger. He was right there, doing card tricks with the now-free Houdini.

Apple pulp sprayed down around me, the juice sticky and sweet as it stuck to my face and neck. The crowd surged to its feet, bringing their hands together. The knight had dazzled them with his blades once more. I couldn't concentrate on the here and now, however. Andreas lifted his plague-doctor mask and stole a quick sip of water. Jian took a slow, deliberate bow, eyes fixed to mine. Cassie smiled down from above, her mask glinting like a blade. I swallowed hard, attention straying to Anishaa, who swung twin ropes of flames and then spit them perilously close to where I stood. Each of them was beautiful yet deadly. And perhaps they were all guilty.

I stumbled across the stage, thoughts circling clues like crows circling a carcass, when an arm came down around my shoulders, tugging me near.

"Everything all right, Miss Wadsworth?" Mephistopheles asked.

"If you don't smile and take a little bow, you're going to frighten the audience."

I went to comply when recognition finally struck me. "The stolen fabric..."

"Later," Mephistopheles said. "Please bow and take your seat."

"No," I whispered. "Jian's the murderer. We have to get him off the stage. Now."

"What?"

"Jian's the murderer!" I nearly shouted.

Across the stage, Jian cocked his head, spinning a knife in one hand as someone might do with a pistol. "What did you just say?"

A row of cancan dancers emerged from behind him, kicking their limbs high, their skirts in shades of vermilion, chartreuse, and cobalt. They were the only splashes of color in a moonlight palette. And they were currently making Jian's progression toward me quite difficult. He wove through the line of dancers, ducking back from their kicks, gaze hard as he towered over me.

"You've got no proof for that accusation, do you?" Jian demanded.

Mephistopheles somehow managed to tug us behind the dancers and their voluminous skirts, almost as if he'd also predicted this and wanted the scene to be blocked from the audience's view.

"That fabric you're wearing? That was stolen days ago," I said, nodding to his waistcoat. "We believe the murderer is to blame. And here you are, wearing it for the whole audience. Tonight is your big finale, isn't it?"

Jian stared down at his waistcoat, blinking as if he'd only just noticed it. "This was a gift."

"A gift from whom?" I asked, unconvinced, although the hurt flashing in his eyes was hard to miss.

He glanced at Mephistopheles while the dancers retreated behind the curtain. "From—"

"Ladies and gentlemen," an accented voice boomed through the dining saloon. "Please direct your attention to our grandest performance yet! May I present...the Hanged Man!"

Mephistopheles, Jian, and I stared at one another, expressions matching masks of dread as all the lights in the room went out at once.

THIRTY-NINE
SPECTACULAR SPECTACLE

DINING SALOON
RMS ETRURIA
8 JANUARY 1889

A floodlight flashed on near the end of the stage, illuminating a shadowy corner in a ghostly white blue. Next to the unmistakable, old looking glass, Dr. Arden swung slowly from a noose. His eyes bulged, and a black tongue protruded from his gaping lips. His left arm was missing at the elbow. All sounds in the room ceased, even the mournful violins screeched to a halt at the sight. My attention, however, snagged on something worse, and my blood chilled at the impossibility before me.

Thomas sat facing the magic looking glass, blindfolded, a garrote around his neck. His hands were bound behind his back. The fortune-teller must have lured him onstage—a feat that wouldn't have been hard, considering how much Thomas had wanted to join me for the finale.

"If anyone moves," Andreas said quietly, his voice projected from some mechanical device, "this young man dies."

Mephistopheles shifted beside me, but held his hand up, stalling the performers from making any sudden movements. I glanced back at Jian and the knives he still held. Jaw clenched, he fixed his focus only on his friend. I didn't know if he was involved, but given the look of complete and utter betrayal playing out on his features, I had a feeling Andreas was the person who'd gifted him the waistcoat.

"You," Andreas barked at Anishaa, "put the flames out slowly." The fire-eater glanced at Mephistopheles, eyes wide. "He's not in charge! Do as I say, or I will kill him now."

Anishaa didn't hesitate this time, she stumbled forward, drenching her torches in buckets of water, the hiss of the fire meeting the steam the only sound in the room. Aside from my pounding heart.

"The knives. Drop them, by the blades, off the stage. Now."

Jian wordlessly did so as Andreas stood behind Thomas, expression guarded as he gripped the garrote around my friend's neck. I wanted to take a step in their direction, but forced myself to comply to his warning. I had to remain calm, think. I would get Thomas out of this situation, or die trying. There was no other option.

"Andreas…" I said slowly, "please let Thomas go. He's done nothing wrong."

"We're about to begin the divination of Mr. Cresswell's future, Miss Wadsworth. Fate chooses its mark," Andreas replied. "Some people have faith in the magic looking glass. It will show him his future bride. He believes in the beauty of true, fated love. As I once did."

I tried to keep my voice steady, to keep the entire situation calm. Out of the corner of my eye, I saw diners fidgeting in their seats. I hoped their movement didn't enrage Andreas. His knuckles were turning white. "Thomas's future is most certainly brighter without the looking glass. If you let him go, we can assist you. I'm sure you had a very good reason for what you did. All you have to do is let Thomas go and we can discuss this."

He gave a quick, stiff shake of his head. "Afraid I can't do that, Miss Wadsworth. He wants to know his fate and I will give it to him."

Thomas made a strangled sound, his fingers tugging uselessly at the restraints on his wrists.

"I already know his fate," I said, near pleading. "He and I are going to live happily in the country. He'll have his laboratory and I'll have mine. We'll—" I blinked the tears back, angry with myself for letting my emotions get the better of me. "Andreas...please stop. I—I love him."

"No." He held an arm out. "You do not deserve him, running around with the ringmaster, forsaking his love. The looking glass will show him a different fate, one that is free of hurt. I insist that you sit down and watch the show."

"Enough, Andreas." Mephistopheles stepped up beside me. I could clearly read the panic in his expression, though his voice held that familiar edge of authority. "Put the garrote down. The captain and his men are on their way. The dining saloon has been locked and there is no escape. Crew members are standing guard outside—we had them as a precaution."

"Escape?" Andreas snorted, his grip tightening on Thomas's bindings. If he pulled any harder, Thomas was going to die. I clenched my fists. "I never imagined I'd escape from this, Ringmaster."

Thomas, lips just beginning to turn blue, made a sudden movement to stand, and Andreas shoved him down, eyes flashing as if he could take all of us on at once and win. I went to charge forward, but Mephistopheles snatched the back of my skirts, keeping me in place and probably saving Thomas's life.

"You all have two choices," Andreas said. "Either handle this civilly and with dignity, or I will have to make this much harder and more painful."

"Where's Liza?" I asked, hoping to distract him. "Is she still alive?"

He turned unfathomably cold eyes upon me. "For now."

It was hardly comforting, but it was better than her being dead.

He set his attention back on the garrote, tugging it a little tighter. Thomas wheezed and I nearly lost my mind.

"I know why you've murdered those women," I shouted out, ignoring the gasp from the audience. I'd nearly forgotten them. "Revenge. Correct? You said Liesel sold roses. Lord Crenshaw paid her a compliment and Lady Crenshaw falsely accused her of theft. Out of nothing more than jealousy." A simple story of a broken love turned lethal. "The Crenshaws. The Prescotts. They conspired to put Liesel in prison, didn't they?"

I closed my eyes. Suddenly a new image sprang into my head. I felt as though I were Thomas Cresswell, traveling into the mind of a murderer once more. In my mind I saw a girl with a sweet smile and kind eyes. A girl who didn't have much but made the most of her simple life. A girl who'd captured the heart of the young man before us.

"Lord Crenshaw had your betrothed arrested, didn't he?" I asked, venturing a step closer. Andreas didn't answer. "Mr. Prescott is the chief magistrate who sentenced her without a fair trial." I shook my head. "Conditions in prisons are atrocious. Your betrothed got sick there. Something that could have been treatable, but Dr. Arden refused to tend to her in the workhouse."

"It all started with that horrible woman." Andreas clenched his teeth so hard he all but growled the words. "Confessed right before drinking the poison I'd laid out. Said she couldn't live with what had happened to her daughter. She'd overpaid for the flowers, even though Liesel tried to refuse." His expression turned colder than the winter sea slapping against the ship. "Her husband confronted her over missing money and she claimed it must have been that thieving flower girl. The one with the funny accent. Lady Crenshaw knew how her husband would react—apparently he's got a history of locking people away."

Andreas turned his furious gaze in my direction, grip lessening. "They killed her. All of them." A muscle in his jaw ticked. "They took my beloved from me, so I took what they cared about most in return. An eye for an eye. I will not stop until they've tasted from the well of despair that I've been drowning in these past few months."

A noble family. A doctor. A chief magistrate. Six of Diamonds. Ace of Spades. Five of Hearts. Ace of Clubs. Their roles, laid out. Seven of Swords, the Star—punishments fitting their crimes. A story of jealously, love, loss, betrayal, and revenge.

He wrapped the garrote more tightly around Thomas's neck, and I could have sworn I felt the phantom sensation of losing my own breath. My world seemed on the brink of annihilation.

"Each of them murdered her. All of their hands are dirty, stained in blood. Everyone gets their hands dirty in this business, right, boss? You taught me that. Even you betrayed me. You sent me out to fetch those flowers that day. Without you I wouldn't have met Liesel and she'd still be alive in Bavaria. This cursed carnival should burn. And after this voyage? After this I don't think even *you* can recover, Mephistopheles. Though I do thank you for that money; without it, none of this would have been possible."

"Money?" I asked, glancing between them. "What money?"

Andreas looked at me, eyes narrowed. "I arranged for them all to receive paid first-class passage on this ship. Our glorious ringmaster felt so bad about Liesel, he agreed to give me a handsome sum for her grave marker. Being as she is dead, I didn't think she'd mind me using the money to avenge her. See?" he said, momentarily letting up on the garrote. "My hands are filthy now, boss."

"Oh, Andreas." Mephistopheles slowly shook his head. "I never meant…that wasn't the point of my story. I was speaking of living well as the best revenge. And getting your hands dirty—that's just stage talk. Not something literal. My hands are usually covered in grease from engineering new mechanisms. Not the blood of innocents."

"'Innocents'? Haven't you been paying attention? *None* of them was innocent!" Andreas shook his head. "What world could I ever live in after they killed my love? The only thing keeping me going is the thought of vengeance, making those men pay. My hands are no more stained than the hands of those who are in supposed good standing in society. How many others have they killed, and yet they still walk free? How many lives destroyed by their whims?"

Murmurs went up from the crowd. With Thomas gasping for breath, I'd again forgotten the audience was watching every moment of this. I was focused on two things: the steady war-drum beat of my heart, and the realization that I'd fight a thousand battles and die a thousand ways before I allowed any harm to befall *my* love. Andreas would be revealing his spectacular spectacle soon, especially now that his whole plan had been laid bare.

"But…you didn't kill those men," I said, maneuvering closer. "You murdered their daughters, and Mrs. Prescott."

Andreas barely flicked his gaze in my direction. "I hurt them where it did the most damage. Once each of those men has lost everything he's ever loved, that's when this will be made right. Leaving Prescott and Lord Crenshaw alive is the best form of torture for them. Let them live out their days in misery. As they did for me."

"You cannot take justice into your own hands," Mephistopheles said. "You should have told the detective inspectors."

Andreas snorted. "If you believe they would investigate the death of a poor, sick flower girl from the slums, and put the rich men who killed her behind bars, then you're as bad as they are. Justice is only given to the powerful, and that's not really justice, is it?"

Thomas's eyes rolled back and he began to go limp. The audience gasped, and I involuntarily took a step forward, then halted at Andreas's command, brimming with anguish and frustration.

I cried out as Andreas released the garrote, but my relief was short-lived when his knife flashed in the bright lights. Someone screamed behind us, but I shut out all distractions, my focus set only on the blade. He'd swiftly removed the new weapon from his boot, eyes trained on Thomas, who was struggling to draw in breath. He was going to kill Thomas, then do the same to me and Mephistopheles as his grand finale.

Soft whistling from the rafters drew my attention; I glanced up beyond the maimed body of Dr. Arden as it twisted on the rope, where Cassie and Sebastián stood near their trapezes. They pointed to Andreas and a large bag of whatever they held, signaling their plan. Mephistopheles and I wouldn't be alone in our attack. We'd likely tackle Andreas before any true harm could be done to us, or Cassie and Sebastián would drop the sack and knock him out, but Thomas...

Sounds of diners crying faded into one throbbing pulse—the beat of my heart, the only rhythm urging me on. Andreas was going to slay Thomas right before my very eyes. He saw him as just another wealthy elitist, one more problem in a broken system.

I would never allow Cresswell to become the final showpiece in his warped finale.

For a moment, all of us were frozen in a horrifying tableau. Then Andreas drew his leg back and kicked Thomas halfway across the stage. I knew he was giving himself room to show off his knife skills. My entire body felt as if it had been dunked in ice, then immediately set ablaze. In that moment, watching Thomas stagger and fall to his knees, I understood with startling clarity what Andreas had been through watching Liesel die needlessly.

There was no world I wanted to live in where Thomas Cresswell wasn't a part of it. No matter the odds stacked against us, I'd fight for him until I drew in my last, shuddering breath. Even in death I'd never stop coming for those who threatened my family. Because that's what Thomas had become. He was mine—I'd chosen him just as he'd chosen me, and I'd defend him with everything I had. Our friendship had caught fire and blazed with something powerful and untamed. Something I'd been foolish to ever doubt.

"No!" Cries and shouts went up around me, and I could have sworn I heard the performers charging their friend. A bag of resin missed its target and smashed onto the stage, the powder puffing out like one of Mephistopheles's smoke entrances. I ignored it all, my focus as sharp as a bone saw.

Andreas raised his knife, and I knew he'd fling it into Thomas's chest. He'd been practicing with Jian all week, and his aim had gotten frighteningly true.

I didn't think. I didn't need to. I simply needed to act. I'd been practicing sleight of hand all week, never realizing that I would apply those tactics in a moment such as this. My body was in motion without a second thought.

I slipped my hand under my skirts, seized the scalpel strapped there, and threw it as hard and fast as I could. I didn't bother aiming, there was no point. I wasn't a marksman, nor did I possess Jian's skills. I would not hit a moving target. But the smashing of the precious looking glass would land the deepest blow anyway. Just like murdering the wives and daughters of his enemies inflicted the most pain.

The sound of glass shattering caused the moment of distraction I'd hoped it would, a moment I pressed to my advantage like any magician worth her salt in tricks.

Andreas screamed, guttural and unhinged. I'd taken the last of his Liesel from this earth. Mephistopheles yelled my name, perhaps in warning, but I was already aware of the danger as he ran at the fortune-teller, barreling into him. I didn't cry out as I crashed into Thomas, wrapping my arms around him, knocking us both to the ground, nor did I make a sound as Andreas's knife sank deep into my flesh.

It struck exactly where I'd imagined it would. In that moment, I felt darkly victorious. I'd gone up against the monster and protected the one I loved. I'd banished my doubts. At first there wasn't any pain, and I foolishly believed he'd missed hitting anything vital. That Thomas and I were both going to escape from this nightmare whole and unharmed. That the two of us would live out our days in the country, exactly as I'd said we would. That I'd spend as long as it would take to make things right between us, to earn back his love and prove mine.

But that blissful nothingness didn't last. A moment later a sharp, searing sensation tore through me, wrenching a scream from deep within. The sound was more animalistic than human, and I'd no idea I could emit such a terrible, feral noise. Tears streamed down my face and dripped into my mouth, salty and warm.

"Thomas!" Everything became hot and sticky, though shudders simultaneously racked my body. Fingers slick with blood gripped mine. "Thomas," I said again, more softly.

"Wadsworth"—Thomas's voice was strained—"stay here. Stay here with me."

"I'm not...going...anywhere." There was nowhere in the entire world I'd rather be. Though the part of me not consumed by the searing heat in my leg worried I'd just told another lie...that wishing to or not, I might leave Thomas Cresswell yet. I wanted to cry or laugh out, but the pain was overwhelming. Blessedly, bits of darkness sneaked in, dulling some of my agony.

My medical deductions were slow in coming, but in and out of the blackness throbbing through me, I became aware that I was dying. That warm sensation rushing down my stocking was blood. And there was a lot of it. Too much for a person to lose.

"Thomas..." My voice was barely a whisper, but he heard me. He gripped my hand tighter, and leaned in. "Don't leave me."

"Never." Something dripped onto my face, but I was too tired to open my eyes. My head felt as if I'd swallowed too much champagne too quickly and little white stars clustered around the edge of my vision. The more warmth I lay in, the colder my body became.

It seemed like sweet justice, that a blade would be the end of me.

"Wadsworth..." Thomas sounded as if someone held a knife to his throat, but the danger must be gone. The thought comforted me as I drifted off to sleep. A hand clapped my cheeks, slowly at first, then more steady. It should have stung, but I felt too far away. A beautiful dream was beginning—one where Thomas and I were waltzing around a ballroom that reminded me of a star. Everything was white and pure and smelled of peonies and magic.

"Audrey Rose! Look at me." Thomas's face came into view, hovering above mine. He swore like the Devil, but in this moment he might have been an angel sent to guide me somewhere. His lips, no longer tinged blue, were moving, but sounds drowned out as waves of white and black crashed around my vision. I stared into his wide eyes. He was alive. He was whole. Death was not victorious. The thought carried me further into a peaceful nothingness.

Words melted into one another and I could no sooner listen to Thomas than I could command my wound to stop bleeding. My pulse was a quiet refrain as the beat slowed. Warmth flowed freely around my body, dragging me further and further toward the promise of a blissful rest. I now had two pulses, each warring with the other. One in my leg and one in my chest. Both seemed to fade the more they fought. Which was all right by me; I wanted to drift off and succumb to the darkness. It was much more pleasant than the wild pain unleashing itself upon me. I wanted to fall back into that wonderful dream where we could dance amongst the stars.

Thump.   *Thump.*   *Thump.*

One moment there was euphoric calm, an acceptance of release; the next there was a pressure on my leg, heavy and uncomfortable. It jolted me from that serenity. I wanted to shriek again, to make the suffering go away, but I was too tired. I wriggled away from the pain, blinking up at whoever was torturing me, but my lids grew heavier, more unwilling to obey even as the beast of agony ripped into my body again and again.

The pressure mounted and I finally managed to scream until I tasted blood in the back of my throat. Part of me knew I had to fight as viciously, had to try to live, if only to shove off the person inflicting the pain on my leg. I barreled my focus and squinted through the impending dark. Thomas's hands were a vice on my bare thigh, tears dripping down his face onto mine. I had the impression of him shouting orders to someone nearby, though I couldn't hear them or be sure. I was too fixated on his tears. In my mind I reached up to wipe them away, though it must have been another dream.

I love you, I thought, rallying against the blackness. More than all the stars in the universe. In this life and ever after. *I love you.*

Thump.   *Thump.*   *Thump.*

Thump.

I battled and raged with everything I had for a final glimpse of my dearest Thomas Cresswell, but the darkness descended like a vengeful army and claimed me for good.

FORTY

FAREWELL

Light streamed in from a window, pulling me from sleep. Gulls called to one another and muffled voices joined in from somewhere outside. The sharp scent of antiseptic made my stomach flip, taking the remainder of my peace. I blinked until the blurriness subsided. Cots and small tables came into view—I was in an infirmary.

I gasped when Thomas leaned forward, his chair creaking as he shifted his weight. I hadn't seen him sitting there, and now that I was looking, he appeared truly wretched. Dark circles marred the skin under his eyes, his face paler than I'd ever seen it before. There was an aura of hollowness to him that made gooseflesh rise on my arms.

I wondered if he'd seen a ghost.

He reached over, clasping my hand in his, eyes red rimmed. "I thought..." He gripped my hand tighter. "I thought I'd lost you for good, Wadsworth. What in the bloody hell were you thinking?"

Bits and pieces came back, though it all seemed too foggy to be real. "What happened?"

Thomas drew in a deep breath. "Aside from you rushing to save me from certain death? Taking a knife precariously close to your femoral artery?" He shook his head, and this time there was nothing lighthearted in his face. "The blade went in so deeply it stuck to the bone, Audrey Rose. Your uncle was able to remove it while Mephistopheles and I held you down, but we cannot be certain how much of the bone was fractured. Thus far we don't believe it's shattered."

I winced, as if his story had given my wound permission to cry out once more. "Sounds as though you've all been busy. What day is it?"

"You've been out for only one evening. We've reached port in New York." Thomas drew lazy circles on the back of my hand, his voice a near whisper when it came out. "Andreas confessed to all."

"Even the body found in the crate?" I asked. "Did he explain why that victim was different from the others?" Thomas fiddled with the cuff on my dressing gown, doing a poor job of pretending he didn't hear me. "Thomas? I'm all right. You don't have to treat me as if I'm made of porcelain now."

"It's not you." He sighed. "When we asked Andreas about that crime, he claimed to have no knowledge of it. He's in the brig until detective inspectors come to fetch him. They're not sure where he'll face trial yet, since most of his crimes occurred at sea. We may need to return to England."

"But why wouldn't he have confessed to—"

"Your uncle and I believe it's possible there might have been a second killer on board," Thomas said. "Passengers have already begun disembarking, so if Andreas didn't commit that murder, then—"

"Then we just delivered a Ripper-inspired murderer to America."

We both sat in silence, allowing the gravity of that possibility to settle around us.

"For now," Thomas finally said, "let's hope we're wrong and Andreas was simply feeling uncooperative."

I met his gaze and nodded. It seemed we'd allow ourselves one more half truth at this journey's end.

"Was he the one who stole the fabric?" I asked, remembering Jian's waistcoat. "Or was it an unrelated crime?"

"He admitted to stealing it—apparently he's a petty thief when he's not murdering for revenge. It's an old habit he brought with him from Bavaria. He used to steal clothes from people he'd tell fortunes to. One woman recognized a missing garment and reported it to the police, which is why he left and joined the carnival."

"Speaking of that, what of the Moonlight Carnival? How are Mephistopheles and Houdini?"

"They've both bid you farewell," Thomas said, and I could see he was watching me carefully. "Mephistopheles sends his apologies—and two tickets to their next show, free of charge. He and Houdini said we won't want to miss what they're working on, it's going to be—"

"Spectacular?"

Thomas snorted. "For their sake, I hope so. They've got to find something to distract from the multiple murders committed by their famed fortune-teller. Though knowing Mephisto, he'll find a way to work with it. Infamy is a draw for most. We're all fascinated by the macabre. Must be our dark, twisted human souls."

"I'm glad it's over," I said. "I sincerely hope the families are at peace."

Something else important slithered around the edges of my thoughts, but my mind was still so foggy.

"Liza!" I wrenched myself up and collapsed back. Agony shot through my body, reminding me how injured I was. "Where is she? Is she all right? Please, please tell me she's alive. I cannot bear it."

Thomas adjusted my pillows and gently pressed me back. "She's all right. Andreas drugged her and had her chained in his rooms. But she's recovering. Much faster than you."

I exhaled. "I'm not worried about me."

"But I am. There's something else you should know...about your injury," he said, slowly moving about his seat, eyes cast downward. "You'll be able to walk, though it's possible you'll have a permanent limp. There's no way of determining how it will heal."

The burning ache in my leg flared at the reminder of my injury. A limp. Though some may find their worlds destroyed by such news, I did not. My future would see me moving not across a ballroom floor but within a close laboratory. And corpses did not care how gracefully I walked.

For my own benefit, I needed to lighten the mood. Things were far too glum, and regardless of how badly I'd been hurt, I needed something positive to cling to. I was alive. All other details would be worked out. I smiled to myself; I truly was sounding like Mephistopheles.

"The price of love doesn't come cheaply," I teased. "But the cost is worth it."

Thomas abruptly stood, leaving my hands craving his warmth. I reexamined my joke, wondering which part of my statement had pierced him.

"You ought to rest now," he said, avoiding my gaze. "Your uncle will be in soon to discuss travel arrangements. And I know Liza has been stomping around outside, too."

"Thomas...what—"

"Rest, Wadsworth. I'll return again soon."

I pressed my lips together, not trusting my voice to conceal my hurt. I watched Thomas gather his hat and overcoat and hurry from the room, as if the sight of me now disturbed him. I tried not to take it personally, though a few tears managed to sneak past the dam I'd erected. It seemed Thomas Cresswell was disappearing from my life along with the carnival.

Another presence in the room stirred me from sleep. I rubbed at my eyes, though I didn't bother trying to sit up. "Thomas?"

"No, my love. I'm the much-handsomer one. I blame the loss of blood for that slip."

Despite the amount of pain I was in, I grinned. "Thomas said you'd left with Houdini already."

"Yes, well, I made it halfway down the docks and figured you'd go mad with want." Mephistopheles tentatively clasped my hands in his. They were rough and calloused in places, a testament to how often he worked with them. He ran his thumb over my knuckles, the movement calming. "I didn't want you missing me so much that it affected your recovery."

I shook my head. "Always such a charmer." I made to lean over the side of the bed and winced. "Open that drawer, would you?"

"There's not a snake inside, waiting to sink its fangs into me, is there?"

I rolled my eyes. "Fine. I wouldn't mind hanging on to your signet. The rubies would fetch a decent amount."

I'd never witnessed Mephistopheles move quite so fast, not even while performing his fancy tricks. He held the ring up, eyes misting before he blinked it away. "Thank you."

"How else will people blackmail you? Couldn't have you running off without it."

"Indeed." He smiled. "Promise you'll miss me just a little?"

"I might think of you one cold, dreary December, many, many years from now."

"And?" he prompted, expression hopeful.

"And wonder if you bathe in your mask."

His chuckle was dark and deep. "No need to wonder, my dear. I'm more than willing to show you firsthand. Shall we go to my chamber or yours?" He eyed my bandages. "Perhaps we ought to delay our tryst. I wouldn't want you bleeding all over this suit. It's bad for business."

"I am going to miss you," I said, because it was the truth. Something I hadn't been acquainted with in a good, long while. Sleight of hand had been interesting to learn, but I was no good at playing that role long term. I wanted to offer nothing but honesty in the future. Pretending had not only confused me, but nearly hurt Thomas irrevocably.

"I know. It's my cross to bear that I am so incredibly irresistible." Amusement left his eyes, replaced by something more uncertain. "Tell me...did I ever truly stand a chance at winning your hand? Or was everything between us a lie? The dancing, the laughter...surely it wasn't all an act."

I stared into his dark gaze, pulse picking up as I imagined a different sort of future. One that still included science and freedom. Passion and theatrics. In that future I could be happy, more than happy. We'd use science to build impossible machines and magic, dazzling crowds and earning praise. I could travel the world and never settle into a role society deemed appropriate. Mephistopheles would make a wonderful husband—never chaining me up unless it was for the stage. I could be very content in that future. I would be more free than the acrobats soaring from one trapeze to the next.

But my heart and soul would always belong to another more fully. Thomas and I were partners in every way. And while imagining life without the magic and easy smiles of Mephistopheles was a little sad, thinking of a world without Thomas Cresswell was unbearable. I could no more walk away from him than I could abandon my heart and still live.

I leaned over and pressed my lips to Mephistopheles's cheek. "In another world, or another life, I think we could have done amazing things together. You're going to make someone very happy one day—but that person isn't me. I'm sorry."

"I'm sorry, too." I watched the column of his throat bob and squeezed his hand as tightly as I could manage. He held me a moment more, then stood. "I'll work on a bit of engineering genius and name it after you, my lost love."

I couldn't stop myself from laughing, full and loud. "Goodbye, Mephistopheles."

"It's Ayden, please." He moved to the door and paused. "Until we meet again."

Thomas stood rigidly beside me, gloved hands gripping the frosted railing as we watched passengers disembark. They would all certainly have stories to tell about the ill-fated ship. Not even Houdini would escape from the scandal, though I was certain he would turn out fine in the end. A group of policemen made their way through the crowd, heading into the brig to collect the criminal the papers were calling the Bavarian Ripper. It wouldn't be long now. My breath caught, and I had the sudden urge to hold my center. I did not want to say goodbye. I dreaded it.

"I'll be with you again soon enough, Wadsworth. You won't even know I'm gone."

I stared at his profile, heart thudding dully. He hadn't looked me squarely in the face since I'd taken the knife. I knew my sleight-of-word act had worked a bit too well, and I deserved his anger, but this was too cold to bear. "That's it? That's all you have to say?"

"The fact remains I am needed here, in New York, as your uncle's representative." He took a deep breath, eyes fixed on the people still exiting the ship. I wanted to clutch his overcoat, shake him until he was forced to look at me. But I kept one hand at my side and the other firmly on my borrowed cane. He had always granted me the freedom of choice. I would not steal his from him. If he wanted to stay here, I would not selfishly beg. "I will join you as soon as I can."

I ignored the tear rolling down my cheek. I did not wish to part like this—with him as cold and distant as the shores of England. We had been through far too much. Though perhaps it wasn't the act I'd put on—it was possible he couldn't bear to see me after I'd been injured.

Maybe my broken leg was a reminder of how close we'd both come to losing our lives. I may have realized what I was willing to give up, but that didn't mean he'd come to the same conclusion.

I gathered my emotions, proud of how much control I had of them now. "Aren't you supposed to say something like 'I'll miss you terribly, Wadsworth. These next few weeks shall be a slow sort of torture, I'm sure.' Or some other Cresswell witticism?"

He finally turned to me, eyes lacking their usual glimmer of trouble. "Of course I will miss you. It will feel like my heart is being surgically forced from my chest against my will." He inhaled deeply. "I'd rather be run through with every sword in Jian's arsenal. But this is the best for the case."

He was right. Of course he was. The case had to come first, but I didn't have to like it. I gripped my cane tighter. My entire life I'd wished for the bars of my gilded cage to disappear—all I'd ever wanted was to be set free. To choose my own path. First my father had let me go, and now it seemed Thomas was doing the same.

Freedom was both heady and terrifying. Now that it was in my grasp, I wanted to shove it back. I had no idea what to do with it or myself.

"Then I wish you well, Mr. Cresswell," I said, ignoring the wrongness of my formal words. "You're right. Being upset is silly when we shall meet again soon."

422

I waited for him to snap out of this cool persona, to don the warmth of his affection for me, but he remained unmoved. A detective cleared his throat behind us, destroying the last of our moments together. I didn't know whether to burst into laughter or tears. Only eight short nights before, we'd stood on this very promenade, wrapped in each other's arms, kissing beneath the stars.

"Mr. Cresswell? We're taking the bodies ashore now. We require your presence en route to the hospital."

Thomas nodded curtly. "Of course. I'm at your disposal."

The detective tipped his hat to me before disappearing back into the ship. My pulse roared and my leg ached. This was truly it. The moment I'd been dreading since the Ripper case. I was finally saying goodbye to Mr. Thomas Cresswell. It felt as if there was not enough oxygen left on earth to sustain me. I dragged in breath after breath, cursing my corset for being so fashionably tight. I was fine. This was all fine.

I remained a filthy liar. There wasn't anything fine about this situation.

Thomas stared at the door that would lead him to a path divergent from mine. For the first time in months, we would not be adventuring together. I felt his absence already as if a part of me had been carved away, and my body still yearned for its missing piece. I was whole on my own. I did not need another person to complete me, and yet the way we were parting made me feel ill. It was not right, but I didn't know how to make it so. Perhaps that was the ultimate lesson in letting go—accepting that which was out of our control. I could only do my best and my part; it was up to Thomas to meet me halfway or not at all.

He slowly turned and faced me, jaw tight. "Farewell, Miss Wadsworth. It has been an absolute pleasure. Until we meet again."

I ignored the similarity to how I'd parted with Mephistopheles.

When he'd said goodbye, I didn't feel as if the world had ceased to spin on its axis. Thomas tipped his hat and began to leave.

In my mind, I rushed after him, clutched his overcoat, and begged him to stay. To take me with him. To forsake my uncle's command to remain here and see this case through in New York, and to marry me in the chapel this instant. Grandmama lived close by—though given the fact she'd not responded to any of my letters she might be traveling the Continent—and would be a witness, if only to spite my father.

In reality, I forced my lips together and simply nodded, watching him walk away for however long we'd be apart. Maybe a few weeks. Or maybe forever. Whatever he chose, I would live with it. However hard, I'd find a way. He paused, his back to me, fingers tapping the doorframe. I waited, breath held, for him to make a joke or run back and sweep me into his arms, but after another moment, he pushed himself forward and disappeared into the ship.

A sob tore its way from my chest before I stuffed it back in. I stood there for a few breaths, heart pounding. I had no inkling as to why this goodbye felt permanent. But I knew, somehow, deep within the marrow of my broken bones, that if I did not stop him, Mr. Thomas Cresswell would exit this ship and my life forever. I wrapped my unoccupied hand around the railing, allowing its icy bite to distract my thoughts. I'd need to seek warmth soon—the dull pain in my leg was turning vicious.

I focused on the physical pain instead of the new, more prominent ache in my chest.

Together Thomas and I had burned bright as a shooting star, and flew apart just as fast.

We'd stopped the Bavarian Ripper. Cleared the rest of the Moonlight Carnival of wrongdoing. Thomas was simply giving forensic aid here while Uncle and I traveled to our next destination, where he would, surely, eventually join us. All would be well soon enough—I was simply making more out of our goodbye than what it was. After all of the death I'd faced, it wasn't hard to find a logical explanation for my hesitancy to say farewell to someone I loved. I reminded myself of earlier sentiments: *Science is an altar I pray to. And it offers me solace.*

I silently chanted the words like a refrain, staring out at the sea long after Thomas had left.

EPILOGUE

Liza walked down the promenade deck, hood tugged over her brow to stop the blasts of wind blowing over the Hudson from destroying her stylish coiffure. She stepped up beside me and gazed down at the circus crates that were being unloaded. I admired the painted moons on them—the dark black circles with silver crescents on their sides.

The Moonlight Carnival was off to entertain a new crowd in a new city. I had no doubt that Mephistopheles would steal the hearts and minds of everyone he met. Houdini had a stunningly bright future, too. He was well on the way to becoming legendary. I had a feeling it wouldn't be the last time we'd hear from either of them.

Which I wasn't sure was a good thing.

"After everything you did, I would have thought you'd be brave enough to tell him the truth," she said, gaze fixed on the crates below.

"Who?" I asked. "Mephistopheles?"

"Don't be purposefully daft," she slapped my arm.

Andreas had given her a tincture that had knocked her out. Apparently a few hours after my heroic act, she'd come stumbling back to the room, unharmed. He'd grown fond of Liza, her passion-ate spirit reminding him of his beloved Liesel, and spared her from further torture or death. I crinkled my brow and Liza sighed.

"Honestly? You carve open the dead, seeking the truth behind their deaths. You crave dissecting things to solve puzzles. Yet you are hopeless, dear cousin, when it comes to being truthful. Most espe-cially to yourself." She faced me, hands on her hips. "Did you tell Mr. Cresswell that you love him? That you cannot wait to see him again? That you are afraid he blames himself every time he sees your injury?" She studied me and shook her head. "No, you didn't. You stuffed it all inside and pretended everything was well. But that isn't the truth, is it? You're worried."

"I . . . it's—it's all very complicated."

Liza actually snorted. "It's truly not that complicated at all, Cousin. Thomas—cunning as he is—believes every half-truth you tell him *and* yourself. He cannot see through your mask. It's likely the only thing he cannot puzzle out, and I'd wager it's because he feels too much for you. I guarantee he believes he's doing the gentle-manly thing by leaving—he's giving you a choice to follow Mephis-topheles, even if it breaks him apart. Did you notice the red rimming his eyes? He's not slept since you were hurt. Uncle tried removing him from your rooms and your Mr. Cresswell nearly turned feral at the idea of leaving your side. You're both so intelligent in matters involving the mind, but the heart? It's as if beings from other galaxies are puzzling out fried potatoes."

"He . . . what?" I could not even wrap my brain around the absur-dity of the thought. "Why would he believe I'd choose anyone else? I jumped in front of a blade for him. I'm fairly certain that indicates my preference. His leaving has nothing to do with that."

"Are you certain?" Liza gave me an exasperated look. "How did the two of you part? Let me take a stab at the scene—oh . . . sorry."

She cringed, motioning toward my leg. "That's probably the wrong term for a while."

I huffed a laugh. "What am I going to do with you?"

Liza wrapped an arm around me, holding me close. "You're going to love me by heeding my romantic advice. Now, then, I wager Thomas formally bid you farewell. Cold. Not an ounce of flirtation to be found. I bet he even tipped his hat instead of kissing your gloved hand." She grinned at my scowl. "Shed your mask, Audrey Rose. Tell him your fears. I promise you he doesn't care about your cane or broken leg. It's your soul he fell in love with. He's giving you the opportunity to decide your own fate, but trust me, he loves you deeply."

I turned away, suddenly not wanting Liza to see the tears that had begun streaming down. "What about you and Houdini?" I asked, deflecting. "He didn't lie to you, you know."

Liza shifted her attention back to the circus crates. "I know that. We just—while I adore him, I want a different sort of future. The carnival was exciting, but, hard as it might be to believe, I miss Mama." Now I was the one who snorted and she nudged me. "Harry will find a woman who makes him happy, and I will find someone, too. Now, then, stop trying to hide from your own truth. Tell Thomas you love him, or you'll spend the rest of your days regretting it."

"But what if he is leaving because of the accident? What if he—"

"Pardon me." Liza cleared her throat and nodded toward the opposite end of the promenade. "I think I see Mrs. Harvey waving all the way down there. I must go to her at once."

"Honestly?" I swiped the wetness away and turned, annoyed by my cousin's swift departure. My scolding died on my lips when I met Thomas's gaze. He'd managed to slip in beside me, a magician in his own right. I shook my head as Liza winked over her shoulder and hurried away. Tears slipped freely over my cheeks again while he studied me. I angrily brushed them away, hating that, while I could mostly corral my emotions during an investigation, I had no control over them outside the laboratory.

"Cresswell," I said, lifting my chin. "I thought you had business to attend to."

"I did," he said simply. "You see, I happened to ask Lord Crenshaw where he had such a handsome walking stick made when your uncle and I conducted our final interview. Imagine my surprise when he said he'd purchased it here in New York. There's a shop right up the block, actually." He moved closer, pointing in the general direction of where the store must be located. "I believe this rose beats the one Mephistopheles tried to give you."

"I . . . What?"

Thomas tossed a cane into the air with one hand, caught it with the other, then handed it over to me on bended knee. It was a beautiful ebony cane with a carved rose knob. The shaft looked like the stem of the flower complete with thorns. I stared at it, unable to formulate words. It was stunning—a piece of art.

"Thomas, it's—"

"Almost as handsome as me?"

I laughed, though more treasonous tears burst out, too. "Indeed."

A seriousness entered his eyes, making my heart flutter. "Our work will always be important to each of us. But you have my heart wholly, Wadsworth. No matter what. The only way that will be taken is in death. And even then I will fight with every piece of me to hold your love near. Now and forevermore."

I'd had nearly the same thoughts before everything went to hell on that stage. I ran my fingers through his hair, twisting a lock around as I gazed into his eyes. They were filled with adoration as real and true as anything. What we had was no illusion, but it was magical. I let my hand fall away from him and gripped my new cane, testing its weight. "You know? I believe this is the most precious rose I've ever received."

He gave me a slow, playful smile. "My magic trick was fairly impressive, too. Do you think Mephistopheles will take me on? I could practice. Actually," he said, taking my arm in his, adjusting his gait as I moved unsteadily beside him, "we ought to do an act together. What do you think of 'the Amazing Cressworths'? It's got a pleasant sound to it."

"Cressworth? Did you honestly combine our names? And why does your name go first?" I stared at him out of the corner of my eye, mouth curved upward despite my best efforts. "I think the most amazing part of our act would be not lulling the audience to sleep with your wit."

"Devilish woman," he said. "What name do you suggest?"

"Hmm." I leaned on my cane, pretending to think long and hard. "I suppose we'll have plenty of time to figure it out."

"Mmm. Speaking of that," he said, "I've been thinking."

"Always a troublesome thing."

"Indeed." Thomas managed to slip his hands around my waist. "We've already lurked in London alleys, explored spider-filled castle labyrinths, survived a lethal carnival..." He brought his lips close and I tilted my face up, heart fluttering as he brushed his mouth against mine softly. His kisses were an intoxicating form of sorcery. "Perhaps now we can try one of my suggestions? Might I offer—"

"Just kiss me, Cresswell."

His crooked grin set fireworks off inside me, and without uttering another word, he obliged.

AUTHOR'S NOTE

The RMS *Etruria* had many lavish rooms for first-class passengers, but the dining saloon described is from my imagination. I used real elements and added many of my own—creating the backdrop for a traveling carnival, complete with a stage and a black-and-white checkered floor. (Though the ship did truly have refrigeration and electricity.)

Funnel cake: the earliest recipe I found for funnel cake came from a German cookbook published in 1879. The description Thomas gives of a pastry fried in butter comes from it, though it's not mentioned by name.

Harry Houdini would have been fifteen in 1889, which was a little too young for the story, so I took the artistic liberty of making him seventeen. Houdini began publicly performing magic in 1891, not 1889, though he did perform as a trapeze artist at the age of nine. He met his wife, Bess, in 1893 and they had a wonderful love story.

I hope Houdini fans and historians won't mind my use of his famous escape tricks, even though they occurred later in his career. "The torture cell" was actually named the "Chinese Water Torture Cell" and was first publicly performed in 1912.

"The Milk Can Escape" was performed in 1901. When Mephistopheles says "...failure means a drowning death..." in that introduction sequence, it's the actual tagline from the Houdini promotional poster. The "Metamorphosis" trick was performed by other magicians, but Houdini's act caught attention in 1894 because both he and his wife performed it on stage. (Other acts only featured men.) Houdini was incredible at marketing himself and his tricks, which I tried to show a glimpse of when Liza talks to Audrey Rose in their cabin and says, "He claims there's power in how you sell something."

Houdini's magic career spanned from dime museums, to vaude-ville, to being part of a sideshow in a traveling circus. After altering his acts to draw larger crowds and create higher stakes, he became known as the King of Cards, the King of Handcuffs, and the escape artist/master illusionist we admire today. There are rumors he met someone early on who helped clean up his grammar, and I imag-ined that mysterious figure as Mephistopheles. Later in life, Harry famously fought to debunk frauds when spiritualism became popu-lar. It was a fun detail I added when Liza dreams of speaking to the dead and he yells from the stage, "Spiritualism is a hoax."

For more information on Houdini's life I recommend reading *ESCAPE! The Story of the Great Houdini* by Sid Fleischman.

Andreas Bichel, also known as "The Bavarian Ripper," was the true-life inspiration for the killer. I reimagined him using his fortune-teller "talents" as part of a traveling circus and altered his crimes to reflect tarot cards. By the time this novel takes place, the real Bichel had already been executed. Killing method: He'd lure young women into his home, promising to show them their future with his portend-ing mirror, tie their hands behind their backs, blindfold and murder them. Just like Andreas in this story, he stole fabric from his victims, which is ultimately how he got caught. The sister of a missing woman went into town, asking shop owners if they'd seen her sibling, when she saw the tailor making a waistcoat from her sister's petticoat. He provided the name of the man who'd given him the material and placed the order, and she summoned the police. They later found the bodies of the missing women buried in Bichel's woodshed.

One of my father's friends was a VICE cop in NYC, and he'd talk about the dangers of getting too into character during under-cover operations. While crafting Audrey Rose's performance, I fash-ioned her acting in a way that not only seemed slightly out of the norm for her, but had her succumbing to that very danger. Audrey

Rose worked so hard at crafting an illusion, that it almost became real. Many thanks to my dad's friend for the inspiration behind the undercover operation.

Any other historical inaccuracy or creative liberty not mentioned was done to (hopefully) enhance the reading experience of this extravagant, yet fictitiously doomed, luxury liner.

ACKNOWLEDGMENTS

Strangely enough, publishing a book is not unlike the circus. There are many performers, all juggling different aspects of the process, working together to turn a simple document into something show-stoppingly spectacular.

Many thanks to Barbara Poelle, who keeps me in constant awe of her ability to switch between fierce agent and gentle friend as quickly as Andreas demonstrates the switch-change card trick to Audrey Rose. To the team at Irene Goodman Agency, Heather Baror-Shapiro at Baror International Inc., and Sean Berard at APA, for continuing to work your sorcery. I don't need a magic mirror to see how bright the future is for Audrey Rose and Thomas.

Jenny Bak, your incredible edits take a dull first draft and shine it up until it sparkles more than Mephistopheles's flashiest tailcoat. You're my partner in all things gory and glitzy; thank you for always indulging my dark side. Sasha Henriques, you continue to add layers of awesome with your notes—many heartfelt thanks! To the entire troupe of wondrous performers at JIMMY Patterson Books and Little, Brown, and the talented ringmaster who brought everyone together: James Patterson, Sabrina Benun, Julie Guacci, Erinn McGrath, Tracy Shaw, Stephanie Yang, Aubrey Poole, Shawn Sarles, Ned Rust, Elizabeth Blue Guess, Linda Arends, and my copy editor Susan Betz. From marketing and publicity to an incredible sales and production team to interior art and cover magic, I'm forever grateful for your support and hard work with this series.

Mom and Dad, you've always believed in the power of dreams, and I'd be lost without your love and support. (And going with me to all those doctor's appointments, especially when they take blood. I die.) Kelli, keep slaying your dreams in the most spectacular fashion. (I made a *Dogwood Lane Boutique* pun!) As always, thank you for being my personal stylist and keeping both myself and my house on trend. I think I'll keep you as a sister. Ben, Carol Ann, Brock, Vanna, Uncle Rich and Aunt Marian, Laura, George, Rich, Rod, Jen, Olivia, Gage, Bella, Oliver, and every fur baby in the family, much love to you all.

Irina, Phantom Rin, maker of otherworldly art. Once again you took images from my imagination, improved them, and turned them into stunning pieces. Many thanks for the idea of including moons and stars on Mephistopheles's gloves, and for bringing the Moonlight Carnival characters to life with your custom tarot and playing cards.

Traci Chee, from traveling together for book events, to being hotel roomies (and foodies), to always being there through all the good stuff and hard medical stuff, I cannot tell you how much your friendship means both on the publishing stage and off.

Stephanie Garber, I honestly don't know what sort of supernatural powers you possess, always calling EXACTLY at the right time, but I'm forever grateful for you! All of our talks about plot and characters and bookish recommendations and life are general is pretty legendary. :)

Sarah Nicole Lemon, Renee Ahdieh, Alexandra Villasante, Nicole Castroman, Gloria Chao, Samira Ahmed, Kelly Zekas, Sandhya Menon, Riley Redgate, Lyndsay Ely, Hafsah (and Asma!) Faizal—getting to hang out with you at events is the best.

Librarians, teachers, booksellers, book bloggers, booktubers, and bookstagrammers—thank you for telling your students, friends, and the whole internet about your love of this series. Special shout-out to Sasha Alsberg, Katie Stutz, Rec-It Rachel, Kristen at *My Friends Are Fiction,* Stacee a.k.a. *Book Junkee,* Bridget at *Dark Faerie Tales,* Melissa at The Reader and the Chef in its place. Brittany at *Brittany's Book Rambles,* Brittany at *Novelly Yours,* and the entire goat posse.

And to you, the person who's read all the way to the end, thank you for reading and dreaming and going on another murdery adventure with me.

EXCLUSIVE BONUS CONTENT

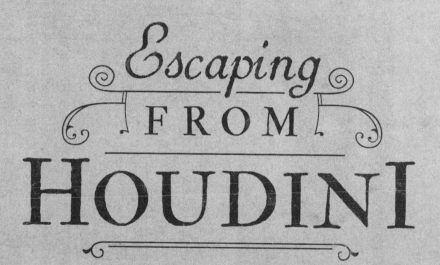

Escaping FROM HOUDINI

Tarot cards
with handwritten notes from
author Kerri Maniscalco

INFINITY SYMBOL ↓

MORE
MOONLIGHT
CARNIVAL
SYMBOLS

INFINITY SYMBOL

THE CIRQUE D'ECLIPSE TAROT PLAYED SUCH A HUGE ROLE, AND I ADORE HOW CLOSE THIS IS TO THE ORIGINAL IMAGE IN MY HEAD. RIN EVEN INCLUDED THE INFINITY SYMBOLS JUST LIKE MEPHISTOPHELES PAINTED IN HIS TAROT DECK!

THESE ARE DESCRIBED IN CHAPTER 18. ♡

PHANTOM RIN ADDED CRESCENT MOONS TO THE RINGMASTER'S
GLOVES, AND I LOVED IT SO MUCH I CHANGED THE DESCRIPTION
DURING COPYEDITS!

The Magician

HIS MASK ALSO FEATURES A MOON.

CAN YOU SPOT ALL THE MOONLIGHT CARNIVAL DETAILS? IN THE FAUST LEGEND, "MEPHISTOPHELES" WAS A DEMON WHO WORKED FOR THE DEVIL, MAKING BARGAINS. I BASED HIS STAGE PERSONA ON IT.

(HINT: CHECK HIS SUIT, TOP HAT, & THE BORDER :))

AUDREY ROSE'S OUTFIT WAS INSPIRED BY A VINTAGE COSTUME
I FOUND ON PINTEREST. SHE WORE IT THE NIGHT SHE DRANK THE
GREEN FAIRY.

I LOVE THAT HER MOTHER'S
LOCKET WAS INCLUDED !!

THIS
IS
MY
FAVORITE
CARD

I ADORE THE DETAILS ON THOMAS'S SUIT.
IF YOU LOOK CAREFULLY, YOU'LL SPOT THE DRAGON
ON HIS WAISTCOAT. A FUN NOD TO HIS FAMILY !

THOMAS IS ALSO WEARING A ROSE BECAUSE
HE CLEARLY CAN'T HELP HIMSELF ☺

CASSIE (CASSIOPEIA)

The Empress

I'M SUCH A HUGE FAN OF HER POSE & HER MASK.
THE BODICE IS ALSO ANOTHER FAVORITE!

HER NAME, ROLE, PERSONALITY, AND COSTUME WERE ALL
INSPIRED BY THE CONSTELLATION.

I TOOK A BIT OF THE GREEK MYTH
AND INCORPORATED IT INTO HER PERSONALITY
TOO.

MOONLIGHT CARNIVAL SYMBOL ↙

One of my favorite details are the flames swirling into the border. ↗

I'M A HUGE FAN OF ROBERT FROST, AND EVERY TIME I IMAGINED ANISHAA SWALLOWING FLAMES, I COULDN'T STOP THINKING ABOUT HIS POEM "FIRE & ICE." IT WAS THE INSPIRATION BEHIND HER COSTUME.

Ace of Wands

♡ ♡ HER JEWELRY REMINDS ME OF PIECES I'VE GOTTEN FROM MY SISTER'S BOUTIQUE ♡ ♡

THE CONSTELLATIONS IN THE BACKGROUND ARE ANOTHER FUN DETAIL!

FUN FACT: I CHOSE "JIAN" AS THE KNIGHT OF SWORDS'S NAME FOR TWO REASONS. 1.) IT MEANS "STRONG" (WHICH IS HOW I PICTURED THIS CHARACTER.) AND 2.) IT'S ALSO THE NAME OF A DOUBLE-EDGED STRAIGHT SWORD.

JIAN'S ARMOR - BREASTPLATE, BELT, BOOTS, & GAUNTLETS ALL HAVE THE MOONLIGHT CARNIVAL SYMBOL, TOO!

Knight of Swords

THE SADDLE HAS HIDDEN CRESCENT MOONS.

SEBASTIAN CRUZ: THE CONTORTIONIST.

The Hierophant

ONE OF MY FAVORITE THINGS TO WRITE WAS AUDREY ROSE'S REACTION WHEN SHE FIRST SAW SEBASTIAN. HER SCIENCE-FOCUSED MIND COULDN'T STOP WORRYING OVER THE (SEEMINGLY) ANATOMICAL IMPOSSIBILITY OF IT.

RIN ALSO MANAGED TO SNEAK THE MOONLIGHT CARNIVAL SYMBOLS ONTO HIS COSTUME, TOO.

HIS COSTUME WAS ALSO INSPIRED BY A VINTAGE CIRCUS PHOTO I FOUND.

HIS CONSTELLATION SUIT IS EXACTLY HOW I PICTURED IT IN THE BOOK!

THE RINGS, MASK, CANDLES AND SMOKE CURLING AROUND THE BORDER ARE SO MAGICAL!!

I LOVE EVERYTHING ABOUT THIS CARD! ONE OF MY FAVORITE DETAILS IS THE TAROT CARDS SPREAD ACROSS THE TABLE. THEY MATCH THIS CUSTOM DECK AND REALLY BROUGHT THE SCENE FROM CHAPTER 18 TO LIFE.

The Fool

EVERY TIME I LOOK AT THIS CARD I SPY ANOTHER COSMIC DETAIL - LIKE THE STAR TABLE!

THESE CUSTOM PLAYING CARDS ARE DESCRIBED IN CHAPTER 3.

♡ ♡ I FELL MADLY IN LOVE WITH POE AS A TEEN, AND THIS DESIGN WAS A COMBINATION ♡

♡ OF "THE RAVEN" MIXED WITH MEPHISTOPHELES'S LAST NAME. ♡

♡ ♡ ♡ IF YOU CAN'T TELL... I LOVE HOW THESE CAME OUT! THE RAVEN! THE MOON! THE THORNS! THE

DETAILS MAKE MY DARK HEART SO HAPPY!

♡ ♡ IN COLOR, RIN MADE THE RAVEN'S FEATHERS LOOK IRIDESCENT.

CHAINS & CARD SYMBOLS - A NOD TO HOUDINI'S TITLES! ↓ ↓ ↓ ↓ ↗

I LOVE THE SMIRK ON HOUDINI'S FACE - LIKE HE KNOWS HE'S ABOUT TO BANISH THE WORD "IMPOSSIBLE!"

THE CHAINS MATCH THE PLAYING CARD DESIGN. (THE RAVEN + MOON CARD.)

FUN FACT: THE BORDER ON THIS CARD IS FROM THE ORIGINAL ART. IT WAS LATER CHANGED TO BECOME A TAROT CARD.

LIZA'S COSTUME IS SAVED ON MY PINTEREST BOARD.

LIZA AND HOUDINI'S CARDS ARE THE ONLY TWO PLAYING CARDS - A CHOICE I MADE TO CELEBRATE HIS EARLY TIME OF "THE KING OF CARDS."

ONCE AGAIN, RIN ADDED THE MOONLIGHT CARNIVAL SYMBOL. SPY IT IN THE FAN?? SHE ALSO ADDED SO MANY HEARTS IN THE CURTAINS

HER CARD IS THE QUEEN OF HEARTS, WHICH IS WHY SHE HAS A THORN BORDER. (TO MATCH THE RAVEN BACK!)

The final villain.

The unexpected redemption.

The ultimate devastation.

How will Audrey Rose's story end?

READ ON FOR A SNEAK PEEK OF

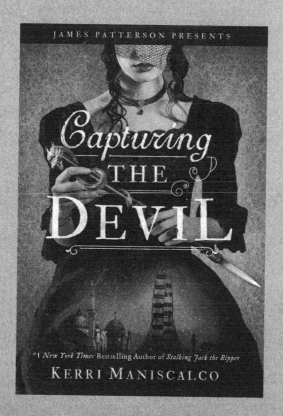

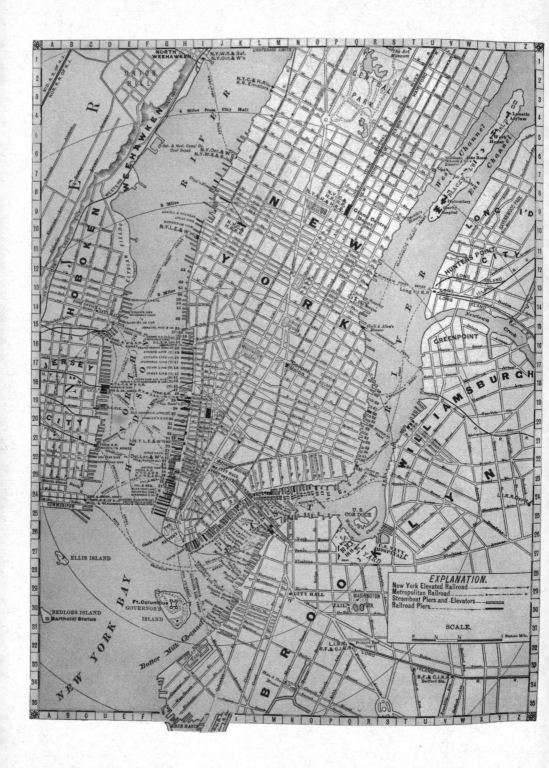

ELEVEN
THE COLOR OF BLOOD

AUDREY ROSE'S ROOMS
FIFTH AVENUE, NEW YORK CITY
22 JANUARY 1889

I was too stubborn to admit it, but Uncle was correct again—tonight my bones ached worse than they usually did. Standing for extended periods was difficult enough without wintry weather sinking its claws in, wreaking more havoc on me.

After we'd sewn up the last cadaver, I had the kitchen send a dinner tray to my room, hoping my warm quarters and thick blankets might help. Once I finished eating, I sat in front of the fireplace, scalding tea in hand, and accomplished only burnt fingers. The aching chills refused to leave. Knowing I'd hurt worse in the morning, I limped to the bathing chamber and turned the copper faucet, filling the bath for a good, hot soak.

I stepped out from my robe and gingerly maneuvered into the water, wincing a bit until I acclimated to the heat. I leaned my head against the lip of the porcelain tub, my hair piled in a messy knot, and inhaled the pleasing herbal scent. Liza had taken to concocting more than tea blends—she'd made the loveliest aromatic salts for me, claiming medicinal properties would help different ailments. This particular blend would assist with drawing out toxins and calming my nerves, amongst other things, she told me.

Whether that was true or not, it smelled divine. Steam rose in fragrant tendrils of lavender, lemon balm, and eucalyptus, relaxing both my muscles and soul. I was constantly moving as of late, always rushing from one problem to the next without pausing to restore myself. I wasn't used to taking careful note of each of my movements, and found the learning of it to be tedious at best. Though my body was a stern professor—it let me know when it had had enough and would continue teaching the same lesson until I became an apt pupil. I must learn to pace myself or suffer the consequences.

Death. Murder. Even while relaxing I couldn't escape such horrors. I closed my eyes, trying to erase images of the most recent mutilated corpse from my mind. I loathed that a woman might be brutalized by her killer and then again by the men investigating the crime. It was an unfair world—one that showed no mercy for those who needed it the most.

Hoping the bath salts might draw those thoughts away, I sank lower, the water now tingling against my earlobes. A door to my outer rooms opened and closed, the soft click reminding me of a bullet sliding into the chamber of a pistol. I sighed. So much for stealing a few restorative moments alone. I silently prayed my aunt hadn't come to read any more passages of scripture. I was one prayer away from losing my mind. I dipped further into the water and pretended I hadn't heard her enter, focusing instead on unkinking each muscle. Soon enough, footsteps approached and I wished a thousand unpleasantries upon the intruder.

"Wadsworth?" Thomas called quietly, then pushed the door open, halting as I nearly splashed him in my haste to cover up. Of all the...

I crossed my arms in a feeble attempt at modesty. "Have you lost your senses?"

"If I hadn't before, I certainly have now." He blinked slowly, trying and failing not to stare at me in the tub. He didn't have the courtesy to even blush—he looked positively dumbstruck. As if he'd never encountered a body without clothing before. Perhaps just not one with a still-beating heart. I'd be flattered by his obvious response if I wasn't so flustered.

"Get out!" I whispered harshly. "If my aunt or father sees you in here—"

"It's all right. We're engaged." He shook himself from his stupor and knelt beside me, a small devilish smile playing on his lips. "That is, if you'll still have me?"

"Father agreed?" Forsaking propriety, I almost leapt from the water into his arms, stopping myself at the last moment. "I can't believe you kept that from me all afternoon!" I sat back and his focus shifted to where my bare shoulders met the water. His gaze darkened in a dangerously seductive manner, awakening a growing need in me. "At least be a gentleman and turn around."

His expression hinted that he was far from a gentleman at the moment, and a quick inspection of my face confirmed I liked it. Excitement thrummed through my veins. I couldn't deny enjoying the power of his deductions when he directed them at me, and I wondered what that extreme attention to detail focused entirely on my body would feel like.

"As a properly engaged couple, we're permitted a few more liberties. For instance, we might spend time alone, behind closed doors." He purposely scanned the bathing chamber, nodding toward the door. "Seems a shame to let those liberties go to waste."

The scoundrel had the unmitigated *gall* to indicate joining me in the bath. As I turned that thought over, my entire body heated up, having nothing to do with the steaming water. I found the idea of bathing together to be—I splashed water onto my face. When I looked at him again, I noticed a slight furrow in his brow. "Was there something else?"

"Other than informing you that we're finally, truly, engaged, dear fiancée?" I nodded, the word sending a little thrill through me. As if recalling he had a purpose more important than flirting, he pulled a small velvet pouch from his jacket pocket, his attention now fixed on it. "My sister arrived bearing gifts."

I almost jumped from the bath again, but settled for craning my head around Thomas to see if his sister was making an appearance in my chambers, too. "Daciana's here?"

"She and Ileana arrived shortly after supper." He ran his thumb over the velvet pouch, seemingly lost in another place and time.

"Cresswell?" I gently prodded. "What is it?"

"A letter."

He sounded so sad, my heart nearly broke. I motioned to the little pouch, wanting to drag him from his despair. "That's the strangest letter I've ever seen."

He glanced up through thick lashes, humor flickering in his eyes before he looked away. "Instead of being terrified of her imminent death and thinking only of darkness, my mother wrote us letters. She wouldn't survive to see either of us married, but..." he shook his head, swallowed hard. His emotions were on full display, unlike earlier during the autopsy when he'd seemed so cold and remote. "She wrote one for me to read upon my engagement."

Forgetting about any cursed rules of the world, I reached over, water dripping onto the hexagon tiles, and laced my fingers through his. "Oh, Thomas. Are you all right?"

A single tear slipped down his cheek as he nodded. "I'd forgotten, almost, what it was like. Listening to my mother's advice. Her voice. The soft accent that was never quite British or Romanian, but somewhere in between. I miss her. There isn't a day that passes where I don't wish for another moment with her. I'd hoard it away forever, knowing how precious it was."

I gently squeezed his hand. In this most unfortunate circumstance, we understood each other too well. I missed my own mother terribly. While I was thrilled Father had finally agreed to our engagement, the wedding planning and celebration would be difficult to go through without her. Her absence—along with Thomas's mother's—played a large role in our second request to my father. I hope he'd consented to that as well.

"It is a gift, having her letters to look forward to," I said. "They're invaluable little mementos—proof that some things are truly immortal. Like love."

Thomas swiped at his nose, smiling, though his expression

was still too despondent for my liking. "Beyond life, beyond death. My love for thee is eternal."

"That's beautiful. Was it in the letter?"

"No. It's how I feel about you." I swore my heart stuttered a moment. The young man who London claimed was nothing more than a cold automaton had created poetry. Thomas quickly opened the velvet pouch, tipping its contents onto his palm. A ring with a large crimson jewel lay there like the deepest drop of spilled merlot or crystallized blood. I gasped as he held it up to the light. The unblemished stone was quite literally breathtaking.

"Red diamonds are the rarest in the world." He turned it one way then the next, showing off its magnificence. I couldn't stop staring at it. "My mother told me to follow my heart, no matter what others might counsel, and give this to the woman I choose to wed. She said this stone represents an eternal foundation, one she hopes is built on trust and love." He inhaled deeply. "I'd already jotted down those lines for you, '*beyond life, beyond death; my love for thee is eternal*.' " At this admission, he blushed. "When Daciana brought me this letter today—the very day your father gave us his blessing—and I read that line, it felt as if my mother was here, offering her own blessing not just for me, but for you, too. She would have welcomed you as her daughter."

He took my left hand in his, his gaze now locked onto mine. All teasing and shyness had vanished. I knew him well enough to realize how serious he'd become, how important these next words would be. His coldness this afternoon in the makeshift laboratory was self-preservation; he was preparing to open himself more fully than the corpse we'd flayed apart. I remained still, as if one unexpected movement might frighten him away.

"This ring is a gift from my mother, passed along from her mother and so on. It was once owned by Vlad Dracula." Without breaking my stare, he nodded toward the jewel. "It's yours now." Gooseflesh rose along my arms, catching his attention. "I'll understand if you'd rather have another diamond. My family legacy is rather—"

"Majestic and incredible." I cupped his face, noticing a slight tremor go through him. I didn't think it had anything to do with the bathwater. Thomas Cresswell still didn't believe he was worthy of love. That his lineage was some sort of dark curse. I thought he'd banished his doubts by the end of our voyage here. Some monsters were harder to slay, it seemed. I'd gotten chills because I was honored he'd share his deepest fears with me. With this blood-red diamond, he was giving me another piece of his heart. It was a gift rarer and more precious than the stone he wished to place upon my finger. "I will wear it proudly and cherish it forever."

I worked my mother's pear-shaped diamond off and put it on my other hand, pulse racing as Thomas slipped his family heirloom onto my ring finger. It fit like it was always meant to be mine. Thomas kissed each knuckle, then drew my arm around his neck, uncaring that he was getting his shirt wet.

"I love you, Audrey Rose."

Without prompting, I placed my other arm around him. My shoulders were now completely out of the bath and I was perilously close to being exposed further, but I didn't care.

Thomas's body was both a shield and comfort as he pressed it firmly against me.

"I love *you*, Thomas." When we kissed, I swore the earth shook and the stars burned brighter. Thomas moved out of my grasp long enough to hop into the tub, fully clothed, and pulled me onto his lap. Heat shot through me at the unexpected but welcome contact. "Are you quite mad? I'm not wearing any clothes!" I whispered, laughing as he dunked under the water, then shook his head like a dog. Droplets pelted me. "My aunt will die from the scandal!"

Thomas brushed a piece of hair from my face, then slowly moved his lips from my jaw to my ear and back, kissing my bare skin until I was convinced we soaked, unhurt, in a pool of fire, and each of my fears and worries of being caught burned away. "Then we ought to be very quiet."

He lifted me higher and I stared into his eyes, losing myself in the sensation of running my fingers through his damp hair. He looked at me like I was a goddess—like I was fire and magic and spell work combined in human form. I traced a finger down to his collar, teasing the first button open. I suddenly wanted to see more of him, I *needed* to. I tugged his jacket off, leaving his shirt on, though it might as well have been off. Soaked through, it left little to the imagination. A faint image bled through the fabric. I leaned in. "What is that?"

He glanced down as if he hadn't a clue, then shrugged. He unbuttoned the first few buttons and pulled his shirt open, revealing a tattoo. They'd become quite popular with the upper class, but I hadn't thought he'd be interested in such fads. Not that I minded. It was...tantalizing. I touched it with my fingertips, careful to avoid the red splotches around its edges indicating it was fairly new. He watched me, his attention intent and focused, while I inspected it.

"A skull and rose?" I finally asked. "It's beautiful. What does it mean?"

"Oh, lots of things." He drew back, exhaling, a self-satisfied smile in place. "Mostly it's a study in contrasts: light and dark, death and life, decay and beauty." His expression turned thoughtful. "To me it also symbolizes good and evil. Placing it on my heart proves love conquers everything. Naturally I needed a rose on my body forever, too." He kissed me, slow and sensuous, as if to make sure I didn't misinterpret his innuendo. "When you saw Prince Nicolae's tattoos you seemed intrigued, so I deduced you'd enjoy it. I hope that's true."

I gave him a bemused look. "You're free to ornament your body however you'd like. No permission needed."

"Truthfully, I thought it'd be a good reason for you to take my shirt off."

I grinned. Thomas enjoyed saying shocking things to gauge my response. There was no reason I couldn't match him in that area. "Your deductions might not be as sharp as you think if you believe I lack motivation, Cresswell."

His jaw practically hit the floor. Immensely satisfied, I bent my head, kissing the inked area above his heart. With or without the rose tattoo as a permanent marking, Thomas Cresswell was mine. When a small gasp escaped him, I covered his mouth with my own, claiming him fully.

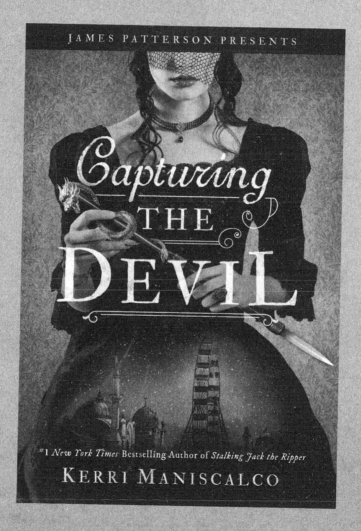

ABOUT THE AUTHOR

Kerri Maniscalco grew up in a semi-haunted house outside New York City, where her fascination with gothic settings began. In her spare time she reads everything she can get her hands on, cooks all kinds of food with her family and friends, and drinks entirely too much tea while discussing life's finer points with her cats. Her first novel in this series, *Stalking Jack the Ripper,* debuted at #1 on the *New York Times* bestseller list. She's always excited to talk about fictional crushes on Instagram and Twitter @KerriManiscalco. For updates on Cressworth, check out Kerrimaniscalco.com.

JIMMY Patterson Books for Young Adult Readers

James Patterson Presents

Stalking Jack the Ripper by Kerri Maniscalco
Hunting Price Dracula by Kerri Maniscalco
Escaping from Houdini by Kerri Maniscalco
Capturing the Devil by Kerri Maniscalco
Gunslinger Girl by Lyndsay Ely
Twelve Steps to Normal by Farrah Penn
Campfire by Shawn Sarles
When We Were Lost by Kevin Wignall
Swipe Right for Murder by Derek Milman
Once & Future by Amy Rose Capetta and Cori McCarthy
Sword in the Stars by Amy Rose Capetta and Cori McCarthy
Girls of Paper and Fire by Natasha Ngan
Girls of Storm and Shadow by Natasha Ngan

The Maximum Ride Series by James Patterson

The Angel Experiment
School's Out—Forever
Saving the World and Other Extreme Sports
The Final Warning
MAX
FANG
ANGEL
Nevermore
Maximum Ride Forever

The Confessions Series by James Patterson

Confessions of a Murder Suspect
Confessions: The Private School Murders
Confessions: The Paris Mysteries
Confessions: The Murder of an Angel

The Witch & Wizard Series by James Patterson

Witch & Wizard
The Gift
The Fire
The Kiss
The Lost

For exclusives, trailers, and other information, visit jimmypatterson.org.